HOME BY CHRISTMAS

BY

BRIDGET BERESFORD

MAJOR RICHARD WAYGOOD MBE

ACKNOWLEDGEMENTS

Many thanks to:

The Imperial War Museum, London.

John and Janine Lloyd at the Household Cavalry Museum, Windsor.

Musée de la Première Guerre mondial 1914-1918, Péronne.

The Néry Historical Society.

The Historical Society of Soissons

The Museum at the Château de Pierrefonds, Oise.

The Museum at Rethondes, Compiègne, Oise.

The late Monsieur André Bocquillon.

Monsieur Jean Bocquillon.

Monsieur Benoit Verdun & 'Une Incroyable Odyssee 5ème Division de Cavalerie.'

Captain D. Holden.

Kay Hambrook for the loan of her books.

Phil Wooler for the loan of his books.

Sue Cameron.

Dedication

This book is dedicated to all those men who fought and died in the Great War. Also to their trusting and courageous horses who perished while they carried out their duty.

We will remember them.

5.0 out of 5 stars Home by Christmas., 16 Jan 2

This review is from: Home By Christmas (Kindle Edition)

The full horrors of WW1 and the fictitious King's Own Cavalry regiment are vividly conveyed by Richard Waygood and Bridget Beresford in this book. It certainly brings home the realities and the true atrocities that the soldiers and horses of the First World War suffered. It graphically describes the events that they lived through on a daily basis. The relationships between the men who are from different social backgrounds is fascinating and complex, which then develop into a respect for both each other and their senior officer, Captain Andrew Harrington-West.

It tells the story of Andrew and his experiences in both the war and his personal life and his relationship with his fellow soldiers, the horses and how he deals with the prejudice of class barriers. Compulsive reading and hints at maybe a sequel?

5.0 out of 5 stars Home By Christmas, 30 Nov 2013

By hobbyhorses

This review is from: Home By Christmas (Kindle Edition)

Worth reading, I'd recommend it to anybody; the bond between man and horse, and between men, in those difficult days of WW1, and the spirit found to battle on, with a twist of romance to complete the story. Well done to the authors in their dedication to all the research needed to write this novel.

5.0 out of 5 stars Fantastic book, 29 April 2013

By Barbara Cooper

This review is from: Home By Christmas (Kindle Edition)

Bought this for my daughter on kindle. She absolutely loved it - so much so that not only does she have it on kindle but wanted the printed version too for those times when a book is the best thing to read!

CONTENTS

CHAPTER ONE

Somewhere in Northern France – August 1914

'Give me strength.' A tall good looking trooper sneered at the little cockney with sticking out ears. 'Is that all you can say? We're going into battle for the first time and all you're worrying about is your bleedin' horse.'

'I said the 'orses look 'appy grazing the grass. They don't know they're gonna fight.'

'What's wrong with that, Turner 64?' retorted a wiry young man.

'You can keep out of it, Marsh. I was talking to Shrimp.'

'He isn't Turner 64, I am.' Another tall trooper, the spitting image of his twin brother, joined in the conversation.

'So bloody what? A Turner is a Turner, you're both the same to me,' said Shrimp.

'I'm Turner 4865 and he's Turner 4864, 'cos we joined up together, see. Our numbers run one after the other.'

'We know why you're 64 and 65. Shift your 'orses, they're coming too close to mine,' retorted Shrimp.

'What's so special about your horse? He'll probably be dead meat after this ambush anyway.'

'Get lost, Turner,' said Marsh. 'That's if the Hun turn up.'

'You and Shrimp hoping they won't? Getting windy are you?'

Shrimp turned to a tall, aristocratic looking lance corporal and asked, 'Williams, do you think they're gonna come?'

'Why ask him?' Turner 65 sneered sarcastically. 'He's only a La-di-dah boy who went to a posh school. What will he know, old boy?'

'The captain's sure they're coming,' replied Williams in his educated accent. 'That's good enough for me.'

'God give me strength,' repeated Turner 65, turning to his brother. 'It's just our luck to have to fight with a bleedin' cockney and an upper class nob who should be an officer but who's only a lance corporal.'

'You go to the other side of the river and join Lieutenant Somerville, then,' retorted Shrimp. 'Anyway, Williams chose to be a NCO.'

'We don't want to be with that bleedin' excuse for an officer.' Turner 64 moved his horse closer to Shrimp. 'It's a pity you ain't with him though.'

'Shut up, 64. The captain'll hear you,' said Williams.

'He knows Somerville's a bloody fool. We all do,' said Turner 65.

'Don't talk like that. You could be put on a charge.'

'Says who?'

'I do. Anyway, Sergeant Armstrong's with Somerville. He fought in the Boer war, he knows what's what,' retorted Williams.

'The captain's comin' over 'ere.' Shrimp whispered, as he watched the dark haired officer striding towards them. 'You'll be for it now,' the cockney added, noticing his superior's deep blue, almost violet eyes glaring at the twins.

***

Captain Andrew Harrington-West had been surveying the plain below him, watching out for the enemy, as he idly listened to the fifteen dismounted troopers. He looked at his watch, shrugged his shoulders and walked towards his men.

'The enemy seems to be somewhat tardy,' he addressed them. 'I was reliably informed that they are coming. You all know what to do?'

'Yes, sir,' came a chorus of voices.

'We hold the enemy in the ford. Lieutenant Somerville on the other side of the river will attack them from the front. They won't be able to escape out to the left, it's too boggy. Impassable for a horse. Nor will they be able to jump down the waterfall on the right-hand side. There's a ten foot drop into deep water and, as you can see, below us the banks are far too steep to allow a horse to climb out.' He paused. 'Although we were sent out today to reconnoitre, the information I received regarding the enemy cavalry patrol presented an opportunity that was too good to miss. I know you'll all fight well.' He turned and stared at the twins. 'Turners...' They jumped and paled under their tanned faces. 'I expect exceptional courage from you two. You've both shown outstanding skill in training so I'm sure you won't let the King's Own Cavalry down.' He turned to the rest of the men. 'Our regiment, the King's Own, as you all know, has an excellent battle record. Let's keep it that way.' He turned and walked back to his post on the hill and raised his field glasses, training them on the stony road below him. His heart raced as he saw the tell-tale cloud of dust in the distance. 'Bring my horse,' he ordered. 'Girth up and mount.'

His eyes narrowed as he turned in his saddle and watched his men hurriedly take up their positions. A fractious horse pushed its way up through the file of waiting troopers and stood close behind his own gelding.

It swung its hindquarters from side to side and stamped its front feet. 'Let him eat that branch,' Andrew snapped.

The horse lunged at a twig of silver birch and pulled at it until it broke off. It kept him occupied, chewing and tossing his head, while the branch flew up and down narrowly missing the haunches of Andrew's horse.

'Draw swords,' Andrew ordered.

Mechanically, in a much rehearsed movement, the men quietly drew their long sharp swords and tilted them back against their shoulders into the slope position. They waited, all of them stony-faced, for the order to charge.

As the elite Uhlans, their pointed helmets glistening in the sunlight, came into view below them, a trooper gasped, 'Look at them fucking long lances'. Someone threw up and Turner 65 muttered, 'For God's sake'.

Andrew turned and said, 'This is what we've come to France for, to free Europe ... fight hard, lads'.

'Yeah, we'll be home by Christmas,' Turner 65 said to his brother. The troopers fell silent. The enemy had arrived at the river and walked into the ford. The German horses stopped with a jerk as they put their heads down to drink. 'Move along,' shouted the Feldwebel, a German sergeant, to the head of the column. They kicked their irritated horses further into the river. Eventually the last of the forty five riders reached the water.

Andrew was aware that Sergeant Armstrong, across the river, was watching him for the order to charge. He could feel the anticipation of the men behind him. He sat alert and poised, his hunting instinct telling him to wait. Then, to his disbelief, the senior German officer dismounted the first twelve men at the head of the column. They stood on the edge of the ford, letting their horses graze. Not only were they off guard, but some soldiers had begun to stow their carbine rifles back on their saddles.

Andrew let out a sigh, hardly able to believe his good luck. He raised his sword arm twice as the signal to charge. The British cavalry poured down the steep banks on either side of the river. When they met the flat ground, they spurred their mounts into a gallop, leaning forward over their horses' necks, their swords now in the thrust position, the lethal tips extended menacingly towards the enemy. The horses' nostrils flared red in the sunlight, and the whites of their eyes flashed as they galloped into battle for the first time.

***

The surprised Germans at the head of the column stood mesmerized as Rupert Somerville's troopers, led by Armstrong, pounded towards them. Pandemonium followed as those on foot tried to mount, but their horses, frightened by their shocked riders, began to pull back, rear up and swing round. The men jerked their reins, shouting and adding to the confusion and fear. Some horses broke free and galloped past the British, snorting and carrying their tails high in the air.

Letting the sergeant lead his troop into the Germans lines, Rupert found it easy to claim his first kill, a dismounted German. He plunged his sword into the soldier's back as he tried to flee. The sharp weapon seemed to slide through human flesh more easily than into the sacks of straw that they used in training. He felt elated as he searched for his next victim and shouted to a trooper who was galloping towards a dismounted man, 'Out of the way Ashton, he's mine'. He felt the same excitement as his sword found its mark and the German fell to the ground.

***

The enemy at Andrew's end of the ford tried to turn their horses, which, oblivious of the danger, were only concerned with quenching their thirst. The riders had their hands full as they struggled to raise the horses' heads and face the rapidly approaching British.

The fractious English horse, with the branch of silver birch stuck in his bit and flying out of his mouth like a tattered flag, cannoned past Andrew completely out of control.

'Hold hard!' yelled the captain. But the runaway galloped on towards the Germans, heading straight for a young soldier. He was one of the few who had been able to turn his horse to face the oncoming British. As if in a trance the German held his lance pointing at the upper body of the trooper on the bolting horse.

The sharp four-edged point ran straight through the Englishman, who let go of his reins and clutched at the weapon with both hands. The horse reared up and twisted round. His rider's weight falling backwards wrenched the lance out of the German's hand. The heavy tubular-steel weapon struck the German on his jaw as it sprang into the air. Andrew saw the look of shock and horror on the young man's face. He drew his revolver and fired a bullet into his chest, sending him reeling into the water to join his victim beneath the feet of the plunging horses.

The cavalrymen, incensed at the killing of one of their own, galloped into the ford and fell on their enemy. The Turner twins hunted like a pair of lurchers after a hare, each instinctively knowing what the other was doing. They quickly saw the problem that the Germans were having with their cumbersome ten-foot lances. Riding up on either side of their quarry, one twin grabbed the lance and forced it up out of harm's way, while the other drove his sword into the enemy's body, before moving rapidly on to deal with their next target.

A German soldier who had lost his horse crouched low in the water at the side of the ford. Shrimp noticed him spear an English horse as it came within his reach. The horse fell as the tip of the lance pierced its heart. The rider struggled to get up out of the blood-red water.

Shrimp, enraged with the German for killing the horse, rode at him like a man possessed. He dropped his reins and grabbed the wavering lance. His horse stopped on command and he drove his sword at his enemy's head. The German let out a roar of pain, dropped his lance and clasped his hands over his face. Shrimp continued pushing and pulling his sword until the man fell silent and toppled into the water. As the trooper withdrew his weapon he saw the German's eyeball lodged at the tip like a bead on an abacus. The Turner twins, seeing what had happened, smiled. The small thin boy seemed to grow in stature and grinned back.

Out of the corner of his eye, Andrew saw Lance-Corporal Williams heading for a dismounted German standing precariously on the wall of the waterfall. The young NCO charged, but as he drew near, a German officer drove his lance into the hindquarters of Williams's horse. The horse took off, leapt over the wall and landed in the river below. Andrew only had time for a brief look to see the rider disappear beneath his gelding and both sink under the water. He thought what a waste of a young life, but he had no time to reflect as he ducked out of the way of the same Hun, who dropped his lance and drew his revolver. The man fired, but the bullet zinged passed the captain and buried itself in a fresh faced German lad who was coming up behind the English officer.

Andrew heard a German bugle. He watched as his scattered enemy restored some form of discipline and bunched together. They stumbled over their fallen colleagues, slithering on the paving stones that were slippery with blood mixed with viscera. Riders pulled their walking-wounded comrades up on to their mounts; the tight cluster of men and horses pushed its way past the British cavalrymen and burst out of the ford. They galloped up the hill and on towards the edge of a forest.

The men with Rupert, having tasted blood and near victory, yelled with anger and frustration. Without waiting for the order they gave chase, whooping and hollering as if after a hunted animal. Rupert caught sight of a wounded German trying to get to his feet. He had a hole in his right arm which hung uselessly down beside his body. Blood poured from his right leg, his lance lay a distance away and he had no other weapon. The boy stared at Rupert: he pleaded with his eyes and raised his left hand above his head in a gesture of surrender.

Rupert felt jubilant as he drew back his sword and drove it into the boy's body. Turning, he noticed a young trooper staring at him with a look of disgust on his face.

'What are you looking at, Ashton? We can't take prisoners. Now get going.' Rupert spurred his horse and galloped after his men.

***

Andrew stood and watched the Germans as they careered up the hill. He silently cursed Rupert for recklessly galloping after them. He knew that they were very nearly behind enemy lines. His bugler had sounded the retreat, but the men, their blood up and their adrenaline flowing, were already half way up the hill.

Andrew collected his stragglers. 'Draw rifles,' he ordered. 'Turners, come with me.'

Holding his revolver in his hand, he waded back into the water to dispatch the badly wounded horses and to check for surviving Germans. As he bent down to put his gun to a horse's head a shot rang out. He spun round to see Turner 65 fire again at a German officer.

'He was going to shoot you, sir,' explained 65 as the man slumped under the water.

'Thank you, Turner.' Andrew stared at the dead German.

'We'll go and check the rest, sir. Shall we take any prisoners?'

'Yes, as long as they don't try to kill us. Make sure they're disarmed.' Andrew continued the grisly business of dispatching the wounded horses, British and German. Then he counted the dead soldiers, his only satisfaction being that the Germans outnumbered the British. Having removed the personal papers from the bodies of his men, he ordered two troopers to collect the saddles, bridles and kit from the dead British horses.

'Sir,' called Turner 65. 'We've found a live Hun.'

'Are there any more?'

'No, me brother's checked them all.'

'Good, good, bring him over here.'

The prisoner was bleeding from a chest wound, his face was grey and his breathing was laboured. Andrew thought that he hardly looked old enough to fight. 'Try to make him comfortable,' he ordered. Looking around he added, 'We must water the horses. The ford is out of the question'. He glanced at his boots and shuddered; they were soaked with bloodied water and festooned with pieces of human and equine remains.

Andrew counted his collection of men which, including himself, amounted to ten, plus seven horses, two thirds of the soldiers who had stood under the trees with him that morning. All of them had blood stains on their uniforms except for a trooper called Stone; he was caked in mud and his horse was missing. None of Rupert's men had been killed at the ford, but he wondered how many would return after chasing the Germans.

Andrew led his diminished half-troop into a stubble field and on towards the forest. A bunch of riderless horses, some German and some English, grazed together at the edge of the river bank. He ordered Shrimp to catch them; Marsh was missing, so he told Trooper Stone to help instead.

Shrimp was still carrying his sword erect, proudly aware of his trophy. Stone looked up at the eyeball which now resembled a hard boiled quail's egg on a skewer and retched. 'Fisher,' barked Andrew, 'get rid of that thing and clean your sword.'

Shrimp wiped his sword on the ground. The offending object bounced along the stubble and came to rest staring sightlessly up at the sky.

'Now go and catch those horses.' Andrew, pleased that the boy had come through the battle unscathed, hid a smile.

'The Hun ones too, sir?'

'Of course, they're not going to attack you. How's your German?'

'I don't speak no German, sir.'

'Talk to them nicely. I'm sure they'll understand. Get a move on, we'll meet you down in that corner of the field.' Andrew pointed to the edge of the forest.

***

Rupert arrived at the top of the hill in time to see the tail end of the German patrol disappear into the cover of the forest. Killing had given him a new power and a sense of supremacy which carried him forwards into the forest at the head of his men. He didn't look behind for Andrew.

The wide forest ride stretched out in front of him in a straight line. Rupert could see the Germans ahead and he began to gain on them. They abruptly turned off the main ride, and cursing, the British lost sight of them. The path they followed twisted and turned before it ended at a junction with six straight rides. The Germans had vanished. Rupert rode around the *carrefour*, telling his men to look for hoofprints, which they quickly found and followed, but the trail soon disappeared into the undergrowth. Rupert returned to the junction. He had expected to see Andrew; his feeling of elation suddenly evaporated and he felt vulnerable as he realised that he was alone. Sure that unseen eyes were watching him, he wanted to return by the way they had come.

'This way,' he ordered.

'No, sir, it's this one, here are our hoofprints,' shouted a trooper.

'There're hoofprints coming down this one, too, sir,' another man called out.

Rupert turned his head this way and that. He was on the verge of panicking as Sergeant Armstrong approached him. 'The path we came down twisted, sir. The others are all straight. It's this one.'

'Of course, Armstrong, that's what I was looking for.' Rupert moved his men off at a canter, but the horses were tiring and some of the troopers found it difficult to keep going. The Sergeant rode up beside the officer. 'Sir, we need to water the horses before they collapse.'

'We haven't time for that,' Rupert snapped. The sergeant shook his head, and, as if on cue, one of the horses stopped. Although the rider flapped his legs, the horse wouldn't move.

'Dismount,' cried the sergeant. The trooper slid to the ground. His horse stood and trembled. Rupert stopped impatiently.

'There's some water further along this track,' said Armstrong. 'I noticed it earlier.'

Rupert continued begrudgingly at a walk until they came across a ditch. It was almost dry, but there was just enough water to allow the horses to snatch a few mouthfuls.

At a noise in the bushes, the men hastily reached for their rifles. A man emerged from out of the undergrowth pushing a bicycle. The troopers let go a sigh of relief when they saw that he was dressed in the blue trousers and jacket of a French workman.

'*Les Boches sont partout, ils faut que vous en allez,*' the man cried. '*Les Boches, partout. Allez! Allez!*'

While the sergeant fished in his pocket for the small French phrase book that had been issued to every serving British soldier, Rupert, glad to feel superior, said in a patronising tone, 'It's all right Armstrong. The man is saying the Germans are everywhere and that we need to leave, which is rather an understatement. I think we know that'. The men looked anxiously around, shifting in their saddles.

'Perhaps he can direct us out of this forest,' the sandy-haired sergeant suggested. 'We have to get these horses watered as soon as possible. Ask him if he knows of a safe place.' Rupert had seen the slow progress of the exhausted horse as it had made its way towards the ditch and he was obliged to agree.

'All right,' he snapped. He spoke in French to the cyclist, who replied, '*Suivez-moi*'. Rupert felt better when he saw the look of respect on the men's faces at his knowledge of French but he soon began to feel frightened again as the Frenchman took them off the track and deeper into the forest. He blamed Andrew for not following him.

They emerged into a small clearing with a large stone house standing in the middle of an overgrown garden. The place looked deserted. The French worker led them to some tumbledown sheds at the back of the house.

Sergeant Armstrong dismounted the men. 'Put your horses in them sheds, then detach buckets and fetch water from that pump. Corporal Clark, start pumping.'

The men took their canvas buckets from their saddles and made their way to an iron pump that stood near the house. Clark moved the rusty arm up and down, but nothing happened.

'Keep going,' ordered the Scotsman. Eventually there was a gurgle. 'Here she comes,' exclaimed Clark, as, with a hiss of air and more gurgling, the pump delivered up a trickle of yellow water. The two NCOs looked at each other in relief while the corporal renewed his pumping with vigour. The water began to run clear and the men queued up to fill their buckets.

The Frenchman left, saying that he would send a guide to help them return behind their own lines. Rupert paced up and down until Armstrong tactfully suggested that he might be more comfortable in a shed. He sat down on an old wooden crate and stared at the ground. He grew irritated and frustrated as he listened to the troopers talking amongst themselves while they filled their canvas buckets with handfuls of grass. Someone said, 'Somerville don't know his arse from his elbow. That bloody fool will get us all killed. He's too good looking for a soldier. He looks like a nancy boy to me. We all drew the short straw being in his lot and not with the captain'.

'Just supply them horses with grass and keep your mouth shut, Nash,' someone replied. 'You all right?' he added, as Nash swayed and nearly fell over.

'No, me head hurts.'

There was a pause and then Rupert heard the second man say, 'Bloody hell, that looks bad. You'd better go and sit down. I'll get the sarg to patch you up'. Rupert sat seething at the remarks. It needled him when he heard the men calling Andrew *the captain* while they spat out his name, *Somerville,* without his rank.

He listened to the NCOs organising a guard rota. He felt lonely and isolated, aware that the Germans could arrive at any moment. He held his head in his hands trying, unsuccessfully, to stem his tears.

***

Whilst Rupert was lost in the forest, Andrew arrived at the river, well below the ford. The water was shallow and the thirsty horses quickened their pace as they walked into the middle.

'Don't let them drink too quickly. I don't want any colic tonight,' Andrew ordered, as the horses dived at the swiftly running water. But they drew back, snorting, curling up their top lips and shaking their heads.

'The river's full of blood, sir!' exclaimed Turner 64.

Andrew looked down and saw the frothy red scum that had washed down from the waterfall. 'I thought we might have beaten this filth.' He looked up as Shrimp and Stone arrived, leading five horses, three German and two English. 'Well done, Fisher. Did you have a problem catching the enemy horses?'

'No, sir. They seem to speak pretty good English.'

'Good, good.' Andrew smiled. 'We'll cross the river and move downstream away from this debris.'

They rode in single file between the river and a steep wooded bank. The wounded German soldier sat clutching the pommel of the saddle while a trooper led his horse.

Turner 65 called out, 'Sir, there's some water, but not much more than a trickle, coming down from the forest over here'.

Andrew went back to investigate. 'Well done, Turner. It looks like a spring. Dismount, all of you, and use your buckets to water your horses.'

The men were halfway up the steep bank when Shrimp put up his hand. 'What's that noise, sir?'

'What noise?'

'That,' replied Shrimp. Everybody froze, voices could be heard, and the sound of horses sloshing down river towards them. The German looked hopefully in the direction of the noise.

'Draw rifles and keep a close eye on the prisoner,' ordered Andrew. The men dropped their buckets beside their startled horses. The animals sensed the alarm and one stepped sideways into the river. He stood broadside on and refused to come out.

'Leave him,' barked Andrew. He realised that the enemy would have no difficulty in picking off his men. He held his breath as the unknown soldiers stopped before the bend in the river.

He ordered the Turner twins to advance along the bank and find out who they were. The remaining men hid behind trees, trained their guns up river, and waited.

***

Lance-Corporal Williams strode through the water leading his horse. Marsh followed him with two horses. He stopped dead as Williams held up his hand. 'Soldiers,' he hissed. 'Wait here. If I don't come back, mount your horse and bugger off up the river as fast as you can. Hold my horse.' Williams crept downstream, keeping close to the bank under the cover of the overhanging trees. He stopped beneath a weeping willow at the bend in the river. He carefully and quietly parted the branches and found himself looking straight into the barrel of a Lee Enfield. 'Fucking Hell, if it ain't La-di-dah Williams,' said a familiar voice.

'Turner 65,' Williams breathed. 'I never thought I'd be so pleased to see you.'

'What the hell happened to you?' asked Turner 64. 'We thought you was dead.'

'It's all right, sir,' called 65 as he made his way back to Andrew. 'It's Williams and he's got Marsh.'

'Thank God. Good to see you. Tell me what happened later. Right now we need to get up that bank and into the forest.' Andrew was relieved to see both men return alive. Williams had attended his own school, Harrow, although he had left well before the boy had arrived there. Andrew was acquainted with the lad's mother. He guessed that he was only 16 and had lied about his age when he joined up. Marsh was the son of his father's huntsman. Andrew had seen him grow up to reach the army's required age of eighteen.

Once they reached the top of the hill, the men relaxed. Williams looked around and asked one of the Turners, 'Is this all that's left of us? Where's Somerville? And who's the Fritz?'

'That's my prisoner. Somerville buggered off on a wild goose chase after the Hun,' replied 65. 'The captain sounded the retreat, but they took no notice... They just kept galloping towards the forest, but way over there.' 65 waved his arm towards their left. 'They're probably lost or dead by now.'

Andrew had a good view from the top of the hill through the beech trees and into the fields surrounding the ford. He could see no sign of the enemy. He lowered his field glasses and called Marsh to join him. 'What happened to you?'

'My horse lost his head in the skirmish, sir. He went berserk. He made for the wall in the ford. I thought he was going to jump, but he dropped his shoulder at the last minute and ducked out. I went clean over the wall without him. I landed in deep water and, thanks to his Lordship, your father, for making us learn to swim in the great lake at home, I swam downstream and waited, not knowing what to do.'

'Go on,' Andrew prompted.

'I saw a Hun fall into the water, but he couldn't swim. I could have saved him, but I let him drown.' He shivered and looked at Andrew. 'They say drowning's an easy death, but actually I'd rather be run through with a sword. It took quite a long time. I'll always be grateful to his Lordship, reckon he saved my life. Would... would you thank him for me when you next write to him, sir?'

'Of course I will. He'll be very pleased to hear you say that.' Andrew smiled kindly.

'Sir, should I have saved Fritz?'

'No, we're fighting a war, Marsh,' Andrew said. 'If you had, he would have killed you. You did well.'

'Thank you, sir.' Marsh joined the others and Andrew heard Turner 65 ask, 'How come the captain's father taught you to swim?'

'My father's his huntsman. He has a pack of hounds, owns a big estate does the captain's father. He's Lord Hawkenfield. He's in the War

Cabinet.'

'Does that mean the captain will be a lord one day?' asked Shrimp.

'No, his older brother Bertram will be the next Lord Hawkenfield. He's just been promoted to a Lieutenant-Colonel. In the guards, he is.'

'Yeah,' retorted Turner 64. 'The captain's bound to get promoted, too. They look after their own, them nobs do.'

As he heard the remark Andrew snapped, 'Turner! Go and fetch some water and wash that horse over there, he looks over-heated.' He watched as both twins spun round, gave their horses to Shrimp, and walked back down the hill to the spring.

Andrew sighed. He also agreed with the popular belief that, in fact, Bertram had achieved his promotion through his father's position.

CHAPTER TWO

The Enclave

Andrew stood on the hill and scanned the surrounding countryside for Rupert, but he could see no sign of him. He then inspected the horses while they cropped the grass under the trees. 'Most of them have got minor injuries of some sort,' he remarked to his men. 'We need a place where we can bathe their wounds and feed them.' He paused as the Turner twins came back, each carrying a canvas bucket full of water. 'Thank you, Turners. We'll wash the worst of the cuts and then move on. Williams, over here please.' Andrew took some maps from his saddle bag. 'How's your map-reading skill?'

'All right, I think, sir.'

'These maps date from the time of Napoleon III. Wouldn't you think the French would have updated them?'

'Maybe the forest hasn't changed that much since then. I know when I stayed with a family in France they were very proud of their forests and gave me a detailed history of them. The only trouble is I've forgotten what they said.' Williams smiled ruefully.

'Let's hope you're right.' Andrew indicated a small clearing in the middle of the forest. 'I would like to make it to this enclave before dark. I only hope that it still exists. There seems to be a dwelling and fields; at least we could graze the horses. The road we came down isn't marked, although here's the river. This could be the ford by this marshy ground... and I think we must be on the top of this hill... here.'

Williams's grey eyes narrowed as he studied the map. 'Yes, because this could be where Lieutenant Somerville was heading. The forest follows the fields round to the north-east in exactly the same pattern.'

'Yes, that's what I thought.'

'If we follow this ride down the hill towards the south west and then take the third ride from the right at this sort of roundabout...'

'Yes, and continue to the next junction, which is called... *Carrefour du Sanglier Noir*, and then take the second left, hopefully we'll arrive at our destination. Thank you, Williams. Sometimes two heads are better than one. By the way, what happened to you? I saw you go over the waterfall.'

'Yes, sir.' Williams grinned. 'Luckily the water was very deep. I thought I'd had it as we jumped the wall, but the landing was soft and I managed to swim free of my horse. Fortunately, he followed me towards the shallows and I was able to catch him. He was unscathed, except he kept shaking his head; I think he got some water in his ear. Then I was joined by Marsh. After that we found two horses. One of them was the German horse and the other was Stone's. He was stuck on the bank.'

'Stuck? What do you mean?'

'His head was jammed between two trees, a bit like a cow in a byre. You know, the cow puts her head in the manger, the cowman shuts those metal things and she can't get her head out.'

'How extraordinary. I know what you mean.' Andrew smiled. 'I can't quite picture how a horse could, or would, do that in a wood. Do you know how he got there?'

'I've no idea, but we had a devil of a job to get him out.'

'Well, it was a good thing you did, otherwise he might have starved to death.' Andrew would have liked to have had a word with Stone, but he wanted to move on and it would keep. He gave the order to mount.

'Well La-di-dah, where are we going?' Turner 65 asked as they moved off.

'Somewhere to graze the horses, I hope.'

'Are we going far?'

'Don't know,' replied Williams.

'Oh come on, La-di-dah,' said Turner 64. 'We saw you talking to the captain.'

'He doesn't confide in me,' replied Williams.

The twins looked at each other. 'The little creep puts on that accent to crawl round him,' said one.

'Yeah, bloody little brown-noser,' replied the other.

'Did you see Stone reclaim his 'orse?' Shrimp spoke in a hushed voice. Marsh shook his head. 'Well, it hates 'im... didn't want to go near 'im.'

'Your imagination, Shrimp,' Turner 64 sneered.

'No, straight up, the captain noticed too, I saw 'im look. He was as surprised as me.'

'I think he was astounded that Stone had lost it in the first place and at where we found it,' remarked Williams.

'Yeah, that was weird,' Marsh said.

'I'm so pleased you made it, Marsh.' Shrimp changed the subject. 'I was worried when I saw you was missing, but I knew you'd turn up.'

'No you didn't,' remarked Turner 65. 'You looked like the boy in the nursery rhyme who lost his sheep.'

Williams turned in his saddle. 'How does that one go, 65? We don't know any nursery rhymes.'

'Very funny, La-di-dah,' retorted Turner 65. 'That horse you're leading, Number 49…'

'I know his name, thank you. You were supposed to wash him off because he was overheated, but you didn't do a very good job. He's dripping with sweat.'

'I did wash him off, know-all; he keeps swishing that short stubby tail of his. It looks like he has colic.'

'I'm well aware of that. He keeps trying to kick my horse. I think you should look after your Fritz, he looks as if he's going to fall off.'

Turner 65 swung round to see the prisoner hanging on to the pommel of his saddle. He was taking shallow rasping breaths and his blue tunic was soaked in blood. Turner 64, who was leading the young German, remarked, 'I think he's going to snuff it'.

'This is the *Carrefour du Sanglier Noir*,' Andrew remarked to Williams, as he looked at the name on the five-pointed signpost at the next junction. 'You must be right about the forest not changing very much over the centuries. But I do think the French should take these signposts down. They're going to be invaluable to the enemy.' He looked at his men and noticed the state of the prisoner; also that Number 49 was showing signs of distress. A trooper, who had a deep cut in his thigh, was bleeding badly and, although he had been patched up with the emergency field dressings they all carried, Andrew knew the man desperately needed stitching up.

He took the second path on the left. The track seemed endless as it twisted and turned. Andrew was beginning to forget about the enclave and thought about setting up camp in the next clearing when they rounded a corner and he sighed with relief. On his left stood a cluster of farm buildings beside a vegetable garden and a large field. At the front lay a long single storey farmhouse.

He dismounted, walked up the worn stone steps and knocked on the sun-baked door. The crooked shutters were closed and pale green paint was peeling off the Z-shaped cross timbers. The place looked deserted except for a wisp of smoke curling up out of the chimney. He knocked again, harder this time, and stepped back, looking and listening for a sign of life. A ghostly sound of two large dogs baying came from one of the outbuildings. Those horses which had been hunters before being bought by the army lifted their tired heads and pricked their ears.

'They sound like the hounds at Hell's gate,' said Turner 65. One or two troopers shifted uneasily in their saddles.

'Could be Count Dracula's castle,' remarked his brother as the eerie baying continued.

'It's just a couple of bloodhounds,' said Marsh.

Andrew was about to bang on the door again when it suddenly opened. A pretty round-faced girl, her dark hair covered by a head scarf tied back at the nape of her neck, stood in the doorway.

'*Oh, c'est vous. Ou est le docteur?* ' She looked the captain up and down, her eyes moving on to the motley group of dirty bloodied soldiers mounted on their tired and shabby-looking horses.

'The doctor?' Andrew replied in French. 'What do you mean?'

'*Marie-Claude, j'arrive.*' A girl's voice came from inside the cottage. The door opened wider and a tall, slim young woman moved into the doorway and stood on the top step.

Andrew looked up into a pair of twinkling grey eyes set in a pretty face with high cheek bones and skin like fine porcelain.

'You got here quickly. I wasn't expecting you until after dark.'

'I didn't know you were expecting us at all,' replied Andrew.

'Where's the doctor?' The girl continued in good English.

'The doctor... I don't understand...'

'You have a German prisoner... No matter, bring your horses in.' She turned to her companion. '*Ouvre la porte*, Marie-Claude.'

The shorter girl ran to the side of the house and dragged open the heavy gate. Andrew ordered the men to ride through while he walked beside the tall, elegant young woman.

'Do you mind about my prisoner? I can't very well leave him in the forest.'

'*Non*. He looks very young and he's covered in blood. My name is Francine.'

'Captain Andrew Harrington-West.' Andrew removed his hat and shook her hand.

'Sir!' A trooper called.

'Yes.' Andrew replaced his cap, and hurried forwards. 'What is it?'

'It's Bright, sir.'

The badly wounded trooper, his face as white as a sheet, was swaying on his horse, while blood oozed from his leg.

'Bring him indoors. The Boche too,' said Francine. '*Marie-Claude, viens vite.*'

'Turners,' called Andrew. 'Help Bright and the prisoner into the house.'

65 jumped off his horse, saying to Marie-Claude, 'Here, let me, Miss.' Bright leant on heavily Turner as he assisted him into a bedroom and laid him on a narrow bed. His brother helped the German who wheezed and coughed and brought up blood.

'Where shall I put him, Miss?' asked Turner 64.

'Lay him on the bed next to our man. I don't think he's going to kill anyone,' said Andrew. 'That's if you don't mind,' he asked the girl.

'*Non*, you can put him there.'

Turner 65 stood in the middle of the room, staring at Marie-Claude. 'It's all right, Turner, you can go and see to your horse now,' said Andrew. The trooper left reluctantly, still trying to catch the girl's eye, but she was busy attending to Bright.

'What did you mean about the doctor?' Andrew asked Francine again.

'He's bringing in some English cavalry who are lost in the forest. Who are you?'

'Also British cavalry. Good Lord, maybe he's found the other half of my troop. How many men... do you know?'

'About fourteen, I think, with fourteen horses.'

'Thank God. They galloped after the Germans and I've not seen them since.'

'Well, they're lost very close to the Boches, at the other end of the forest. They'll have to travel by night. But don't worry, the doctor knows the forest like the back of his hand.'

'How close are the Germans?' Andrew asked.

'They're not close to here... yet. The forest, she is big.'

'You seem very cool about it.'

Francine smiled. 'We'll cope when they come closer. I'll leave Marie-Claude with your wounded man. She'll make him comfortable until the doctor arrives. She has a gun; she can shoot the Boche if he moves.'

'Don't worry, I'll send a man in to guard him.'

'All right, come outside and we'll settle your horses.'

Francine led Andrew to a building. 'Will they be happy here?' she asked, opening a door.

Andrew saw a row of over twenty stalls. Fourteen were bedded down with straw. He gasped, 'You've prepared them for us. That really is too kind'.

Francine smiled. Andrew looked at her shabby dress and stout boots. The thin material emphasised her neat figure and pert breasts. He quickly turned to his men. 'Get these horses watered and settled down,' he ordered. 'Then feed them from their nose bags.'

'*Non, non*, it's all right, we have feed also,' Francine replied. 'Follow me, I'll show you the feed shed.' Andrew walked behind her, noticing the way the thin material fell, revealing her swinging athletic hips. He found it difficult to concentrate on what she was saying and so he glanced around him. They walked past a deserted kennel that looked as if it could house a considerable number of hounds. 'What is this place?' he asked.

'The hunt kennels,' replied Francine.

'Where are the hounds?'

'Gone down to… Le Marquis' chateau in the Loire valley… for safe keeping, along with the huntsman, all except these two hounds.'

Andrew looked at the two canines in a smaller kennel. 'What breed are those? I've never seen black and white hounds before.' They had stopped baying and stood waving their sterns. Their pointed aristocratic noses sniffed the air, while their long ears framed their heads like judges' wigs.

'They're Gascon Saintongeois, French deer hounds, Monsieur. That one is Dagobert and this is Daguet. We keep them to *faire le bois*.'

'What?'

'To track the animals in the forest.' She opened the door to a shed. 'The Marquis said I must give our store of corn to the British or the French. If the Boches come they will take it all.'

'That's very generous of you. I'll tell my NCOs to help themselves, shall I?'

'Please do.'

Andrew went to check the wounded men. He frowned as he heard Bright's fast, shallow breathing and saw that the blood from his thigh was beginning to stain the linen sheets. 'A doctor will be coming to see you soon,' Andrew tried to reassure him.

'Thank you, sir,' whispered the white-faced trooper, closing his eyes.

The German was struggling to breathe and every now and then he coughed, bringing up blood.

Andrew returned to Francine in the kitchen. 'Bright looks worse and I think the prisoner is close to death. When do you think the doctor will get here?'

'Not until after midnight, I expect.'

Andrew cursed Rupert again for galloping off in pursuit of a prey that was bound to lose him in the forest. He called for Williams.

Without any preamble, he asked the lance-corporal, 'Pilson was in our half-troop, wasn't he?' Williams nodded. 'But he wasn't among the dead, so I presume he must be missing. I don't see how he could have made it through the ford and off with the lieutenant. Did you see him?'

'No, sir, I didn't.'

'You don't think he could have... Well... absconded?'

'No, definitely not.' Williams was adamant.

'No... No I thought not. He's a good man. Let's hope he's with the others and that they arrive before too long. You can bring the men in for their meal. The food is ready. Leave two troopers on guard outside.'

The men ate in silence and then left to rest in the hay loft, leaving Andrew alone with Francine.

'Get some sleep.' She smiled. 'Your men may take a long time to get here; we'll hear them arrive soon enough. You'll be of no use to anyone if you're too tired. You can sleep in Marie-Claude's room. She can share with me. I'll take you there. ' Andrew looked at her slim figure with her dark hair falling to her shoulders. For a moment he felt vulnerable. Since leaving home and arriving in France, nobody had showed him that sort of kindness. He nodded and followed her to the sparsely furnished bedroom. He stood in the doorway and said awkwardly, 'Thank you for looking after us.' She nodded and hurried away.

***

While Andrew's men were eating their supper, Rupert's troopers were waiting impatiently for their guide.

'We're all starving. Have you got anything to eat?' A trooper asked Corporal Clark.

'No. Drink your water while we have plenty of it.'

'It tastes funny.'

'Stop complaining. It's the same for all of us.' Clark hurried away to talk to Armstrong. 'I see you've patched up Nash,' he remarked.

'Yes, I don't like the look of his wound. He says he's seeing two of everything and feels drunk... Listen! There's a horse coming. Let's hope it's our guide.'

'Let's hope it's not the Hun,' Clark remarked. He stood with Armstrong and watched a man dressed in tweeds riding towards the sheds. Rupert came out to greet him.

'Good evening, I'm Doctor Lejeune. I've come to help you.'

'You've taken ages. What kept you?' Rupert said.

'I'm sorry, the Boches are everywhere. I had a devil of a job to get through.' The Frenchman spoke good English.

'You did well then.' Armstrong smiled, trying to make up for Rupert's rudeness.

The doctor looked down at him. 'You need to go to the hunt kennels in the middle of the forest. The Boches are only two kilometres away from here but fortunately they're not moving.'

'Two kilometres!' gasped one of the men who had gathered round. 'That's just over a mile.'

'We'll have to be careful in order to avoid them,' continued the doctor. 'The German cavalry are everywhere, I had to hide in a thicket while two patrols met and exchanged information. Unfortunately, I couldn't hear what they were saying. I've brought some bread for you. It's all I could get.' He opened a rucksack and brought out a baguette spread with butter and filled with ham, which he gave to Rupert.

Armstrong heaved a silent sigh when he saw that the rest of the baguettes were hard and spread with nothing. He passed them to the men, saying, 'We have a sick man, Doctor'.

'Most of the men have something wrong,' snapped Rupert. 'Have them girth up and we'll be on our way.'

Armstrong addressed the doctor again, smiling, 'If you wouldn't mind... please'.

'Of course.' The doctor glanced briefly at Rupert and followed the sergeant.

'I'm worried. This man can hardly stand up.'

After examining Nash, the doctor said, 'He has severe concussion; by rights he shouldn't be riding'.

'You'd better inform the lieutenant,' said Armstrong.

***

'He'll have to ride,' said Rupert.

'He could drop dead at any moment. I've known people with a bad blow to the head do just that, with no warning,' replied the doctor.

'We can't leave him here,' retorted Rupert. 'The Hun could find him.'

'Yes… I understand. Put him on a quiet horse.'

'They're all quiet. They've been in a battle, most of them are lame. Hurry up, we need to get going. It's beginning to get dark.'

The horses were nearly all stiff as they set off after their rest. Armstrong hoped that after a bit they would loosen up and most of them did, although they weren't helped by the amount of equipment that they had to carry. A leather bandolier was wrapped around each horse's neck holding sixty rounds of ammunition. A leather bucket was fixed to the right side of the saddle, containing the trooper's rifle, plus a metal mess tin and a feed bag holding seven pounds of oats. A sword-frog and scabbard, also spare horse shoes in a pouch, plus another seven-pound feed bag and a folding canvas bucket were attached to the near side of the saddle.

The right front saddle-arch held a pair of leather wallets containing small kit; this was covered by a rolled-up mackintosh cape. A rolled-up greatcoat was attached to the rear arch. Underneath the saddle were two blankets, one for horse and one for the rider.

Added to this weight, each rider carried a bandolier over his left shoulder with thirty rounds of ammunition and a felt-covered water bottle. A haversack was slung over his right shoulder containing his personal belongings. Including the rider, each horse carried around eighteen stone.

The half-troop rode away from the main rides and down paths rutted by the tracks of wagons that had removed logs during the winter. A horse stumbled and Nash fell to the ground. Rupert sighed with impatience and barked at a trooper, 'For God's, sake put him back on his horse'. The doctor, who was riding beside Rupert, looked round anxiously. 'Hurry up,' shouted the lieutenant, and the cavalcade began to move again.

The doctor shook his head. 'I don't think he should be riding.'

'He has no choice.'

They carried on in stony silence, while Nash swayed in his saddle. After a short distance a trooper cried, 'He's fallen again, sir'.

'Nash is having a big problem, sir.' Armstrong told Rupert as they rode back to the afflicted Nash. 'We have to hold him in place.'

'Keep moving,' Rupert ordered, and then he smiled. 'You ride up with the doctor. I'll stay at the back and help Nash.'

'Are you sure, sir?'

'Quite sure. Keep going,' he replied pleasantly.

The men rode on, occasionally looking back at Rupert and Nash, who were making very slow progress and falling further and further behind.

Nash fell off his horse again. Rupert dragged the trooper into the undergrowth at the side of the track. Then he mounted and quickly caught up with the others.

'What's happened to the sick man, lieutenant?' enquired the doctor.

'He did precisely what you predicted; he suddenly fell off his horse, only this time he was dead when he hit the ground.'

The men stared at their officer. 'Shall I go back and look?' asked the doctor.

'No need, I know he was dead.' The doctor looked undecided. 'Come on.' Rupert was impatient. 'We're wasting time.'

'Shouldn't we take his body, sir?' asked Armstrong.

'No, we don't know where we're going. Someone will find him and do the necessary.'

The men rode on in uncomfortable silence along a track that bordered farmland. It was just possible to see the forest curve around a farmyard that stood in the middle of the fields.

'We have to get to the forest on the other side of that little farm, but we'll have to continue all the way round by way of the trees.'

'How much longer will that take us?' asked Rupert.

'It'll add over an hour to our journey.'

'Then we'll cut across.'

'That's unwise,' replied the doctor. 'There are dogs. They may bark and wake up the farmer.'

'Does that matter? He's French, I presume.'

'Of course he's French.'

'Then we'll take that chance and cut through. How much further do we have to go once we're on the other side of that farm?'

'I should say about another hour's ride, at the pace we're going... maybe an hour and a half.'

'Then we'll definitely cut through.'

'All right. *On your head be it,*' he muttered under his breath.

Clark, hearing the exchange, looked anxiously at Armstrong, who shrugged his shoulders.

They crossed a boundary ditch and continued through a stubble field. They managed to push their stiff horses into a canter and then a gallop. Rupert was pleased that things were speeding up. At that moment a flock of geese in a pen began to march up and down beside the wire, honking. In the next pen guinea fowl began to run hither and thither making a high-pitched staccato noise.

Rupert stopped his troop, but it was too late: the two large dogs that were chained to their kennels began to bark.

An upstairs window flew open and the farmer fired two barrels of his shotgun into the air. The men grabbed their rifles.

'It's all right, Monsieur Boudain,' shouted the doctor. 'Come down and quieten your animals.'

The irate farmer came running down the stairs and into the yard. A furious conversation began in French between the two men.

'Look!' shouted Sergeant Armstrong. He pointed at lights and movement in the fields at the far end of the farm.

'*Les Boches!*' cried the farmer.

'We must get out of here!' the doctor said.

Rupert turned his men and they galloped back to the point in the forest where they had entered the fields.

'Back to square one,' Clark said under his breath to Armstrong. The gallop to and from the farm hadn't helped the lame horses. The men continued riding in silence along the track that followed the edge of the forest. From time to time they caught the sound of raised voices coming from the farm, but the enemy didn't seem to want follow them.

All the lights went on in the house and Rupert could see through his field glasses that some of the riders had dismounted and were milling about in the yard.

'I expect they'll take Monsieur Boudain's poultry and his eggs,' remarked the doctor.

'That's not our problem,' replied Rupert tetchily.

Suddenly shots rang out, quickly followed by the sound of a woman shouting. Her screams were cut short by more gunfire. The troopers shivered and kicked their tired horses into a faster gait. They were all glad when they could leave the perimeter and take a path that led deeper into the forest.

'How much further do we have to go?' demanded Rupert.

'Quite a way yet,' replied the doctor. 'Your horses look exhausted.

Can they keep going?'

'Maybe we should dismount and walk, sir,' suggested Armstrong. 'Or find some water.'

'Yes.' Rupert replied to the doctor's question.

'Dismount,' ordered the sergeant. The men gratefully slid off their horses.

'What are you doing?' demanded Rupert. 'I didn't give the order to dismount.'

'Sorry, sir. I thought you said, yes.'

'I was talking to the doctor.'

'A misunderstanding on my part. I see there's a stream up ahead. Shall we water the horses?' Rupert waited impatiently while the horses drank. 'I think the horses are walking faster without riders on their backs, sir,' Armstrong said.

Reluctantly Rupert dismounted. The troopers plodded on, too weary to talk. They constantly glanced over their shoulders, looking and listening for a pursuing enemy.

At last the doctor said, 'We're here.' Their spirits rose as they stopped beside the entrance to some buildings. Their hopes were dashed and their fears returned as they heard the movement of soldiers behind the high wooden gates.

'You idiot, you've brought us to a Hun encampment,' snarled Rupert. Then they heard the unmistakable voice of Williams giving the order to mount. 'Thank God,' Armstrong said under his breath.

CHAPTER THREE

Reconnaissance and an Encounter

Clark jumped off his horse and opened the heavy gates, his young face lighting up when he saw Shrimp, the Turners and Williams.

Turner 65 shouted, 'We've been waiting for you. You're only five hours late.'

'What do you mean?' Clark asked, then he said, 'Good morning, sir,' as Andrew came out to greet them. Andrew noticed Rupert's glare as Clark added, 'We were lucky to make it back at all'.

'Thank God you're all safe. Well done.' Andrew addressed the rest of the arrivals. 'Get these horses fed and watered. Attend to any injuries. I'll be out to inspect them later.' He turned to Williams. 'Dismount the men, we'll postpone the reconnaissance.'

It wasn't until he had cast his eyes over the returning troopers that he spoke to Rupert, 'I see you've lost Nash and you haven't got Pilson'. He looked at Lejeune. Rupert hastily introduced him.

'So you're the intrepid doctor. Excellent. Please refresh yourself, and then maybe you could look at an injured man.'

Rupert watched Francine run into the yard and escort Lejeune into the house. He jumped as Andrew said, 'Rupert, come with me'. His heart sank as he followed his senior officer into the privacy of the feed shed. 'Now, what happened?' demanded Andrew. 'I blew the retreat and yet you continued galloping after the enemy. It was obvious what would happen once you entered the forest.'

'I didn't hear the command.'

'Didn't you?'

'No, I didn't.' Rupert avoided Andrew's eyes. He didn't want to tell Andrew that he hadn't issued the order to pursue the Germans. The men had done that all by themselves. Andrew continued: 'You have to learn to listen for orders, Rupert. Your duty is to look after the men'.

'I thought it was our duty to make them fight.'

'You're being obtuse. You know what I mean. Perhaps you would like to explain how you lost another soldier. He wasn't among the dead at the ford. How did he die?'

'He died after the battle. In the forest. From his head wound.'

'But you had a doctor with you. Didn't you ask his opinion?'

'Yes, of course. He told me that Nash could drop down dead at any moment and he did. You can ask him if you want.'

'I intend to.'

Rupert looked up. He felt sick as he saw the angry look in Andrew's deep blue eyes as they bored into his. 'I... I couldn't leave him behind. The Hun were on our tail. I wanted to get him back to the squadron... or at least into friendly territory so he could have the best possible care.' He paused. 'I even rode beside him to help him.' He noticed Andrew's features beginning to soften and added, 'I was devastated when he dropped dead'.

'All right, as long as you did your best. How did your men fight? Is there anyone whom I should mention in my report?'

Rupert realised that he hadn't noticed which men had fought well. He thought for a moment. 'They all did a good job... except for Ashton.'

'Why? What did he do wrong?'

'Between you and me, I thought he could have done better. It... it was more a case of what he didn't do.'

'I see. You've got blood on your arm. Are you injured?'

'No.'

'Then whose blood is that?' Andrew pointed to a large stain on the inside of his right sleeve. Rupert lifted his arm to look and felt his colour heighten. 'I...   we've been in a battle. I don't know whose blood it is.'

'You'd better go and get something to eat from the kitchen and clean yourself up.' Rupert let out a long sigh as he walked away.

Andrew noticed Rupert relax as he left the shed. He began to follow him when he heard Clark talking to Williams. He stopped to listen.

'We wouldn't have made it back if it hadn't been for the Frenchman and Armstrong.'

'As bad as that, was it?' asked Williams.

'Somerville was out of his depth. He didn't want to stop and water the horses, or let us dismount to take the weight off their backs. Then the farmer got shot.'

'What farmer?'

'Although we can't really blame him for that, I suppose. The Hun would have taken the farm in the daylight. They were very close.' Clark went on to explain what had happened.

'Good Lord. Luckily they didn't come after you.'

'Yes, thank God. They would have made mincemeat out of us.'

'We've got a prisoner.' Williams changed the subject.

'Have you? Somerville wouldn't take any prisoners. Ashton saw him kill a wounded Fritz. He had his hands up and wanted to surrender, but he ran him through with his sword. Ashton said he enjoyed it.'

'What, Ashton?'

'No, Somerville enjoyed it. Ashton saw him do it.'

Andrew walked on thoughtfully and went into the house to find out the doctor's prognosis on Bright and his prisoner. As he entered the room he heard the short rasping breaths of the German.

The doctor stood beside Bright. 'I can't stitch up the wound. I fear his cut, which is deep and jagged, has become infected. He has a fever. I've done what I can and I've given instructions to Marie-Claude. I would like to take him to *les bonnes sœurs* at the Convent in St. Anton.' He glanced at the other bed. 'The German is dying. I can't do anything for him.'

As Andrew looked at the young man his upper body went into spasm. He coughed and gasped. Blood poured from his mouth and his face twisted in agony. He stared at Andrew and then fell back against his pillows and lay still.

'He's gone.' The doctor hurried to the bed and held his pulse. 'You'll have to bury him,' he said as he covered his face with the bed sheet. 'If you ask your soldiers to dig a grave, I'll send for the priest. You must move on from here, certainly by tomorrow.'

'Thank you, Doctor; I'll bear that in mind. I need to rest my men and horses. I'm sure that by tomorrow we'll be able to make the journey. Francine has suggested that we go to a château about twenty miles from here.'

'That would be an excellent idea.'

'I'll go on reconnaissance this afternoon and see how the land lies. You've been very kind. How much do I owe you?'

'Nothing, I do this for France, *Capitaine*. I'll take my leave now; à bientôt.'

***

After Rupert's men had eaten and gone to rest in the hay loft, Andrew inspected their horses. Number 49 had died in the night and his body had been removed to the skinning shed. Andrew walked down the row of stalls and suddenly stopped beside a new arrival.

'I'm not happy with this one. Bring him out, Fisher.' Andrew ran his hand down the horse's swollen hind leg and the animal lashed out. 'Whoa!' he exclaimed, and caught hold of the leg again. 'I can feel the bones moving in his pastern. I don't know how he made it back here. Take him to the skinning shed.'

Andrew watched as the reluctant animal limped towards the shed, then he stopped, snorted and refused to move. Shrimp stood and stared at the horse. 'Fisher, you're being very half-hearted. Give him to Marsh and fetch the twins.'

By the time Shrimp came back, the body of the horse lay on the tiled floor beside that of Number 49.

'Marsh, you know how to skin out an animal; can you show the Turners? Fisher, are you up to skinning out?'

'Yes, sir.'

'Right, get these horses done as quickly as possible. Mademoiselle Francine assures me that we may use any equipment that we find in here. You'll see knives in that rack, and wear the rubber aprons that are hanging beside them.'

The four men quickly attached chains around Number 49's hind legs and winched him up off the floor.

'You all right, Shrimp?' asked Marsh.

'Yeah, once they're dead, I don't mind. It's the in-between bit I don't like.' He and Marsh worked on Number 49, while the Turners started on the other horse.

'Look at this,' exclaimed Shrimp. 'There's a tear in this 'orse's gut.' The Turners and Marsh gathered round.

'It's a small puncture. It looks as if it was made by one of our swords. Fritz had big lances. They would have made a much larger hole,' said Turner 65.

'I've never seen a horse with such violent colic before. It was horrible. No wonder... poor devil,' added Marsh.

When Andrew came back to see how they were progressing, they showed him the tear. 'Well spotted, Fisher,' he said. 'Very curious. Unfortunately, his rider was killed so we can't ask him what happened.'

Andrew returned to the house, where he found Francine in the kitchen. He told her that she could make use of the dead horses in whatever way she wanted. 'It's thanks to you that we could use the facilities here. Otherwise we would have to leave the carcasses in the countryside, as we did at the ford.'

'Thank you, I'll tell the villagers, and I'll take some meat for Daguet and Dagobert. I expect a farmer will remove the horses that were killed in the ambush.' She shuddered.

'I'm going to take out a patrol: I wondered if you could accompany us as a guide. I... I presume you can ride.'

Francine stared at him. 'Yes, I can ride.'

'Good, good.' Andrew didn't notice her surprise at his remarks and called for Williams. He told him to get the horses ready and that Francine would be joining them.

'Have you seen Mademoiselle Francine's horses?' asked Williams.

'No, I haven't.'

'Two cracking thoroughbreds, a bay and a grey. I'd fancy my chances around Aintree on either of them.' Williams grinned at Francine, who smiled back.

Andrew turned to Francine. 'I'll look forward to seeing them. Now we'd better get on. Excuse me,' he said, as he leant across her to pick up a map. He paused in surprise as he smelt her perfume. He was sure that it was identical to the expensive fragrance he had given to an old flame. 'I... I want to go back to the ford and look for Pilson. Also survey the surrounding area, see where the Boches are, that sort of thing. It could be dangerous. You may not wish to come?'

'Danger and I are becoming good friends and my horses need exercise.' She smiled.

'Which horse are you thinking of riding? The grey would have to be camouflaged.'

'What do you mean?'

'All grey horses have to be painted with permanganate of potash dye. The entire regiment of the Scot's Greys had to paint all their horses.'

'Good heavens!' exclaimed Francine. 'In that case I'll take my bay.'

'I'm sure there's someone who knows how to saddle a horse with a side-saddle. Would you like us to...?'

'No, thank you, that won't be necessary. I'll go and change. I'll be with you in a flash.'

Andrew found his party lined up and ready to set out. Francine appeared leading her horse. She was wearing men's breeches and boots. He knew that some women were beginning to ride astride, although his sister would never be allowed to ride in that fashion. He was about to ask if he could help her to mount when she swung herself lightly into the saddle. Once mounted, her magnificent horse sidled towards the men, tossing his head and snorting. Andrew hoped that she would be able to control her mettlesome animal. He was beginning to wonder if asking for her help had been a good idea; he didn't want the repetition of a runaway horse. He quickly mounted the horse that Williams had saddled for him and, looking down, realised that it was German. He shot a sharp look at the lance-corporal, who was apologetic. 'He's the freshest and soundest horse we have, sir.' Andrew nodded, moved the men forwards. He asked Francine to ride up beside him at the front of the small cavalcade. She skilfully brought her dancing horse next to Andrew's well-behaved mount.

'Take this path.' She pointed with her whip to a narrow gap in the trees. As soon as the path widened, Andrew asked her to trot on. He watched her slim back and supple hips as she rose gracefully up and down in the saddle. He wondered why her features were so different from those of her sister. She was taller, more elegant and had a finer bone structure. Maybe she was born on the wrong side of the blanket, he thought. Then the words of his great aunt Agnes came into his head when, on his eighteenth birthday, she had paid for him to visit a lady of easy virtue. 'I don't want you practising your lust on the servant girls. I can't abide so called *gentlemen*, who litter the countryside with their offspring. Nothing is so nauseating as to be served at table by one's neighbour's bastard.'

'A penny for your thoughts? asked Francine. 'You seem to be miles away.'

Andrew jumped and blushed. Francine had stopped just before a wide straight ride. 'Oh, I … I see we have to cross here. Turner 65, dismount and see if the coast is clear. Take these.' Andrew recovered his composure and handed his field glasses to 65. All lustful thoughts were chased out of his head as they crossed the open expanse of the ride.

They arrived safely at the river, but a long way downstream from where they had watered their horses the previous day. Andrew shuddered as he saw the pieces of viscera that had been washed up on to the banks.

They crossed the water and carried on up a hill, but the path dwindled away into undergrowth and it soon became impassable. Andrew halted the patrol, dismounted, and continued on foot with Francine and Williams. He was glad that Francine was wearing men's breeches and boots; a riding skirt would have severely hampered her progress through the dense, thorny bushes. When they reached the edge of the forest, Andrew pulled out his field glasses and focussed them on the stony road where Rupert had chased the Germans the day before.

'Good God, look!' he exclaimed.

'*Mon Dieu!* My poor France.'

'Great Scot!' Williams stared, horrified.

The road was alive with Germans. A seemingly never ending convoy of infantry, cavalry, troops and heavy artillery was pouring down the hill. They passed through the ford and travelled in the same southerly direction that Andrew and his troop needed to take in order to get back to their squadron.

'We have to move closer,' Andrew said to Francine. 'They're clearing the ford... and digging something.'

'Follow me.'

'You stay with the horses. Just tell me where to go.'

'Rubbish,' Francine whispered and hurried back down the hill.

They rejoined their horses and, before Andrew could say anything, Francine had mounted, crossed back through the water, up the hill and was heading along the top of the riverbank towards the ford. Andrew had no choice but to follow her. The men, in single file, galloped after him, dodging the trees and the overhanging branches.

She stopped when she came to a small clearing. 'If you continue on foot you'll reach the ford.'

'Yes, I think I know where we are. This comes out at the place where we waited for the Hun.' Francine nodded. 'Williams come with me.' Andrew was relieved to be back in charge. He addressed the others: 'If we don't come back, look after Mademoiselle Francine and return to the enclave as quickly as possible'.

Turner 65 spoke for all of them when he said, 'It'll be an honour, sir.'

Andrew gave him a sharp look, then he and Williams walked cautiously along the ridge. They were nearly at the ford when they heard some movement in the river below. They froze. German soldiers were fishing a body out of the water.

'Marsh's Fritz?' Andrew mouthed. Williams nodded.

They fell quietly on to their stomachs and wriggled forwards until they could clearly see the men working on the other side. They were digging two long graves. One for the British bodies; he counted them and wondered again what had happened to Pilson. The other trench contained the fallen Germans. As soon as the body of the drowned man had been laid to rest, they filled in the two trenches and planted a crude wooden cross on each.

The convoys of the enemy army came respectfully to a halt while a chaplain held a brief burial service over both the British and the German graves. Andrew and Williams offered up their own private prayers.

As soon as the short service finished, the German war machine set in motion once again. Great cannons, each hauled by six pairs of horses, lumbered through the ford. Motorised food wagons, ammunition lorries, columns of infantry and cavalry marched past like a gigantic hostile python, snaking its way slowly yet relentlessly towards the Allied positions.

Both men crept away from the scene. Andrew stopped to break free from a bramble. He spun round as he heard a noise. He saw a German officer standing a little way away under the shade of the trees staring at him. He thought he was the officer who had been in charge of the burial party. His hand flew to his revolver but he hesitated and stared at the German, who stared back. Andrew knew that if he fired he would summon the army below. Time stood still as he waited for the officer to shoot, but the man continued to stand and stare.

Andrew felt compelled to say, 'Thank you for awarding my men a Christian burial.' He saluted the German, who, to his amazement returned his salute, turned round and disappeared back the way he had come.

Andrew ran towards Williams, who was rooted to the spot.

'I think... I'm not sure,' Andrew gasped. 'They know we're here, now. Just run.'

They ran for their lives, stumbling as they glanced over their shoulders, expecting to see German soldiers hot on their heels. Their backs bristled, anticipating the thud of a bullet.

As they reached the waiting men, Andrew gasped, 'We need to leave this place fast.' He flung himself on to his horse.

Francine set off at a gallop down through the trees, jumping the ditches as she crossed the wide rides.

Andrew slowed the patrol to a walk when he was sure that they weren't being followed. Suddenly, above the noise of the horses' blowing, he heard a short burst of machine-gun fire. He abruptly halted the men. The men clutched their rifles and stared through the trees in the direction of the sound. The "*tat-tat-tat*" sounded again, hollow, echoing and sinister. Andrew looked at Francine and smiles broke out on their faces. He heard Shrimp whisper, 'What's so bleedin' funny?'

'It's a woodpecker, townie,' replied Turner 65. 'Makes his nest in trees, eats bugs in the bark.'

'Oh,' Shrimp breathed, 'is that all?'

Andrew moved the men forwards at a jog trot, until Francine unexpectedly held up her hand and stopped.

'What is it?' whispered Andrew.

'You hear the birds?'

'Yes, they're jays, what about them?' Andrew looked ahead in the direction of the noise.

'They follow *les grands animaux*. When the deer are disturbed by something, usually humans or dogs, the birds fly up and squawk.'

Andrew's throat went dry and he noiselessly moved his men off the path and into the undergrowth. They waited in silence; even the horses sensed the necessity for quiet and stood still.

Although straining his ears, Andrew didn't hear the arrival of an elegant party of red deer until they appeared, walking in single file, led by the smallest hind, to within a few feet of the seven horses. They stopped in unison. The patriarch, a magnificent stag, his splendid head of antlers held high, gazed at Andrew. The captain, fascinated by the fourteen-pointer, stared back. With great accuracy and precision, the stag then moved his females forward. Andrew despaired of ever being able to teach his troops the same simultaneous halt to canter movement. He turned to smile at Francine, then jumped and swung his head round as he heard voices approaching. Two young women came into view, walking towards them under the trees. As they came closer he saw that they were carrying baskets filled with fungi. They stopped to pick a cluster of yellow mushrooms, chattering all the while to each other. The troopers held their breath until the girls walked away, never realising how close they had come to the group of armed men.

When he was sure that they were out of earshot, Andrew moved the men forwards again at a canter. The Turner twins looked at each other and grinned. 'I'll have the one on the right,' whispered Len Turner.

'That one's mine,' stated 65.

'All right, we'll share her,' replied Len under his breath.

Shrimp looked at Williams, who pulled a face and whispered, 'Cocky so-and-sos, they'll be lucky.'

Unexpectedly the path they were following opened out into the enclave. 'We're back already,' exclaimed Andrew. 'Thank you for piloting us so expertly.'

'It was a pleasure.' Francine smiled. 'I haven't enjoyed myself so much since the end of the hunting season.'

Andrew watched her nimbly dismount and return her horse to his loosebox. He was relieved to see that everything was normal. The soldiers who had been left behind were busy grooming their horses or cleaning their kit, unaware of the advancing proximity of the Germans.

'We need to leave this place tonight,' Andrew informed Rupert who had come out to greet him. 'The Germans know we're in the vicinity.' He went on to tell the lieutenant what he had seen, but he didn't mention his encounter with the German officer. 'We'll leave at nightfall; make sure everything is ready.'

Andrew went into the house and told Francine. 'That's not a problem,' she said. 'I'll take you to the Château de la Croix, but first I must send word that we're coming.' She turned to Marie-Claude. 'You know what to do.'

'*Oui Mm…* Francine,'

'*Attends,* the wounded man, he cannot ride.'

'I'm afraid he must, how else…?' said Andrew.

'*Non, non*, he can go by farm cart.'

'What!'

'Marie-Claude will fetch Albert, he will take him. They can leave as soon as he gets here, and he can take your spare equipment. We'll hide it under something.' Andrew was beginning to wonder who was in charge of the operation.

***

It didn't take long for the cart to arrive, pulled by two great white Percheron horses and laden with unthreshed sheaves of oats. Albert, the driver, spoke no English but he helped the men stow the extra saddles and bridles under the straw. They left a gap big enough for Bright. The Turner twins helped the sick man to walk across from the house and settled him into the makeshift bed.

As Andrew watched his equipment trundle away, he desperately hoped the Germans wouldn't want to commandeer the oats.

***

Just before nightfall the men went out to saddle up. Most of the horses were sound and rested, but some were still stiff and sore from their exertions the day before. Four lame horses were being led; however, they still had to carry extra bandoliers containing sixty rounds of ammunition.

As darkness fell, the men, with their full kit, were lined up ready to move off. A bright waxing moon lit the yard with a soft glow, and Andrew, glancing to see if Francine was ready, gave the command to move off. He heard the arrival of a galloping horse. With a racing heart, he revoked the order.

'*Docteur* Lejeune,' Francine cried. 'Q*u'est que c'est*?'

'The Boches are *sur la route*; you must go through the forest, cross the plain at *le Vieux Chêne,*' shouted the doctor.

'*Oui*, I know where you mean.' Francine explained to Andrew, 'We must go south east through the forest to start with, and then cut to the south west. That way we'll only have about one and a half kilometres of open country to cross, instead of eighteen. But it'll take much longer'.

'We have no choice,' Andrew replied and, turning to the doctor, he asked, 'Do you know what has happened to Albert and the cart?'

'He must have met the Boches, certainly, but I don't know if he got through. I'm sorry.'

'Thank you for coming to warn us so precipitously.'

'*De rien, mon Capitaine,*' replied Dr. Lejeune. 'I wish you a safe journey.'

Andrew said goodbye to the doctor and moved his troops out of the safe enclave that had sheltered them so well. As they set out on their way in the moonlight he worried about Bright. If caught, he was not in good shape and it wouldn't take much persuasion to make him talk. If that were the case, the Hun would be out there waiting for them.

CHAPTER FOUR

The Chateau

Guided by Francine, Andrew led his men down moonlit forest rides; the surreal light made the trees throw ghostly shadows on to the path in front of them. Andrew could hear the chinking of the bridles and the soft thud of the horses' footfalls on the sandy floor. He kept his eyes trained on the path ahead, relying on Rupert and the NCOs to keep an all-round watch.

The moon disappeared behind a racing cloud and the trees began to whisper, the breeze became stronger and Andrew had to slow down.

An eerie roar erupted from the undergrowth. The men froze in their saddles. Another bellow was quickly followed by the sound of clashing weapons.

The horses lifted their heads and pricked their ears. Some shied violently and tried to bolt. The men drew their rifles with one hand and tried to control their mounts with the other. Andrew, together with a few men, managed to turn and face the trees. The others were running backwards and sideways on plunging horses.

'You bloody idiots. Stand fast!' yelled an NCO, whose horse stood with his ears pricked, intently watching the undergrowth.

'All right lads, calm down,' Sergeant Armstrong shouted, as he gained control of his horse. Andrew could hear heavy breathing and the sound of brushwood being trampled underfoot. The battle drew nearer. One of the led horses reared up and broke free.

The noise stopped. A stag shot across the path, his damp coarse coat shining in the moonlight. He jumped a ditch and disappeared under the trees. A larger stag followed and, with saliva dripping from his mouth, stopped on the path, raised his head and let out a roar of victory. He glanced at the riders, shook his antlers and returned to rejoin his females.

Andrew smiled as he heard Shrimp say to Marsh, 'Cor, 'struth! What in hell's name was that?'

'Only a rutting stag.' Marsh grinned. 'Mating season. We get a lot of red deer down our way, but I've never seen one so close or so big.'

'All these wild animals over 'ere.' Shrimp shuddered. 'Give me London any day. You don't get mad bellowing creatures in London.'

Andrew looked across at Francine. 'You took that very calmly. What a magnificent sight.'

'I should have warned you. The stags collect in this part of the forest.'

'He could have been the Imperial stag we saw this morning.'

'Perhaps.' She smiled.

Andrew turned back to his troop, who by now had their horses under control. 'We have two horses and a man missing, sir,' said Sergeant Armstrong.

'Who?'

'Stone. His horse barged into mine,' replied Turner 65. 'He jabbed it in the mouth, so it reared up and took off. The led horse followed him.'

'Clark, go and get him.' Andrew turned and addressed his men. 'That was a disgraceful display of soldiering and horsemanship. What on earth do you think you were doing? If an animal can cause so much havoc, what hope have we got against the Hun? You're lucky that we're behind enemy lines; otherwise you would be doing extra duties and training. Now, for the rest of this march I want to see you acting like fighting men. Control your horses and do not behave like schoolgirls on a picnic. Do I make myself clear?' The men nodded and shuffled in their saddles.

Clark set off as fast as he dared in the darkness, but he didn't have far to go before he found the riderless horse. As he gathered up the broken reins he heard a commotion further along the ride. Stone was on his feet. His horse flew in circles around him while he hit and jabbed at it with his sword.

'What the hell are you doing?' yelled Clark. Stone dropped his sword and stared at the NCO. The corporal rode up to the little man, leant over and punched him. He stumbled backwards and fell to the ground.

'Stand up. Pick up your sword and mount.'

Stone scrambled to his feet holding his stinging cheek. 'I'll report you. You can't hit me.'

'Report me to who you like. I'm reporting you for horse cruelty. Now get on your horse.' Stone's horse shied away from him. 'For God's sake!' Clark held the horse while Stone mounted. It was wet with sweat and thin wheals from the sword lashes were beginning to stand out on its skin. 'Now ride in front of me, you little bastard, so that I can see what you're doing. You'll pay for this.'

As soon as they joined the troop Andrew moved the men forwards. He didn't notice the state of Stone's horse.

They rode on in silence, stopping occasionally for a few minutes' rest. Andrew heaved a sigh when at last Francine slowed down and said, 'We're coming to the plain now.' He halted the troop and sent the Turners to scout the road ahead. They came back saying that the coast was clear.

Once the troop was crossing the open countryside, Francine pointed. 'Look, you can see the château.'

Andrew could just make out the turrets and spires of a large medieval castle standing on a hill silhouetted against the light of the moon. He was tired and his mind began to wander. He stared up at the sky and became mesmerized by the racing clouds as they sped across the heavens. He was reminded of a poem about a ghostly galleon tossed on cloudy seas, and a highwayman who came riding along a moonlit road.

He shook his head and stared. Horsemen were coming towards him. He went cold as he saw the moonlight glinting on the helmet of the first German rider approaching over the brow of the hill. He was followed by a patrol of enemy cavalry. They were set on a collision course. There was no cover and nowhere to hide.

'We'll take them. You want us to behave like fighting men,' Rupert remarked. Andrew turned his troop off the road and galloped through a field that had been partly ploughed. Then he pulled up and signalled for the men to carry on past him.

The Germans continued up the farm track towards the forest without giving a hint that they had seen the British Cavalry. Andrew spurred his horse back to his men. 'The quickest way to the château?' he threw at Francine as he galloped towards her. She pointed with her whip and swung her horse right-handed across the plough. The troop followed at a gallop, their horses struggling in the deep going.

They crossed a small stream and then up the steep rise to the château. 'This way,' cried Francine. She took them up under the ramparts of the castle and, to Andrew's surprise, stopped in a shrubbery beside the ivy covered walls.

'We can go through here,' she said, 'but first... Ah, here he is.'

Andrew jumped as an old man appeared from nowhere and spoke to Francine.

'*Merci,* Henri.' Francine turned to Andrew and translated. 'All's well, the Germans are not near the château, they go through the village. We can go in here.'

'In where?'

'It's low, the men will have to dismount and there are a number of steps.'

Andrew watched Francine insert a large iron key into the ivy and unlock a door. Once she lit a lantern he recoiled as he saw a flight of steps.

'How the… are we going to get the horses up there?'

'Don't they go upstairs? If not, we have to go through the village to reach the main entrance. But the Germans are traversing the village.'

Andrew heaved a sigh. 'Well, we'll just have to give it a try. I must say that at the Royal Military College, the Academy Adjutant rides a horse up the steps and into the entrance hall during the Sovereign's Parade.'

'Well, there you are then.' Francine looked triumphant. Andrew smiled at her, thinking to himself, yes, but the steps are fewer, and they train the horse first.

Francine continued: 'At least it isn't twisty, you know?' She made circular movements with her hand.

'I can't quite imagine horses going up a spiral staircase.' He smiled.

'I've taken a horse up this one, mine he will do it. Come up and look first.'

Andrew followed Francine into the bowels of the château. Medieval sconces holding thick candles were set at intervals up the stairs. When lit, they threw a pale flickering light on to the stairway and made shadows dance on the stone walls.

The tread of each step was fairly wide and not too deep. Andrew counted thirty five as they led up to a wide stone corridor. Francine lit more candles set in lanterns on the walls and he could see that the passageway ran in both directions. There were no windows in the thick walls, only occasional chimney-like air ducts which whistled with each gust of wind, making the lights splutter.

'We call this *La Ceinture*….. The Belt, she goes all the way round the château running underneath the courtyard. Come, hurry.'

Francine turned to the left and walked quickly round a corner, only stopping briefly to light the lanterns. Narrow spiral staircases descended and ascended at intervals on both sides of the passageway. A foul smell arose from one of the downward exits and Andrew stopped. 'What's down there?' He shivered.

'The dungeons.' She looked at him and smiled. 'We don't use them anymore, but there is a way out through here.' She stopped by an outer wall that curved into a turret and fiddled with a protuberance. A small entrance appeared, just large enough for a man to crawl through.

'If you go down to the bottom, you can get to the cells. This castle has been besieged many times over the centuries, and sometimes it was the chatelains themselves who were taken prisoners. The third Marquis built this secret passage.' She laughed. 'He made several alterations to the chateau. He was, how you say... a resourceful man?'

Andrew shut the rotating hatch. They hurried on down the passage until they came to another flight of steps. The stairway was wider than the previous one and the ceiling was higher. He counted thirty seven steps to a landing outside a wooden door. He helped Francine slide it open and saw a brightly lit stable of nearly thirty stalls. Most were bedded down with straw and the hay racks were full.

'Good Lord. This is amazing.' He smiled. 'You really have been incredibly kind.'

She looked up at him. 'It is nothing.'

He looked into her twinkling grey eyes, took a step towards her, and then quickly spun round. 'We must hurry back before the Hun spot us.'

When Andrew returned to the men waiting under the ramparts of the castle, he decided to send Shrimp and Clark up first as they could do anything with their horses.

''Struth!' exclaimed Shrimp, as he saw the steps. He patted his horse. 'My lad will go up there. I took an 'orse up the steps of St. Paul's Cathedral once for a bet. It was easy going up, but it was a bit tricky coming down. He didn't fall nor nothing. I won me bet, sir.'

'Good, good.' Andrew smiled.

'My horse will go anywhere,' announced Clark. 'He's the cleverest horse in the army, sir.'

'Oh, yeah.' Turner 65 sneered as he took a quick look at the steps. 'We'll see about that when you get to the top with your soppy horse.'

'Turner, get back to your own horse,' snapped Andrew. He turned to the men waiting by the ivy-covered door. 'On the command you'll all follow Fisher and Clark. Don't look back at your horses and keep walking. Are you all ready? Then walk march.' The captain mounted the first few steps praying that there would be no trouble. He turned and saw Shrimp, his reins held loosely in his hand, talking to his horse. It followed him up the steps like a well behaved dog. Clark's horse also followed his rider, and the other horses willingly followed them. When they arrived at the top Andrew congratulated them.

'It wasn't difficult, sir,' said Shrimp. 'Them steps seemed to fit the 'orse's stride somehow. It was easier than St. Paul's.'

'He's right, sir,' remarked Clark. 'The horses did find it easy.'

'How strange.' Andrew started to walk round the *ceinture* towards the stables. 'What is it?' He asked as Clark approached him.

'I need to speak to you, sir.' Andrew nodded. Clark quickly told him about the incident with Stone and how he had mistreated his horse. 'Thank you for that information.' Andrew's face hardened, although he had to smile to himself as he heard the men's remarks when they smelt the odour issuing from the dungeons.

The next flight of stairs offered no problem. When the door to the stables was opened the horses eagerly scrambled up the steps towards the smell of hay.

Once they were settled Andrew called for Rupert. The lieutenant followed his senior officer to the end of the stalls. He stood staring at the ground as Andrew asked, 'Have you got a problem with the way I run things?'

'N... No, of course not.'

'Then why did you find it necessary to make an insolent remark in front of the men.'

'What insolent remark?'

'Let me remind you. It was when we came on the German patrol.'

'Oh, I... I said something like: "Take cover". I really can't remember. Everything happened so quickly.' Rupert lowered his eyes under Andrew's steady gaze.

'I'll let it go this time,' said Andrew. 'But if it happens again, I won't be so lenient. Now pull yourself together. Come with me to inspect the horses. There's something I would like you to see.'

The horses, grateful to have the heavy equipment removed from their backs, stood pulling at their hayracks as the two officers walked down the line. Most were unscathed by the journey, although one had lost a shoe in the plough. The officers were pleased with their condition, until they reached Stone's horse. They glanced at each other. The welts stood out on the horse's haunches and neck. Although Stone had washed away the flecks of blood, they could see the scratches on his belly.

'What happened to your horse?' asked Andrew.

'I don't know, sir.' Stone stared at Andrew with vacant eyes. The horse lifted its near hind and kicked out. Stone flinched.

'Lieutenant,' said Andrew, 'what's that mark near his stifle?' Rupert bent down and looked at the base of the horse's flank.

'There's a hole in the loose skin.'

'How did that happen?' demanded the Captain.

'Don't know, sir.' Stone stared at the floor.

'Look at me when you're speaking,' snapped Andrew.

'I don't know sir.' Stone heaved a sigh.

'Clark, come here.' The NCO marched over.

'Sir!' He stood to attention. The other troopers became curious and started to gather around the stall.

'Explain this.' Andrew pointed to the marks on the horse.

'Well, sir,' replied the corporal, when I went to fetch Stone I found him on his feet and hitting his horse with his sword. Then I saw him stab the horse, about there.' He pointed to the wound. There was a deathly hush.

'I see,' said Andrew. 'What have you got to say, Stone?'

Stone shook his head, looked at the captain, and said, 'It's lies, sir, all lies, he's got it in for me. I never done that.' The troopers began to murmur.

Clark stared at Stone. 'It's not lies, sir. It happened like I said.'

'Look behind the horse's ears,' Andrew ordered.

Clark moved the horse's head collar back and revealed some scratches which continued down his neck under his mane.

'He obviously got those while trapped in the wood,' said Andrew. 'How did he become stuck between two trees, Trooper?'

'I don't know nothin' about that,' replied Stone.

'Trooper Stone, I'm placing you under close arrest: you'll be charged with horse cruelty.' Andrew signalled to the Turner twins. 'Guard this man.'

As he walked away, Andrew remarked to Rupert, 'I don't like the way the horse is behaving. He's showing the same symptoms as Number 49. Make sure you keep an eye on him. I don't want to lose another horse'.

He left Rupert repeating his orders and went to look for Francine. He eventually found her in a loosebox.

'Is everything alright?'

'Yes perfectly, thank you, I have had to arrest a man and I need a secure room in which to hold him.'

'Why, what's he done?'

'Stabbed and beaten his horse.'

'The dungeons!'

'No. Somewhere closer, more like a bedroom with a lock on the door.'

'The dungeons would be more fitting for a man who stabs his own horse, I think.'

Andrew replied, 'We're British. We don't throw our own soldiers into medieval prisons, at least not these days'.

'What a pity. Follow me.' She took him across the quadrangle and up a staircase.

'The horses found it easy going up the steps.'

'*Oui*, they would.' Francine laughed.

'Why is that so funny?'

'Because the third Marquis made the steps to fit a horse's stride.'

'Why on earth would he do that?'

'He had a mistress in the next village. She used to enter the château on her horse that way. Also when he visited her, he could come home unobserved. His wife was a gorgon, I don't blame him.'

'You could have told me it would be easy.'

'I did.'

They arrived in a broad gallery hung with portraits. 'Who are these people?' Andrew asked.

'The Marquis' ancestors.'

'Who's this?' Andrew looked up at a handsome man staring arrogantly down. He had Francine's features and the same intelligent grey eyes.

'The present Marquis.' She hurried on through the gallery.

So that's it, thought Andrew. She's the bastard daughter of the Marquis. She must be a favourite of his, no wonder the workers do as she says.

'This is the third Marquis' wife.' Francine stopped under a portrait of a dignified woman with masculine features and a disdainful look on her face. She reminded Andrew of his great aunt Agnes.

After the gallery they turned into a long corridor with several bedrooms leading off it. Francine opened a door. 'Your wounded man,' she said with a flourish.

'He got through. Thank God! Why didn't you tell me?'

'I just have.'

Andrew frowned as he walked up to the sleeping Bright. He felt his forehead. He was burning up. The trooper opened his eyes and tried to sit up in bed. 'Lie still, old chap,' said Andrew.

'There're hundreds of Germans...' the trooper murmured. 'Everywhere... cannons, lorries, cavalry, infantry ... I could just see them… through a gap in the straw. The driver kept going and they didn't give us a second look… Thank God… Fair frightened me though… You be careful, sir.'

'Yes, I know, I saw them travelling through the ford yesterday. Try and get some sleep.'

'*Capitaine*,' called Francine. 'Will this do?'

'I'll see you later,' he said to Bright and joined Francine, who had opened a door off the bedroom. The room contained a narrow bed and a wash stand. He went over to the small window and looked out at a sheer drop down to the road a long way below. 'Perfect.' He checked the lock on the door. 'And rather more salubrious than the dungeons.'

'I thought you might like your two men together.'

'Thank you, that was very thoughtful of you. I'll put a guard in with them.'

They looked round in surprise as a maid ran into the room. She spoke very fast. Francine looked in alarm at Andrew.

'What is it?' Andrew grew cold.

'She says the Germans are camped in the village. You must speak to the Mayor.'

Andrew hurried after Francine, following her downstairs, along more corridors until she led him into one of many drawing rooms. He found Doctor Lejeune standing with his back to the fireplace anxiously watching the door; his face was serious and troubled.

CHAPTER FIVE

Honour before Glory

Andrew strode up to the doctor and shook his hand. '*Bon jour,* so you're the Mayor as well as the Doctor. I understand you have some bad news for us. The Hun are camping in the village.'

'Some officers are staying, *oui*, but the rest are marching through. It's becoming very dangerous. Fortunately for us they're heading towards Paris. You need to leave tonight.'

'I have to return to my regiment, but I have no idea where they are. My CO will be wondering what has happened to us. Is there any way of sending a message?'

'The British Expeditionary Force is retreating in a south-westerly direction. If you make for Chavigny-Le-Matz you'll be heading the right way. You can learn more from the villagers *en route*. In any case, I'll send a man on a bicycle... don't worry, he'll find your regiment. The King's Own Cavalry, is it not?'

Andrew nodded. 'We cut across the plough coming here and a horse lost a shoe. The Hun could easily follow our hoofprints.'

'Monsieur Lefevre is ploughing there this morning. I'll make sure he covers your tracks and removes your lost shoe. In fact I'll ask him to drive his herd of cows over that field.'

'You're very kind, Doctor. While you're here perhaps you could look at my wounded man again.'

'Kind, you say?' The doctor smiled. 'We're all fighting the same enemy. Of course I'll look at your man. Take me to him.' They returned to the bedrooms.

After the doctor had spent some time with Bright, he came out of the room, saying, 'He has an infection and a high fever. We must get him to St. Anton. I'll arrange it. Now I must go. *Bon chance*'.

***

A meal had been prepared for the men in the servants' hall. Williams sat opposite Stone, who was placed between the Turner brothers at the long table. He watched as 65 picked up Stone's plate. Then he felt sick as the twin cleared his throat and spat a dribble of mucus into the food.

Len Turner and a few troopers began to giggle. Williams glanced around at the others. Most of them looked shocked.

'I say, that's disgusting.' Williams said to the Turners. 'I know he's despicable, but there are limits.'

'Yes,' agreed Marsh. 'He'll get his comeuppance. Let the condemned man eat his last meal.'

'I don't like bullies,' retorted 65.

'That's the pot calling the kettle black,' said Williams. 65 looked across the table and imitated his educated accent. 'Why aren't you an officer... old boy?'

Williams ignored his jibe. He had no intention of telling him, or the others, why he had chosen to enlist as a trooper. He replied, 'Let him eat in peace, otherwise you sink to his level. I know our CO, Major Falterstone; he's an avid horseman. He'll deal with Stone severely enough.' Then he added, knowing that Falterstone was, in fact, a ditherer, 'They don't call him *Old Falters-not* for nothing. He'll go for the jugular. You might like to bear in mind that the last cavalryman to be flogged was for horse cruelty'.

'Cor! What did 'e do?' asked Shrimp.

'He did something rather nasty to a mare with a broom handle. He got 150 lashes.'

'Blimey.' Turner 64's eyes gleamed. 'What Stone done is worse.'

'Yes.' 65 stabbed Stone in the arm with his fork.

'That's enough! Eat your food.' Williams was worried that the Turners might incite the rest of the men into some sort of lynch mob. To his relief, 65 heaved a sigh, shrugged his broad shoulders and began to eat. Williams was pleased that nobody seemed to want to tell Stone that flogging was no longer allowed in the army. He noticed the prisoner shiver as he picked nervously at his food, taking care to avoid the globule of spit.

***

Rupert and Andrew sat down with Francine at a highly polished table in the ornately furnished dining room. Rupert hardly spoke and as soon as he had finished his meal he excused himself, left the table and asked for someone to show him up to his room.

'He's very tired.' Andrew felt he had to explain to Francine.

'He looks very young. He has a pretty, sensitive face.'

'What do you mean?'

'Well, he shows his emotions rather easily for a man. He has deep, smouldering dark eyes. They go with his dark hair and make him look romantic. That's how I imagine the poet, Lord Byron.'

'Really, I hadn't noticed.' Andrew felt uncomfortable. 'I'm sure he isn't mad, bad and dangerous to know, like Byron.'

'No, of course not. He's a little frightened of you, I think.'

'I hadn't noticed that either.'

'Strange, you seem to notice most things.' Francine smiled.

Andrew quickly turned away and looked up at a portrait of the third Marquis' wife hanging above the sideboard while she stared arrogantly down at him. 'Why is her portrait in this room as well?'

'She brought an enormous dowry to the family. She was the last in a line of wealthy aristocrats, the third Marquis was lucky to marry her. It was her money that paid for the alterations to the château. There must always be a girl christened with her name in the family, otherwise they say that there will be no more male heirs. The family Du Byard Du Moulin would die out.'

'Like a curse?'

'In a way. When she found out about the mistress in the next village she wasn't pleased. So I suppose she did curse the family. She hangs over the sideboard to remind everybody it was her money that kept everything going.'

'How extraordinary. You must know a lot about the family?'

'*Oui*, I have known them all my life.' Francine's grey eyes twinkled.

'You must excuse me, too.' Andrew got up from the table. 'I need a short sleep.' He suddenly felt very tired and, after a few glasses of wine, quite mellow. 'I don't know how to thank you for everything that you have done for us, I feel overwhelmed.'

'Think nothing of it.' She stood up and walked towards the door, tossing her dark shoulder-length hair away from her face. 'We do it for France.'

'I had rather hoped that you might do it for me.' Francine turned round and looked into his eyes, holding his gaze. He took her hand and without thinking kissed her. He felt her breath quicken and pulled her into his arms. He found her lips and held her close; she quivered as her slim body moulded into his. He was surprised to smell her expensive perfume again.

Francine suddenly sprang back and turned away from him, trembling. She felt consumed with a feeling that she had never felt before.

She wanted him to continue, but everything she had been taught held her back. She was nineteen years old and she hadn't had much experience of men. She knew they found her attractive, which amused her, but she had never met one who she was interested in. She preferred to spend time with her horses.

Her upbringing came to her rescue as she recovered her composure. She turned to face him, stood to her full height and said, 'I'll find someone to show you to your room. I presume you want to be awakened later this afternoon'.

'I'm sorry. I didn't mean... the wine... I... Please forgive me...'

'Think nothing of it.' Francine felt she was back in charge of the situation and mellowed. While she walked to the bell pull, she kept a space between herself and Andrew. She turned to face him. 'I understand you would like to go over the route you intend to take tonight?'

'Yes, thank you. That would be very useful.'

'We'll do that once you're rested. Ah, Marie-Claude,' she addressed the small dark-haired maid, in French, as she appeared. 'Would you take the captain to his room please?'

Andrew followed the girl through corridors and up staircases, until they stopped outside a door on the other side of the quadrangle from Stone and Bright.

'*Merci,* Mademoiselle.' Andrew entered the bedroom and walked over to the window. He felt mortified and stared morosely out at the surrounding countryside. He could see the edge of the forest and the road that they had come down in the night. He noticed a small herd of cows walking over the strips of ploughed land; a boy and a dog were trying to round them up without much success. Two large roan horses patiently pulled a plough in tedious straight lines. But he saw no Germans. Strange to think we're fighting a war, he thought, as he drew the brocade curtains, obscuring the peaceful pastoral scene.

He took off his outer clothing and lay on the bed. He tossed and turned, saying to himself, *'How could I have been so stupid? If she were a lady, I certainly would never have kissed her.'* Then he realised that, in the dining room, she *had* behaved like a lady. He went cold as he thought '*what if ...* ' He quickly dismissed the idea. A lady wouldn't ride astride and work with the horses. He was convinced that she was born on the wrong side of the blanket. He wondered where she had got the perfume and decided that she had a lover. That would explain why she took fright at his advances.

And yet he felt sure that she was interested in him.

His aunt Agnes had told him: 'Andrew, do not look for lust in your wife, if you do you can be sure that you have married beneath you. Your wife must be well bred. She will be required to run your house and control your servants, and at the same time she should bring you a reasonable dowry. When she becomes blessed with children you need no longer bother her in the bedroom. If she has been well instructed by her mother she will expect no more from you in that department. Take your lustful pleasures elsewhere, if you must, but don't cause a scandal.'

He shuddered. He would rather have a bride like Francine than some tense, bad-tempered aristocrat. After all, he thought, I'm only the second son. I don't have to provide an heir and a spare.

He decided that when he woke up he would set about making it up to Francine, even if she did have a lover who could buy her expensive perfume.

***

He awoke to a quiet knock on his bedroom door. A maid entered carrying hot water for his wash stand. 'Mademoiselle Francine is waiting for you in the dining room, Monsieur.'

He looked at his watch and saw that it was four o'clock in the afternoon. He had been asleep for six hours. He still felt exhausted, although a little fresher after he had washed and shaved. He made his way downstairs and found Francine sitting at the table talking to Rupert. She greeted him stiffly.

'Good afternoon,' replied Andrew breezily.

There was a copious meal laid out on the sideboard. He said, 'This is marvellous.' Then he addressed Rupert. 'I trust the men and horses are resting.'

'Yes, I set a guard-duty roster. It allowed them plenty of sleep, more than us at any rate.'

'Good, good. And the prisoner, what of him?'

'He's having more sleep than any of us.'

'Well, he can make the most of it, it won't last. What of his horse?'

'Much better; it ate up earlier.'

'Excellent.' He turned to Francine and smiled. 'May we go over the route back to our regiment?'

'Certainly.' She unfolded a map and pointed with a table knife.

'You can follow these tracks and cut across farmland well away from the big roads. Head for Chavigny-Le-Matz... here. Then you should be within easy reach of the British or French as they march south.'

Andrew leant over as far as he dared without getting too close to her. He looked at the map and nodded. 'As long as everyone holds the same course. Rupert, what do you think?'

The lieutenant got up and peered over Andrew's shoulder. 'Yes, I agree, it looks quite straightforward.'

'There're plenty of farms along the way where you'll be able to find food for your men and horses,' Francine said. 'Luckily the harvest was a good one and the barns are full of corn at the moment, although it is... *pas battue*... how you say? The grain is still on the stalks.'

'Unthreshed.' Andrew smiled at her description of the stored corn. He was pleased when she met his eyes and gave him a brief smile. He looked down at the map and sat studying the proposed route. 'Your maps are very good; none of these little roads and farms are recorded on ours. So we're looking at a journey of ... we're travelling in the dark... nearly two nights' ride I should think.'

Francine nodded in agreement. 'I have to go to Paris, on an errand for the marquis. I cannot come with you tonight because I have to ride over to see some people first. But I could meet you here.' She pointed to a farm. '*Domaine du Beauregard*. You should be there early tomorrow morning. I can accompany you on the last leg and then join up with the British or French armies, whichever one we find first. It would help if I had an escort, if that's all right with you.'

'It'll be a pleasure. How will you get to this farm before us?'

'I'll go by daylight. Doctor Lejeune assures me that the Germans are not stopping civilians. I plan to start straight away. Also it's necessary to take some dynamite with us. I wondered...'

'Dynamite! Whatever for?'

'For the villagers in Chavigny; they'll use it to blow up these bridges... here and here.' She pointed to the map. 'I would feel safer if you took it. If I am caught with it...'

'Of course we'll take it.'

'*Bon*, I'll see you at the *Domaine du Beauregard*. If we miss each other, *Capitaine*, you must take the dynamite to the Mayor of Chavigny. According to my information the Boches are not in this area.'

'That's settled then. I'll see you there very early tomorrow morning.' He smiled to himself, wondering again who was in charge of the operation. 'Rupert, you'd better go and check the men and horses. Make sure Sergeant Armstrong has re-shod the horse that lost a shoe.' Rupert stood up and took his leave of Francine, thanking her for her hospitality.

'It's nothing, Lieutenant, *à demain.*' She gave him a smile.

When Rupert had left the room, Francine said, 'You may also take these maps if they are better than yours'.

'Thank you, Mademoiselle. I think they'll be invaluable.'

'I go to find my horse.' She stood up. Andrew walked to the door and opened it for her, saying, 'I'll come and see you off'.

Francine brought out her grey horse. 'He looks even more splendid than your bay,' said Andrew, as he held it while she mounted. He was pleased that she was riding astride. If she found herself in difficulties then she would be able to ride faster. Although he couldn't picture any German army horse which might out-gallop her grey thoroughbred, he added, 'Would you like me to send a couple of troopers with you?'

'*Non, non*, thank you. I have Jean-Pierre, the stable-boy. Your men would not be able to get past the Boches.'

'No, of course not.' He put his hand on her horse's neck and looked up into her eyes. 'Please take care.'

She smiled down. 'Don't worry about me. The Boches are not stopping civilians. I shall be safer than you. I'll see you tomorrow morning.' She waved and clattered out of the stable yard.

Andrew told the twins to bring Stone down to the stables to tend to his horse and make ready for their departure that night.

***

The troop, taking a French boy as guide, left the château by the main entrance as soon as it was dark. They rode in single file, their horses' hooves wrapped in sacks to muffle the sound.

Andrew had divided Francine's sticks of dynamite between himself, Rupert and the NCOs. He carried his in his tunic. It made him feel very uncomfortable.

He was pleased when they could leave the road but, as they turned into a wood, the horses began to lose their footing. Andrew halted the troop and ordered everyone to remove the sacking.

Once on the move again, they rode in tight formation, with Andrew at the front and Sergeant Armstrong at the rear. They were able to keep up a steady trot interspersed with bursts of canter through the fields.

The route they had chosen was proving to be free of Germans, allowing them to stop every hour for a short rest. During these breaks they followed the same routine. Some stood guard, while the others dismounted to rest their horses' backs and to answer a call of nature. When they stopped at the edge of a wood, Stone watched Turner 65 dismount and walk away, leaving his brother on guard.

'Shush, I can hear something,' exclaimed Stone, pointing to the front of the group of men. Everyone stared up ahead. 'There it is again, can't you hear it?' One or two men nodded.

Stone kicked Turner 64's horse in its stomach. The horse shot forwards into Marsh, who snapped, 'What the hell are you doing? Can't you control your horse?'

'Of course I bloody can. Something spooked him.'

'Well, nothing spooked my horse. You need to learn to ride.'

'Don't give me riding lessons. I've been riding all my life.'

'Mount,' ordered Sergeant Armstrong. The men jostled each other as they hastily obeyed.

65 ran back. 'Where's Stone?' Both twins looked round. 'The little shit's scarpered!'

'He's there. Not far away,' cried 64. 'Hurry up.' The prisoner, heard them coming and spurred his horse on, but the touch of colic it had suffered the day before had weakened it.

'Got you, you bastard!' 65 grabbed the lapels of Stone's tunic and pulled him to the ground, then he jumped off his horse and hit him. The prisoner cried out in pain. 'Shut up, you little runt.' 65 hauled him to his feet and threw him on to his horse. The twins sandwiched Stone between them as they galloped back to the troop.

'What are you doing?' Rupert demanded.

'Stone was answering a call of nature, sir. We went with him,' said one of the twins.

'You mean he nearly absconded,' remarked Williams under his breath.

'Shut up, La-di-dah,' retorted Turner 65. 'We've got the little bastard under control now.'

'Let's hope so,' Williams replied.

The scout Andrew had sent up ahead came back reporting that the coast was clear. The captain moved them forwards.

They were able to keep up a fast pace until the guide announced that they were nearly at the farm where they were to meet Francine. Andrew could just make out the fortified buildings standing out on the plain and he relaxed as they turned up the long drive.

Sergeant Armstrong rode up beside him. 'Sir, I can see movement.'

Andrew held up his hand and brought the troop to a halt. He thanked God for the tall trees that lined the farm track and ordered Armstrong to investigate.

'Soldiers.' The sergeant returned breathlessly. 'I'm sure of it. I heard hooves and then I heard an NCO give orders.'

Andrew swung his horse around and headed back the way they had come. He kept the troop under the trees. Once in the lane he turned right and slowed to a walk. He studied his map again. 'We'll head towards the village of Chavigny,' he told Rupert. 'There's a large farm about three miles further on from here.'

They continued trotting in the field beside the lane when suddenly Armstrong shouted, 'Sir, look right'. Andrew looked up and saw the outline of a group of riders silhouetted on the far edge of the field. They kept up a parallel course, shadowing the British.

'They're Germans,' shouted Andrew.

He broke into a canter. The Germans did the same. The British quickened their pace and so did the enemy. Andrew felt his horse tire and looked behind him at the others. They were blowing hard and their gallop was becoming laboured. He knew that if it came to an out and out race against the Germans, the English horses wouldn't be able keep going for long. He looked for a way out or somewhere to hide.

He saw a small wood in front of them, surrounded by a field of drying corn, lying just beyond a river. He spurred on, galloped over the bridge and made for the copse. He couldn't understand why the Germans still held their course on his right, but it gave him the time he needed to position his men. He dismounted some and the others took cover behind the trees. Six men crept behind the stooks of corn on each side of the lane.

Andrew saw the Germans gallop up to the river and cursed as he realised that they were going to cross higher up. Just as he was about to move his soldiers, he saw the enemy turn down the field. They galloped parallel to the river and headed for the bridge. He jumped off his horse and yelled at Rupert to take control of the troop should anything happen to him. He ran towards the bridge, diving on to his stomach behind a stumpy willow tree. As the Hun approached he heard the laboured breathing of their horses and the rasping orders of the officer.

The enemy began to cross the bridge. Sergeant Armstrong yelled, '*Fire!*' The leading officer fell on to the wooden planks. His horse reared up, spun round and spooked the horse behind. He turned and cannoned into the horse following him. Chaos ensued while soldiers piled on to the bridge in the wake of the baulking horses.

The men behind the stooks continued firing and another German fell from his horse and into the river. One of the British rifles in the cornfield fell silent.

Andrew pulled the bundle of dynamite out of his tunic. He shortened the fuse with his teeth and lit it with shaking hands. The bridge was heaving with men and horses as he hurled the lighted sticks into the midst of the morass of soldiers and animals. He ran for his life back to the copse. Andrew felt a bullet graze his arm as he flung himself into the spinney.

Two Germans had managed to cross the bridge just before the explosion. As one of them turned round to see horses and riders fly into the air, he was shot by a trooper sheltering behind a stook of corn. The other leading German fired several rounds into the stook. Then, although wounded, he galloped hell-for-leather towards the copse, firing frantically at both men and horses. He reminded Andrew of an angry wasp that had been crushed yet still kept moving. He calmly took aim and fired. The German fell from his horse. He remained silent and still on the ground.

A German soldier who had been on the edge of the blast jumped into the river screaming. His clothes were on fire. He was pushed under the water as a horse fell on top of him. There wasn't a body of a horse or soldier left intact on the bridge. The wooden floor and railings had splintered and floated down stream like a flotilla of burning toy boats, joined on their journey by the rags of German uniforms torn from the bodies of the wearers.

Silence fell. The smell of burning flesh filled the air. Shrimp covered his face with his hands, murmuring, 'Those poor bloody 'orses'. Marsh crouched next to him and put his hand on his friend's back. 'Its war, mate. We've gotta do this if we're to be home by Christmas.'

Two German riders, who had never made it on to the bridge, had been thrown from their horses by the blast. Although injured by flying debris, they were making their way back across the field as fast as they could.

'I'll take some men and go after them.' Rupert stood up.

'No, you won't. Do you want to end up back in their hands?' said Andrew. 'Our route lies south west of here. I'll not be drawn into their territory by two men who look to be on their last legs.'

'We could easily take them,' retorted Rupert, but Andrew had already turned away to find out what damage had been done to his men.

He was pleased to see that they had lost no time in doing their best to patch each other up using their field dressings. He walked towards the stooks and saw a trooper crouching down behind a sheaf of corn. He put his hand on the young man's shoulder. He fell to the ground still clutching his rifle, his frightened eyes wide open and yet sightless. Andrew closed the dead man's eyes. He looked up to see Clark still crouched behind a sheaf. 'Are you all right?'

'Yes, sir. That could have been me.' The corporal was shaking.

'I know. It could have been any of us. You'd better go and find your horse.' Dawn was beginning to break as Andrew wearily followed him.

'Let me dress your wound, sir.' Armstrong had noticed the blood on Andrew's tunic.

'You're bleeding too.' Andrew observed. 'Let me take a look.'

'It's only a flesh wound.'

'Nevertheless, let me see.'

Armstrong reluctantly took down his breeches, revealing a glancing wound in his thigh. He assured Andrew that there was no bullet lodged in his leg. Andrew dressed his wound and then removed his own tunic, allowing the sergeant to look at his upper arm. He winced as Iodine was poured on the open cut, thankful that the bullet had also passed through.

As soon as Armstrong had finished, Andrew found a trooper sitting on the grass leaning against a log, surrounded by men.

'What is it?' he asked.

'Cole is badly wounded, sir,' said Shrimp. Andrew bent down and looked at the man, who was having difficulty in breathing. 'He has a bullet lodged in his shoulder.'

'He's been hit in the leg, too, sir,' added Williams. 'He caught the full force of that mad Fritz. The one you shot.'

'Yes, so I see. Armstrong, patch him up as best you can.' Andrew turned to Cole, smiling. 'Don't worry old chap, we'll be joining the regiment shortly. Soon get you to a medic.'

He looked at Shrimp, whose right hand was a bloodied mess. 'What's happened to your hand, Fisher?'

'Don't know. Sarge thinks I might lose me finger, sir.'

'Let's hope not.'

'You've got nine more,' said Turner 65. 'Better than Bright; he might lose his leg so I heard. And Cole for that matter.'

'All right, Turner,' snapped Andrew. 'I'm sure Fisher will be most gratified to hear that.' Then he looked around and asked tersely, 'Where's your prisoner? I placed a man under close arrest in your care. Where is he?'

'I...er... I don't know, sir,' replied 65

'You mean, you have time to stand here making facetious remarks and yet you've lost your prisoner.'

'I... we were coming to report to you, sir.'

'Were you indeed? Well, I don't see any reporting going on. I can see you making yourself obnoxious, though. What's happened to Stone?'

'We haven't seen him since we crossed the bridge, sir,' replied 64. 'You dismounted some of us, but I don't remember seeing him after that.'

'No, sir,' continued his brother, 'and then the action started.'

'Has anyone else seen him?' The captain looked round.

'I didn't see 'im cross the bridge,' answered Shrimp. The twins glared at him.

'Neither did I,' agreed Marsh, glaring back at them.

'No, nor did I,' added another voice.

'Right, I'll deal with you two later,' snapped Andrew. Then he called to Rupert and took him to one side. 'I still have the feeling that you're not always in agreement with my orders.'

Rupert blushed and replied, 'No... no, not at all'.

'I think you should know that in the Peninsular Wars a troop of over- zealous British Cavalry, while their blood was up and in the heat of the moment, galloped wildly after the French. When the enemy eventually lost them, the British realised that they were twelve miles inside enemy territory. They, the hunters, had now become the hunted.'

Rupert stared at the captain. 'I know, I've read the account of the Peninsular Wars, sir.'

'Then you should know that it is one of the oldest tricks in the book and it is one that I do not wish to fall for.'

'No,' Rupert replied with a little more respect.

'Don't get carried away, use your head and think of the bigger picture. Think of your men before yourself, because they'll be the ones who'll save your bacon after the glory of your hour has faded. You fell for the same game at the ford, but luckily you had Sergeant Armstrong to help you out, and the doctor. Otherwise you wouldn't be here. Remember that.

If you think I would be stupid enough to gallop after two Germans with this bunch of exhausted men and horses, you need your head examined.'

Rupert stared at the ground.

'Right,' Andrew continued breezily, 'we'll go and inspect the horses.' He felt that he had been a little hard on the man, but the condition of Cole, together with his act of throwing the dynamite and the subsequent carnage, had affected him more deeply than he liked to admit.

The German who had galloped into the copse had fired randomly at the horses' legs and it was obvious that Clark's horse had a shattered limb. Andrew glanced at Clark. He was facing his horse leaning on its neck and staring at the ground hoping the other men couldn't see that he was crying.

Before he realised what was happening, Andrew pulled out his revolver and, holding it close to the horse's forehead, pulled the trigger. The horse crumpled to the ground and lay dead at Clark's feet. The trooper knelt beside the animal stroking its neck, feeling totally bereft, tears flowing freely down his face.

Andrew suddenly felt exhausted and sickened at the unconstrained killing of horses and men. He felt a stab of the loneliness that his father had talked about before he left home. He had told him that the higher up the ladder he went, the lonelier he could become. His father reminded him of the family motto, *Honour before Glory,* and advised him to respect his men and then they would respect him. He told him to honour his enemies in defeat.

These words gave Andrew courage. He sighed, wondering how he was going to move his collection of wounded men and tired horses on to the next farm, let alone find the regiment. He looked at the sky. The sun was coming up and the Germans could arrive at any moment.

CHAPTER SIX

Betrayal

Stone made his escape from the troop just before they crossed the bridge. He spotted a steep gully and spurred his horse down into the ditch. He dismounted and waited, standing in water and hidden in the shadow of the bushes.

The blast of the dynamite lit up the countryside. The trooper could see that the ditch ran alongside the road that they had just galloped up. Yanking at the reins, he led his horse as fast as he could away from the explosion. When he thought it was safe he came out of the little channel, remounted and galloped along the grass verge. The road divided into two. He pulled up and stood dithering for a moment before deciding to take the right-hand fork. It was beginning to get light but he was already over a mile away from the blown up bridge. He followed the winding road until it turned into a track and suddenly came to a dead end in a field. Seeing no sign of habitation, he turned round and rode back the way he had come.

He was covered with pieces of debris from the explosion and was picking the bits off his tunic with disgust when his horse stopped abruptly. He looked up and froze as he saw a bloodied German soldier standing in front of him holding a rifle.

'*Halte*!' yelled the German. Stone turned round only to see another equally tattered and bleeding German behind him, also holding a gun. He put up his hands and his horse wandered over to the bank and began to nibble the grass.

'Get off your horse,' shouted one of the soldiers, in English. Stone's legs buckled as he dismounted and he fell to the ground.

The Germans laughed. 'That's what we like to see, a Tommy on his knees.'

'Don't shoot, please don't shoot.' Stone knelt in the road. One of the soldiers kicked him in the chest; he fell back, hit his head and began to sob uncontrollably.

The German stood over him. 'We've found a coward; what we will do with him, Hans? We could have some fun, with him, *ya*?'

'Good idea, Helmut.' Hans joined his companion and stood leering down at their captive.

'No, please... I... I have information for you.'

The Germans looked at each other. 'What information?'

'About the French and where the English are going.'

Helmut prodded the muzzle of his rifle into Stone's chest. 'Why would we believe you?'

Stone stared at Hans, who was looking through his things in the wallet on his saddle. 'What are you doing?' he shouted and tried to get up. Helmut pushed him down again. 'Keep looking, Hans, he has something hidden on his saddle.'

'No, I haven't. Don't you want to know where the English are going?'

'All in good time... Ah, what have we here?' Hans unrolled Stone's Mackintosh cape and out fell a wad of French Francs.

'Where did you get this?'

'I... half inched it.'

'What?' exclaimed Hans and looked at his friend; neither understood the rhyming slang.

'I... I'm carrying it... to give to my commanding officer.'

'Why?'

'Because I'm an envoy.'

'Do you have papers?'

'Yes... No. I lost them in the water. I was nearly blown up.'

'I don't believe you.' Hans hit him again.

'All right, I stole it... from the castle... there's plenty more.'

'What castle?'

Stone told the soldiers all about the château, the enclave, and the doctor. He allowed himself to be threatened every so often, until he told them where Andrew was taking the men to rendezvous with Francine.

'Where are your weapons?' Helmut asked.

As Stone had been under close arrest, he had no weapons. 'I... my rifle was blown out of my hands.'

'Where's your sword?' Helmut looked at the empty sword-frog.

'I... It... I don't know.'

The Germans stepped back and talked to each other; they recognised the château as the one they had ridden past a couple of days before. There were several farms in the area, but they decided that it wouldn't take long to find the right one.

'Shall we kill him?' Hans asked his colleague.

'*Nein*, I make him unconscious. He's a deserter. The British will shoot him if they find him. He won't get far with no horse and no weapons.' Helmut slammed the stock of his rifle into the side of the Englishman's face. Stone fell back and lay motionless on the road. The Germans searched through the trooper's pockets, taking everything else that they could find. Then both men mounted his horse and, digging their spurs into its sides, they rode away.

When Stone came round, he stood up slowly. His head throbbed. He leant against the bank holding the sleeve of his tunic to his bloody nose, trying to get his bearings.

He thought it might be safer to make his way back to the blown up bridge. He concocted a story as he went. As he came within sight of the river he saw a group of people clustered around the bodies of the dead soldiers and horses. He crept closer, keeping to bushes at the side of the road until he could see that there were no Germans or British. They seemed to be a party of French farm workers.

He dropped down into the ditch that he had stood in earlier and walked towards the river. He was covered in blood from his nose bleed. He had an angry bruise on his face from the blow of the rifle butt and more blood on the back of his head where he had fallen on the road. He knew that he looked as if he had been hit by the periphery blast of the dynamite.

When he reached the remains of the bridge he stepped out of the ditch into the river and shouted. The French looked up in surprise. A man in a tweed jacket and tie came towards him, clambered halfway down the opposite bank and held out his hand.

'Are you all right? What's your name?'

Stone stared at him, shaking his head, pretending not to understand, although the man spoke in English. The Frenchman helped him out of the river. The trooper stood in the field staring at the scene of devastation. Some of the party were digging trenches, the rest were collecting the dead bodies and pieces of human remains that were scattered around the area. A priest, dressed ready to perform a Mass, blessed each body as the men laid them on the grass.

'My name is Leblanc, I'm the mayor of the village, and this is Father André,' explained the Frenchman.

'Where am I? What's happened?' Stone looked at the British cavalryman lying dead and flinched.

'Have a drop of brandy and sit down over here.' The mayor handed him a hip flask. As Stone painfully sat on a log, the Frenchman said, 'Let me look at your wounds; perhaps I can help.'

Stone pulled away from him. 'No, no, don't touch me. You're going to kill me.'

'*Non, non, mon vieux*, of course not. Tell me what happened.'

Stone took several gulps from the hip flask. 'I don't know. I woke up over there.' He pointed to the ditch beyond the river. 'I don't know how I got there.'

'I see. You must have been knocked unconscious by the blast.'

'Yes. My head hurts like hell.'

'You have a nasty bruise on your face and some blood on the back of your head.'

'I must have been hit by something.'

'Sit here and rest while we finish tidying up this bloodbath.' Stone began to feel queasy as he watched the French search the area for the remains of the Germans and their horses. They placed the human body parts in the trench, and the animal bits on to a farm cart.

At last they could find no more. The workers gently placed the body of the British soldier into a grave on one side of the road and the Germans into a mass grave on the other.

The mayor called to Stone, 'We're ready to bury your countryman now'.

The trooper stood up and moved closer as the priest performed the burial service. He sat back down on his log while the two graves were filled in. When they had finished the doctor returned. 'Come with us to the village and then we can make arrangements to return you to your regiment.'

'I don't know what my regiment is. I don't know who I am or what I'm doing here.'

'We'll sort things out when we get to my house.'

'How?'

'You have an identification disc around your neck. Let me look at it. You don't want to be shot as a deserter, do you?'

Stone cursed himself for forgetting to destroy his tag. He had no option but to show it to the Frenchman.

'Your name is Trooper Stone and you are with the King's Own Cavalry Regiment. We'll find out where they are and I'll take you back myself. They can't be very far away.'

Stone forced himself to smile. 'Thank you.' He had no alternative but to climb into the mayor's car along with the priest and accompany them to their village.

***

While Stone lay unconscious his fellow troopers were struggling through the countryside to find a farm. They had gained two new German horses which, like their British counterparts, were laden with ammunition and spare equipment.

The badly wounded trooper rode but the rest, including the officers, walked beside their mounts. Andrew glanced back to see Cole swaying in the saddle, hardly able to hold his reins, while Williams led his horse. He heard Clark making friends with his new mare and he thought how resilient these young men were. He felt proud.

At last they came to a farm, enclosed within high stone walls. They marched into the farmyard, entering through high wooden doors set in a stone archway.

A cart, laden with belongings and pulled by two sturdy farm horses, stood in the courtyard ready to move off. The farmer's wife and three children were saying tearful goodbyes.

'I'm sorry,' said Andrew. 'We seem to have arrived at an inopportune moment.'

'*Non, pas du tout.* Come in.' The farmer continued in English. 'Have you seen the Boches along the way?'

Andrew told him of their encounter and added that as far as he knew the Germans were ignoring the French civilians.

The man turned back to his wife, kissed her and his children and then signalled to the driver to continue on his way. Andrew felt for the children, who were half excited and half frightened. But his heart went out to their mother who was doing her best to hide her fear and her tears.

'They're going to my cousin in Normandy,' explained the farmer. 'I shall stay here and look after my farm with a few faithful workers. Many left yesterday with their families.'

'I'm sorry,' repeated Andrew.

'It's not your fault. Come, we must feed and rest your horses, and then you must leave. Perhaps you could help me make some coffee for your men.'

'No, no, we won't disturb you.'

'Nonsense, they'll find food in the barn for the horses. I'll look for something in the kitchen for your men.'

Andrew came out with a steaming jug of black coffee, and the farmer followed with baguettes and a stick of Salami. While the men ate and drank, Andrew asked the farmer where they were. 'I need to know the Allied positions; have you any idea?'

He looked at Andrew's map and pointed. 'You're here... and the British are here... and here.'

'My God! Are you sure? I can't believe the BEF are retreating at such a rate.'

'Unfortunately, yes. I heard this morning that the Boches are close on their heels. That's why I've sent my family away, and when I heard your explosion, well...'

'We'll press on. We're way off course and much further south than I thought. If we ride towards the west we should, by rights, find the British.'

'After your explosion, the Germans will come looking for you. I think you should go.'

Andrew agreed and, having given the horses a short rest, mounted his men. As they were lined up he rode out in front of them. 'I want to say how well you fought last night and at the ford. You all acted with tremendous courage. We mustn't forget the men whom we have lost. They too fought well and we can be justly proud of them. I know the men who fell at the ford had decent Christian burials. The farmer assures me that the villagers will arrange the same for our fallen colleague of last night.

'On a happier note, I have good news for you: the British Expeditionary Force is not far in front of us and I believe we'll catch them up before long.'

He turned the line of men, made his way to the head of the small cavalcade, saluted the farmer and rode out of the farmyard.

The men's morale was high as they made their way along straight roads lined with lime trees. Their horses strode out well in spite of their soreness. As they rode up a steep hill Andrew sent Clark off in front to reconnoitre.

He came cantering back. 'There are troops in the valley,' he exclaimed.

Andrew halted the troop. 'Who are they?'

'I don't know. I think they're ours!'

Andrew advanced alone on foot, leaving the men hidden behind the brow of the hill. He lay on his stomach looking through his field glasses. The road they were following met another road passing at right angles, and that was full of lorries, infantry and horse artillery.

Andrew ran back to his men. 'Thank God! We've found the

retreating BEF. Come on, we'll catch them up in no time.' He spoke to the wounded Cole. 'I'm sorry, this may cause you considerable discomfort, but we need to move on fast. Are you up to cantering?'

'Yes. The sooner we join them, the better,' Cole murmured through gritted teeth.

'Good man. Williams will lead your horse. You hang on tight.'

Andrew mounted his horse and set off at a gallop down the hill.

The infantry looked exhausted and dirty. Some had their arms in blood-soaked slings and others had bloodied, grimy bandages around their legs or their heads.

A few soldiers looked up at the arriving cavalry troop but most of them kept their heads down. They needed all their energy to keep marching.

Dispatch riders wove their way past the marching men, whilst horse drawn wagons trundled along, sandwiched between the columns of soldiers.

Andrew let a battery of Royal Horse Artillery pass him by, watching the teams of tired and dusty, sweating horses as they hauled their gun carriages. He acknowledged a Major riding behind the teams. Andrew saw him looking anxiously at his lame horses and guessed that he was wondering how long they would be able to keep going before he would have to halt his men and deal with them.

He reined in beside an infantry officer riding with his men, saying, 'Good afternoon, Andrew Harrington-West'.

'Afternoon to you, George Trenchard.' He turned to look at Andrew's men. 'You've seen some fighting. Been earning your keep in a rearguard action?'

'No. Out on reconnaissance. Where have you been?'

'Mons, old chap. A few losses but we're still here, what.'

'Yes… yes, you are indeed.' Andrew looked at the pinched grey faces of the walking wounded. 'I need an ambulance.'

'Don't we all, old boy,' replied Trenchard with a short laugh. 'You'll be lucky to find one with any room inside it.'

Andrew smiled briefly and catching sight of a grey horse-drawn wagon with a red cross on its side, he left Trenchard and rode towards it.

The co-driver of the ambulance slept on the box beside the driver, who also nodded in and out of sleep. Andrew ordered them to halt. The man jumped, glared at the captain and said, 'What do you want?'

'Pull over and stop,' ordered Andrew.

The driver turned his pair of horses on to the stubble field at the side of the road. The co-driver awoke with a start as the ambulance lurched to a halt. 'What the fuck.....?' he exclaimed, then seeing Andrew he said, 'Oh'.

'I have a badly wounded man, and I need you to take him,' said Andrew.

'We don't have room,' replied the driver. 'Half the bleedin' infantry want me to take them. We're full up.'

'We are the Cavalry.'

'Can't you ride your bloody horses?' muttered the co-driver.

Andrew glared at him. 'I beg your pardon?'

'I wondered about the horses,' replied the man, turning away to light a cigarette.

'We don't have room,' the driver repeated.

'Well, we'll have a look, shall we?' Andrew went to the rear of the wagon and dismounted. He pulled back the canvas curtain and recoiled at what he saw. Badly injured men, their bandages soaked in blood and their faces taut and white with pain sat squashed up beside each other on the floor. Their eyes were staring and frightened. Two men lay on blood soaked blankets laid over raised wooden slats. Both men had parts of their bodies shot away. One lay very still, no blood seeped from the mangled mess that had once been his leg.

'See,' snapped the driver. 'I told you, no bloody room.'

''E's dead. Are we at the field hospital yet?' One of the wounded soldiers stared at Andrew expectantly.

'Not yet, old chap,' replied Andrew. Then, turning to the driver, he ordered, 'Move that man off there and my trooper can have his place.'

'And where am I going to put him?' asked the driver.

'He can go under the bench,' replied one of the injured soldiers. 'He won't mind. He's snuffed it.'

'Good idea.' Andrew smiled at the private, then ordered, 'Turner, help Cole off his horse and bring him over here.'

Turner 65 dismounted and gently helped the trooper down from his horse. Cole looked grey and exhausted. He would have sunk to the ground but for Turner's strong supporting arms. The ambulance men, realising the extent of Cole's injuries, fetched a stretcher from the side of their vehicle and carefully laid him on it while they made room inside the wagon.

Some of the injured men began to complain as they had to move in order to allow the dead man to be taken off the narrow bench. A young private retched as he saw the mutilated body. 'For Christ's sake boy, don't throw up, it fucking stinks in here already,' said a soldier. The boy stared miserably at the floor.

'Leave 'im alone,' retorted an older man. 'The bloke next to me has been dead a while and you want to smell what's coming out of him.'

'If we move him, too, then my mate can lie down,' suggested a man with a bandage wound around his head. The ambulance men looked at the friend who was slumped against the front of the wagon. His eyes were closed and his breathing was fast and shallow. Blood seeped through the dressing wrapped round his upper body. Again with much moaning and complaining from the other passengers they rearranged the man. At last they placed Cole on the bench.

'Thank you, sir,' murmured Cole.

'Good luck, old chap,' replied Andrew. 'Safe journey.' As he mounted his horse, several wounded infantrymen limped up to the stationary ambulance and demanded a ride.

'They all want a bleedin' lift now,' the driver grumbled.

Andrew moved his troop forwards and left the incensed medical orderlies to deal with the crowd of walking wounded who were now flocking around their vehicle.

'Fucking officers,' remarked the co-driver, then, turning to the soldiers, he shouted, 'Bugger off the lot of you'.

CHAPTER SEVEN

Coalescence

Andrew knew the rest of his Squadron was riding somewhere up ahead, so he pressed on in spite of the heat, only stopping when and where he could find water for his horses.

The cavalrymen were glad to be riding as they watched whole swathes of troops collapse on to the grass verges as soon as they heard the order 'fall out'. Some men lay stretched out, resting their heads on their haversacks. Others sat drinking from their water bottles, most of them lighting up cigarettes, and all of them thankful for the respite.

Fleeing French civilians cluttered up the road with their over-laden carts, trudging wearily away from the advancing German army. Andrew wondered if they knew where they going or where they would be spending the next night.

Armstrong rode up beside Andrew. 'Sir, I heard the scout from the artillery saying that there was plenty of water about two miles up ahead, also a field of barley stooks.'

'Well done, Sergeant, we'll head there.'

They found the field and rode across it towards a stream. Andrew dismounted the men while they watered their horses and allowed them to eat the unthreshed straw.

A company of riflemen were sitting on the ground resting. Shrimp strolled over to them and was soon in deep conversation.

'What's he doing?' asked Turner 65.

'Passing the time of day with the infantry. Does it matter?' replied Williams.

'Fraternising with the plant life, more like,' retorted Turner 64.

'We're all on the same side,' snapped Armstrong.

'Yeah, but they're cannon fodder.'

Williams and Armstrong glanced at each other. 'What do you call these?' Williams asked as they watched a battery of Royal Horse Artillery clatter across the field in a cloud of dust.

'At least they have horses.' 65 grunted.

The drivers quickly dismounted and the gunners jumped off the limbers. They unhitched the horses and led them to the stream.

'Good job we've finished,' remarked Turner 64. 'There won't be any bleedin' water left after that lot have been at it.'

'Yeah, and look at them over there,' added his brother. The group of troopers turned to watch men from the RHA filling their flat based wagon with sheaves of barley straw.

'I hope we've got enough fodder for our horses,' remarked Clark.

'Of course we have,' retorted Turner 65. 'The captain knows what he's doing.'

'Yeah, but the poor bleedin' farmer who owns this field won't have enough feed for his stock this winter,' remarked his brother.

'No,' added 65. 'Thank God we haven't got this lot traipsing all over our farm.'

'That's why we're all out here fighting the Hun, so that they don't invade England,' said Williams.

'Oi, Shrimp, we're going now,' yelled Turner 65 as they were given the order to mount. 'What were you doing talking to them plant life?' he asked as they rode away from the field.

'They was telling me how they march. They start at dawn and keep going all day. Then at ten to the hour they have ten minutes rest.'

'What every hour?'

'Yeah, they keeps looking at their watches, them that has watches, that is, and then they drops like stones to the side of the road on the command.'

'They've been here nearly an hour now.'

'They're waiting for orders, but they're standing up now,' said Shrimp. 'I'm glad I got me 'orse.'

'Soft bugger.'

'Let's see you get off your horse and march, 65,' said Marsh.

'Fuck off,' retorted the twin.

'Fuck off yourself, country bumpkin,' said Shrimp.

'Shut up,' snapped Sergeant Armstrong before 65 could reply.

'Anyway, they was telling me this story about an angel at Mons.' Shrimp's eyes lit up as he told the story.

'Oh yeah, they saw you coming,' Turner 65 scoffed.

'No, deadly serious they were.'

'Go on.' Armstrong prompted him. 'I heard some soldiers talking about that as we were loading Cole into the ambulance, something about St. Michael the Archangel, they said, with a sword and riding a white horse.'

'That's right,' exclaimed Shrimp. 'He appeared in the sky above them. The German prisoners saw him, too, only then 'e had an army of English bowmen behind him.'

'What was it doing, this angel?' asked Turner 64. 'Saving them all?'

'Don't know,' replied Shrimp. 'But some Coldstream Guards saw this young eth... eth er...'

'Ethereal?' Williams joined in the conversation.

'That's right, this beautiful ethereal woman beckoning to them.'

'There would have to be a bit of skirt in it.' 64 grinned at his brother.

'Go on,' said Williams.

'Well, they followed her across this piece of open land and into the safety of a bunker that they hadn't noticed before. Then a shell fell where they'd been standing. They would've all been killed if they hadn't followed her.'

'They were drunk,' said 65. 'They get a ration of rum before a battle you know. 'Spect they had too much... angels and ghostly women, my arse.'

'No, straight up, that's what they said. They wasn't pulling my leg, some of them said it was a good omen.'

'And you believed them.' The twins grinned at each other.

'It could well be a good omen.' Everybody looked at Williams in surprise, and he continued: 'The Battle of Crécy was fought in 1346, on the 26th August to be specific. So it's almost the exact anniversary of that battle. Our bowmen beat the French there in the Hundred Years War. It meant we won Calais and it was a turning point. Crécy isn't very far away from here'. There was a stunned silence.

'Cor.' Shrimp shivered. 'Maybe the angel was telling Fritz to beware 'cos we're going to win the war.'

'Do me a bleedin' favour,' Turner 65 scoffed.

'Exactly, Shrimp.' Williams nodded. 'Maybe that was precisely what they were doing.'

'You would believe that,' said Turner 65, ''cos you went to a posh la-di-dah school where they teach fancy things.'

'My education has got nothing to do with it,' retorted Williams. Then he asked, 'Have you got a better explanation?'

'Yeah, too much liquor,' repeated 65.

'The prisoners didn't have no rum,' said Shrimp.

'I think it's a sign to say we're going to win this war. I mean that's three supernatural things happened, told you we'd be home by Christmas.' Marsh was adamant. Williams agreed and the others nodded.

'Oh my God, you're all soft in the head,' exclaimed Turner 65.

They rode on arguing about the angels until Armstrong told them to be quiet.

'Tell us about your farm,' Williams asked the Turners.

'We live in Kent and we grow hops.'

'For beer?' asked Shrimp.

'Yes. But we don't get no free beer,' retorted 64.

'We have the brewers' grains back for the stock,' 65 eagerly told the men. 'We have a few Romney sheep up from the marshes in the winter, and a herd of milking cows. We keep pigs and poultry and grow a bit of corn.'

'Keeps you busy then,' said Williams.

'Yeah, we work all day, every day. The winter's hard,' 64 joined in.

'The summer's hard work, too, gathering the harvest. There's something to do all year round, but we wouldn't do nothin' else, would we, Len?' added 65. His brother shook his head.

'Who's working in your place while you're over here?' asked Williams.

'Our two younger brothers,' answered Len Turner. 'Our sister Fanny and our Ma do the chickens, the ducks and geese, and they feed the pigs. Fanny's learning to milk. Our Ma weren't pleased when we left to fight. We didn't have to, 'cos we work on the land, see. Our Da were proud of us, but he said our brothers have got to stay and help on the farm. Anyway I reckon we'll beat the Hun and be back home before long.'

'Yeah, 'specially now you've told us about this angel,' 65 grinned.

'Don't start that again,' snapped Armstrong.

'We must be stopping here,' remarked Williams, as they rode into a busy village. 'It looks like a defended bivouac area. Look at that field full of infantry.'

They all turned to look at rows of resting soldiers smoking and chatting, their rifles stacked together in neat wigwam shapes beside them, looking like giant kindling wood ready to be lit.

'There's some more friends for you, Shrimp,' said 65.

'If you don't believe me you go and ask them,' retorted Shrimp.

'We ain't that stupid,' Len sneered.

Andrew halted at a junction in the centre of the hamlet. He asked a dispatch rider if he had seen the rest of their squadron.

'Yes, sir,' replied the man. 'Proceed down that road and you'll find them in the field, along with the RHA.'

They found the cavalry mounts picketed near a battery. Andrew marched his men into the field and across to the horse lines. They were met by the familiar sound of hammers ringing on anvils as the farriers went about their business. Their forges were alight and the smell of burning hooves filled the air. The men began to relax, feeling safe at last, at home amongst the well-known sounds and smells.

An officer watched them ride across the field. 'Good God, Harrington-West's lot!' he exclaimed.

'Captain Dickson-French. What a pleasure to see you again.'

'Likewise, old boy, we thought you were dead.'

'No, no, I'm afraid not. It takes more than a few Hun to kill us off.'

'Old Falters will be pleased to see you, can't think why,' replied Charles. He cast his pale watery eyes over Andrew's men and said with a short laugh, 'Your troop looks a bit diminished old bean, and dirty, covered in blood some of them. Looks like you've been hunting and got them all blooded, what!'

'They have been er... blooded as you put it,' replied Andrew. 'But not riding to hounds I'm afraid, fighting a war instead.'

'Well, as long as you took some Hun, that would explain your long absence I suppose.'

'We took a few of them.'

Charles turned to Rupert. 'Somerville, glad to see you're in one piece, nearly had to write to your mother to say you were missing. Good thing I waited, what.'

Andrew didn't think it was common knowledge that Charles spent a lot of time with Rupert's mother. He was surprised that he declared so blatantly that he was in touch with her. Rupert's father had been a crony of Oscar Wilde before the writer had died at the turn of the century. Andrew knew that he spent most of his time away from home in his rooms in London.

'Have we been reported as officially missing?' Andrew asked Charles.

'No, not yet.'

'Good, good. I have men who need medical attention. Where...?'

'You'll find the medics over there.' Charles pointed to a small farmhouse next to the field. 'Old Falters is next door. I'm just going over to secure a decent billet for myself in the village; want me to bag you one too?'

'No, don't worry.'

'Just as you like old boy, but what with these dammed cyclists swarming everywhere and the Royal Engineers, the bloody signals too, it's a blasted scrimmage to get anything reasonable.'

'Please don't worry,' repeated Andrew. 'I have a lot to attend to first.'

'Can't think why, old boy, let your NCOs do it, that's what they're for, don't you know. Come and have a drink, bound to be some sort of alcohol in these Froggy cottages.'

Andrew shook his head, replying, 'Not yet thank you'.

Winking at Rupert, Charles said, 'Please yourself. See you later young Rupe.'

Newly released carrier pigeons suddenly flew up with a loud flutter of wings and circled overhead. Dickson-French looked up at the sky and remarked, 'These dammed pigeons flying off all over the place makes one want to shoot the buggers. I have to keep a tight control of my rifle when they fly up, what'.

'I'm sure you do.' Andrew tried not to sound exasperated. His men had been watering their horses and were beginning to settle them in the horse lines. He wanted to inspect their injuries.

'And these dammed Froggy interpreters,' continued Charles. 'The silly arses, mad as hatters some of them. They can't ride, old boy, think they can, but they can't. They get under your feet most of the time. Best to avoid them if you come across one of them; I do.'

'Well, don't let me keep you from securing your billet,' answered Andrew. 'You need to get there first before any interpreters or the artillery.'

'Good God, yes.' Much to Andrew's relief he hurried away, calling back over his shoulder, 'I'll bag a place for you, Rupe'. Rupert grinned and nodded.

'Rupert,' said Andrew. 'See the horses are settled in and send Armstrong and Fisher to the Dressing Station. I'm going to report to Major Falterstone.'

He found the officer-in-command in a long, low, stone-built farmhouse. He was sitting at a table in the dimly lit kitchen, surrounded by men and papers. Falterstone looked up as Andrew entered and said distractedly, 'Andrew, dear boy, pleased to see you're back. Glad I haven't got to write to your father with any bad news. Although a Frenchman on a bicycle told us what had happened'.

It took Andrew a little while for his eyes to adjust to the gloom of the oppressive room with its low beamed ceiling. 'I have a list of my missing and dead men. We fought another skirmish and blew up a bridge.'

'Good, excellent, let me have a report.'

'I'll write it this evening.' Andrew paused and then asked, 'This Frenchman, did he say what happened to our guide? We were supposed to meet her at a farm, but due to unforeseen circumstances we ended up at the wrong one'.

'No. What guide? One of our interpreters?'

'No, no, only a French girl.' Andrew tried to sound unconcerned. 'The Hun were quite close at the time. I hope she got home safely, that's all.'

'No, he didn't mention any guide... Well, what is it?' asked Falterstone as Andrew still stood in front of him.

'I have a report on a man who was abusing his horse and who may have deserted.'

'I can't deal with that now. Lamentable, I'm sure, but there are more pressing matters at the moment. Go and find a billet, then get something to eat in the village hall. Villagers are putting on some sort of officers' mess, don't you know. I'll see you there later. Talk to me then.' The harassed major turned to one of his juniors and Andrew left the house.

He walked to the Dressing Station. He sighed as he saw the long queue of battered, tired men leaning against the smoke stained walls of the dirty cottage. Andrew looked at their drawn, pain-ridden faces and shivered at their expressions of helplessness and fear. He hoped that the war would be over as soon as the Allies turned the retreat around.

He shuddered as he saw horse drawn ambulances rumble up to disgorge their sorry cargo. Many men had not survived the uncomfortable ride over the cobbled roads of Northern France while squashed into the hot interior of the swaying vehicles. Their mutilated bodies were taken to the garden at the back of the house and lined up side by side on the grass with their hats placed over their faces.

Those wounded who could not walk were immediately transferred to motorised vehicles. Andrew watched in horror as stretcher after stretcher was carried across to the waiting lorries. Men lay still, covered in blood-soaked blankets, their faces grey with pain. He could clearly see by the way the blankets lay on the bodies that most of them were missing parts of their limbs. He could only guess that after another agonising, bumpy journey to the Field Hospital, all that awaited them there would be amputation.

Harassed orderlies carried stretchers, cigarettes hanging out of their mouths. Every now and then they would bend down and offer a drag to their patients. Some of the wounded men gratefully took several puffs. Others opened their pain filled eyes and stared incomprehensibly at their bearers. They closed their eyes again, as if to shut out the agony.

Andrew jumped as someone called, 'Sir… sir, this way, please.' As an officer he was ushered straight through to the nether regions of the cottage. He passed a painful few minutes as the wound on his arm was hastily stitched and soused in Iodine. He emerged from the house bandaged up and his arm in a sling. On the way out he passed Sergeant Armstrong.

'You all right, sir?' The sergeant looked at the sling.

'Perfectly, thank you. It's just a scratch.' Andrew smiled. 'How's Fisher?'

'He's all right. Once his finger was cleaned up it didn't look so bad. I believe he had a stitch in it, that's all.'

'Good, good. Your turn now, good luck.' Armstrong gave a wry smile as he reluctantly went in to see the medic.

The village street was bustling with officers trying to find billets, batmen sent on errands and soldiers going about their business. Desperate French civilians struggled through the crowd of military personnel, unsuccessfully looking for lodgings. They blocked the road with their laden handcarts until they were angrily moved on by frustrated NCOs.

Andrew was sent, by the billeting officer, to a small but clean cottage to share a room with an artilleryman. He introduced himself. The officer held out his hand. 'Lieutenant John Martin. I'm just writing my report. Then shall we go and get something to eat?'

Andrew replied, 'Excellent, I also have a report to write.'

As they walked together to the *Mairie,* two teams of tired and dusty artillery horses clattered past, laboriously pulling their 13-pounders. The bullet proof shields were pitted and bent showing evidence of a recent encounter with the Hun. The two officers watched as the fatigued drivers, their uniforms torn and soiled, dropped to a walk when they entered the field. A party of drivers and gunners ran across from the horse lines to relieve the riders who thankfully slid off their horses. The weary animals, knowing they were home, quickened their steps towards food, water and rest.

'You've seen a lot of action,' Andrew remarked.

'Yes,' replied Martin. 'A lot more to come, I think. I must say that the new bullet proof shields they have provided us with seem to be doing their job. I've had fewer casualties from enemy small fire.'

'That's good,' replied Andrew. 'We don't have bayonets yet, and our horse shoes wear out very quickly. But then you'll have the same problem, with the shoes that is.'

'Yes; so, I expect, do these men.' Both officers stepped back as a company of infantry, their faces haggard, marched past and into a field.

'I can smell their McConnachies army rations from here,' said Andrew.

'Yes, it smells quite good. Have you tried it?'

'Of course, but I wouldn't recommend it. I think I prefer bully beef. However, I am becoming quite partial to strong tea with Nestlé Condensed milk.'

'Yes, it certainly gives one energy.'

Andrew and Martin walked into the *Mairie* and found dinner being served in a long room with high windows looking out on to a rose garden enclosed within a high stone wall.

They found a table, sat down and glanced around at their fellow diners.

'There's a lot of top brass at that table over there,' remarked Martin.

'Yes, that's Brigadier-General Wheatcliff. He fought in the Boer war. He's a cavalryman.'

'He must be the man who pulled off that incredible rearguard action when heavily outnumbered. It was his successful fighting withdrawal which led to an important British victory.'

'Absolutely correct, my sergeant speaks very highly of him. By God, I'm glad we've got him with us,' said Andrew. 'He's the man to get us out of this retreat and turn the tables on the Hun.'

'That major is an artillery officer and the colonel on his right is from the infantry,' continued Martin. 'The half-colonel with them is a Royal Engineer. They're all pretty good blokes.'

'Yes, I've heard Wheatcliff is a great one for local protection and liaison amongst the different regiments, infantry, cavalry, and artillery, etc. You know, for mutual support.'

'That's what we need,' replied Martin. 'We're all on the same side. But to hear some of the men talking you wouldn't think so.'

Andrew laughed. 'Yes, some of my troopers believe they're better than the *plant life,* as they call the infantry. Changing the subject, we're lucky that the Quartermaster-General has had the foresight to drive ahead and drop provisions off in the villages along our route. It means that the cooks can prepare meals. This is very good.'

'Yes, considering we're fighting a war, it's excellent. But I believe the French actually cooked it.' Martin paused. 'Tell me what you've been up to.'

Andrew told him about his two battles and then the lieutenant recounted his exploits. They had finished their meal and were just getting up from the table when Andrew saw Dickson-French, Falterstone and Rupert bearing down on them.

'I need to have a word with my OC,' said Andrew.

'I'll head back, going to turn in, had a hard day,' replied Martin.

'I'll join you shortly. I'll try not to wake you.'

'Don't worry, you won't. I'll be dead to the world.' He smiled and left.

'Thought you'd like us to join you, old boy.' Charles sat down and placed six bottles of red wine on the table. 'Requisitioned these from my billet, don't you know. Sorry your friend has gone.' He gave the retreating Martin a cursory glance. Then he brought out a large red and white spotted handkerchief and wiped his ginger moustache which had been dampened by his running nose.

''Evening.' Falterstone took off his hat and smoothed down his grizzled crinkly hair. 'What's on the menu?'

'Its beef stew, and very good,' replied Andrew.

Dickson-French grunted. 'Looks pretty awful to me.'

'It's a whole lot better than the food the soldiers are eating,' said Andrew.

'So I should hope,' retorted Falterstone. He then said to Charles, 'Good thing you had the forethought to bring red wine, what'.

'My thoughts exactly.' Charles began to fill up the glasses.

'Not for me, thank you.' Andrew turned to the major. 'I mentioned a trooper who may have deserted.'

'Did you?' replied Falterstone.

'Yes.' Andrew began to tell him, again, about Stone. Falterstone interrupted, 'How would you know if he's deserted? Soldiers are going missing all the time. They're not always with their right regiments. People have got mixed up, some have been killed and some taken prisoner. You can't go making assumptions. Impossible to say what has happened to him.

Everything's in disarray. Look at you, we thought you were dead.'

'I know,' Andrew replied patiently. 'But this man was already under close arrest for horse cruelty.'

'Horses are abused all the time out here. Alive one moment, wounded and dying the next. What do you call cruelty, eh?' snapped Falterstone.

'If your man was under close arrest, how did you lose him? That was a bit lax of you, Harrington-West,' remarked Charles.

'We were being pursued by the enemy and had to turn and fight.'

'Well then, the man's been killed; there you have it in a nutshell,' said Falterstone.

'I don't think so.'

'He'll turn up. He's got nowhere to go, you see, or he's been killed, or captured by the Hun. One or the other. Don't waste time thinking about him, more important things going on. Put him down as missing.'

'I've already done that.'

'Good, that's the end of the matter. As for horse cruelty, no time for that… Out here? Have a glass of wine.'

'You'll have to excuse me. I'm going to return to my billet, I've had a long day.'

'The night is young,' remarked Dickson-French. 'What on earth are you going to do there? And after I managed to lay my hands on this rather good wine too.'

'Turn in, old chap. We march at 5 o'clock tomorrow morning.' Andrew turned to Rupert, who was smirking at his exchange with Falterstone. 'I expect to see you at the horse lines at 4 a.m.'

'4 a.m.!' exclaimed Charles. 'Whatever for? I won't get there until 4.50.'

'That's up to you, but I want my junior officers to set an example. The men will be up at 3.' Andrew noticed the look that Rupert exchanged with Charles. He did his best to keep his anger hidden. 'Now, if you'll excuse me, I'll say good night.'

'Good night,' replied Falterstone airily.

CHAPTER EIGHT

Reinforcements

The next morning Andrew mounted and stood in front of his squadron of six officers and a hundred and fifty two other soldiers. He watched as Major Falterstone and Charles Dickson-French arrived to mount their horses. The major nodded at Andrew with a pained expression on his face.

'Good morning,' Andrew responded cheerily.

'Morning,' said Charles, his runny eyes heavy from lack of sleep.

'You look the worse for wear,' Andrew remarked.

'Yes, old boy. Let's hope there isn't too much shooting, not 'til lunchtime at any rate. You missed a good evening.'

Once the two officers were mounted the cavalcade left the field. Andrew smiled to himself, thinking how Charles's head must be objecting to the noise of over three hundred sets of steel horse shoes hammering on the paved road.

The troop of soldiers who had fought at the ford rode directly behind him. Andrew's mind wandered between thoughts of home and the war as he idly listened to the men chatting.

'I 'ardly slept a wink last night,' Shrimp remarked to Marsh.

'No, neither did I.' Marsh looked at the Turners. 'I expect you two slept like tops.'

'No, we bloody didn't if you must know,' retorted 65. 'I found a molehill under my ground sheet. I was kept awake by the stench of horse's sweat on my blanket which was still wet from being under my saddle for God knows how many days.'

'And those bastard dispatch riders coming and going all bleedin' night,' his brother complained.

'It was scarcely all night, Len,' said 65. 'We were up at 3.00 hours to feed the horses, if you remember.'

'I thought you country boys always got up at the crack of dawn,' Shrimp taunted.

'You're getting very cocky,' retorted Len.

'Yeah, about time we sorted you out,' added 65.

'Just try it, hedge-kickers,' replied Shrimp.

'Don't you lot ever stop arguing?' Williams sighed.

At that moment a fraught dispatch rider rode up; he had been weaving his way through the long cavalcade of soldiers looking for Andrew and his patience was wearing thin.

The captain moved his squadron off the road and halted them in a field while the motorcyclist handed him a sealed envelope containing orders from Brigadier-General Wheatcliff. As soon as Andrew signed the receipt, the dispatch rider rode thankfully back towards his mobile H.Q.

Andrew read the papers and explained to Rupert. 'We're to return without delay to the rear of the column, take an easterly direction and relieve a company of Riflemen who are holding a village. We're to take two guns from a battery of the RHA... Oh excellent, with Lieutenant Martin. I shared a billet with him last night. Also another troop of twenty five men with...' He paused and read from the orders. 'A Vickers machine gun under the command of Lieutenant Fields, horse drawn ambulance number three and ammunition lorry number fifty six. You'd better go and find them while I turn the squadron. We'll rendezvous at the crossroads. Can you remember the names?'

'Yes.' Rupert looked as if he was about to be sick.

'Pull yourself together.' Andrew glared at him. 'I told you to be in the horse lines at 4.00 hours but you didn't turn up until 4.30. What were you drinking last night?'

'Charles sent his batman out to find some brandy. It wasn't very good quality,' replied the white faced Rupert.

'I've no sympathy. A hangover like yours is considered to be a self-inflicted wound. I could put you on a charge. As it is I hope you're suffering enough to learn not to do it again. Now write down the names I have just given you.' Rupert pulled out his note book and, whilst balancing it precariously on the pommel of his saddle, wrote down his instructions.

When he finished Andrew said, 'Try to look as if you're not a dissipated young fool. You're setting a bad example. Hurry up, we haven't got all day'.

The squadron made their way back against the heavy flow of traffic. They were able to ride on the stubble and cut hayfields beside the road most of the time. Although, when they had to march on the road itself, their way was hampered by the escaping French civilians who spread themselves in straggly rows across the dusty cobbles.

'Fucking Frogs,' exclaimed Turner 65, as they wound around donkey carts, wheelbarrows and perambulators piled high with belongings.

'Poor little blighters.' Marsh looked at the children, their eyes wide, staring in awe at the soldiers. Turner 65 grunted a reply and then added, 'Where are we going anyway?'

'Here apparently,' replied Williams, as Andrew suddenly took a right hand turn and halted them in a field.

The captain looked back through his field glasses and was relieved to see Rupert cantering towards him. He was followed by two teams of artillery horses hauling their 13-pounders.

He cheerfully greeted John Martin and told him to let his men graze and water their horses while they consulted his map. They both agreed that it would take about two hours to reach the village. The ambulance trundled up, and also the troop of twenty five riders with their machine gun and its limber. The officer in command rode up to Andrew and said, 'Lieutenant Fields reporting'.

'Good morning,' answered Andrew. 'And this is the Vickers Gun?'

'Yes, accurate up to 2,900 yards.'

'Good, good. You can rest your horses while we wait for the ammunition lorry and then we'll get going.' Andrew paused and added, 'Ironic that the mechanised vehicle is taking longer to reach us than the equines'.

Once the ammunition arrived, Andrew mounted his men and the small army continued on its way towards the besieged village. Lieutenant Fields and John Martin rode up beside him.

After they had been riding for nearly an hour, Fields said, 'Listen… That's gunfire. Not far now'.

The men tensed up. The horses pricked their ears and quickened their steps; gunfire and explosions were becoming a part of their everyday life.

'Thank goodness we're out of the sun,' Marsh remarked to Shrimp, as they entered a section of woodland. The temperature had dropped noticeably as the tall trees shaded the road.

'I'll say.' Shrimp patted his sweating horse.

'We're going to see some action again soon,' continued Marsh.

'I expect so.' Shrimp sounded unenthusiastic.

'Getting windy?' Turner 65 butted in.

'You've been very quiet.' Marsh turned in his saddle to look at the twins. 'We thought you were asleep or too frightened to talk.'

'Fuck off,' retorted 65. 'We can't wait to fight, got the taste for it now. It's too hot to talk.'

'Quite right,' agreed Shrimp. 'We don't want your hot air adding to the heat.'

'Very funny,' replied 65.

As they were emerging from the wood with their destination in sight, Fields said, 'Do you hear that?'

'Yes, a plane,' replied Martin.

'Take cover!' yelled Andrew. 'It's German.'

The squadron of cavalry rapidly disappeared out of sight. The RHA galloped down a dry woodland track. The ammunition lorry accelerated after them in a cloud of dust and the ambulance followed the lorry at a more sedate pace, arriving under cover just as the plane had finished circling the village and headed towards the wood.

The soldiers looked anxiously up at the sky through the canopy of trees as the aeroplane drew nearer. The horses shook their heads, struggling to rid themselves of the insects that clustered around their eyes; some kicked at their stomachs trying to dislodge clinging horseflies.

'Fucking flies,' exclaimed Turner 65. 'You'd think there would be less under these trees.'

'Quiet,' barked an NCO.

'I suppose he thinks the pilot can hear us,' Len Turner whispered.

The men stood craning their necks to look at the aircraft as it circled the wood.

'He's not going to drop anything on us,' said 65 scornfully, as a young trooper ducked. 'The pilot only has a revolver and a camera.'

'They can drop bombs,' declared Shrimp.

'Bollocks,' retorted Len Turner.

'Straight up, they can. I've seen one of ours with a passenger leaning over the side carrying a bomb.'

'Quiet,' shouted the NCO.

The plane circled only once over the wood. Andrew waited until it was out of sight before yelling, 'Get these units moving fast, we've little time to waste'.

They galloped across the open farmland towards their objective. As they clattered down the main street of the village, a group of wounded British soldiers came out of a house waving and cheering. Andrew slid his squadron to a halt beside them. Through the open door he could see the rows of wounded men lying inside. More British heads appeared at the upstairs windows.

'Good God! How many wounded are there?' he exclaimed to Martin. Then he shouted, 'Which way?'

'Keep going to the end of this road, sir,' replied an NCO, leaning on the side of the door, his head bandaged. 'You'll find Major Hardwick there.'

'Thank you, Sergeant.' Andrew moved his men off to the cheers of the wounded soldiers. He had no difficulty in finding the OC, who ran up the street to greet them. He was overwhelmed to see the small army that had come to relieve his men.

'Thank God you've arrived,' he exclaimed breathlessly. 'We couldn't keep this up for much longer. We had a hell of a battle yesterday and the men are exhausted. Halt your squadron here, Captain. They'll be well out of range. The Hun are collecting their dead at the moment, which makes me think they're going to advance as soon as they've finished. You're a Godsend. Follow me.'

Andrew left an officer in charge of the squadron, took Fields and Martin and followed the major to the eastern edge of the village. Hardwick pointed to a small wood which lay across a strip of farmland. The fields swept down to a narrow valley and then climbed up again to the wood. The stubble was littered with the carcasses of fallen German horses, the aftermath of a battle.

Andrew watched the German stretcher parties through his field glasses. The bearers held white flags tied to branches; they hung limp in the hot sun.

'We're very short of ammunition,' said Major Hardwick. Thank God you brought replenishments. As you can see, their cavalry charged unsuccessfully. Some of the wounded Germans struggled here to give themselves up. Luckily we managed to keep the infantry at bay. We, too, have been licking our wounds and burying our dead. I've seen a movement of horses in the wood and I fear they've also received reinforcements. The Hun must know very soon how few we are. An aeroplane flew over here nearly an hour ago and the pilot will have reported in by now. We have to hold this village. It's on a vital supply line. You see that road which goes to the south?' The officers nodded. 'That joins up with the retreating armies. It's a cut through for our supply transport.'

'Yes, we saw the plane. I only hope that he didn't see us. Luckily we were in a wood,' Andrew replied.

'Let's hope so; at any rate we don't have much time.' The major took the officers into a garden to the right of the main street. The enemy had shelled the first few houses and the riflemen had had to withdraw out of their range. 'Most of the inhabitants have left. Some French civilians have taken over the rifles of the dead men and others are ready with their shotguns or anything else they can lay their hands on,' continued the major.

Andrew was appalled to see only a handful of walking wounded propped up behind a garden wall. They were joined by a few elderly Frenchmen, some with rifles and some with shot guns, their cartridge belts crossed over their chests like bandits. 'Have you got more men in the farmyard across the road?'

'A few more.' The major managed a wry smile and walked on until they came to two 13 pounders. 'This is Captain Wiltshire from the artillery.' Major Hardwick introduced the tall young man who joined the officers. He looked exhausted and dirty.

'Good to see you.' Captain Wiltshire shook Andrew warmly by the hand. 'We had three 13 pounders. One has been put out of action. We're very low on ammunition.' He gave Andrew a quick smile. 'Thank God you've arrived.'

'You'd better discuss where you want to position the reinforcements,' interjected Major Hardwick. 'I don't think it'll be long before the Hun advance.'

'I agree,' replied Wiltshire, who immediately began to discuss where to place the newly arrived guns with Martin and Fields.

Andrew heard Captain Wiltshire say, 'I think you could position your machine gun in a second floor window of the farmhouse beside the church. It's the highest accessible point. There's a first-rate view over the open country. Also it's well out of range of the enemy artillery in the wood. That's if you can manhandle it up the stairs'.

'I'll have a look. It shouldn't be too much of a problem,' replied Fields.

'I think it best if we take the left flank,' Wiltshire continued, speaking to Martin and Andrew. 'There's a spinney beside the farm entrance. We can put one gun just inside the farm and the other two in the copse.' He turned to Andrew. 'Take your squadron to that outlying stockyard on the right flank.'

Andrew looked at where he was pointing. 'How are we going to get there without being seen by the enemy?'

'The ground falls away to the right of the stockyard. If you skirt around the back of the village and approach it from there you'll be in the lee of the hill. Once in the yard you have the stone walls for cover.'

'Right you are.' Andrew looked at Major Hardwick for confirmation. 'Perfect.' The major nodded.

Andrew ordered his squadron to go at once to the stone barn at a gallop. He watched while the gunners in the copse made ready their guns. The teams of horses retired a short distance away into the wood, and the drivers sat tight in their saddles ready to move the weapons at a moment's notice. The gunners and bombardiers stood or knelt in their positions beside the concealed guns, ready for action.

The enemy had now finished collecting their dead and the British officers became aware of movement in the wood. Major Hardwick called an abrupt end to their conference.

Andrew mounted his charger and galloped round the back of the village to join his men in the stockyard, closely followed by his cover. After he arrived he didn't have to wait long before he saw the Germans beginning to emerge from the wood, led by a squadron of Uhlans. They fanned out to the left and right of a company of infantry who were strung out in a line between them.

Andrew's heart sank as he saw the numbers of foot-soldiers. But he was pleased to see the Germans had divided their squadron of cavalry in half. He jumped as an enemy shell landed with a loud explosion to the east of the village close to the old position of Captain Wiltshire's guns. Andrew hoped the Germans hadn't realised that they had been moved. As another shell landed within a few feet of the first, he thought his hopes had been confirmed. The enemy had just advertised the new position of their own guns.

While Andrew watched the advancing army he could feel the tension of his soldiers. He knew that the troopers who had been with him at the ford would give a good account of themselves, but there were a lot of young lads in the squadron who had never fought before. He turned in his saddle and looked behind him.

Some men intently watched the advancing enemy. Others looked pale, their faces pinched and their eyes wide and staring. Andrew guessed how their stomachs churned as they clutched their swords. Their horses fidgeted, sensing the tension.

'God, they look young, some of them will surely die', he thought. He turned back to watch the Germans. They were riding close to a high park wall which ran alongside the field. He noticed that the ground was steep and the Uhlans were holding back to the pace of the marching men.

The horses at the rear were jogging and treading on those in front. Through his field glasses, Andrew could make out the body language of an irate NCO. The riders had loose seats, their legs stuck forward and they were hanging on to their reins in order to keep their balance. They can hardly ride, Andrew thought in astonishment. His eyes travelled to the riders at the front of the column: they looked as competent as his own troopers. He signalled to Armstrong to join him and quickly told him what he wanted him to do when the squadron attacked. He told Rupert to stay with the sergeant.

Andrew swung his glasses round to his far left and watched the cavalry on the other flank. He knew that Captain Wiltshire's artillery would make short work of them. He shivered, knowing that the horses wouldn't stand a chance.

The enemy guns continued firing without much effect, the shells landing in more or less the same place. The British guns didn't return the fire. Andrew noticed that as each time a gun fired the badly ridden horses became more unsettled.

Most of the horses in Andrew's squadron remained quiet, although some of them jumped with their heads in the air and their ears back at each explosion. Their riders stroked their necks and spoke to them and they stood still.

Suddenly all hell broke loose. Three British 13 pounders roared into action. They fired salvos at the Germans in the opposite wood just as the advancing enemy had begun to mount the slope up to the village. The fourth British gun sent several rounds diagonally across the approaching army. They landed very close to the back of the cavalry on the enemy's left flank. Although the horses were just out of range, some of them were sprayed with spent shrapnel. It was all that was needed to set them off. Their riders lost control and at least twenty horses began to stampede. They broke through the ranks in front of them and galloped uncontrollably towards the village.

Andrew realised that Captain Wiltshire must have noticed the bad riding, and silently thanked him. Seizing the moment, he ordered his bugler to sound charge. His Squadron cantered out of the gate and on to the plain with their swords in the engage. They came under fire from the advancing line of enemy infantry, a few troopers were hit and fell, but the horses kept galloping. The Vickers gun instantly barked into action, quickly backed by the British riflemen on the ground. The enemy Infantry fell on to their stomachs to avoid the fire. Andrew galloped relentlessly on towards the

German cavalry.

Armstrong, taking thirty men and Rupert, peeled away from the main body of cavalry and raced after the runaway German horses.

The rest of the enemy horsemen were surprised by the full squadron of British cavalry. They were vastly outnumbered. Their officers shouted orders while the NCOs desperately tried to instil calm and order.

The leading German officer, carrying his lance, galloped towards Andrew. After his experience at the ford, he ducked dexterously out of the way of the wavering length of steel and drove his sword home into his opponent's upper body. The German lurched in the saddle and fell to the ground. His lance flew up in the air and landed under the feet of a following horse. It stumbled and threw its rider.

The men behind Andrew, spurred on by their captain's performance, vigorously attacked the remaining horsemen. The German NCOs managed to keep their formation together, in spite of their fallen officer and the distracting stampeding horses. They rallied and fought like fury against the overwhelming number of British. The battle wasn't as easy as Andrew had anticipated.

Then the enemy started to throw down their lances. They were far more skilful with their swords and quickly began slashing their way through the attacking British troopers.

A German hacked at the right hand of a young lad; the trooper looked down in astonishment as he dropped his sword, blood soaking his forearm and running down his horse's shoulder. He fell to the ground in shock, the pain temporarily masked by his flow of adrenaline.

Andrew realised, with respect mixed with regret, that the Germans were making short work of his inexperienced young troopers. He called a hasty withdrawal. The Bugler's call was not easy to hear above the noise of the British guns, and some men didn't notice the tactical retreat. Andrew quickly ordered the men who had obeyed the order to form a tight half circle around the fighting soldiers, cornering them against the park wall. He shouted 'draw rifles,' and ordered his crack shots to fire several rounds into the mêlée, picking off the NCOs and the officers first. His Bugler continued sounding the retreat until the British left the battle as best they could.

Andrew glanced at Shrimp. He had no weapon in his hand. 'Fisher, where the hell is your rifle?'

'I give it to Marsh, sir.' Shrimp pointed. 'He fell and his horse took off, wiv his rifle.' Andrew saw Marsh lying between the legs of a dead horse, using it as cover. His own right leg was sticking out at a very strange angle, obviously broken. He was firing at the Germans as calmly as if he was shooting rabbits.

The Germans, realising that they were cornered, started to panic. Andrew ordered his men to open fire. Some of the enemy, looking for an escape route, began riding their horses at the wall. The horses found it too high, except for one who took off and landed straddled on top, its hind legs lifted off the ground. The spikes ripped through the girth and the saddle slipped off taking the rider with it. The horse fell backwards and lay beside the wall, unable to get up. The trapped rider screamed in pain, not helping the morale of the depleted Germans.

A German officer, still in the saddle but with blood pouring from a wound in his side, realised that they were surrounded and vastly outnumbered. He yelled the order to surrender. Andrew watched as the enemy dropped their weapons and lifted their hands above their heads. The officer saluted Andrew who returned his salute. The encounter was over.

Armstrong had successfully rounded up the bolting horses and incompetent riders with very little loss to his own troops. He and Rupert were now shepherding them back to the village.

Andrew gritted his teeth as he heard the screams of the badly wounded horses. It was a noise that went right through his body. He knew that he would never get used to it. He left a small party of men including, a farrier to dispatch the animals and a medic to attend to the wounded men. He gave orders that the disarmed Germans were to be taken to a house off the main street and the enemy horses to a farm.

Those of his troopers who didn't have a sound mount hastily grabbed a loose horse whether it was German or British. They followed their captain back to the eastern side of the village to report to Major Hardwick.

The German infantry, now a ragged line, were still lying on their stomachs half hidden by the slope. They fired fruitlessly in the direction of the village. As soon as they stood up they were cut down by the machine gun fire. Andrew shuddered as he saw yet more German horses brought down by the British artillery and hastily looked away.

'Well done.' Major Hardwick congratulated the squadron as they arrived in the village. 'We have the enemy in a stalemate situation at the moment. We need to flush these buggers out from under the lee of the hill.'

The sound of clattering horses' hooves rang out from the village. The two officers stared in the direction of the street. Major Falterstone came round the corner at the head of his squadron.

'Hello, old bean.' Charles Dickson-French's unmistakeable accents reached Andrew's ears. 'We've come to help you out, don't you know. Looks like the artillery have had quite a party.' He nodded towards the morass of dead men and horses. 'Hun didn't quite make it to the village, what.'

'I hope your hangover's better.' Andrew tried to smile.

'We'll take over now,' Falterstone addressed Hardwick.

'That'll give us an opportunity to water our horses,' remarked Andrew.

'Where's Rupert?' Dickson-French asked.

Andrew waved his arm in a south-westerly direction. 'Over there with the prisoners.' He led his men back into the village without waiting for an answer.

Major Hardwick explained the situation to Falterstone, who replied, 'Dickson-French will flush out the Infantry and then go after the guns in the wood. Harrington-West will act as back up, when he returns. Watering horses, indeed, in the middle of a battle. Ours have made it here without any water and are ready to go, fresh as daisies. Right Charles?'

'Absolutely.' Dickson-French took a long swig from his water bottle.

Captain Wiltshire turned up and addressed Hardwick. 'We've still got three guns in working order.'

'Good. How many have the Hun got?'

'Only two firing now, but we're keeping them busy.' Sporadic gunfire backed up his statement. Captain Wiltshire looked at the newly arrived horses, some standing with their heads low and their hind legs stretched out behind them, and he said, 'Shouldn't you water your horses before you continue?'

'Don't give me lessons in horsemanship, man,' retorted Falterstone.

'No, sir,' replied Wiltshire. He turned his attention to Hardwick, who clarified the battle plan and Falterstone's orders. He returned to his guns, happy in the knowledge that his horses had been watered and fed. They were fit and ready to move his guns at a moment's notice.

Falterstone looked at Major Hardwick, who said, 'We're ready when you are.'

'Carry on Charles,' said Falterstone.

Dickson-French spurred his hot, tired horse out of the village, followed by the weary squadron. They galloped down the hill towards the line of German infantry. The Germans, pleased that at last they could see their enemy, opened fire with gusto. Charles galloped towards them and they were forced on to their feet.

Unfortunately the cavalry came between the enemy and Lieutenant Fields' line of fire. The riflemen managed to fire some rounds, but they too were hampered by the British.

The Germans began to turn and run back towards the wood. The British gave chase, cutting down the fleeing enemy with their swords. The Vickers gun burst into action again and Lieutenant Fields, to his chagrin, inadvertently killed one or two British riders. The German artillery fired a salvo into the conflict, aiming at the British. But the shells fell short. Not many German soldiers made it back.

Andrew returned to the eastern side of the village and watched in horror at the number of British horsemen and their mounts that were being hit. Loose horses careered off in different directions. Some of them stopped to eat grass as soon as they found themselves at a distance away from the fighting. A few galloped blindly in the direction of the park wall. Andrew watched as one by one they fell to the ground. He knew that a horse could take a large number of rounds before it would come down. He guessed that as their adrenaline stopped flowing their life force ran out and they gave in to the loss of blood.

Suddenly there was a succession of explosions in the wood. Fire and debris shot into the air. 'Captain Wiltshire must have hit an ammunition dump,' Andrew shouted to Falterstone, who replied, 'Yes, Charles is doing very well'.

'Yes, he's lost most of his squadron already.'

'Glad you agree,' replied Falterstone.

When the noise eventually stopped Andrew realised that none of the German guns were firing.

Dickson-French, still on his horse and relatively unscathed, also noticed the silence. He called the remains of his men and galloped into the wood.

Falterstone sent Andrew after them. His squadron raced down the hill well to the right of the fallen Infantry. He arrived at the entrance to the woodland with no resistance from the enemy. He stopped to listen. He heard movement and light gun fire towards the east. Following the sound he caught sight of a team of German artillery horses. Gunners hung on to the swaying limber as it bumped over the ground and out of the wood. They were followed by another team who were hitched together but had no gun. All six horses had two riders on their backs. They were closely pursued by Dickson-French and a few of his men. Much to Andrew's surprise the Germans were gaining ground. Charles's horses looked done in.

Andrew spun round as suddenly shots came from above and behind him. One of his troopers fell wounded from his horse. He yelled at an officer to divide the men into groups and sweep the woodland for snipers.

The men spread out like beaters on a pheasant shoot and combed the woodland, pushing the enemy back towards the village and the British guns. They took no prisoners.

Andrew, riding on the far left of his men, heard a rustling in the bushes. He tightened his hold on his revolver and left the track. He saw a German officer riding a grey horse and followed him. His eyes were drawn to the German's good looking mount. He recognised it, without doubt, as Francine's horse.

The German looked back and galloped out of the trees. Andrew gave chase. He didn't worry that he couldn't keep up with the thoroughbred. He knew that the German was heading for the high, spiked park wall and would have to come to a halt. He emerged into the fields to see the rider galloping alongside the obstacle until he reached a point where the ground rose slightly, making the wall appear lower.

To Andrew's amazement the man galloped into the field, stopped and turned back towards the wall. Andrew heard himself shouting '*No!*' for the sake of the horse. He was sure that it would suffer the same fate as the German horse earlier that day. Instead of taking aim with his rifle and trying to bring the man down, he stood rooted to the spot. He stared as the German grinned, saluted, and then cantered steadily at the obstacle. He spurred the horse on. It took off at precisely the right spot and sailed over the wall, spikes and all. Andrew watched open mouthed in admiration of a good horse and rider. Something about the German's style of riding began to ring bells in his head, but he couldn't think why. The officer sped away across the parkland and out of range.

Andrew turned his horse around and rode back to the wood. He looked up, surprised to see Armstrong galloping towards him. 'What is it, Sergeant?'

'There you are, sir. You had me worried.'

'No need. I came to no harm. I thought I saw…' He stopped in mid-sentence thinking, '*where the devil did that Hun get that horse?*' He pulled himself together. 'Where're your prisoners?'

'I left Lieutenant Somerville in charge of them. I wanted to get back to the action.' Andrew looked distant as Armstrong continued: 'We've cleared the wood. No more snipers, sir. The Hun artillery has done a bunk, and Dickson-French has gone off after them.

'Yes, I saw them in full cry. Their horses looked exhausted.'

'How did Falterstone reach the village so quickly, sir?' asked Armstrong. 'We left them way back on that crowded road.'

'They came in by the other road I imagine. The village is strategically placed. All roads seem to lead to it.' Andrew lapsed into silence. His thoughts drifted back to how the German had ridden the grey horse and how he had come by it.

'Sir, are you all right?' asked Armstrong. 'Your arm not bothering you? You're not wounded?'

'No, no.' Andrew smiled. 'I'm absolutely fine. What about you?' He stared at a patch of blood on the sergeant's arm.

'I'm as right as nine pence.'

'Are you?' Armstrong nodded.

As they crossed the plain, Andrew looked at the grisly sight of the dead German horses. He could hear the flies as they swarmed over the blown up bodies of the horses that had been killed the day before. He put his hand over his mouth and nose as the full force of the stench hit him. The horses tossed their heads and some blew down their nostrils.

Andrew gave a short laugh. 'La Croix de la Belle Dame.'

'What did you say, sir?' asked Armstrong.

'That's the name of the village, the Crucifix of the Beautiful Woman. There's nothing beautiful about it today.'

'No.' Armstrong shuddered. 'More troops have arrived by the looks of things.'

They hurried on up the hill and entered the village to find a battalion of British infantry lined up in the main street. The soldiers jumped to attention and saluted as a heavily guarded staff car squeezed passed them and drove up towards Andrew's tattered squadron.

A high ranking officer stepped out of the car and barked, 'Captain Harrington-West'.

'Sir!' The captain saluted. He found himself staring into the weather-beaten face of Brigadier-General Wheatcliff.

'Good work,' remarked the Brigadier to the assembled officers as he looked over the gruesome remnants of the battlefield.

Major Hardwick and the open mouthed Falterstone gazed in curiosity tinged with awe at the top brass as he repeated, 'Captain Harrington-West, I want a word. In the *Mairie*. Don't bother to clean up'. He then strode back to his car, which whisked him away to the village hall.

'Huh, well you're obviously for the high jump,' remarked Falterstone. Andrew gathered his wits together and hastily rode to the *Mairie*.

He handed his horse to a soldier. The guard on the door saluted and someone ushered him into the dim entrance. He crossed the tiled floor and a door swung open in front of him. He entered a long conference room heaving with activity. Papers were laid out on the wide oval table and carafes of water were placed in a line down the middle. Empty glasses stood beside each chair. Andrew realised how thirsty he was and wanted to grab a carafe as he walked past.

Aides-de-Camp were huddled and talking in low voices. One or two looked up as the dishevelled cavalry officer entered the room. Someone approached him, flung a door open and said, 'In here'. The stunned officer walked into an office to find Brigadier-General Wheatcliff seated behind a kneehole desk. He stopped and saluted.

'Sit down.' Andrew wanted to sink into the comfortable chair with a long drink in his hand, but he sat perched on the edge of his seat.

'Drink?' Wheatcliff asked. 'I expect you're thirsty.'

'Yes, a glass of water would be…' Andrew wondered if the man was a mind-reader. The Brigadier nodded to his orderly who handed him a glass. Andrew sipped it steadily.

'I expect you're wondering why you're here.' The Brigadier continued without waiting for an answer, 'I understand you met the daughter of the Marquis du Byard du Moulin: indeed, you stayed in his château'.

'I… We stayed in the Château de La Croix, certainly, but I didn't meet Mademoiselle du Byard du Moulin.'

'I hope you're not wasting my time. I'm informed by a…' The Brigadier frowned and looked down at a piece of paper, 'Doctor Lejeune that you did. Mademoiselle Francine du Byard du Moulin, the favourite and youngest daughter of the marquis apparently looked after you and acted as your guide. Is this true?'

'Y…yes, yes, sir,' replied the shattered Andrew. 'She helped us to escape and provided food for the men and fodder for the horses.'

'For God's sake man, answer my questions correctly. Have you left your wits on the battlefield?'

'No, sir... that is I ...'

'Now this lady has been kidnapped by the Hun.' Andrew jumped and nearly choked. 'They're holding her in her father's château. Her father, the marquis, is essential to our relations with the French. He's privy to our plans and has a lot of clout with the French army. He wants his daughter back, and so do we, before he spills the beans to the Boches. I have it on good authority that he might well be tempted to do so, under the right kind of pressure. His daughter is very dear to him, maybe more so than the fate of his country. Do you follow my meaning?'

'Yes sir.'

'Do you know the château well?'

'Yes, sir. Mademoiselle Francine showed me round. It's vast, and very beautiful.'

'Right, can you rescue this woman? They're apparently holding her in the dungeons of all places. I ask you, what sort of barbarians are we dealing with? The cells are well hidden I understand.'

'I know where they are. I believe I can get her out. How long have they been holding her, sir?'

'Since two or three days. They picked her up at a farm. God knows what she was doing gallivanting around the countryside at night on a grey horse. But there you are, that's the French for you. Riding astride too if you please. Clearly out of control, inviting herself to get caught if you ask me.'

'I'll get her back, sir.'

'Excellent. Take who and what you need. You'll leave by lorry immediately you're ready.'

'Can I take members of my squadron?'

'I've just said so. The chateau is now behind enemy lines. You will release a carrier pigeon when you arrive there.' Andrew stood up and looked at the map that the brigadier showed him. 'You will RV here... with this Doctor Lejeune. Be very careful who you speak to. Release another pigeon when you have the girl... And Harrington-West, if it's impossible to get her out you will have to eliminate her. Do you understand me?'

'Yes, sir.'

'We cannot afford to have any weaknesses in the French government. I'm expecting you and your men to do your duty as regards your King and Country. You make what personal sacrifices are necessary. Is that clear?'

'Perfectly, sir.' Andrew stood up and saluted. Wheatcliff was already turning the pages of another document on his desk, although Andrew heard him say, 'God speed, Captain'.

CHAPTER NINE

Infiltration

Andrew was stunned now that he had discovered Francine's status. He cringed when he remembered how he had kissed her and he racked his brains trying to recall if he had talked about her being a servant. At least he hadn't mentioned that he thought she was a bastard.

He realised that if he had shot the German who was riding her horse he could have taken him prisoner and found out more. '*Wheatcliff is right*', he thought, '*I have left my wits on the battlefield.*'

He banged the pommel of his saddle, sending shock waves up his injured arm, as he began to think what might be happening to her. He kicked his horse into a trot, but had to slow down to a walk in order to weave in and out of the troops who were arriving in the village.

He found his squadron settling their horses into horse lines in a field, and he called his officers to tell them that he was going on a mission for Brigadier-General Wheatcliff. Only three of the five he had started out with that morning were still there: one had been killed and another wounded. Rupert was still with the German prisoners. Then he summoned Sergeant Armstrong. His face fell when he saw blood on the sergeant's upper arm and thigh. 'You have a new wound and opened the old one.'

'They're only scratches, sir.'

'Don't be ridiculous, I can see from here that they're not. Go and get them seen to immediately. You're far too good a soldier to lose with an infection. I wish I could take you with me, but I can't. When you're sorted out I want you to rest and take some leave. I'll see you when we return.'

'Yes, sir. I'll have the lads fall in and then I'll find the dressing station. Which men do you want?'

Andrew told him to fetch the Turner twins, Williams, Clark and Shrimp. When they arrived he was relieved to see that none of them were seriously wounded. He ordered them to go and get something to eat from the mobile cookhouse that was setting up in the field and then report to him in the empty farmhouse. As they were leaving he called out, 'Fisher, come here please. Where's Marsh?'

'He's going to the field hospital. His leg is badly broke. They say he'll probably go home.'

Andrew listened to Shrimp's directions and then found Marsh just as he was about to be loaded into an ambulance.

'How are you?' Andrew looked down at the trooper's pain ridden face. The lad smiled. 'I'm fine, sir. Is Fisher all right?'

'Yes, a few bruises that's all.'

'He saved my life… giving me his rifle. You're not going to charge him with losing his weapon, are you, sir? Because it's me you need to put on a charge.'

'No.' Andrew busily wrote a letter on a page torn from his note book. When he finished he handed it to the wounded man. 'I want you to give this to your father when you arrive home. I'll be writing to my father shortly. When you eventually get there, you'll tell them that I'm well and that we'll soon have the Hun on the run.'

'Yes, sir. As soon as my leg's mended, I'll be back.'

'I'll look forward to seeing you, but I expect we'll be back in England by then. Have a safe journey. You fought exceptionally well and your shooting was first class. Well done.'

The pain-pinched face broke into a smile. 'Thank you, sir.'

Andrew walked back to the horse lines deep in thought. It seemed strange that the young man on the stretcher would soon be seeing his own family. The tranquil English countryside seemed far away from the stench of blood and death and the noise of battle.

He looked round as a petulant voice called, 'Harrington-West, what did Wheatcliff want?'

Andrew swung round. 'Major Falterstone, I didn't see you there. Has Charles returned yet?'

'No… No sign of him. You can saddle up and go and look for him.'

'I'd like to, but unfortunately I have orders to go elsewhere.'

'Who from? Where are you going?'

'Brigadier-General Wheatcliff. Not quite sure where yet.'

Falterstone grunted and, much to Andrew's relief, abruptly turned and walked away. He hoped that he wasn't going to ask any of his squadron to go off on a wild goose chase after the missing officer and men. But he feared that he would.

***

Andrew's chosen troopers were assembled in the deserted salon of the farmhouse when he arrived. As he walked into the house he heard the men talking.

'What are we doing here?' asked Turner 65.

'Don't look at me,' replied Williams.

'Well you're the know-all. You know everything, or reckon you do,' said Len Turner.

'I'm not psychic.'

'We'll find out soon enough,' remarked Shrimp.

'I saw you throw your rifle to Marsh. You'll get done for that.' 65 nodded knowingly.

'Rubbish, he saved Marsh's life,' retorted Williams.

'We're all probably in trouble.' Shrimp looked grave. 'That's why we're here. You lost Stone, remember.'

'Speak for yourself. We're here because we're crack troopers,' replied Turner 65.

Andrew entered the room, saying, 'Turner is correct. You are all here because you're the best'.

The men jumped to attention. Andrew smiled to himself as he saw the look on their faces. 'We have a dangerous assignment to accomplish. It involves going behind enemy lines. If there is anyone amongst you who feels that he is unable to take part, please leave now.' Nobody moved. 'Once I've told you the brief outline, you'll be unable to leave. If you breathe a word to anyone outside this room you'll be shot. Do I make myself clear?' The men nodded. 'Do you all want to come?'

There was a chorus of voices. 'Yes, sir.'

'Good, good. Williams, check that there's a sentry on the front door.' Williams returned with an affirmative answer and Andrew continued: 'We're to return to the castle which is now in enemy hands. When we arrive in the vicinity I'll tell you what our objective is. For the moment that's all you need to know. You will collect your saddles, bridles, weapons and haversacks containing the minimum amount of personal belongings and be at the entrance of this farm in thirty minutes. Any questions?'

There was a slight pause before Shrimp asked, 'What about our horses, sir?'

'You leave them behind. We'll be travelling by lorry.'

Shrimp's face fell. 'Who'll look after them, sir?'

'I'm sure the rest of the squadron will be able to look after your horse, Fisher. We managed before you arrived in the regiment.'

'Yes, sir.' Shrimp looked crestfallen.

'Williams, you'll go to Signals and collect a cage of carrier pigeons. They're expecting you.' Andrew turned and left the room.

'Carrier pigeons,' 65 scoffed.

'Hurry up and get going,' ordered Williams.

65 turned to Shrimp. 'You trying to back out? 'Cos of your soppy horse?'

'No.'

'65, we don't have time for your polemical quibbling. Get a move on.'

'All right, La-di-dah,' 65 replied testily.

'Pole what?' asked Len.

'Don't ask him, brother. He thinks he's being clever. Gets ideas above his station he does.' But Williams had hurried away to find the pigeons.

***

The co-driver sat with the men on the hard benches in the back of the lorry as they drove to the rendezvous.

'Why are we going to...?'

'Shut up Turner.' Williams interrupted, lighting a cigarette and nodding towards the co-driver. 'I have no idea. I suggest you catch some sleep.'

'Here, here,' added Shrimp. 'Then we won't have to listen to you.'

Williams turned to Shrimp. 'You can shut up too; you egg them on, you know.' Shrimp smiled into the darkness and shut his eyes.

'You'll gas them pigeons with your fag,' remarked one of the twins.

'Thank you Turner; if they die of carbon dioxide then so will we all.' Williams looked down at the six pigeons huddled together on the floor of a small wooden box.

'Shouldn't they have water?' Shrimp opened his eyes. 'And food? You don't want them to die.'

'I expect they'll survive until we get to where we're going.'

'How are you going to carry them?' asked Len.

'Someone will carry them on their back. The cage has straps.'

'Well as long as it ain't me,' declared 65.

'They would die of gas, if it were you.' Shrimp laughed.

'You think you are so fucking funny, don't you, Shrimp?'

'Yeah, funny how they find their way home.' Shrimp ignored the taunt. 'If they had any sense they'd fly back to Trafalgar Square, lots of mates for 'em there.'

'For Christ's sake, stop your drivel. They would be much better in a pie. Is that what you want to do, to fly back to London?'

'Shut up, 65,' snapped Williams. 'Sometimes we wish you would fly back to England and stay there.'

'Here, here,' agreed Shrimp.

'Get some sleep. We don't know how far we're going, so make the most of it,' Williams added before 65 could answer.

One by one the men fell asleep as the lorry swayed and bumped over the cobbled roads.

The driver entered a village and suddenly swung into a farm yard, waking up his sleeping passengers as he stopped in front of a barn. The men alighted and the lorry drove away.

Andrew was pleased to see Doctor Lejeune emerge from the gloom of the building. 'Captain, a pleasure to see you again. But under what unfortunate circumstances, *n'est ce pas*?'

Andrew shook him warmly by the hand. 'Tell me what's happened.'

'I'll take you into the house. Someone will bring food for your men. You all look worn out and, if may I say so, a little battered.'

'You could say that.' Andrew agreed that his men did look tired and dishevelled. He smiled. 'We're all fit, you know.'

'Come, follow me.'

Andrew followed him into the back of the farmhouse. He smelt something cooking on the stove. It reminded him of the enclave and the seriousness of their mission. As soon as they entered the salon he asked, 'What happened? How did she get caught?'

'Francine went to meet you at the farm as arranged. The Boches raided it. Luckily for you, you managed to avoid them and went to the wrong farm.'

'But not Francine.'

'*Non*. Someone alerted them. There are traitors everywhere. One has to be very careful. They knew who she was.'

'I had no idea who she was.'

'*Capitaine*, how could you not know?'

Andrew looked away, hoping the doctor didn't notice his heightened colour. 'I... I wasn't thinking straight. The moments of our first meeting were... misleading. I thought she was the huntsman's daughter. We met at the hunt kennels. She was wearing a ragged dress and helping in the house and the stables. I thought the other girl was her sister.'

'I agree that you didn't see her at her best and her demeanour wasn't that of a great lady. She was a tomboy. She liked nothing better than to ride and hunt.'

'Why are you using the past tense? She's not…'

'*Non, non,* I talk of her childhood. She's still headstrong and does exactly what she wants. She's aware of her beauty. She knows men are attracted to her.' He shrugged. 'But she has no thought of marriage. She has all she wants in her life, money, freedom… why saddle herself with a husband?'

'Ye… yes…' Andrew tried to hide his feelings. 'How do you know where they're holding her?'

The doctor's face clouded over. 'Some servants have escaped from the château and they told us that she's in the dungeons. They stink. The sewage outlet runs down beside them and they are infested with rats. Regrettably, they are truly the dungeons of the romantic novelists of the 19th century.' The doctor saw Andrew's face harden. '*Oof,* don't worry about her courage. She played in those dungeons as a child. *Non,* I worry more about disease.' He gave a short laugh. 'But I hear the German guards are not happy either. We have set rumours about human vampires living in the castle. I understand that they're expecting to see Count Dracula visiting them in the night.' Both men gave a weak smile.

'What condition is she in?' The doctor turned away and Andrew felt cold. 'How is she? Have they harmed her?'

'I… I don't know.'

Andrew raised his voice. 'Yes you do. What have they done to her? Tell me.'

'I'm not sure… but we need to get her out of there as quickly as possible.'

'We'll go now. We haven't time to eat.'

'Your food is coming and your men already have theirs.'

'I couldn't eat a thing.'

'Try to eat as much as you can. You don't know when you'll next have a meal.'

Andrew looked sharply at the doctor and began to pick at a plate of food that a woman had placed in front of him.

As soon as she left, the doctor continued: 'The enemy lines are just on the other side of this village. The château is several hours ride from here'.

'Then we must hurry.' Andrew put down his knife and fork.

'Let me explain your route as you eat. You'll have to go by the woods, avoiding the open plain. It's a roundabout way, but it's as safe as it can be. It should still be dark by the time you arrive at the next rendezvous. Your horses are in the barn. I think there are twelve: you take what you want. The men have their saddles?' Andrew nodded. 'I have a good guide for you, a young lad who will join the French army himself soon. His father is a high ranking officer.'

Andrew's patience was beginning to run out. He pushed his plate to one side and stood up. 'I've had enough to eat. We'll start straight away.'

As he entered the barn he heard the men arguing over which horse they wanted.

'We need big horses,' declared Turner 65. 'We'll take these two.'

'The captain will take first pick,' replied Williams.

'I'm having this one.' Shrimp had his sights set on a little mare who backed away, shook her head, and laid her ears back at anyone who went near her.

'She looks half wild to me,' said Williams. 'Do we need her?'

'Yes, I'll ride her.' Shrimp remained adamant.

'Right,' said Andrew as he looked at the assortment of horses. 'The Turners can have the two big geldings.'

'This one looks like an officer's charger, sir.' Williams showed him a good looking thoroughbred.

'Yes, I'll take him. Clark can ride this one.' Andrew looked at a small quality chestnut mare with four white socks and a broad white blaze on her pretty dished face.

'Yeah, she looks like a soppy girl's horse. That'll suit Clark,' muttered 65 to his brother.

'Turner,' barked Andrew. Both twins looked up. 'I don't want to hear any more of your fatuous remarks. We're all here to look after each other. Now, if you're incapable of doing that, you'll have to leave us. Unfortunately you can't return to the squadron, so I will, in effect, have to shoot you. And, believe me I will shoot whichever one of you makes the next absurd and insulting comment. I will not have our mission put in jeopardy by your constant gibing at the other members of our team. Do I make myself clear?'

'Yes, sir.' The Turners, seeing the grim look on their captain's face, believed him.

'As you're identical, I shall have no qualms about shooting the wrong twin by mistake. Do you understand?'

'Yes, sir.'

'All right the rest of you, saddle up.' He looked at three shabby horses together in a pen. 'We'll leave these, they look old and thin. We'll take nine horses. Fisher and the Turners will each lead a spare horse. We can sort things out as we go along, if we have to change horses *en route,* then we will. Williams, you take the pigeons.'

A tall boy came into the barn, leading a horse, accompanied by the doctor. 'This is your guide, François de Gillan; he speaks very good English and he has hunted around here all his life. He knows the countryside inside out, even in the dark.'

The boy shook hands with Andrew, who then lost no time in mounting his men. Shrimp's mare immediately stood on her hind legs, but he sat tight, clinging to her back like a monkey up a stick.

'Clark, take the spare horse,' ordered Andrew. They left the farmyard under a stone archway, riding out on to the plain. The horses were fresh, but Andrew trotted them on at a brisk pace and most of them settled quickly. The moon was coming and going behind the clouds and it reminded him of their ride to the castle with Francine.

Shrimp's horse stood on her hind legs again and lunged forwards in a series of kangaroo hops. She overtook the other horses and landed in the ploughed field at the side of the track.

'Keep her on the plough until she settles.'

'Yes, sir,' Shrimp managed to reply, as the mare flew through the air.

'That's Monsieur Copain's filly.' François informed Andrew. 'I don't think she's properly broken in.'

'Don't worry,' Andrew smiled. 'She will be by the time we arrive at our destination.' The filly continued prancing and bucking until, at last, she stopped abruptly in the middle of the field and refused to move. Shrimp tried all the methods he knew to make her move forwards, but they failed. When she saw the other horses passing her on the track, she threw up her head and stared after them. Shrimp sat still in the saddle, feeling that the mare was making up her mind, rather like a recalcitrant child, deciding that, in the end, it might be a good idea to co-operate with authority. She took a tentative step forward, shook her head and tried to rush after the other horses. Shrimp made her stop and he patted her whilst she stamped her feet and pawed the ground. Then he released the reins and let her canter through the plough after the other horses. He joined the track and slotted in at the rear. The mare trotted along, her ears pricked, looking as if butter wouldn't melt.

Andrew looked round and smiled. 'Glad you could join us, Trooper.' Shrimp grinned and patted the filly, who tossed her head. The Turners turned round and grinned too. Shrimp waited for a sarcastic comment, but none came.

'The German territory starts in this wood,' the guide told Andrew, as they slowed to a walk before entering the dense copse. 'They patrol along the main path but if we skirt round by the lake, then through Monsieur de Pracin's garden, we can reach the next wood quite easily.'

'Go ahead.' Andrew stood aside and let the young man lead the way. He turned back to his men. 'Single file. Clark, bring up the rear, behind Fisher. Don't get yourself kicked by that lunatic filly.'

They snaked their way along a narrow path. The horses occasionally stumbled over tree stumps and protruding roots that littered the middle of the winding trail, but no one came to grief.

Andrew was becoming impatient by the slowness of their progress when at last they emerged into a clearing beside a lake.

François explained, 'We ride around the lake, past the little château and on to the next wood.'

'Right you are. Lead on again, please.'

'I think we must ride slowly over the turf. Monsieur de Pracin is a loyal Frenchman, but he values his garden. He likes to think his grass is as good as an English lawn.'

'Then we'll take great care. Please inform him that it is as good, if not better, than any English garden. Everyone, please make sure that we do the minimum amount of damage.'

They cautiously crossed the lawn. Even Shrimp's temperamental mare behaved herself. Andrew's face fell as they came to the end of the garden. He saw that they had to jump down a walled-up bank into a deep gully. Once in the gully they had one horse's stride to gather momentum in order to jump up the other side into the parkland.

'You go first,' Andrew said to François. The young Frenchman jumped neatly down the bank and up into the park.

The Turners followed. Then Williams's horse jumped down, but the pigeon cage bumped about on the lance-corporal's back. The frightened occupants fluttered and the horse stopped dead.

'Help him, Clark,' Andrew ordered.

As Clark dismounted, Shrimp remained standing in the garden holding his horse. 'Sir, there's movement in the park. I think it's an enemy patrol.'

'Get back into the gully and dismount,' ordered Andrew. 'Fisher and Clark, either get your horses down now or go back into the garden.'

Clark looked at Shrimp, who nodded, and they both dropped their horses down the bank and into the gully.

Andrew put his field glasses to his eyes, trying to see into the darkness. He eventually caught the movement of riders coming towards them.

'Well done, Fisher. You're right, it is a patrol. Keep your horses still... and Fisher, twitch that mare. Williams, keep those pigeons quiet.'

Shrimp thought for a moment and then rummaged in his haversack pulling out a ball of string. He cut off a length and tied it into a slip knot ready to slide over the nose of his horse. Williams threw his mackintosh cape over the wooden box and prayed.

The men stood beside their horses, anxiously holding them tight. If the moon stayed behind a cloud and the patrol didn't come too close, they wouldn't be seen. Andrew wished that they had their own trusted army horses; he didn't know how these French mounts would behave if there was any gunfire. His heart sank as the Germans, riding at a walk, came closer.

'Keep your heads down,' hissed Andrew. The men in the ditch froze. Shrimp quietly slipped his piece of string over the mare's nose and pulled it tight. He then wrapped the end round and round his wrist until it dug into his flesh. The mare lowered her head, closed her eyes and silently sulked.

The patrol of about a dozen Germans headed for the perimeter of the park, well away from the hiding British. Andrew heaved a sigh of relief. But when they reached the double banks that separated the garden from the parkland, they turned towards the British troopers, riding about thirty yards in from the bank.

The men in the ditch heard the clink of metal from the horses' bits, and the conversation of the riders as they approached. Andrew wished he could understand German and prayed that the moon would continue to stay hidden behind the clouds. The French horses seemed to understand the urgency for quiet. Luckily the dozen German riders were above their line of vision.

Andrew began to breathe as the last pair of horses passed him by. He froze as a small ball of fire flew in his direction. He barely had time to reach for his revolver when the butt end of a cigarette landed a few feet away on the bank. He stared at it in relief as it continued burning, sending a thin column of smoke spiralling upwards.

A sudden noise erupted from the park. The cavalrymen in the ditch started and the German riders turned their heads to look in the direction of the sound.

'*Was ist das*?' someone exclaimed.

'*Eine koo,*' another replied, accompanied by some laughter. The patrol relaxed and the animal continued to vociferate.

'How many times a night do they patrol?' Andrew asked François, when the enemy had at last disappeared from sight.

'I don't know, but they were talking about returning to their billets. They're not very happy at the way the French villagers are treating them.'

'You speak German?'

'Oh yes. It sounded as if they wouldn't come this way again tonight. But...'

'We cannot be certain. How much further have we got to go?'

'We're about a third of the way there.'

'Is that all? We need to hurry.' Andrew became agitated. 'Get moving fast,' he ordered.

The men hurriedly mounted and the horses, again feeling the urgency of their riders, either scrambled or jumped up the bank and into the park. Andrew took them at a sharp canter across the open land between the oak trees. 'How do we penetrate this wood?' Tall pine trees climbed steeply up a nearly vertical hill, their dense, outspread branches obliterating any light from the moon.

'We have to take the path that winds around the circumference. The Boches have installed themselves in a large house on the summit. It commands a good view over the surrounding countryside.'

'A good thing they can't see in the dark,' remarked Andrew.

'Yes, we would be sitting ducks if they could.'

The soldiers slowly wound their way through twisty narrow paths, and once more Andrew became irritated in spite of inhaling the soothing, therapeutic smell of the pine trees. He thought the smell would forever remind him of this journey that was beginning to turn into one of those nightmares when the dreamer, try as he may, is unable to reach his destination.

They arrived at another lake and another clearing.

'Haven't we been here before? Aren't we going round in circles?' Andrew asked.

'*Non.*'

'Do we go around the water?'

'*Non,* the lake is long and narrow. We have to cross this one.'

'How the hell are we going to do that?'

'There is an old causeway, reputed to be Roman, which crosses the lake. It's nearly one and a half metres wide and lies about a foot below the surface. When the hunted stags come here they run across it. They look strange, as if they are galloping on top of the water. Most people never ride along it, except me and the hunt servants. It's easy to find in the shallows, but you must all ride one behind the other in exactly the same footsteps. The hunt has put gravel down on the other side of the lake, to help the huntsman launch his boat if he has to kill the stag. That's if it stays at bay in the water. But there is a bog on each side of the gravel.'

Andrew explained to the men what they had to do and again he wished they had their army horses. However, all the horses entered the water readily enough.

They splashed through the shallows and found the causeway. All went well until they were about half way across. Turner 65's horse stopped and began to paw the water. Shrimp managed to grab the led horse, while Turner urged his horse onwards. It panicked, shot forwards, lost its footing and fell off the walkway into the deep water. It then began to swim out of control into the middle of the lake.

The rest of the group continued gingerly head to tail behind François. Shrimp couldn't swim, so he sat very still and prayed that he wouldn't fall off.

Williams felt the pigeons flutter their wings and was glad that he had left his cape covering the cage.

All the men heaved a sigh of relief when they arrived on the gravel at the other side. The first few horses walked safely out of the water. Shrimp's mare suddenly swung her head round to look at Turner's horse. He couldn't keep her straight and she veered off course into the boggy ground.

The other riders watched Turner 65 steadily heading for an island in the middle of the lake.

'Can your brother swim?' asked Andrew.

'Yes, sir.'

'Get off it,' Andrew hissed, not able to shout. 'And for God's sake, don't land on that island.' Much to Andrew's horrified astonishment; Len Turner put his cupped hands to his mouth and gave a series of owl hoots.

'What the devil are you doing?'

'Telling him to dismount and swim back, sir.'

'What?'

'We have a code. We used it when we were children, playing soldiers.'

'Did you? Then tell your brother to swim back here with his horse, immediately.'

'I just have, sir. Here he comes.' The others looked on in amazement as 65 dismounted into the water and swam back, followed by his horse.

'Well done.' Andrew congratulated him as he walked dripping out of the water. 'Your boyhood games have served you well.'

'Yes, sir.' 65 coughed and spluttered and wiped his wet face on his soaking sleeve.

'Fisher's stuck, sir,' exclaimed Clark.

Andrew looked up and saw the mare floundering in the mud. '65, you're already wet, go and help him.'

'Yes, sir.' 65 grinned, pleased to be back in his captain's good books.

'The rest of you make one long rope out of your lead ropes.'

The more the mare struggled, the deeper she became embedded in the mire. Turner 65 waded out into the soft sticky mud, carrying the end of a line that had been hastily knotted together. Shrimp was standing up to his thighs in the mud holding his mare's head, desperately trying to sooth her.

'Don't worry mate, we'll soon get you out of there.' 65 threaded the rope through the stirrup iron, flipped it behind the mare's hind quarters, and passed it back through the stirrup on the other side. Then he floundered his way back to the gravel.

The men, slowly but surely, dragged the mare towards them, aided by Shrimp who pulled on her head collar. She co-operated, sensing they were trying to help her. Then the rope broke.

'Whose fucking knot was that?' snapped someone.

'Just re-do it. And hurry.' Andrew was becoming increasingly annoyed at the time that was being wasted. But Williams had already waded into the mud to re-tie the knot.

After frantically lurching forwards the filly at last extricated herself from the bog and stood trembling on the bank.

'Fisher, ride another horse and lead that mare. If she causes any more trouble we'll leave her in a field somewhere.'

'She won't cause any more trouble, sir.'

Andrew had to smile to himself, in spite of the situation. 'How much further now?' he asked the guide.

'We follow this river…'

'What river?' Andrew spun round and noticed a narrow stream that flowed into the lake. 'Not more walking in single file.'

'Yes, I'm afraid so. It takes us deep into the forest, very close to the château.'

'How long will it take us?'

'*Ooof*, maybe a small hour.'

'Get mounted. Ride in single file,' Andrew ordered.

It was possible for the riders to walk briskly up the narrow stream until it entered the forest, where it twisted and turned. They had to stop every now and then to negotiate low branches.

Andrew looked up at the night sky which was beginning to lighten.

'It's all right, *Capitaine*, we're nearly there now. Just round the next bend and we see the fields.'

Andrew wasn't at all sure that he wanted to see open fields as the dawn rapidly approached. However, when they rounded the bend in the river he recognised the farmland and his heart leapt as he saw the familiar château towering above them.

'We go to Monsieur Lefevre's farm,' said François.

'The man who covered our hoofprints by ploughing his field.'

'The very one. We stay in the river and then we have to cross one field, maybe… two hundred metres. He's leaving his cows by the river. We'll cross the field in the middle of the herd.'

They plodded on. Andrew's spirits lifted when he saw a herd of assorted coloured cows, with a large white bull, standing in a hollowed out watering place beside the river. They were held in position by three boys and a shaggy dog.

One of the boys ran into the river and removed a strand of barbed wire that stretched across the water. Andrew ordered his men to dismount and lead their horses into the middle of the cows. They obligingly moved apart to allow the British into their midst. Once the soldiers were encircled by the herd, the boys and the dog began to drive them up the field towards the farmyard.

'Keep your heads down,' ordered Andrew. He was confident that they were camouflaged enough, providing the Germans weren't being too vigilant.

The bull closely followed a roan cow. Every now and then she swished her tail; each time the bull tossed his head and snorted. Shrimp, who was nearest to the two animals, watched them uneasily.

'It's all right, Shrimp, the bull won't hurt you. He's got other things on his mind at the moment. Don't get between him and his lady-love and you'll be all right.'

'Oh. Thanks 65.' Shrimp looked up and grinned.

The men arrived in the farmyard and quickly settled their horses in a barn. There was neither sight nor sound of the enemy.

'Sir, what shall I do with the pigeons?' asked Williams.

'We'll release two, then feed and water the others. Bring the cage over here.' Andrew left the barn and walked into the yard. 'I've got the rings and the message. Bring one out.'

'Which one?'

'It doesn't matter.'

Williams opened the trap door on the lid of the box. 'Careful.' Andrew slammed the lid shut on Williams's hand. 'Don't let the whole lot go.'

'Sorry, sir, I'm not used to pigeons.' Andrew didn't add that neither was he. Williams extricated a bird and together the two men, after much fiddling, managed to fix the ring and the capsule on to its leg.

'Let it go… just throw it up in the air,' Andrew added as Williams hesitated.

'Like that?' Williams let go of the pigeon. It flew upwards and began to circle the farm yard.

'Oh my God!'

'What now?' exclaimed Andrew.

'Look, sir.' Andrew hastily looked around for patrols of Germans. 'No, up there.'

'Oh Lord!' Andrew saw a bird of prey glide gracefully towards the flapping pigeon.

'Shall I shoot it?'

'And summon the entire German army? Don't be stupid.' The two men, joined by the troopers, watched helplessly as a peregrine falcon swooped down and in a spray of feathers carried the pigeon back to the wood.

'Release another quick, sir… while she's occupied with that one,' said 65.

'I think you're right. Williams, another bird please.'

Williams repeated the procedure and this time the released pigeon circled round and then flew safely away in a northerly direction. 'What about the message on the other one: won't the Hun find it?' asked Williams.

'It's in code. Let's hope they don't understand it.'

'The falcon might eat it, sir,' declared Shrimp. 'Then we'll have to wait until it passes through her.'

'I hope we'll be long gone by then.' Andrew replied.

CHAPTER TEN

Imprisonment

While Andrew was joining up with the British Expeditionary Force, Francine lay on a straw paillasse in her own medieval prison. She shivered with cold. The dungeons were below ground level and the stench from the ancient sewers hung in the chill air, mingling with the tang of decay. The filthy smell stuck in her throat, in her clothes, her hair and on her body. The spluttering light from the torches outside the cell threw strange jumping shadows on the walls and the reek of the tallow made her nauseous.

The iron bars of the cell ran from ceiling to floor. Francine could not avoid the prying eyes and leering looks of the two German guards in spite of the flickering gloom. She would have to use the bucket in the corner of the cell before long. She wished she wasn't wearing breeches. It would be a much easier exercise in a skirt.

She cursed herself for having mistaken a troop of German cavalry for Andrew, and again for her extreme folly in running out to greet them.

She remembered the unpleasant hour of questioning, which had ended with the enemy ignominiously bundling her into a lorry. She didn't know what fate had befallen her beloved horse. All she could do was pray that Andrew had not fallen into the trap that the Germans had set for him. She thanked God for giving her the sense to tell him about the dungeons in the château and fervently willed him to come to her rescue.

She jumped as she heard the clatter of soldiers' boots approaching the dungeons and looked up as the guards stood to attention. A handsome German officer stood outside her cell.

'*Bonjour, Mademoiselle.*'

She stood up gracefully and inclined her head. 'Are you going to let me out? It's a disgrace that you keep me here.'

'You may come upstairs, certainly.' He spoke with respect.

She thought the man had a kind face in spite of being the enemy. She followed him up the stone steps and into the *ceinture*. As they walked around the stone corridor she glanced anxiously at the number of guards posted there. Her heart sank as she wondered how anyone would ever be able to rescue her.

She was incensed as the officer took her to her father's study. 'How dare you use this room? What are you doing?' She gasped as they entered to see cabinet doors open and bundles of private papers on the floor. German soldiers were methodically stacking them into tea chests.

The officer barked an order and the room emptied immediately. '*Mademoiselle*, you would be annoyed at whatever room we used. I can understand that.'

Francine secretly agreed with him, but she said, curtly, 'I need a change of dress and I need to visit the W.C.'.

'No problem.' She watched, indignantly, as the officer used the hand-embroidered bell-pull to summon a servant. She started, even more aggrieved, when Mathilde, her father's housekeeper, entered the room. However, she was slightly mollified when the stiff elderly servant disregarded the German and addressed her by saying, 'You rang, *Mademoiselle?*'

The officer replied, '*Mademoiselle* would like a change of clothes. Please fetch what she needs.'

Francine said, 'I'll come with you, Mathilde'.

'No, you will stay here.' The women looked at each other, trying to ignore the German, but the servant recognised his air of authority as that of a well-bred gentleman. Her training as a servant made her give in to his orders.

Francine was not so influenced by his manner and retorted, 'Where can I change? I told you I need the W.C.'.

'Someone will escort you down the corridor and then you will change in here.' She glared at him. Before she could argue he added, 'I'll leave the room'.

Francine addressed Mathilde. 'Please fetch my brown skirt with the woollen jacket, beige silk blouse and my brown walking boots.'

'*Oui, Mademoiselle.*'

The German ordered, 'Also bring hot water, a basin, soap and a towel so that *Mademoiselle* may wash. But I warn you, do not play any silly tricks. We'll search the things you bring back'.

'*Oui, Monsieur.*'

'Go... go.,' the German snapped. The old lady slowly left the room, glancing back at Francine for approval. He added more kindly, 'Your mistress will be safe with me.'

Francine bore the indignity of being escorted down the corridor by two private soldiers. At least it was better than using the bucket in the cell.

When she returned she sat on an elegant chair and looked out of the window, trying to disregard the fact that the enemy officer was now sitting behind her father's desk. He stood up, walked round and sat down beside her. She quickly folded her arms because, for one moment, she thought he was going to take hold of her hand. He smiled kindly. '*Mademoiselle*, as you know, the British are on the run. It is only matter of time before we take Paris. We would greatly appreciate your help.'

'I'll never help you. Even if it was in my power to do so, which it isn't,' she snapped.

'It is in your power to help your father. I don't want to mistreat you. My war is not against beautiful girls such as you. I implore you to co-operate with us.'

'Never.'

'I hope you'll change your mind, my fellow officers are not so *gentille*. They will not treat you so well. I fear for your safety… please do as I ask.'

Francine stared at him. 'What is it that you do ask, *Monsieur*?' At that moment the door opened and Mathilde came in carrying her clothes, water, soap and a towel.

'Put those things down.' The German officer watched intently as the guards methodically went through every article of clothing, including the silk underwear. Every so often his eyes flicked to the faces of the two women in the room.

Francine glanced at her servant and then back at the German. The old woman suddenly flung her arms around her, sobbing. '*Mademoiselle*, I cannot bear this.' Then she whispered very quickly in her mistress's ear, 'Have courage, we have sent for the *Capitaine*.' The guards dragged her away and threw her into the corridor.

'How dare you treat an old woman like that?' Francine's eyes flashed.

'What did she say?' demanded the German.

'You heard what she said.'

'She whispered something, what was it?'

'I heard no whisper. Are you going to leave me to get dressed?'

'*Mademoiselle*, do not play games with me. What did the woman say to you?'

'Oh, you mean that between her sobs she said. "*soyez courageuse*?" But of course if you are hard of hearing, you may have missed it.'

'Perhaps.'

'Are you going to leave me?'

'Certainly.' The officer withdrew, taking the guards with him.

As soon as he left the room, Francine allowed herself to smile and thought, *'I know Andrew will come. I don't believe this talk of the British being vanquished'*.

The German politely knocked on the door before he entered the room again. 'If you assist me I can escort you to your father in Paris.'

'What do you want of me?'

'We want to make sure that the Marquis cooperates with us.'

Francine stared at the good-looking face and retorted, 'He'll never do that'.

'He will, to save his daughter from a ghastly, slow death.'

She inwardly shivered but continued looking straight at the German. 'He will not know what you do to me.'

'We'll tell him.

'He won't believe you. You're wasting your time. He is a true and loyal Frenchman. *La France* will come first, not me.' She tossed her head and added, 'I, too, will never betray my country'.

The German leant forwards and lowered his voice. 'He will not want his much-beloved and favourite daughter to be tortured.' He leant back in his chair, watching her face. Francine refused to let him see her fear, looked him in the eye and repeated, 'I will not betray *la France.* You do not frighten me, *Monsieur*'.

'*Mademoiselle*, I implore you. I hope very much that I frighten you. I would not enjoy throwing a beautiful creature like you to the wolves.'

'Then you won't do it.'

'I can assure you, *Mademoiselle*, that someone will do it. The officer who relieves me this afternoon is ambitious. He comes from a family of powerful aristocrats and he needs to prove himself. I have seen how he treats his horses and I believe that he enjoys such things.'

'What things?'

'The torture of innocent civilians.'

Francine tossed her head. 'You will not make me betray my country and my father. We are aristocrats. We have gone through periods of repression and abuse over the centuries and we have survived. We will not give in to your idle threats.'

'*Mademoiselle*, please listen to me, these are not idle threats. You do not understand. He will probably begin by shaving your hair…'

'It'll grow again.'

'Then there will be certain parts of your body that will be cut off.

They will be sent to your father.' Francine looked away. '*Mademoiselle*, this man, this Oberleutnant von Krutz, he will do everything in his power to break you and your father. Please believe me. You will be wise to do as he says. Please write to your father and entreat him to meet our demands.'

Francine tossed her head. '*Non, non,* I will do no such thing. If you out-rank this man then you can give him certain orders.'

'*Nein*, the orders come from much higher up. I can do nothing… except beg you to do as we say.'

'Never.'

The tall blonde German stood up. 'Then you will return to your cell in the dungeons. My name is von Meyer. Ask for me when you change your mind.'

'I'll never change my mind, Monsieur von Meyer.'

'Rittmeiste*r* von Meyer, if you please.'

'*Non, Rittmeister*. I will not change my mind.' She paused. '*Rittmeister*? That means Riding Master, does it not?'

'Yes.' Von Meyer nodded.

'Then, *Rittmeister*, what has happened to my horses?'

'I have them both. I will soon use your grey. He's stabled close to a battlefield. I go there later today.' Francine's face crumpled and she turned away so that the German could not see that he had reached her weak spot. He continued: 'I'll make sure nothing happens to your horses… for the moment. It is only I who will ride them. But of course if you do not cooperate, then maybe…'

'They are only horses,' Francine managed to say. 'We eat them in France.'

'We eat them in Germany too. But yours are of a quality… too good for eating I think.'

'They will not make me change my mind.' Francine believed that she could trust him with her horses, but she didn't know why.

'I regret, in that case, I have no choice but to return you to your cell.'

Francine was marched away back down to the bowels of the castle. As she lay on the filthy palliasse, covered by a damp horse blanket, once more inhaling the vile stench, she wished she had agreed with the German Riding Master. She shut her eyes and thought of Andrew. '*He will rescue me,*' she continually repeated to herself until she fell into a fitful sleep.

The days passed and no one came near Francine except the guards who brought her food. In between pacing up and down her cell she plaited tiny corn dollies made from the straw out of her mattress. She put the completed ones around the edge of her cell. The rest of the time she lay on her paillasse wishing for Andrew to come. Sometimes she slept.

On the fourth day she awoke with a start as an iron key rattled the medieval lock of her cell gate. A short, stocky German officer stood in the doorway and stared at her with steel grey eyes. His thick flaccid lips drew back to show his uneven, discoloured teeth. Francine sprang to her feet.

He was at least an inch shorter than her. She felt intimidated and humiliated as he looked her up and down as if she were a common harlot. 'A pity, I think I would have preferred the breeches.' He shrugged. 'It is of no matter. Sit down.' Francine remained standing. He approached her, jutted out his chin so that his face was close to hers and said unpleasantly, 'I like to be obeyed. The sooner you realise that, the better we will get along'.

Francine stood up to her full height. She turned her head away from the unpleasant odour of stale brandy and cigar smoke on his breath. '*Monsieur*, I have no desire to get along with you: will you please leave my cell at once.'

The man, furious at her superior tone of voice, curled his top lip into a sneer. 'I am a German officer, woman, and you are my captive. It is I who give the orders. You will do as I say.'

'May I remind you that you are in my house?'Francine's body was rigid with anger.

The German gave a snort of laughter, spraying her with a mist of saliva. 'It is no longer your house; we, the German army have requisitioned it. You are but a miserable prisoner. Do not give me orders. You will call me Oberleutnant…. Oberleutnant von Krutz. *Nein*, you will call me sir.'

This time Francine gave a snort of laughter and looked down her aristocratic nose at the angry man. 'I hardly think so.'

There was a snigger from the watching guards. Von Krutz began to lose his temper. Francine glared at him as he approached, so angry herself that she ignored the ugly look in his eyes. She was surprised when he lunged at her, although she had the presence of mind to duck out of his way. He fell against the rough rocks of the cell wall, grazing his hand. The sharp pain infuriated him. He struck Francine across her face.

She cried out. Her father had told her where to kick a man if she found herself in a tight spot. So she kicked the *oberleutnant*, as hard as she could. Regrettably, she didn't kick him hard enough. It only served to make him see red. He caught hold of her and pushed her roughly down on to the bench, falling on top of her.

He held her hands above her head with one hand while he dug his knee into her diaphragm, knocking the wind out of her body. She struggled for breath as he tore at her silk blouse with his free hand. She tried to call out but she couldn't speak. Her body jerked and shuddered as she felt his hand roughly mauling the soft, bare skin of her breasts. He seemed to enjoy the involuntary movements of her body. He pressed his mouth down on to hers. She frantically tried to breathe and took in large gulps of air. She retched as she inhaled his foul smelling breath, while desperately moving her head from side to side to avoid his loose wet lips. He drove his tongue into her open mouth. She caught it with her teeth and closed her jaw. She felt the crunch and tasted his blood.

He yelped and drew back. The pain fuelled his anger and he shouted in fury, splattering her face with his blood. Seeing her look of revulsion, he struck her again and then moved his other knee into the inside of her thigh and prised her legs apart. The more she arched her body and moved from side to side, the more aroused he became.

She fought him as best she could. He roughly ripped away her silk underwear. She wrenched a hand free, tore at his short coarse crinkly hair and clawed his face.

He rammed his hand up between her legs. The pain of his dirty finger nails tearing at her soft tissue was like nothing she had ever felt before. It was excruciating and debasing. She screamed.

The guards shrank back from the bars of the cell. The high pitched scream echoed around the underground prison. It sounded unnatural and eerie. It sent a cold shudder through their bodies.

Francine felt relief as von Krutz withdrew his hand from inside her and his knee from her diaphragm. Her respite was short lived. She felt him unbuttoning the fly of his breeches and recoiled as he released the smell of his unwashed body. She writhed and twisted under his full weight as she tried to dislodge him. It only seemed to spur him on. She had no choice but to endure the humiliation and degradation. His body jerked faster and faster until at last he shuddered, let out a loud moaning sound as if he were in agony and lay still.

He became a lifeless weight lying on top of her and she hoped, in her naivety, that he had had a seizure and that he was now dead. Unfortunately she could still feel him breathing. She struggled to get out from under him. She put her hand up to her swollen face and winced as she felt her cracked cheek bone. She tasted the blood from her bleeding lips, but worst of all was the excruciating pain in her lower body.

Von Krutz suddenly got to his feet and buttoned up his breeches. He left the cell without a word or a backwards glance.

Francine pulled her skirt down over her bruised body. She felt something running out of her and on to the mattress. She lay without moving, but the liquid continued to flow. She sat up, picked the foul smelling horse blanket off the filthy floor and plucked up the courage to look down at herself. She dropped the blanket and froze with fear when she saw the blood. Curling herself up into a ball, she turned her face to the wall, shut her eyes and waited for death. She knew that she was now no longer a virgin and that she was probably pregnant. She understood that no respectable man would ever want her and in effect her life, as she knew it, was over. She welcomed death.

***

The two guards stood to attention as their officer left the dungeons. He had claw-like marks on his cheek and blood oozed out of his mouth. They waited until his footsteps grew faint on the stone stairs and then crept round the corner to look at Francine. They saw her lying motionless. One of them surreptitiously entered the cell and saw the blood seeping into the straw mattress. He nervously listened for her breathing, thinking that she was dead. He was surprised as he heard a faint moan when she moved and clutched her stomach. He quickly left the cell and locked the gate behind him. 'We'd better send for a doctor.'

'*Nein*,' replied the other lad. 'It is best we know nothing. The doctor will ask questions. Do you want to infuriate the *oberleutnant*?'

The lad shook his head. 'But she might die. I thought she was already dead.'

'That is not our problem, Shutz Reimmer.'

'We're supposed to be guarding her, Oberschutze,' Reimmer remarked. 'I'll take her some water.' Reimmer entered the cell with a mug, but Francine didn't move or speak. He put it on the floor beside the bench and retreated behind the bars.

The young Germans waited uneasily, not knowing what to do. Reimmer took a look at Francine every now and then, but she didn't move.

'I think we should fetch a doctor,' he repeated after his fifth trip.

'*Nein*. Sit still and leave her alone,' the *oberschutze* snapped. They both jumped and looked uneasy as they heard footsteps descending towards the cells. A voice said, 'I have your food'.

The men opened the heavy door. A young soldier entered carrying three plates. 'Can I see the prisoner? She is reputed to be beautiful.'

'*Nein*. No one is allowed to see her,' replied the *oberschutze*.

'Why not?'

'Orders. Go.'

'All right, *oberschutze*. You're welcome to this job. The French say Count Dracula haunts these dungeons.' He shivered and looked around. 'I can well believe it. It's creepy in here. I don't envy you spending the hours of darkness down here amongst the rats. But then it is always dark down here. Maybe she's a vampire too. Enjoy your food.' He grinned and ran up the stairs.

'Don't listen to the silly stories. They spread them to frighten us,' said the *oberschutze* as Reimmer looked anxious. 'Eat your food.'

Reimmer replied, 'I'll take her plate.' Francine had not moved. He saw that the circle of blood on the straw was now larger. He covered her with the horse blanket. She didn't move or speak, so he put the plate down on the floor next to the untouched beaker of water. He knew that Rittmeister von Meyer would be coming back the next day and that he would not be pleased to find his much-prized prisoner lying in her own blood.

'She's bleeding heavily. She should have help,' Reimmer told the *oberschutze*.

'All women bleed. It's normal.'

Reimmer wondered what he meant, although he had four sisters and guessed. He shivered. 'This is a horrible place. We can't tell if it's light or dark outside. And this terrible smell... How much longer do we have to stay here?'

The *oberschutze* glared at his inferior. 'Only two more hours. We tell the men who take over from us nothing... Nothing, you understand?' Reimmer nodded.

***

Francine lay motionless. She was unaware of the change of guard. She did become aware, however, of a scuttling and squeaking in her cell. The rats made short work of the plate of food on the floor. Smelling the blood, they jumped on to her bed. Francine felt them scuffling inside the straw mattress. She curled herself into a tighter ball and clasped her arms across her chest while tears overflowed her tightly shut eyes.

CHAPTER ELEVEN

Traitors

Andrew found Marie-Claude in the farmhouse kitchen. She greeted him eagerly and bombarded him with questions about Francine's rescue. He was struggling to answer when Doctor Lejeune arrived and took him into the salon.

'Where's Monsieur Lefevre?' asked Andrew.

'He's outside working; the rest of his family have left. They didn't consider it safe here anymore.'

'Your guide was *extraordinaire*. I'm most grateful to him. Where is he?'

'Yes, he's a good boy. He's left his horse here and has made his way to a relative in the village.'

'Please, thank him for me.'

'Certainly, but you'll see him later. I want you to sleep. We have a meeting at four o'clock this afternoon with some people who will help you with your plan of rescue.

***

Andrew was surprised at how well he slept. Now that he was so close to the château he felt calmer and more focused on the job in hand. He descended into the salon where he stood staring out of the window at the turreted outline of the castle, realising again how massive it was. He started as François came furtively into the room. 'Good afternoon. May I say what an excellent job you did last night.'

'It was nothing. I try to do my duty for France.' François sat down.

'Splendid, splendid,' replied Andrew.

Doctor Lejeune soon arrived with an old man whom he introduced as once being butler to the Marquis. He was accompanied by an elderly governess dressed in a severe black dress with a white lace collar.

They settled down to discuss the plan of action. Andrew opened the discussion. 'Francine showed me an entrance to the dungeons via the *ceinture*. Later she showed me a map of the château and how to avoid that place if it was full of guards. I'm afraid I don't remember where that was.'

'The *ceinture* is indeed full of Germans. You cannot make it through there,' stated Doctor Lejeune.

'I have some plans here.' The old man, his hands shaking, produced large fragments of parchment from a leather briefcase and placed them on the table. The others leant over and pieced them together like a jigsaw.

'I can't make head or tail of this,' said Andrew.

'This is the *ceinture,* and this is the staircase you went up with the horses.' The doctor prodded the map, causing the pieces to separate. Andrew thought he was being unnecessarily impatient and asked calmly, 'Where are the dungeons in relation to these stairs?'

'Along here to the left.' The old man carefully pushed the plans back together again. 'There's an opening off that staircase; it runs along the inside of the wall and joins up with the passage which leads down from the *ceinture.* Nobody has used it since the children were growing up. But you went in there several times, did you not *Mademoiselle*?' He addressed the governess.

'Many times, *Monsieur.* I had to search for *Mademoiselle* and her brother. Sometimes they shut me in the secret passageways.' She shuddered. 'It was foul down there, the smell… it was *épouvantable.*'

'Please explain how you get to the cells from the staircase in question,' asked the doctor.

'There's an entrance about halfway up the stairs. There are thirty five steps, I think.'

'So from the 15th step upwards we should start looking for a way in?' Andrew asked.

'*Oui, Capitaine.* There's a lever on the outside wall. You pull it and you'll find an opening. It's low, you must mind your head.' Andrew smiled patiently at the old lady. 'There's a ladder which descends vertically to the secret passage outside the entrance to the cells. I remember it well. I had to get myself out of there one day. It was very difficult. I was furious and very frightened. I had Monsieur Henri, *Mademoiselle's* brother, thrashed for that.' The old lady began to sob. '*Mon Dieu,* that things should come to this, it is *affreux.* Now, I help my poor Francine by my misadventure and I thank Monsieur Henri a thousand times for shutting me in that terrible passage.'

'I know, *Mademoiselle,* I know.' Andrew nodded. 'We'll get her out.'

The old governess gulped, dabbed at her eyes with a lace handkerchief and continued: 'When I was in there all those years ago, the wooden ladder was rotten. I nearly fell, that is why I was so annoyed and upset'.

'*Mademoiselle*, you are being exceptionally helpful,' Andrew said kindly. 'We could not do this without your help.'

'*Merci, Capitaine.*' The governess smiled up at Andrew through her tears.

The doctor hurriedly took over. 'You must bring Francine out the way you go in.'

'I see.' Andrew was thoughtful. 'Do the Hun know of the staircase we used with the horses? Are they guarding the outside of the château?'

'They patrol the perimeter of the château at ground level. They don't seem to take a lot of notice of that entrance, *non.*'

The old lady became anxious. '*Capitaine*, you must take Marie-Claude with you. You'll need a woman if she is injured.'

'Of course. I understand,' replied Andrew. 'Marie-Claude can join my men outside the château.'

'That is not necessary. You will take Francine immediately to La Maison Forestière de la Grande Biche,' the doctor interrupted. 'I'll be waiting for you there in case she needs medical attention. François will show you the way.'

'Thank you doctor,' replied Andrew. 'Now I need some time with my men. If you'll excuse me, may I…?'

'*Mais certainement*, we'll leave you alone.' The doctor shepherded the two old people out of the room, leaving Andrew and François together.

'It's not going to be easy, especially getting her back up these ladders, but it's the only plan we have,' said Andrew. 'You will go with the others to an RV point in the wood and I'll take Turner 65 and Williams into the château. Come with me and we'll discuss it further with the rest of the men.'

***

As soon as it was dark, the small party rode to the wood bordering the grounds of the castle. Andrew, Williams and Turner 65 crossed the parkland towards the hidden staircase. Williams, who could speak a smattering of German, wore a tweed jacket over his uniform, while the other two wore the blue clothes of French workmen. They noiselessly opened the heavy door and mounted the stairs. They counted to fifteen and then began searching for a lever.

Williams touched Andrew on the arm, drawing his attention to a flat-headed nail not quite flush with the wall. He tried to move it but nothing happened. They continued walking up the steps, but found nothing. The three men walked slowly down, still searching. The nail was the only thing they could find that was in any way out of the normal.

Andrew tried desperately to move it again, but failed. He shook his head in frustration and started to search the wall again. Turner kicked the nail in temper. There was a grating noise and a stone opened, leaving just enough room for a man to put his hand inside the wall. Andrew hurried back and felt inside. He found a knob and pushed and pulled, but to no avail. He withdrew his hand and whispered to Turner, 'It moves very slightly sideways. It's been there for years, maybe centuries, it could be locked solid'.

Turner put his hand inside and yanked the knob towards him. It suddenly moved and he could feel the resistance as a mechanism pushed against the masonry. The soldiers felt a rush of cold air bringing with it a musty, dank smell. A gap had appeared in the stonework. They pulled the door and little by little it pivoted open, making a hole just large enough for a man to crawl through.

The three men stood huddled together in a small recess. They tried to close the entrance, but it wouldn't shut flush with the wall.

'We'll have to leave it like that. Let's hope the doctor is right and Fritz doesn't come down these stairs. Block that crack while I light my torch.' Andrew shone his torch along a narrow, low passage. 'Down here, I think, gentlemen.' As they walked on, they heard a scuttling noise. 'Rats,' Andrew explained.

The floor began to slope downhill until it stopped suddenly in a sheer drop. Andrew shone his torch down into what looked like a well.

'God, what a stench,' exclaimed Turner, as the full force of the ancient sewers hit them.

'You'll get used to it in a minute,' Andrew whispered hoarsely, trying his best not to retch. Williams turned back and threw up behind them.

There was more scampering and squeaking. 'You've fed the rats now,' complained Turner and, much to the others' surprise, he, too, turned back and vomited.

'Never could abide rats,' he explained as he returned, wiping his mouth on the sleeve of his blue coat.

Andrew looked down into the well and saw an iron ladder hugging the rough stones of the wall. He could make out a space jutting out about twenty feet below them. In spite of his usual iron self-control, he too, had to give in and rush back up the passage rather than sully the platform below them.

When he returned, he wound a rope around his waist and looked for somewhere to secure the other end. 'These are the steps leading to the *ceinture*,' he said as he swung his torch around. 'God bless the third Marquis, he thought of everything.' He pointed to an iron ring firmly embedded in the wall. He attached his rope, adding, 'Make sure there's only one man on the ladder at the same time.'

He tested the rungs with his foot and gingerly stepped on to them. The ladder remained firm. He slowly descended to the platform below. 'So far, so good,' he whispered to the others as they joined him. 'We seem to be on track because here is the wooden ladder that may be rotten. There only seems to be about ten feet to the floor below. Fasten your rope to the one already hanging, and make sure it's secure. We don't want another fiasco with knots untying.'

'It weren't my knot.' Turner fastened the two ropes.

Again, Andrew was the first to climb cautiously down. All went well until he ran out of rungs. He lost his balance, grabbed the rope and slid to the floor. The other two men descended slowly and safely to join him in another low passageway. The stench was suffocating.

'God!' gasped Turner. 'How does anything live down here?' Williams dug him in the ribs with his elbow as he saw the look on Andrew's face in the torch light.

The passage continued for a short while then stopped in a dead end.

'This must be it,' said Andrew. 'Where's the door? And more importantly, what's on the other side? Draw your knives.'

'It isn't a door. It's more like a hatch.' Williams traced his finger around a dirt-filled groove. 'Men were smaller in those days.'

'Bleedin' midgets,' Turner grunted.

Andrew extinguished his torch and carefully fiddled with a rusty handle. Nothing happened.

'You do it.' He spoke to Turner. 'You opened the last one.'

Turner yanked the lever and the hatch moved. Andrew winced at the sound of mortar falling on to the ground.

They stopped and listened but heard no hurrying army boots. Little by little they edged the door open, letting in the dim light from the corridor. 'Well, we've reached habitation. Let's hope we're in the right place.' Andrew crouched down and looked along the empty passage.

He emerged out of the hatch and crept along until he came to a stout nail-studded wooden door. He could hear the intermittent sound of voices and then the rasp of hobnailed boots on a spiral staircase. He silently fled back to the hatch. He held the stone entrance ajar and saw a German soldier arrive with three plates of food. The man bandied a few words with the young guard who opened the door. Then he returned up the stairs.

'Now,' ordered Andrew. 'You know what to do.'

They squeezed themselves out of the hatch and walked to the dungeon. Andrew hammered on the door with the butt of his revolver.

'What do you want? We told you, you can't see the girl. Go away,' shouted one of the guards.

'I'm a doctor, I've come to see the woman, open up.' Williams spoke with authority in reasonable German.

Andrew could hear lowered voices in the dungeon. He signalled to Williams to speak again.

'Hurry, I haven't got all night,' ordered Williams.

A young soldier nervously opened the door. The two Germans stood holding their plates of food and stared at the three strangers. While they were wondering why a very young doctor should be accompanied by two French workmen, the Englishmen used their knives.

'Drag the bodies over here.' Andrew shut the heavy door and found the keys to the cells. He stopped as he saw the mound of a body under a filthy blanket, lying on a disintegrating straw mattress. The sweet sickly smell of drying blood mingled with the stench from the sewers. The two men behind him stared wide-eyed at the bench, their hands to their mouths, while Andrew gently lifted the rotten horse blanket.

The girl was lying in the foetal position. Rat droppings littered the straw mattress which was covered in blood.

'Is she…?'

'No,' Andrew managed to say through gritted teeth. 'She has a pulse.'

'The fucking bastards.' Turner's face was full of horror. 'What the hell have they done to her? How are we going to get her back up them fucking ladders?'

Andrew tried to speak, but shook his head.

'You'll have to, Andrew.' The three men spun round and stared at a tall German officer who had silently entered the dungeons behind them.

Turner pulled out his knife. Andrew quickly gestured to him and exclaimed, 'Von Meyer!' A smile broke out on his face. 'Heinrich, of course it was you. The way you rode... Your uniform, I didn't realise... But you knew me?'

'Yes my friend, I knew you straight away.'

'In the wood, at the ford? When you had my men buried.'

'Yes, of course.' The two men warmly shook hands.

'It's good to see you, Heinrich.' Andrew smiled.

The German looked down at his uniform, shrugged and both men laughed. 'I heard you were coming here. I kept the coast clear for you. I want you to take the girl. I haven't seen her, but I heard she was raped.' The tall German walked over to the bench, looked down. 'It's worse than I thought. You must get her out immediately.' Andrew stared at the motionless body, although he was sure she flinched as she heard the word *raped*. Maybe it was his imagination, or perhaps it was he who winced.

Von Meyer continued: 'I'm disgusted by what has happened to her. I'm not a party to this. I fight for my country against other trained soldiers. I do not, knowingly, harm innocent girls. Please take her'.

'Heinrich, my mother always liked you. She said you were an honourable gentleman.'

'I used to think she was a witch. She was often right about so many things that she couldn't possibly have known about.'

Andrew smiled warmly. 'Yes, she is uncanny now and again.'

'You must hurry. I'll see you have a safe passage out of these grounds but further than that I have no power. After that you are on your own. Andrew, take the girl!'

Andrew looked at Heinrich. 'How did you know where to find her, to pick her up?'

'We had a lot of troops in that area, near the farm where you were to meet her, but it was one of your own men who really put us on to her.'

'One of *our* men?'

'Yes, I didn't see him, but he is a little dark-haired man and he had a horse full of holes.'

'Full of holes? What on earth do you mean?'

'My men took his horse and it was covered in sword wounds. It was in a bad way; we're looking after it. It's a good horse.'

'Stone,' gasped Andrew. 'Where's that man now? Do you have him prisoner?'

'No, my troopers rendered him unconscious and left him on the roadside.'

'Then he's still alive, I knew he was.'

'He also had a large amount of French money on him.'

'Where did he get that?'

'He told my men it was from this château.'

'That's extraordinary. How much?'

'Probably the equivalent of £100.'

'As much as that!'

Von Meyer looked at his watch. 'Andrew, my friend, I wish we were on the same side, but we're not. You must go.'

Andrew grasped von Meyer's hand and, much to Turner's shocked surprise, embraced him.

'Take care of yourself, Heinrich. I hope we don't meet again until after the war. Then we can be friends again.'

'I hope so too. Look after that girl; I trust she recovers and I sincerely apologise for what has happened to her. Your small group of men are still waiting for you.'

'You seem to know everything about us.'

'I've been out riding on my own, watching and waiting for you to come. Not all the French are to be trusted, my friend, so be careful. We were tipped off... more I cannot say. You must hurry. I'll keep my troops away from the hidden staircase and the grounds on that side of the château. Then I must officially discover what you have done.' He glanced briefly at the bodies of the guards and then back to Francine. 'Get her to a doctor, but choose him with care. Now go.'

The two old friends embraced each other again. 65 picked up Francine, who stirred, moaned and said something in French.

'What is it, *Mademoiselle*?' Andrew put his head down to hers. He tried not screw up his face at the appalling smell coming from her clothes, her body and her breath.

She opened her eyes. '*Capitaine*?'

'Yes, it's me.'

'I told you not to come, why have you come? Go away.'

'We're taking you to safety.'

'I don't want safety. Let them kill me. It's best... now.' She started to struggle and cry out.

'Shush, you'll summon the guard.'

'I don't care, let them come.'

'Well, I don't want them to take me, or my men. Is that what you want?'

'*Non*, you must go free.'

'Then please lie still and quiet for our sake.'

'All right, for your sake I'll keep quiet. I can die later.'

'Yes, you can die later if that is what you want.'

'Of course it's what I want.'

'Very well, but for the time being please keep quiet.'

Francine shut her eyes, leant her head against Turner's broad shoulder and seemed to fall asleep.

'I think she's delirious,' Andrew said to 65. 'Quick, while she's quiet.'

They hurried silently back down the corridor, towards the little hatch. While Turner and Williams man-handled Francine through the door, Andrew turned to the German officer. 'Good bye, Heinrich. Thank you a thousand times for what you have done. I know the danger you have placed yourself in. I'll not forget.'

'Adieu, Andrew, Godspeed. Go quickly.'

Andrew shone his torch into the small recess. He squeezed through the hatch and fiddled with the rusty handle, but it wouldn't move.

'Turner,' he hissed. 'Come and shut this.' The trooper was almost at the foot of the wooden ladder. He left Francine with Williams and came back. Von Meyer pushed from the outside and Turner pulled until between them they managed to shut the door.

Andrew, who was becoming agitated by the amount of time that they were wasting, had gone along the passage. He stood looking up at the ledge ten feet above his head and at the rotten rungs of the ladder.

Francine was sitting on the stone floor quietly moaning. He knelt down beside her and said, 'We're taking you to safety. You must be very quiet.' Then as an afterthought, he asked, 'Are you in pain?' Francine didn't reply, but rocked back and forth clutching her abdomen. 'I'll get you to a doctor as soon as I can. What did they do to you?'

She turned her head away from him and muttered something. Williams, who was standing on her other side, heard her say, 'They have destroyed me and I will die. I hope it is soon'.

Andrew patted her shoulder and said, 'Be brave, *Mademoiselle*. We'll be out of here soon.' He was shocked at how she flinched when he touched her. He stood up, saying to Turner, 'Williams and I will climb to the top, then you will tie the rope under her arms and we'll pull her up. Stand at the bottom; if she falls, catch her.'

'Yes, sir.'

'Once she's standing with us on the ledge, climb up the rope.' Andrew squatted down beside Francine again and explained what he had planned. 'Can you do that?' he asked.

'I would rather stay here,' she answered. 'You go and leave me.'

'I can't do that.'

'*Oui*, you can.'

'No, I can't.'

Yes, yes, yes, you can. I'm not going up there.'

'Then I'll have to bind you, like a prisoner.'

'Then do so, you are stronger than me, I cannot resist you. Tie me up, better still... shoot me.'

Andrew was beginning to lose patience. 'Francine, please do as I say.'

'*Non!*'

Andrew heaved a sigh and said to Turner, 'Tie her hands and don't let her do anything silly'.

When Andrew and Williams were standing on the ledge, 65 passed the rope under Francine's arms and around her body. Andrew felt mortified as they hauled her up; her limp body swung about like a wrapped parcel on the end of the rope. He was horrified at how thin she was and how light.

Turner soon followed and they stood huddled together on the narrow shelf. Andrew looked up the iron ladder leading to the next landing. He knew that any sound would carry upwards. He whispered to Francine to please keep quiet and do as she was told, or he would have to gag her. He shuddered as she answered, 'Gag me then, or I'll shout and the Boches will shoot me. You too, I expect'.

Andrew sighed and took out his handkerchief. She glared and spat the words at him. 'Put it away, I will not endanger your lives. What do you take me for?'

He hurriedly put it back in his pocket. 'I'll free your hands. Please don't try to jump.'

'I can jump with my hands tied if I want to.' Turner put his arm around her and held her tight.

This time Francine climbed up the ladder between Andrew and Turner. When she got to the top she collapsed. Andrew waited while she got her breath back, but she could hardly stand.

'Turner, carry her,' ordered Andrew.

'Oh, fu...' exclaimed 65, as he slipped sideways and nearly fell over.

'What is it?' whispered Andrew, then he slipped too, realising that this was where they had all thrown up when they had first smelt the sewers.

They were surprised how steep the passage was; although she was so light, Turner found it hard carrying Francine. He was out of breath by the time they arrived at the small recess beside the stairs.

Andrew was pleased that they had left the entrance open. He emerged on to the staircase and froze as he heard the clatter of army boots hurrying around the *ceinture*. They seemed to be running past the top of the staircase and round to the other side of the château. He put his head back inside the passage and whispered to the others to hurry.

They unceremoniously pushed Francine through the gap. Turner carried her as they silently ran down the stairs and out through the heavy door at the bottom. Taking great gulps of fresh air, they thankfully stepped out into the grounds of the castle.

When they reached the safety of the trees, Andrew said, 'You'll not mention what happened in the castle tonight.' The two men nodded. 'We have a traitor amongst us. By remaining silent we may catch him. Now we must hurry. Our horses are in this direction. Give me the girl while you signal to your brother.' Andrew gently took Francine who moaned, but said nothing.

Turner put his hands to his mouth and let out a series of owl hoots. He was answered by a distant call in the direction of the château.

'What the devil are they doing over there?'

'No, sir, that's a real owl.' Turner grinned as another call came from a little way ahead of them.

'Is that your brother? What did he say?'

'All's well.'

'Thank God. Now hurry.'

As soon as Andrew caught up with his men and spare horses, he called to Marie-Claude, who, seeing her mistress, promptly burst into tears.

'*Les salops*. What have they done to you?'

'You have clean clothes?' asked Andrew. Marie-Claude nodded. 'Then clean her up as best you can. I don't know if she can ride.' Andrew walked away and left the two women together.

'Sir, sir.'

'What is it, Fisher?'

'The pigeons are different.'

'What do you mean?'

'They're different pigeons. Look, sir.'

'Williams, come here,' ordered Andrew. 'Are these the same pigeons?'

'I'm not sure.'

'What makes you think that they are different, Fisher?'

'These keep flapping. They sat quietly together when we started out.'

'These do seem to be wilder,' Williams agreed.

'That one has a half-collar of black feathers,' added Shrimp. 'None of them had a collar like that.'

'He's right, sir. They're not the same pigeons.' Williams was adamant.

'Well done Fisher, someone has exchanged them. Gather round. Did any of you see anyone go near the pigeons?'

'No, sir,' came the chorus.

'Who was on guard duty in the barn?'

'We all were at different times, sir,' replied Williams.

'Did anyone go near the pigeons?'

'Yes.' Everyone stared at Clark. 'Well, who?' snapped Andrew.

'Only the doctor. He came in to bring me some coffee.'

'Did he indeed? Did he touch the pigeons?'

'No, but they flapped about and made a noise. They were round the corner and I was going to look at them, but he had brought my coffee to the door and called me over. He said not to worry, it was a cat. Then there was a bang and I did go to look, sir, and a cat ran away.'

'Someone changed the pigeons, you idiot.'

'Yes Turner, I think we've established that. Thank you, Clark,' said Andrew.

'But the doctor...' gasped Shrimp.

Williams looked at Andrew, who asked, 'Where's François?'

'I'm here. I heard what you said.' The men instinctively drew their rifles and surrounded him.

'What shall we do with him, sir?' asked 65.

'We'll see what he has to say for himself first,' replied Andrew. 'Well young man?'

'We've had our suspicions about the doctor since the Germans arrived in the village. Until then he was as true a Frenchman as myself...' 65 grunted. 'But then some Boches officers were billeted in his house. They may have put him under pressure. He has an elderly mother who is very frail... Who knows...?'

'I see.' Andrew nodded. 'Who is suspicious of him?'

'Monsieur Lefevre, that's why he sent his family away. The postman, he heard the Germans talking. My mother…'

'But she let you come with us?'

'Of course, she would have found it hard to stop me. We wanted to find out the truth and now we have. He's the Mayor of the village, you see.'

'Mmmm,' said Andrew.

'What are you going to do with the pigeons?' asked Williams.

'Kill them,' suggested 65.

'No, these must fly to their appointed destination. Otherwise Fritz will know that we have discovered the doctor's duplicity. I believe the original pigeons will be sent on with another message or maybe the same message. I'll sort them out when it's light. We can't release them in the dark. Anyway, we need to leave now. Clark, go and see how Marie-Claude is getting on. François, come over here. 65 and Fisher, prepare the horses.'

Andrew drew François and Williams apart from the other men. 'We will *not* be going to La Maison Forestière de la Grande Biche.' Andrew opened his map and pointed. 'This is the Maison Forestière, here. We need to take a route along here.' Andrew pointed to a westerly direction. 'They'll be waiting for us at La Grande Biche. When we don't arrive they'll guess that we have either got lost, or that we're going to join up with the BEF, which would take us south west, down there. We'll go due west.'

Andrew strode over to Marie-Claude. 'How is Mademoiselle Francine?'

'Not good, *Monsieur*. I have done what I can, but she needs a doctor.'

'I know. We'll find one as soon as possible. Can she ride?'

'Side-saddle, I think. I will ride astride, behind her.'

'No, Turner 65 will do that. Turner, you'll guard her with your life.'

'Yes, sir,' replied Turner. He threw the limp, but compliant, Francine on to the side-saddle. Much to Andrew's surprise, he gently and respectfully arranged her legs around the pommels. Then he vaulted on to the horse and sat uncomfortably behind her, one strong arm holding her tight and the other steering the horse.

Andrew mounted the rest of the men and moved them forwards. Marie-Claude, riding beside Francine, said, 'We're going the wrong way'.

'No, *Mademoiselle*,' Williams replied. 'Have no fear. We're definitely going in the right direction.'

'What did she say?' asked 65.

'She said that she likes you.'

65 held tightly on to Francine and smiled into the night.

CHAPTER TWELVE

Flight

The small party rode fast along farm tracks, through woods and across rivers, but they saw no Germans.

Andrew kept up a good gallop, frequently looking behind him at Francine. She clung on to the pommels of her saddle while Turner held her close with one hand and guided the horse with the other. Williams brought up the rear, listening out for following hoofbeats.

When Andrew's horse began to tire he slowed to a walk and then stopped to let the horses catch their breath.

Francine sat on the ground, exhausted. Andrew bent down and asked gently, 'How are you?'

She stared at him, shrugged and turned her back. He picked up her hand. 'Can you go on riding?' She angrily pulled her hand away.

He stood up and inwardly sighed. 'Turner 65, your gelding needs a respite, change horses,' he snapped. He left Francine to the ministrations of Marie-Claude. 'Fisher, how's that mare?' he asked.

'Sweet as a nut, sir.'

Andrew gave a weak smile. He turned to Williams and said, 'I knew he could do anything with a horse'.

'I wonder if that filly was deliberately put in the bunch to hinder us,' remarked Williams.

'I wouldn't be surprised.' Andrew spoke quietly.

'Luckily they're all French horses and shod with French shoes, just in case anyone is following our hoofprints.'

'Yes, although the doctor knows we have French horses.'

They set off at a gallop again. Francine leant back against Turner 65. Her body was as limp as a rag doll. Andrew hoped that she would be able to hang on until daybreak. As they drew further away from the castle, he moderated the pace, dropping to a trot and walking intermittently.

Dawn was breaking when they reached a small château standing beside a farmyard.

François announced, 'This is our destination'.

'Thank God. I trust they are true Frenchmen.'

'They certainly are, sir.'

'How far are we from the Château de la Croix?'

'Over thirty kilometres. We've covered a lot of ground. This was my third choice.'

'Good God! I hope they're reliable.'

'No, I meant in terms of distance. They would be my first choice as helpful and useful people.'

'Excellent.'

Andrew left the men in a copse and went round to the back of the château with François. An elderly butler opened the door. 'Monsieur François! *Quelle surprise.*' François quickly explained why they were there and without delay the old man said, 'Come to the salon, I'll fetch Monsieur du Gros'.

They were joined shortly by the flustered master of the house wearing a dressing gown, who was quickly followed by a tall, proud-looking woman, also dressed in night attire.

'*Bon jour.*' She continued in English, 'Sit down.'

'No, no, we're a little dirty.' Andrew looked at the elegant chairs with their pristine lemon satin seats and remained standing.

'No matter, you look worn out. Why are you here?'

'We have Francine du Byard...'

'*Mon Dieu.* Where?'

'In the copse.'

'What is she doing in the copse? François, bring her in immediately. We heard she was captured; is she hurt?'

'Yes, Madame,' replied Andrew. 'She requires urgent medical attention.'

'Then why leave her in the copse? *Oh, la, la, la, la, les Anglais!*'

'We had to, just in case... I have some men with her. Perhaps they could come in too?'

'Take them to the farm. Hervé, organise that. I will ...' she ran out of the room calling to her maid. Her husband smiled at Andrew. 'I'm so pleased you have her safe. Welcome to my house.'

The cavalcade of bedraggled men and exhausted horses went to the farmyard, while Turner 65 carried Francine into the house, closely followed by Marie-Claude.

'What have they done to her? *Les bruts,*' cried Madame du Gros. The bruising on Francine's face stood out stark and vivid in the bright light of the hallway. Andrew's face hardened as he clearly saw for the first time the extent of her injuries.

'Take her upstairs.' Madame du Gros had tears in her eyes. Turner 65 carried Francine up the broad sweeping staircase and into a large bedroom. He laid her gently on the soft bed.

'Go. Go.' Madame du Gros shooed him out of the room as he tried to catch Marie-Claude's eye.

The horses were bedded down in a neat row of immaculate looseboxes under the supervision of Hervé du Gros, himself. 'The Boches haven't reached us yet, but they have been to a village fifteen kilometres to the east of here. They have taken horses, fuel and cars. We fear that they'll come here soon,' he told Andrew as he inspected the horses. 'These stables were full of hunters. We gave them to the French army. Luckily your horses are French and will take their place. The Boches will never know the difference, especially if your army saddles are well hidden.'

'You're very kind, *Monsieur.*'

'Nonsense. I'm delighted to find Mademoiselle du Byard in safe hands. But I'm devastated to hear about the Doctor Lejeune. There are some Frenchmen who want to make peace with the Boches and wish the British to go.'

'So I understand.' Andrew's face was grave.

'The majority want to fight of course, to drive the Germans away, but there is a small milieu... Capturing Francine was a good move by the Boches, her father is... Could be... easily influenced. He's not a coward, you understand, but he has a vast fortune.' Du Gros shrugged. 'He could lose a lot of money in this war. I say no more, but you must keep her safe for France. Don't tell people who she is. It would be better to take her to Normandy or Brittany. I'll give you names of the Frenchmen who can be trusted. But I warn you, there's a high ranking English officer, his name is General Littlejohn, and an English politician who would also...'

'General Littlejohn! I don't believe you. He's part of the General Staff. How do you know such things?' Andrew interrupted.

'*Monsieur*, I have spent most of my life in French politics. Believe me, I know. I'll show you some letters, maybe they'll convince you. Trust no one. Take the young lady to the safety of the west of France. Please don't try to reach Paris. You will not succeed.'

Hervé du Gros walked away. Andrew stared after him. Then he called to Williams and took him to one side. 'We need to sort out these pigeons. I have the capsules here.' He opened them. 'Just as I thought, they're in code. They're both the same, and they're destined for the pair of pigeons to be released when we have Francine. How extraordinary, I know this code from my schooldays.'

'We used a code at school when we passed notes to each other in class,' Williams replied. 'We changed the letters around.'

'I'm glad to hear the good old traditions have been passed down to future generations of schoolboys.' Andrew laughed. 'There are twenty-six letters in the alphabet. E is the most commonly used letter. Here the Ls are the most frequent in this message.'

'So therefore if L is E, it becomes the 5th letter of the alphabet. H must be A,' replied Williams.

'Exactly. I'm sure most people could crack this code.'

'Have the capsules been swapped?' asked Williams.

'No, I've carried them in my wallet all the time. No one has changed them, I can assure you.'

'What does your message say? Or perhaps I shouldn't ask, sir.'

'You're an Old Harrovian, your father was an excellent man and I believe your mother is a friend of my mother's. I know I can trust you.'

Williams blushed. 'I haven't told the others of our connection. Because you never met me before I joined your squadron, I didn't think you knew who I was.'

'Sometimes it's best not to ask too many questions.'

Williams's face fell. 'Such as my age?' A stubborn look came into his eyes. 'I don't want to go home.'

'Then I won't ask your age.' Andrew smiled. 'I find you very useful. I don't want to lose you.' Williams relaxed and Andrew continued: 'The message says that we have Francine and we're heading for the Compiègne to Senlis road'.

'Do we want to tell the enemy that?'

'Yes… I rather think we do. It's the route that I was told to take. It may keep the Hun busy looking for us there.' Andrew pulled out his orders. 'We're to release the last two pigeons when we arrive in a village called Verberie. Then we make for the forest of Ermenonville.'

'But we won't go there?'

'Certainly not. For the moment we'll release one pigeon.'

Williams put his hand into the wooden box and extracted an angry bird. Andrew dexterously fixed the capsule on to its leg. Once released, the pigeon circled around without mishap and flew away towards the east.

***

Monsieur du Gros welcomed Andrew into his study, opened a safe and brought out a bundle of letters.

Andrew had to use his knowledge of French to the best of his ability as he deciphered the flowery continental writing. 'May I make notes?' he asked.

'Of course,' replied Hervé.

It took Andrew the best part of two hours to read, understand all the contents and to make notes. Then he sat back in his chair, shook his head and went to find his host.

'You must remember that these are a very small group of men,' explained du Gros, as they returned to the study.

'But rotten. You know what they say about a rotten apple in a barrel,' replied Andrew.

'I do indeed, *Capitaine*. I hope it has alerted you to the danger.'

'Yes, I rather think it has. It's very frightening to find out that Robert Cartwright is the politician in question. He has a certain amount of clout, also access to secrets. But the bitter pill to swallow is General Littlejohn. This is disastrous. He works closely with the Chief-of-Staff; all I can say is that at least he's not over here at the moment.'

'I think you'll find that the General will *do the decent thing*, as you call it.' Du Gros put two fingers to his temple. 'Also I believe that Mr. Cartwright has had his wings clipped and that he, too, will disappear from public life very soon.'

'I'm glad to hear that. I can't thank you enough for allowing me to see these letters. It has made my course of action very clear to me, very clear indeed.'

'And what is that?'

'I'll take your advice and head for Brittany as soon as Mademoiselle du Byard is ready to move on. A doctor has seen her, I presume.'

'Yes, he's here at the moment.'

'May I see him?'

'I don't see why not, in fact I hear them coming down the stairs now.' Monsieur du Gros opened his study door and called to the doctor.

He entered, accompanied by Madame du Gros who acted as interpreter. 'The doctor says there is nothing physically wrong with Mademoiselle Francine.'

'Really.' Andrew glared at the arrogant man and thought for a moment that he almost preferred Doctor Lejeune. 'What do you call the dreadful bruising on her face?'

The doctor shrugged. 'Ah yes, that is bad, but it will heal in time. The cheek bone is fractured. I have given her some powders to help her sleep. As to the other matter, down below.' He gestured with his hand. 'It's nothing more than normal.' Andrew felt very uncomfortable and glanced at Madame du Gros. He looked out of the window and, after a pause, he asked, 'Are you sure?'

'Yes, of course. I've given her a thorough examination. Now I must go.' The doctor looked ill at ease and was visibly relieved to leave the room.

Andrew told his host that he wished to set off that afternoon.

'Do you need anything?' asked Monsieur du Gros.

'Yes, I'm afraid I need rather a lot. A farm cart piled with furniture, two side saddles, and some women's clothes...' There was a knock on the study door.

'*Oui, entréz.*'

The butler came in. 'Monsieur, there is another English soldier in the kitchen. He says he knows the *Capitaine*.'

'What! Whoever...' Andrew hurriedly drew his revolver.

A tall trooper, accompanied by Shrimp, stood up and saluted as Andrew entered the kitchen. 'Pilson!' Andrew put his revolver back into its holster. 'Where the devil did you spring from? We thought you were... Well, missing anyway. How the blazes did you get here?'

'It's a long story, sir. I couldn't get through the enemy lines. I've been skirting round behind the German army and I ended up in the next village. I heard that you were here.'

'Does the whole of France know that I'm here?' Andrew asked.

'I don't know. Well not *you* exactly, an English cavalry captain. I couldn't believe my luck when I found out that it was you.'

'Stone would have let him die at the ford,' Shrimp interrupted. 'He was hiding in the marsh all the time. He never fought, sir.'

'That doesn't surprise me. I haven't time to hear all about it now. You'll have to tell me as we go on our way tonight. Join the other men for now.'

'It's good to be back, sir.'

'It's good to have you back, Pilson, good indeed.'

***

Later that day Andrew assembled the men in the servant's hall.

'Williams, Fisher and Clark, can you all ride side-saddle?' The men stared at him.

'No, sir,' replied Clark and Williams.

'Fisher?'

'Well, sir, I had to break in and train the lady's hacks, see. So yes, I can.' A snort came from the direction of the Turners.

'Have you anything to say, 65?

'No, sir.'

'Fisher, you can give the other two a lesson in the art of riding side-saddle.' The men stared at each other. 'I've chosen you three because you're the youngest and will pass off tolerably well as women. These are your clothes.' Andrew pointed to a bundle of women's garments. 'Choose what you want, that includes the hats.'

'Clark, Turner 64 will be your husband.' There was another snort from the Turners. 'Fisher, you'll pair up with Pilson and Williams, you'll have Turner 65. Marie-Claude will stay with Mademoiselle Francine who will be dressed as a wounded soldier. She will ride in the back of the wagon. The rest of you dress in the men's clothes.

After Andrew had left the room the men exploded into laughter.

'Women eh?' 65 laughed. 'He couldn't have chosen better men for the part.'

'Shut up, 65,' said Shrimp.

'Stop arguing,' snapped Williams. He rummaged through the pile of clothes and picked out a red dress for himself. 'Get dressed.'

'You'll look a right tart in that,' said Len Turner.

'You wouldn't want to pay for it, would you?' said 65. 'You wouldn't even give her tuppence to look at her knickers.'

'You'd have a shock if you did,' said Pilson.

'Yes, by God,' exclaimed 65.

'Never mind what's in my drawers,' said Williams. 'Clark, you can have the pink dress. Shrimp, I think you'd look good in green. I'm going to wear the straw hat with the cherries, and this straw with the pink ribbon would look very fetching with the pink dress. Shrimp, the sage hat with the plums will look good with your dress.'

'That's right, Shrimp, you wear your plums on yer head,' 65 scoffed.

'You'll be wearing your plums on your head, if you don't shut up,' retorted Shrimp.

'And who's going to make me?'

'Me husband,' Shrimp laughed. 'He'll hold you down while I cut 'em off.'

'For God's sake, get on with it,' ordered Williams. 'Here comes François. Which dress would you like?'

'*Merde!*' François looked shocked. 'I'll take the black one. I'll be a widow.'

'You can't, you must be with the captain. Anyway, you look too young to be a widow.' Shrimp was struggling into his green dress.

'*Non*, not really. We are fighting a war.' Everybody suddenly stopped talking and stood still.

Turner 65 said, 'Yeah, we are. So let's get on with it. I'm going to be the French farmer in his Sunday best'.

'Who do you want to impress?' Shrimp mocked. Before 65 could answer, Marie-Claude came into the room.

'How's Mademoiselle Francine?' asked Williams, over the giggles at 65's sudden heightened colour.

'She's not good. She's changed, she hardly talks. It's as if she has lost the will to live. I'm very worried about her.' Marie-Claude gave a little sob. François put his arm around her and she choked back her tears. Turner 65 glared at him.

Marie-Claude suddenly noticed the men and burst out laughing. 'You look so funny. You've forgotten the wigs.'

Williams translated and the men groaned. They each picked out a wig.

'This looks disgusting.' Williams brushed off a dark haired wig. 'I'm sure it's full of fleas.'

Clark was trying to make his fit when Marie-Claude rushed over to him, saying something in French.

'It's upside down,' Williams translated.

Clark altered the wig and looked at Marie-Claude for approval.

'Very good,' she replied in English, smiling at him. She rushed to Shrimp and adjusted his hat, and then to Williams and arranged his dress. 'Ça *va mieux, je pense.*'

'What did she say?' asked 65.

'Learn to speak French,' retorted Williams. 'I'm not going to translate her every word for your convenience.'

***

The men assembled in the stable yard. Four horses were harnessed to a farm cart. The wagon was piled high with furniture and covered with a tarpaulin. Mattresses and blankets lay over the army saddles and bridles, and fodder for the horses was stowed in the back.

The men had to look twice as Andrew arrived to inspect them. He appeared years older. He hadn't shaved and he had rubbed chalk into his hair and on to his face. He was wearing civilian clothes over his uniform.

'You look... tolerably well.' Andrew tried not to smile as he approached the men who were dressed as women. 'If I didn't know differently, I would never guess that you weren't female. Don't slouch, stand up straight and for goodness sake hide your boots under your skirts at all times.' The men smiled self-consciously. 'You look even better when you smile. We pose as a French family fleeing from the Hun. You'll speak to no one. Only Marie-Claude, Williams and François will do the talking. The others will look dumb, which shouldn't prove to be too much of a problem.'

'Turner 64 and Clark will ride. 65 and Williams will stay hidden inside the wagon with Fisher, Marie-Claude and Mademoiselle Francine. Pilson, squash in between me and François, for the moment. Tie the spare horses to the back of the wagon, then mount up and take your places. Someone hold that team. These horses have probably never pulled a cart before. Turner 65, come with me.'

Shrimp helped Clark on to his side-saddle and gave him a brief lesson on how to ride.

Andrew returned with Turner 65 carrying Francine in his arms. Marie-Claude followed, dressed as a nurse and holding a suitcase.

'I'm sorry that you have to lie on top of our saddles,' Andrew apologised to Francine as Turner laid her gently on to the makeshift bed in the wagon. 'I hope you're not too uncomfortable.' Francine turned away and closed her eyes. She wore a French military uniform and her head was swathed in bandages. Marie-Claude settled down beside her. Shrimp and Turner 65 sat down on the hay at the back of the wagon.

Andrew mounted the box, Pilson and François were holding the horses' heads. 'Stay beside them until we know if they'll take kindly to pulling a wagon. Walk march,' Andrew ordered. The horses lurched forwards. They felt the weight in their collars and stopped. 'Fisher and 65, come and help.' The two men jumped down from the wagon. Shrimp promptly tripped on his dress and fell over. 'For God's sake keep on your feet and get these horses moving.' Williams went to help too and between them they persuaded the horses to move forwards and take the weight.

'Fisher, Williams and François get back in the wagon, you look ridiculous,' said Andrew.

'I thought I looked rather fetching in green, sir.' Shrimp was deflated.

'Sorry to offend, but women leading horses are incongruous. Turner 65 and Pilson, stay where you are until they settle.'

The horses began to move and pull together. Andrew practised stopping and starting until he felt confident enough to call Pilson back on to the box. He left Turner 65 at the horses' heads.

'François, go to the back of the wagon for the moment. Pilson, tell me exactly what happened at the ford.'

'Well, during the mêlée, sir, my horse was grazed by a German lance. He leapt over the low wall and into the river on the left-hand side of the ford. I made for the bank but there was a high fence and it was impossible to get out. We kept drifting further away from the ford. My horse was determined not to turn round and re-join the battle. I saw a shallow watering place for cattle, so I headed for that and then we hit the bog. The mud was up to my horse's belly. I jumped off but he was stuck.'

Andrew nodded. 'I get the picture, carry on.'

'Then I saw Stone coming down to the marsh with a horse. It looked like the one we called number 49, because it had a short tail.'

'Go on.'

'Well, it was very odd because Stone was trying to shoo the horse away, but it kept following him.'

'He was dismounted.'

'Yes, I couldn't believe my eyes when I saw him turn round and stick his sword into the horse. Then he jumped over the wall and sat tight on the bank. I shouted at him to come and help me, but he wouldn't.'

'Did he hear you?

'Oh yes, he looked up. He could see me all right, I was having the devil of a job. I kept pulling at my horse, but he just stood there, sinking in the mud with his ears back and his eyes glazed over. I yelled to Stone again but he still didn't move.'

'What did you do?'

'The mud was well above my waist. I took the horse's saddle off and edged my way towards the bank. I put my kit down on the grass and sat looking up at this willow tree. It was hanging over the river. That's when I got the idea.'

'What idea?'

'I tied every piece of long equipment I had together to make a rope. My stirrup leathers, reins, girths, everything, even my braces, until I had a length of line long enough to go round the back of my horse and to tie around the tree. Then I held the other end and pulled as hard as I could. The horse moved ever so slowly towards the bank, but the rope kept breaking.' Andrew smiled. 'It wasn't funny, sir.'

'No, no of course it wasn't. I know the feeling; the same thing happened to us. Carry on.'

'Oh I see. Well, eventually my horse reached the bank and when the next piece of equipment came undone we was on firm ground. He stood shaking and then he collapsed on the grass. I sat on the ground and gathered my strength. When I got up and looked back along the river I saw that Stone had left his hidey-hole and you had all disappeared.' Pilson stopped and swallowed. 'It was a horrible feeling, sir. I was on the wrong side of the river. I thought it wouldn't take long to catch you up once my horse got up, but he didn't, not for ages. By then I had put my saddle and kit back together again and mended the broken things with bits of string.

It was getting dark when he eventually stood up and picked at a bit of grass. I walked away from the ford towards the south-west, the way we had come that morning, but I saw no one until eventually I noticed some lights in the distance. I came to a farm and they put us up for the night. The next day I started back to the ford, but the place was crawling with Hun. Hundreds of them, there was, with cannons and columns of marching soldiers. It fair gave me a fright, sir.'

'Yes, I know. I saw them too.'

'Ever since then I've been riding south-west, trying to catch up with the BEF. But they were always just on the other side of the Germans. I wasn't deserting sir.'

'No, I know, Pilson. That's all right, you did well. I want you to write down all that you saw at the ford concerning Stone, in your own words, as soon as you can. Have you got paper and a pencil?'

'No, sir.'

Andrew tore some sheets of paper out of his note book, took a pencil from his wallet and handed them to Pilson.

'My spelling isn't very good.'

'Don't worry, just put it all down in your own words and then sign it.'

'Like a letter.'
'Yes, exactly like a letter.'

***

By the time they had reached the main road leading to Normandy, the team of horses had settled down well. Andrew called Turner 65 back to the wagon.

Travelling on slowly, they met other French families along the way. Luckily nobody seemed to be inclined to talk.

Andrew suddenly halted the team. He said, 'There's a battery of British artillery approaching fast. Say nothing, remember we're French and we don't speak English. Nobody must know who we are. Look tired and frightened, especially the women'. He added, 'Don't worry. I bet they can't speak French'.

As the battery drew nearer, Andrew hoped he would be able to control his team without having to resort to a man holding their heads. To his horror, an artillery officer halted the first team horses beside the wagon.

'Good evening,' he said in bad French. 'Is there a farm or a village further on where we can bivouac for the night?'

'*Oui*,' replied François, speaking fast in a high pitched voice. 'Just beyond the crossroads and over the next hill there's a village.'

'What the devil is that Froggy woman saying?' The man turned to look at his junior officer riding behind him.

'I don't know, I don't speak the lingo.'

'Any of you lot speak French?' the officer shouted. The men shook their heads. He addressed François again in pigeon French. '*Madame*, is there a village not too far in this direction?'

'Speak slowly.' Andrew spoke out of the side of his mouth while staring at his horses.

'*Oui... oui.*' François pointed back the way they had come and, holding up five fingers, said, '*Cinq kilometres*'.

'Thank you.' The officer turned to his junior. 'The husband's a surly bugger. He looks old enough to be her father. But then that's the French for you. Come on, move this lot forward. We've five miles to cover before it gets dark.'

'*Five kilometres, not miles, you rude idiot,*' Andrew wanted to say.

While the officer had been speaking to François, one of the drivers was looking at Clark, who was smiling back at him. 'That bit of skirt looks

151

all right,' he remarked to the man behind him. 'Why can't they speak a civilized language? If we had more time, I'd fancy my chances with her. She's giving me the eye.'

Clark continued to smile coquettishly from under his hat.

'See, she likes me,' said the driver, winking and leering. Clark winked and grinned back.

'That bloke with her don't look too happy,' said the driver behind him. 'Ugly bugger.' Clark giggled and continued grinning. Len Turner looked like thunder.

''Bye sweetheart, some other time,' the driver called out as they were given the order to move forwards.

Andrew, not trusting his horses, waited until all six guns rattled past before he asked them to walk on. Some of the drivers and gunners sitting on the limbers whistled at Clark as they passed by. He continued grinning and winking back at them.

The men rode on in silence, as they had been ordered to do, until Andrew saw a place to stop. 'We'll camp here,' he said, turning his horses off the main road and into a wood.

As soon as they were clear of any French travellers, the men exploded into laughter and righteous indignation.

'How dare they speak about us like that,' exclaimed Williams.

'You're a harlot,' Len Turner accused Clark and, turning to Andrew, he continued: 'Sir, you've married me to a tart. Did you see how he behaved?'

Andrew said, 'You did well Clark. I thought you were very convincing'.

Clark turned to Len. 'You're just jealous, because they didn't like you.'

'Don't worry Turner 64, they didn't like me either,' said Andrew.

'Yes, I heard,' said 65. 'I wanted to hit that officer, sir. How dare he speak about you like that?'

'Thank Goodness you were in the wagon.'

'They never guessed we were English, though, did they sir?' asked Williams.

'No, they certainly didn't. You all did very well. Let it be a lesson to you. Beware of what you say; you never know who's listening, or who understands what you're saying. Now, get this camp set up, horses fed and watered. Williams, work out the guard rota for the night. Someone light a fire. Turner 65, kill and pluck those last three pigeons and ask Marie-

Claude nicely if she wouldn't mind cooking them. I, for one, am starving. And 65, make sure you don't let them go.'

'You're not going to release them, sir?' Williams asked quietly.

'No. If by any chance they get caught between here and where they are supposed to go, then the Hun will know we're not telling the truth and that we are not at this village, Verberie. They could even find us.'

'Francine is important, isn't she?'

'Yes, she's an expendable pawn in a very nasty game of chess and I'm not going to allow her to remain one.'

CHAPTER THIRTEEN

Flying Visit

The small party of men journeyed on; the roads were busy and their pace was slow. They stopped regularly to feed and water the horses. At night they camped out. None of the other travellers on the road realised that they were no more than just another French family fleeing from the Boches. Eventually they turned off the main western road and travelled north.

Andrew tried to find out what had happened to Francine, but each time he spoke to her she closed her eyes and turned away. Marie-Claude also told him nothing, so he gave up.

Early on the fourth day they climbed a hill. They all gasped as they looked down and saw the English Channel stretching out to the horizon. They rumbled down a windy road in high spirits and stopped on the outskirts of a fishing village.

Andrew assembled the men. 'As you know, Mademoiselle Francine is in grave danger. I'm taking her to England.' They stared at him, their faces breaking into smiles. 'Change into your uniforms.'

The men were happy to be back in their normal clothes and eagerly gathered round as Andrew spoke to Pilson, Clark and François. 'I'm leaving you three to return the wagon, horses, saddles and bridles.' Andrew, noticing their disappointment at not going to England, smiled brightly. 'We shan't be staying long. Pilson, you managed very well on your own in France, for which I congratulate you. Clark, you're clever with horses. I need someone whom I can trust to drive the wagon and return all nine horses safely. Make your way to the nearest BEF Head Quarters. François will guide you. I have a letter here that explains what I am doing, also my orders concerning you. You will hand it to the Commanding Officer. For the moment you'll all wait here until I come back.'

It didn't take Andrew long to find a fisherman who was willing to ferry his party across the Channel for a small fee. When he returned he thanked François profusely for helping them and wished him well. The men shook each other solemnly by the hand and Shrimp said a sad farewell to his filly. The wagon rumbled away.

Andrew had taken the precaution of slipping one of Francine's sedatives into a drink and she dozed in and out of sleep, not aware of where she was going. The four remaining men carried her on a stretcher with

Marie-Claude in attendance, still dressed as a nurse.

They boarded a trawler which smelt of fish and by the time Francine and Marie-Claude were installed below in a tiny cabin they were already manoeuvring out of the harbour.

Andrew felt unable to deal with whatever it was that was disturbing the beautiful French girl. He fervently hoped that he was doing the right thing in taking her to England and that he wasn't going to find himself court-martialed for disobeying orders, abducting a young woman and her maid, whilst involving six British soldiers.

He stood for a long time watching the retreating French coastline. The gaff rigger began to heave as they sailed into the middle of the English Channel. He held on to the side of the vessel, his eyes fixed on the horizon, as he tried to ignore the smell of fish and keep his last meal down.

The other cavalrymen, apart from Williams, weren't so successful. They sat huddled together on the cramped deck, every now and again having to lean over the side.

It was a long and tedious journey. When the sedative wore off Andrew told Francine why he was taking her to England. 'My father is in the War Cabinet. He will know what to do and my mother will look after you and nurse you back to health.'

'Your parents won't want a girl such as me in their house,' Francine replied.

'Of course they will. My mother will be delighted to see you.'

'*Non*, she won't.'

'Francine…'

'*Non*. I tell you, she won't.' Francine spat the words at him. 'I don't want to go to your house. But you have dressed me in these ridiculous clothes, you hold me prisoner surrounded by your men. You even have my maid in your power, what can I do?' She turned her bandaged head towards him and he recoiled as he saw the look of fury. 'I know you're plotting together,' she hissed as Andrew signalled to Marie-Claude.

'*Mais non, Mademoiselle, c'est pas vrai,*' Marie-Claude cried tearfully.

Andrew shook his head and drew the little maid up on deck. With the help of Williams's French input, he told her to give Francine another sedative as soon as she could.

Marie-Claude sobbed. '*C'est difficile, c'est affreux… la pauvre Mademoiselle.*' Williams put his arm around her to comfort her. Turner 65 sprang up and marched over. He glared at Williams, who stood back.

'It's all right, Turner.' Andrew sighed.

Marie-Claude looked up at the tall blonde trooper, smiled through her tears and took a step towards him, the first time she had done anything to show that she was at all interested in him. Andrew and Williams exchanged glances while 65 beamed down into the white frightened face.

Andrew continued explaining to the little French girl what he wanted her to do. She dried her eyes and repeated his words to make sure she had understood.

'Marie-Claude,' Francine called from below. She dived down the ladder and into the cabin, where she tried to reassure her mistress that she was acting in her best interests.

The soldiers' spirits rose when at last they sighted the Dorset coast. Andrew watched as the crew sailed expertly into a rocky inlet hidden from the open sea. The skipper lowered the sails just before a Royal Naval minesweeper steamed round the headland. Andrew stood rooted to the spot, nervously watching as it passed them by, thankful that he wouldn't have to answer any awkward questions.

To disembark they all had to jump into the water and wade up the beach.

'I'll take Mademoiselle Francine, sir.' Turner 65 turned round as he landed in the water. The sleepy Francine allowed herself to be placed in the trooper's arms.

'I'll take Marie-Claude,' Len Turner volunteered. He held the pretty girl in his arms and strode through the shallow water. 65 glared at him and then tripped on a rock.

'You'll drop Mademoiselle Francine if you don't look where you're going,' remarked Williams.

'Shut up, La-di-dah,' snapped Turner 65.

The sodden and bedraggled men found it awkward carrying Francine on a stretcher up a steep twisty path which climbed to the top of the cliff. Once there, they turned to look at the sea. The trawler was still in her hiding place, while the minesweeper carried on up the coast.

They marched on towards a coastal village set on the downs overlooking the sea.

'The countryside is beautiful,' announced Shrimp.

'I thought you hated the country,' remarked 65.

'Yeah, but this is England. The best views in the world.'

'You're right, Shrimp,' said Williams. 'It's good to be home.'

'She ain't home though.' Shrimp looked at Francine as she lay, with her eyes closed, on the stretcher.

As the group of wet soldiers entered the village, people stared. Andrew asked a bright eyed lad where he could find the police house. 'Follow me, sir. It's over here. I want to join the army, sir.'

'Good, good,' replied Andrew. 'You're a bit young yet and the war will soon be over, but we'll always need good men like you.' The small boy grew in stature and marched in front of Andrew to the square, flint-built house.

The village policeman hurried out, hastily pulling his jacket on over his shirt and braces. He asked, 'What can I do for you, sir?'

'I need to use your telephone, please.'

'Come in. What about your wounded man?' The policeman looked at the stretcher.

'He can stay out here in the sunshine.' Andrew didn't know what Francine might say or do. He gestured to the men to lay her on the ground, telling them to humour her and to keep her quiet. Thankfully she slept.

Andrew stood in the dark hallway of the little house, picked up the ear piece of the telephone and jigged the lever up and down. A far-away voice answered. He asked for his home number and waited.

Fortunately his father was at home and came on to the crackling line immediately. Without any preamble, Andrew spoke urgently. 'Father, I've arrived back in England on a flying visit.'

'Andrew, is that you? Have you got the girl?'

'Yes. You know about Francine?' Andrew was astonished.

'Of course. Do you think we do nothing here? Thank God you have her safe.'

Andrew smiled, relieved that he wouldn't have to explain Francine's capture and subsequent rescue. 'I didn't think our exploits would reach the dizzy heights of Whitehall.'

'You've had us all on tenterhooks, believe me. The PM is in quite a flap. You disappeared off the face of the earth, you see, and then to turn up in England. Well done. Where are you, by the way?' Andrew gave him the name of the village. 'By Jove, even better. Is the girl is unharmed?'

'She's... injured, but not seriously.'

'How many are you?' Andrew told him. 'I'll send a lorry. Your mother will be delighted at the news. I'll inform the PM and see you directly.'

Andrew opened his mouth to say 'Goodbye', but the telephone had gone dead.

He joined his men outside the house, followed by the policeman's wife. 'Would you like some tea, sir?' She hovered nervously.

'Yes, indeed, what a good idea.' When she returned to the house he addressed his men. 'Transport is coming and we'll be at our destination before too long. I don't know if you'll have any leave while we are in England.'

'Cor, that would be good, sir,' exclaimed Shrimp.

'Don't count on it, Fisher, but if you do, I want you all to be very careful what you say. You will not discuss what we did in France with anyone. Do you understand?' The men nodded. 'And I mean *anyone*, not your parents, nor your siblings, nor your sweethearts, and especially not any Tom, Dick or Harry who you might meet in a pub, or on a train.'

'What will we tell our families, sir? They're bound to ask,' inquired Len Turner.

'You simply say that you're not allowed to discuss anything, except what is being reported in the newspapers.'

'Right you are, sir.'

'Any further questions?'

'Where are we going, sir?'

'We're going to my home, Hawkenfield Hall, Fisher. Once there I'll receive orders concerning your leave, or the lack of it.' Andrew looked around for more questions, but nobody spoke. 'I must say that I am very proud of the way that you have all taken our exploits in your stride and I'm equally pleased with myself for choosing the right men for the job.'

***

Andrew relaxed at last as the army lorry that his father had procured for them trundled down the drive of his beloved home. He was disappointed because Francine was lying on a stretcher in the back. He had wanted to show her the beautifully landscaped parkland. Fallow deer grazed under the great oak trees, some of which were reputed to have been there since the time of Charles II. The gravel drive curved round to reveal the granite mansion. Expansive lawns lay on either side and swept down to fragrant rose beds. The great lake lay calm and blue to the right of the imposing house.

The lorry scrunched to a halt. The front door flew open and Andrew's sister Caroline, followed more sedately by her parents, ran down the steps.

'Andrew!' The pretty seventeen-year-old flung her arms around him.

'Andrew darling, it's good to see you.' His mother kissed him and held him close. His father shook him warmly by the hand, saying, 'Welcome home. Well done, well done'.

'Where's Mademoiselle du Byard?' asked Lady Hawkenfield. Andrew felt embarrassed as he replied, 'In the back'.

His mother stared at the thin body lying on the stretcher as two men lifted Francine out of the lorry. She looked down with compassion at the pale face swathed in bandages, and said warmly, 'Welcome to Hawkenfield Hall'. Francine opened her eyes and gazed up into the fine-boned face. She smiled weakly. '*Bon jour,* Madame. *Merci.*' Then she shut her eyes. Lady Hawkenfield turned and called out, 'Nanny'. A large, competent woman bustled down the steps. 'Please take *Mademoiselle* upstairs to the blue room.'

The procession of men and stretcher, followed by Marie-Claude, mounted the broad staircase.

'That's young Anthony Williams, isn't it?' asked Lady Hawkenfield. 'I didn't know he was with you.'

'Didn't you Mother?' Andrew felt that he had to say something else, so he added, 'He's a good soldier'.

'Yes, he would be,' Lord Hawkenfield joined in. 'His Father was Commander Sir Archibald Williams, you know. He drowned off The Lizard, while sailing his own yacht. Young Williams should have gone into the Navy as an officer. He shouldn't be an NCO in a cavalry regiment.'

'Apparently he didn't want to be a burden to his mother.' Lady Hawkenfield explained. 'She has three other boys to educate.'

'He's under age I shouldn't wonder,' remarked her husband.

'I'm afraid I don't know, Father, I've never asked him his age.' Andrew spoke truthfully.

Lady Hawkenfield turned to Andrew. 'Marsh would like to put up the men in his cottage, but do you think Anthony should...?'

'That would be perfect, Mother,' Andrew replied.

'I'll see to them, you go and talk to your father.'

Andrew followed Lord Hawkenfield into his study, asking, 'Bertram is away, I presume?'

'Yes, your brother is training his troops somewhere. You know he has been promoted to Lieutenant-Colonel.'

'Yes, that happened before I went away.'

'Of course it did. Now tell me what you've been up to. Tell me what it's like in France.' Father and son spent a long time together while Andrew told him of his exploits.

'You've done well, my boy.' Lord Hawkenfield was proud.

'I thought I might be court-martialed.' Andrew smiled wryly. 'But I had to bring her to safety.'

'You did the right thing.'

There was a knock on the door and Lady Hawkenfield entered. She spoke to her husband. 'It's nearly time to change for dinner, my dear.'

'I'll go and check the men.' Andrew stood up.

'Don't be late.'

'Of course not mother. You know it won't take me long to change.' He smiled as he left the room.

'Before I forget,' Lord Hawkenfield called after him, 'You all have ten days' leave.'

'Excellent. I'll tell everyone the good news.'

Andrew made his way to Marsh's cottage. He shook the tall angular huntsman warmly by the hand and greeted his portly wife. 'It's most kind of you to look after my men.'

''Tis a pleasure, Captain Andrew,' Mrs Marsh replied. 'We're enjoying hearing about our Jo. Trooper Fisher here is his best friend. He saved his life they tell me.' The large comfortable woman beamed at Shrimp.

'Who'd have thought we'd be home before 'im, sir?' said Shrimp. 'Do you think he'll arrive back while we're 'ere?'

Andrew looked at Mrs. Marsh, who replied, 'He's in a military hospital near London. He'll be home before long'.

'How's he getting on?' asked Andrew.

'He's walking on crutches at the moment. He says he can't wait to get on a horse.'

'Good, good.' Andrew smiled. 'By the way, you all have ten days' leave, so I suggest you make plans about visiting your own homes. Marsh, do you have a copy of the railway timetable?'

'I do, sir.

Andrew turned back to the grinning men. 'Sort out your journeys and feel free to come to the servants' hall after dinner. You may all use the telephone in the butler's pantry to ring or to send telegrams to your families.'

160

***

Andrew, his parents and his sister sat down to dinner in the large dining room. The discussion was all about the war until Caroline suddenly asked, 'What happened to Francine?'

Andrew looked sharply at his mother, who replied, 'We don't know exactly'.

'How's she settling in?' Andrew asked anxiously.

'She… she felt more the thing after a bath and a change of clothes.' Lady Hawkenfield paused. 'She's such a beautiful creature. She reminds me of a wounded gazelle.'

'Shall I visit her after dinner?'

'No.' His mother was adamant. 'She wants to sleep, she's still very sore, you know. I… I believe it hurts her to talk.'

'Can I visit her? I could practise my French,' Caroline enquired.

'In a day or two,' replied Lady Hawkenfield.

'That would set the poor girl back, if she had to listen to your dreadful accent,' Andrew laughed. 'Anyway, she speaks very good English.'

'My accent is better than yours,' retorted Caroline, who adored her older brother. 'Miss Pettigrew told me.'

Miss Pettigrew was the semi-retired governess. 'Old Petters probably wants to keep her job,' Andrew chuckled.

'Really, Andrew you shouldn't talk about her like that; she was an excellent governess and she now helps with the flower arrangements in the house and a number of other things. She's very useful to me.' Lady Hawkenfield smiled. 'I'm sure she's right about Caroline's French accent.'

'You see,' remarked Caroline laughing. 'We'll put it to the test with a real French lady.'

'We'll leave the gentlemen to their Port.' Lady Hawkenfield rose gracefully from the table and, followed by her daughter, left the dining room.

'Was she raped?' asked Lord Hawkenfield.

'I think so,' replied Andrew. 'She wouldn't tell me.'

'Tragic for a girl in her position. No French aristocrat will want her for a wife now. The English won't either for that matter. What if she's pregnant?'

Andrew shuddered. 'Father, let's not jump to any conclusions until we hear exactly what did happen. Maybe she was…' He couldn't finish the sentence.

'Well your mother will find out, I shouldn't wonder. She seems to have taken a liking to the girl. Like a terrier with a rabbit, your mother, once she has a bee in her bonnet.'

Andrew turned the conversation back to the war and brought out his notes about the two English traitors.

***

Later, when Lord Hawkenfield retired to his study, Andrew went upstairs to find his mother in her sitting room. He knocked and put his head round the door.

'Here's Andrew,' Caroline cried joyfully.

'Come in and sit down.' His mother smiled fondly at her second son. He sat with his legs stretched out in front of him and watched the fire crackling in the elegant grate. 'I asked Walker to have it lit. I know it's only September, but the nights are chilly and it cheers the room, don't you think?'

'Yes, I love an open fire.' Andrew smiled affectionately at his mother.

'Caroline, it's time for bed,' announced Lady Hawkenfield.

'That's not fair. I've hardly seen Andrew since he got back.' The pretty teenager pouted.

'Sulking doesn't become you,' Andrew told his sister. 'I'll go riding with you tomorrow morning. How does that suit you?'

The girl smiled and tossed her light-coloured hair. She had the same deep blue eyes as her brother and they sparkled as she said, 'I'll show you my new mare. She's the best horse I've ever ridden'.

'I'll look forward to that.' Andrew kissed her. As soon as she left the room, he said 'I hope the army won't take her new horse'.

'Your father assures me that they won't.' His mother's face grew grave. 'Tell me what it's really like in France.'

'Mother, you know Father wouldn't like...'

'Darling, Father isn't in the room and you know my propensity to... to predict certain things.'

'I know and he doesn't like that either.'

'Well, as I said, he's not here, so please enlighten me. I know things aren't exactly as they're being reported. I have dreadful forebodings. The Germans have got us on the run, the powers-that-be are telling us it'll all be over in a jiffy. I believe it'll take much longer.'

'I think you're probably right.'

'I'm sure that you, too, have doubts. So please tell me what they are.'

'Von Meyer called you a witch.' Andrew gave a short laugh.

'Dear Heinrich. I worry for him. He saved your life and that makes me forever grateful. Please go on.'

Andrew smiled. 'You're clearly going to pester me until I do. This is not something I would say to anyone else, in fact I have forbidden the men to speak about our experiences in France. But... you may have more insight into the situation than I do.'

'Darling, I keep my views very much to myself, you know that.'

Andrew's face became serious. 'Well, I saw the might of the German Army as they moved some of their forces into France.' He paused, looked into the fire, then back at Lady Hawkenfield. 'Mother it was frightening. They're not the frenetic, baby-torturing monsters that we're led to believe. They are a disciplined, organised and intelligent fighting machine. They're like us. Kaiser Wilhelm II may be a power-hungry megalomaniac, but their everyday soldier is very similar to our everyday soldier.'

'What you say is interesting. Listen to this article.' Lady Hawkenfield leant over and picked up a magazine that was lying on the table. She flicked through it, saying, 'Here it is.' She read, *'We began to fight because our honour and our pledge obliged us. No power in the world would have respected our flag or accepted our national word again if we had not done so,* which of course is true because of our Treaty with Belgium. The writer goes on to say *although we are fighting Germany, we are fighting without any hatred of the German people. We do not intend to destroy either their freedom or their unity. But we have to destroy an evil system of government.'*

'Noble words, Mother; let's hope we don't lose sight of that sentiment.'

'I hope so too.' She paused and put the magazine down. 'Now tell me about the beautiful young French girl.'

Andrew stared into the fire. 'Francine has changed. Whatever it was that happened to her has altered her out of all recognition.'

'I'll find out what's bothering her.' There was a discreet tap on the door. 'Come in, Walker,' called Lady Hawkenfield. 'I see you've brought the tea tray.'

The butler deftly deposited the tray on the table by the fire and said, 'The men have all completed their travel arrangements for tomorrow, Captain Andrew'.

'Good, good. Thank you, Walker.' The butler left the room.

'Oh, I forgot to say. Lady Williams is driving over to pick up young Anthony. I do feel embarrassed at leaving him with Marsh. I'm sure he should be with us, in the house.'

'No, Mother. He isn't an officer. He must stay with his contemporaries.'

'But they aren't his contemporaries, are they?'

'Well, they are now. He chose to join up as a trooper. He must abide by his decision. Anyway, you would be doing him a great disfavour by inviting him in. He gets on very well with the men and he's useful to me. He'll become an officer before too long, don't worry.'

'But what will I say to his mother?'

'Nothing. I'm sure she feels awkward about it too, but there it is. One can't run with the hare and hunt with the hounds.'

His mother sighed and picked up a small black, leather-bound book. 'I would like to give you this book of poems. I think you'll enjoy them. There are poems for all sorts of occasions.' Lady Hawkenfield paused. 'When you're feeling lonely, I think they'll bring you comfort.'

'Lonely?' Andrew was curious.

'Yes, I'm sure there are times when you feel the burden of leadership. Most great men do, you know.'

Andrew smiled. 'Yes, Father mentioned it to me before I left for France. I do actually know what you mean, although I'm not a great man.'

'Nonsense, you're an officer, a leader and your men trust you. You're in a position of responsibility and as such you'll find yourself in situations that are difficult. It takes a strong person to abide by what they think is right, especially when they have pressure from other directions. Those may be the times when you'll be torn and forced to make decisions that you would rather not make. In your quieter moments you may feel, well... alone. I want you to know that we are all behind you, some of the poems may help you and our love will support you.'

Andrew swallowed and flicked slowly through the pages of the book. 'You really are uncanny; you know just what I'm thinking, don't you?'

'You're my son. It would be odd if I didn't.'

'No, it wouldn't. I'm lucky to have a mother like you, many thousands of men don't. I'll remember your words.' He slipped the little book inside his jacket.

CHAPTER FOURTEEN

A Taste of Honey

The next morning as the family ate breakfast there was a knock on the dining room door. An upstairs maid entered the room.

'Beg pardon, me lord, me lady.' She bobbed a curtsy. 'The Mamselle is taken bad. Nanny said to fetch you, if you please, me lady.'

'Certainly, Lily. I'll come at once.' Lady Hawkenfield stood up. 'Excuse me, my dear.'

Her husband glanced up from behind *The Times* and nodded. 'Look after her well, Adeline. Call Dr. Standsfold at once if necessary.'

'Of course, Arthur.' Andrew looked up anxiously as his mother left the room.

'Good Lord,' exclaimed Lord Hawkenfield.

Andrew jumped. 'What is it?'

'General Littlejohn. He's blown his brains out!'

'Good heavens. When?'

'Yesterday. At his home in Berkshire.'

'How dreadful. His poor wife and family, although...'

'Quite so.' Lord Hawkenfield lifted his head and listened to a motorcycle scrunching on the driveway. 'A dispatch rider. Come to my study.'

'Don't forget you're going to ride with me later,' Caroline said anxiously.

'Of course not,' replied her brother. The two men withdrew.

'I thought you might be interested to know we've just won a battle in France at a village called Néry. Weren't you near there?' Lord Hawkenfield sat down at his desk.

'I don't know. I've never heard of it.'

'It's somewhere close to Verberie, which is between Compiègne and Senlis.'

'Yes, of course. I was supposed to take Francine there.'

'Good job you didn't. There was quite a battle, but luckily we won. Listen to this.' Lord Hawkenfield began to read from his dispatches, 'General von Kluck, commanding the German First Army, has made a fundamental change to the Schlieffen Plan. Instead of continuing in a south-westerly direction and encircling Paris, he's marching southeast. He's attempting to deal with the BEF and to catch the flank of General Lanrezac's Fifth Army, which has escaped across the river Oise. As a result of this, his advance elements caught up with the British on the morning of 1st September 1914 at Néry, a small village in the department of the Oise.

'Néry was chosen as a bivouac point for a large number of the BEF, including No. 1 Cavalry Brigade and the artillery. In all there were two hundred horses and six 13 pounder guns.' Lord Hawkenfield paused and then continued in his own words.

'On the morning in question, a young second lieutenant of the 11th Hussars was sent out on patrol at 4.15 a.m. in thick fog. He caught up with some dismounted Uhlans, who seemed to be lost. His scout saw one and unfortunately fired, thinking him to be an isolated rider. The Germans hastily mounted and charged and the British patrol retreated fast. When they returned to camp, the CO believed the patrol had mistaken the Germans for French Cuirassiers.

'However, one of the Uhlans, staying in a cottage overnight, left in such a hurry that he dropped his cloak. A member of the British patrol picked it up and this persuaded the CO that the riders were indeed Germans.

'In fact, there were a vast number of enemy soldiers, including infantry and twelve heavy artillery guns bivouacking just across a ravine, under a mile as the crow flies from the British camp. They were all camouflaged by the heavy, early morning mist.

'The British patrol had, unfortunately, alerted the Germans to their presence. A fierce battle ensued which we were lucky to win. It all goes to show that we British are always good when we're outnumbered. Then we fight with sheer guts and willpower. If von Kluck has changed the Schlieffen Plan… well, I can only see that as good news.'

'Yes, I agree with you.'

There was a discreet knock on the door and Walker entered the room. 'Her ladyship would like to see Captain Andrew, my lord, as soon as it's convenient.'

'Certainly, we've finished for the moment. Andrew, you'd better go.'

'Thank you for that information, Father. It was most interesting.'

Andrew found his mother sitting at her bureau looking troubled.
'What's wrong with Francine?' Andrew asked.
'She has a raging fever and is in a lot of pain.'
'May I see her?'

'No, darling. She's delirious and slipping in and out of consciousness.'

'Oh, my Lord. What did the doctor say?'

'He's prescribed various things. We're to stay with her at all times. Marie-Claude and Nanny are with her at the moment and I'll relieve them later with Miss Pettigrew.'

'Mother, you mustn't endanger yourself.'

'No, it's all right. Dr. Stansfold says she has an infection picked up from the rats in that dreadful place.'

'What's his prognosis?'

'He says that because Francine is a fit young woman, her chances are good. He... he was quite optimistic.'

Andrew stared out of the window. 'It's my fault, that's why she hates me. I should have forbidden her to meet me that night.'

'Darling, don't be silly. The Germans would have captured her anyway, and without you to rescue her, well... At least here she'll have the best of care.'

'Yes, I know, that's why I brought her. Are you sure there's nothing I can do?'

'No, you go riding with Caroline.' Andrew hesitated. 'Please darling, it will give her so much pleasure.'

***

Andrew found Caroline at the stables, deep in conversation with Williams.

'Anthony says the others have all gone to the railway station. Lady Williams is coming here to pick him up later.'

'Yes, I know,' replied Andrew.

'Can he ride with us?'

Andrew sighed. 'I don't see why not.' *At least Mother would approve*, he thought.

The three set off around the park.

'Do you like my mare?' asked Caroline. 'Anthony thinks she's first class.'

'Yes, she's very pretty.' Andrew looked at the dancing chestnut with four white socks and a broad white blaze.

'She looks like Clark's French horse, only the rider is more accomplished,' remarked Williams.

'Yes, I must say Carro, your seat has improved. You look almost elegant.' Andrew was surprised that his sister, now seventeen, looked like a lady and rode beautifully.

Caroline tossed her head. 'Race you to the end of the park.' She kicked her horse forward and set off at a gallop, jumping a fallen tree along the way. The two men caught up with her at the park railings. For an awful moment Andrew thought she was going to jump them too.

'Oh, I have jumped them.' She laughed at the look on her brother's face. 'She's going to be a wonderful hunter, don't you think?'

'Yes, I do. I only hope Father keeps you under control.' He hoped that Francine wouldn't encourage her to ride astride and shuddered at the thought of them hunting together. However, he admitted to himself that he would be glad if the French girl recovered her zest for life.

They rode home quietly. Andrew dropped in behind the others, deep in thought. When he entered the house he found the place in turmoil. Maids were running up the front stairs carrying basins, towels and jugs of water.

'What on earth's going on?' he asked.

'Mamselle's in a terrible state, I think she's going to die,' Lily blurted out.

'Nonsense, and hurry up with that water.' Miss Pettigrew passed her on the stairs. 'I'm calling the doctor again, Captain Andrew.' She hurried away.

Andrew mounted the stairs two at a time and burst into Francine's room without knocking. She was burning up, soaked in sweat and shivering. She tossed and turned so much that Lady Hawkenfield and Nanny could only stand on either side of the bed trying to stop her from falling out. All the time Francine was shouting in French.

Andrew beckoned to Marie-Claude and told her to bathe the invalid's face, neck and shoulders with cold water. Lady Hawkenfield tried to make her take the solution that Dr. Standsfold had left. Francine swung her head from side to side so violently that she knocked the liquid out of her ladyship's hand.

Andrew, as if he were drenching a horse, clasped Francine's head with one hand and opened her mouth with the other. He told Nanny to place a spoonful of liquid in her mouth. He held her firm until she swallowed. 'One more, Nanny.'

'Master Andrew, I really think one is enough. The doctor said...'

'Another spoonful, Nanny, now,' barked Andrew. The large woman hastily poured another dose. Andrew repeated the performance, holding Francine's mouth tight shut until the medicine went down.

'Andrew, she might have choked.' His mother was shocked.

'But she didn't,' he replied. He released the girl's head and stroked her damp dark hair, again as if she were a horse. Slowly the agitated tossing and turning began to subside and Francine fell into a fitful sleep.

Doctor Standsfold arrived shortly and immediately sent Andrew out of the room. The captain wandered aimlessly up and down the corridor until the doctor eventually emerged from the sick-room.

'While she was sleeping I was able to examine her well. I've left instructions with your mother and some more sleeping powders. She now needs good nursing while we wait for the fever to run its course.' Andrew escorted the doctor to his car. 'Don't hesitate to call me again if you are at all worried, or if there is a dramatic change in her condition. I've told your mother what to expect. I hold out a lot of hope for this patient, she's healthy and strong. However, it's her mental state that I worry about. I don't speak French fluently, but I did understand some of what she's saying. I don't like it, and her little maid looks terrified.'

'Yes, I've heard her shouting, but I'm confident that my mother and I will be able to reassure her on some of the dreadful things that are playing on her mind.'

'I certainly hope so.' The doctor got into his car and drove away.

***

Francine's condition improved, but Andrew was still not permitted to visit her. He didn't know if it was on his mother's instructions or whether it was because she didn't want to see him. He was shaken when two days later a pony and trap turned up carrying the local midwife.

'Is Francine worse? Why have you sent for Mrs. Church?' Andrew stopped his mother in the hallway.

'I don't entirely trust a man in women's matters, even if he is a doctor. Mrs. Church is far more knowledgeable.'

'Mother!'

'Darling, being a gentleman, you couldn't possibly understand.'

'Do you think you should meddle?'

'I'm not meddling; that poor child thinks she's worthless. She wants to kill herself. She feels that she can no longer face her father and her family. You've heard her railing and shouting. Don't you think she needs a little reassurance and help?'

'Well… yes, but how can you do that? It seems pretty clear cut to me. She was obviously raped. Please God she's not pregnant.'

'Oh really Andrew, that's exactly why I've brought in Mrs. Church. It's probably best that you don't think too much about it. As I said, women's matters… never really understood by gentlemen.' She hurried on up the stairs with the midwife.

Francine was sitting up in bed leaning heavily against a bank of pillows when Lady Hawkenfield and Mrs. Church entered her bedroom.

'Well, my dear, how are you feeling?'

Francine smiled; she felt drawn to the elegant English lady and very comfortable in her company. She replied, 'I feel a lot better, thank you Madame'.

'Your bruises are fading.' Lady Hawkenfield gently ran her hand down the pretty face. 'This is Mrs. Church, she's a midwife.'

Francine looked in horror at the kindly woman, and with trepidation at the bag she was carrying. 'You think I'm *enceinte!*' She spat out the word. 'I'm a Roman Catholic, *Madame*. I cannot destroy a life that is growing inside me.' She screwed up her face in disgust. 'Although it is spawned by the devil, I will not add a mortal sin to the burden that I'm already carrying. I have to bear the shame, I know that. I can't understand why you allow me in your house and why you're being so kind.' She turned her head away so that Lady Hawkenfield couldn't see her tears.

Her ladyship spoke gently. 'My dear, you mustn't say that, let alone think it. It's not your fault. Perhaps if you could you tell us what happened, you might feel a little better.' Francine said nothing. Adeline Hawkenfield smiled kindly. 'My dear, I speak French well enough to understand what you were saying when you were delirious.' Francine blushed. 'Please trust me, I have had children. Mrs. Church delivered them. In fact, Mrs. Church has delivered most of the village, including their mothers and fathers as well, so there's no need for you to feel embarrassed. I can assure you that nothing you say will be repeated outside these four walls.'

Francine shut her eyes. She did feel the need to confide in someone: her own mother had died several years ago. Mrs. Church seemed a kindly sensible woman and reminded her of her childhood nanny. She would have confided in her. She opened her eyes and looked at the tall slim elegant lady and the short comfortable figure of the midwife. She made up her mind, sighed and took a deep breath. Very slowly she started to relate what had happened in the foul-smelling dungeon cell.

She was nearly at the end of her story when she shuddered and stopped. Her tears fell unchecked down her face. Lady Hawkenfield was having difficulty in holding back her own tears. She held Francine's hand and patiently waited for her to continue.

Francine swallowed. 'I thought he was dead,' she whispered. 'But he wasn't. Then he left.' Lady Hawkenfield stood up, walked to the window and stared sightlessly through misty eyes at the great lake, not wanting either woman to see the look of anguish and horror on her face.

Francine, mistaking her ladyship's reaction for revulsion, said, 'You're right to be disgusted; as you see I am now beneath contempt'.

Adeline Hawkenfield swung round and hurried back to the bedside. She picked up Francine's hand again. 'No, of course I'm not disgusted. Not with you at any rate, but with that dreadful German; it is *he* who is beneath contempt. I think it best to keep this to ourselves. Gentlemen don't understand these things. We'll say that you have been horribly assaulted by this fiend of a man and that neither you, nor I, wish to discuss it any further.'

'You're trying to protect me, *Madame*. You know what happened and you know how any gentleman will react. I cannot live a lie for the rest of my life.'

'My dear, I think gentlemen are very stupid in these cases. You must understand that there is one rule for the male sex and quite another for the female. I cringe with disgust when I see or hear of innocent young servant girls being taken advantage of by the males of the household. If they become with child then they are thrown out on the streets to fend for themselves. Most of them end up in the workhouse. Some have to earn a living as…' she paused and whispered, 'harlots.'

Francine gasped, 'And what if I am with child?'

Mrs. Church smiled kindly down at her. 'I think that is unlikely, but we'll have to wait a few weeks to be sure.'

Francine stared in horror at the two women. 'My dear, we'll cross that bridge when, and if, we come to it,' replied Lady Hawkenfield. Francine clutched her stomach, her face contorted into a grimace.

'Are you in pain?' asked Mrs. Church.

'Yes.' The girl whispered.

'I have some remedies for you.' Mrs. Church brought herbs out from her capacious bag. 'Perhaps her ladyship will have these made up into a tea. Comfrey and plantain to heal you, you must drink it. Also you must wash yourself with a solution as well. It will help to heal you inside.

Here is some meadowsweet for the pain and St, John's Wort to make you feel happier.'

'I will take nothing to harm the baby. Although I hate it, I will not kill it.'

'There's nothing amongst my remedies that will hurt an unborn baby.'

'Francine, you can safely take what Mrs. Church has given you. I too would not destroy a human life,' Lady Hawkenfield assured her. 'If you prove to be pregnant, you can go and stay with an old family retainer who is discretion itself. When the baby is born it will be taken away and you will never have to see it. Please stop worrying on that score. I'm sure it won't come to that.'

Francine shuddered. 'You're being very kind. I don't deserve it.'

'Well, I think you do.' Lady Hawkenfield smiled down at her.

***

As soon as Mrs. Church drove away, Andrew went to find his mother. He tracked her down in the drawing room with Miss Pettigrew. They were admiring an arrangement of roses that the governess had picked from the garden.

'Aren't they just gorgeous?' said his mother, as Andrew entered the room. 'They smell utterly divine.'

'Yes, exquisite,' he answered.

'Thank you Miss Pettigrew, you have excelled yourself. Hasn't she, Andrew?'

'Absolutely.'

'Captain Andrew, you're too kind,' Miss Pettigrew simpered and left the room. Lady Hawkenfield turned back to the roses.

'Mother,' snapped Andrew.

'Yes, dear, what is it?'

'You know what.'

She took hold of his hand. 'All is well. The poor girl has had a terrible ordeal and now it's over.'

'But is she pregnant?'

'Andrew, Francine has had an appalling experience and we want to forget all about it; please don't mention it again. Why on earth would she be pregnant? That is too ridiculous for words.' Lady Hawkenfield hoped that Andrew hadn't noticed her crossed fingers. 'You may go and sit with her for a little while before dinner, but please don't tire her.'

When Andrew entered Francine's bedroom he was surprised to find her dressed and seated in an armchair. He thought she looked pale but still very beautiful. The bruises on her face had subsided into feint yellow marks. He was pleased to see that she looked straight at him as he walked across the room. That was the first time she had made eye contact with him since her rescue. She allowed him to take her hand briefly and then adroitly turned in her chair and indicated that he should sit opposite her.

'I'm delighted to see you looking so well.' He sat down.

'I must thank you for rescuing me and bringing me here to your beautiful house and charming family.' Francine's speech was stilted. 'I'm very much in your debt.'

'It was a pleasure.' She gave him a brief smile and shook her head. Andrew continued hurriedly: 'It was an adventure and one that I'm proud to have been part of'.

'You are very gallant, *Capitaine*.' There was an awkward pause.

'Francine, I want to apologise for my behaviour, in the château when…'

She turned her head away. 'Please don't.'

'I…. I feel responsible for your capture. I will try to make it up to you.'

'*Capitaine*, please…' She changed the subject. 'Please tell me about your beautiful house. I'm sure it's steeped in history.'

'Well, the park was landscaped by Capability Brown in the 18th century. But long before that it was a Cavalier stronghold and was nearly burnt to the ground by the Roundheads. There's a story that King Charles II himself hid here…' Andrew carried on talking about his much-loved home, although he felt that Francine was feigning her interest.

He breathed a silent sigh of relief when a gong sounded. 'Oh my goodness, that's the dressing gong. I didn't realise it was so late. Will you be dinning downstairs with us?'

'No, I thank you. Not tonight, maybe tomorrow.'

'May I visit you again tomorrow?'

'*Capitaine*, it is your house. I'm sure you can do what you want.'

'Yes, quite.' Andrew smiled. He wished she wouldn't call him *Capitaine*. He withdrew saying, '*Bon soir, à demain*'.

'*Bon soirée.*' She gave a hint of a smile.

***

The remaining days of Andrew's leave passed quickly. Francine joined the family for meals and Andrew proudly showed her the grounds, the horses and the diminished pack of hounds.

While she was in the kennels she began to unbend and ask questions about the hounds. She forgot herself as she admired Lord Hawkenfield's hunters. She even expressed a desire to ride one of them.

'That's his Lordship's four year old. He's just been broken. He'll only do a little hunting this year,' explained Marsh, the huntsman. 'I don't think he would be suitable for a lady to ride.'

'I can assure you, Marsh, Mademoiselle Francine would be able to ride him. She's a most accomplished horsewoman.' Andrew spoke without thinking. He was rewarded by a dazzling smile from Francine. He smiled affectionately back.

As they were returning to the house, engrossed in a conversation about the horses, they encountered Lord Hawkenfield. Francine visibly stiffened and moved further away from Andrew. She nodded to her host and hurried up the steps into the hallway.

'Andrew.' Lord Hawkenfield coughed. 'A word please.' Andrew joined him for a stroll in the garden. 'My boy, I can see that you're very taken with the French girl.' He paused. 'She's a pretty little thing and she has charming manners. But she's not.... How can I put it...?' Andrew gave him no help. 'Well she's not a ...' His father paused again.

'Not what, Father?'

'My boy, she's not the sort of girl I would be happy to welcome as a daughter-in-law.'

Andrew felt annoyed. He asked guilelessly, 'Why ever not? She's well-born and I believe from a very wealthy family. As you say yourself, she has beautiful manners.' He paused. 'Although at present I have no desire to make her your daughter-in-law.'

'Excellent. Your mother and I thought that maybe you had taken a strong liking to her. She won't do, Andrew. Not now she's no longer... You must see that. To have a wife who has been, how can I put it...? Well, tarnished, it won't do at all. You wouldn't want that. You do see what I mean, don't you?'

Andrew looked at his father. He didn't know whether to laugh or to be angry. 'Father, I know exactly what you mean.'

'Good boy, I knew you would.' Lord Hawkenfield walked away leaving Andrew staring after him.

***

After dinner that night Bertram rang to speak to his brother. He told him that he would be going to France shortly. 'I'm having some leave first, but I believe you'll be gone by then.' He went on to ask some questions about the war. Andrew told him a little and then said, 'I don't think we should discuss this over the telephone, you never know who's listening. I've told Father the salient facts'.

'You're right, old boy. I'll look forward to bumping into you over there. Give my love to Mother and tell her I'll be down the day after tomorrow.'

Andrew found Lady Hawkenfield alone in her sitting room.

'What is it, Mother? You seem to be very pensive.'

'I'm worried about that poor girl. Her state of mind, you know. She saw her mother in her room.'

'Her mother's dead, what are you talking about?'

'Exactly; people who are close to passing away sometimes see their relatives who have already passed on.'

'You're not suggesting that Francine's going to die?' Andrew was horrified.

'No. Not at all, that's just it.'

'Then what are you saying, Mother? Excuse me for my stupidly, but you're not making any sense.'

'I don't know, Andrew, only that she's a very troubled young lady. Her mother must have been there to comfort her.'

'Her mother has passed on,' Andrew repeated. 'She couldn't possibly be in the room.'

'She seemed very real to Francine.'

'I hope you didn't encourage her in that line of thinking. She might be going mad.'

'Really Andrew, of course she's not going mad. People under extreme stress sometimes see... odd things.' His mother was affronted.

'Yes, if they're in Bedlam.'

'I'm not going to discuss it with you any further if you're going to take that attitude.'

Andrew picked up her hand and carried it to his lips. 'It's a good thing I know you so well. I believe you; that in some circumstances people can act very strangely. By the way, Father has warned me off.'

'Yes, I thought he would. You must make up your own mind. As far as I'm concerned I grow fonder of the girl as each day passes. She's honest and honourable and someone who I would be proud to welcome into the family.'

'I have no thought of marriage at the moment. Times are too uncertain. Anyway, Francine doesn't like me very much, so the matter doesn't even come under consideration.'

'She likes you more than you think,' remarked Lady Hawkenfield quietly.

Andrew quickly changed the subject and he told his mother about the phone call from his brother.

'Dear Bertram, it'll be lovely to have him home, especially with you going away tomorrow. I have so enjoyed having you here. It's been like a taste of honey.' She smiled fondly at her son.

'Yes, it has for me too. It's been a wonderful break. Though, funnily enough, I'm looking forward to going back to France. I can't think why.'

'I expect your men need you.'

'Yes, I like to think so.'

His mother smiled sadly. 'Lady Williams is bringing Anthony here first thing in the morning. Your train leaves at 11 o'clock, I believe?'

'Yes it does. Take good care of yourself and Father while I'm away. You look so down. It's not like you.'

'This dreadful war. One or two people in the village have lost their sons. I feel that this is just the start of it.' She sighed and managed a weak smile. 'But we must grit our teeth and get on with things. That's the British way.'

'It is indeed.' He smiled at her. She put her hand on top of his and gave it a squeeze.

There was a discreet tap on the door and Marie-Claude entered the room. 'Excuse me, my lady, but *Mademoiselle* would like to see the *Capitaine.*'

'*Capitaine.*' Francine stood up as Andrew entered the room. 'I wish to say goodbye and thank you.' Before Andrew could say anything, she continued: 'I want you to know how much I am in your debt. I'll always be thankful for what you've done. I may not have been very *gentille* with you. I apologise for that'.

'Francine, there is no need...'

'I'm very grateful to your mother. I think your father... but never mind that. I envy you returning to my beautiful country that is being destroyed by *les sales Boches*. I have to stay here for a little while. I will return, whether it is within weeks or months. When I go back I'll cause as much trouble to the Boches as I can.'

Andrew was taken aback by the ferocity with which she spoke. He was pleased to see that she had recovered her spirit but he was anxious that it was turning into such hatred. 'What do you mean?'

'I will become a spy, of course.'

Andrew recoiled. 'Do you think that's wise? I mean... You could be captured again. It would be very dangerous.'

'I told you once; danger and I are becoming old friends. I fear nothing now. The Boches have taken a part of me away, I can never have that back. I have nothing to lose. Now please go and fight for my beloved country.'

Andrew shook her hand. *'Au revoir.'* Without thinking he added, 'I'll write and let you know how the war's going'.

'Thank you. It'll be good to hear from a soldier who's fighting at the front. Godspeed.' She smiled warmly.

He left the room feeling shaken. When he returned to his mother's sitting room the tea tray was waiting for him.

'How was Francine?' asked his mother.

'I... I don't know. She's recovered her old spirit, but she has become very militant. She said something about maybe staying for months in England. Why would she do that?'

'I have no idea.' Lady Hawkenfield looked away.

'Mother, what do you know?'

'Nothing. Francine hasn't told me of her plans,' she answered truthfully. 'Now drink your tea before it grows cold.'

CHAPTER FIFTEEN

Reunions

The atmosphere on the crowded troop train was one of excited anticipation as it headed towards the front line. The BEF had begun to advance north and eastwards, pushing the Germans back.

The long train stopped now and then to fill up the two steam engines with water. The men were able to stretch their legs, although it was raining hard. During one of these stops Williams saw Andrew on the platform and took the opportunity of explaining that Shrimp was riding in a wagon of horses at the end of the train.

'What on earth is he doing there? Our horses are further up.'

'A horse in the wagon at the back of the train went berserk; nobody could do anything with it. It couldn't cope with the noise of the rear steam engine. They wanted to shoot it apparently, but it belongs to a Colonel. His favourite hunter.'

'All right, as long as Fisher doesn't want to adopt the wretched animal when we reach our destination,' replied Andrew.

'No. I don't think so.' Williams grinned. 'The Colonel's own groom will be waiting for the horse at the end of the line.'

The journey seemed to be interminable. The men looked out of the misty window, trying to see between the rivulets of water which ran down the dirty panes of glass.

'This bloody wet weather,' remarked Turner 65. 'Last time it was too hot to move and now it hasn't stopped raining since we landed in France.'

The train shuddered to another halt. This time the NCOs shouted the order to disembark. The carriage doors opened and hundreds of soldiers spilled out on to the low platform. Men jostled one another trying to find their units.

Andrew, catching sight of the Turner twins' heads above the others, found his Squadron. 'What a scrimmage,' he remarked. 'Turner 65 and Williams go and find Fisher and locate our horses. Come back for the rest of the men when you're ready to unload.'

The two men made their way along the platform until they came to the horse wagons.

'These are ours,' said Williams.

'Load of donkeys.' 65 looked in the wagon. 'They've sent us the dregs. Where's that bloody Shrimp?'

'Listen.' Williams heard the familiar cockney voice ringing out further down the train.

'You've got to go and get one of them ramps. The 'orses ain't going to jump down from the train without breaking their bleedin' legs.'

'I ain't taking no orders from some jumped up, donkey walloping trooper,' a private soldier yelled back.

Williams stood to one side and shouted in his upper crust accent. 'What's going on here? Do as the man says.'

The private jumped out of the train and looked around for an officer. He didn't see one, but he yelled to some soldiers who were milling around. 'Get that ramp, the h'officer wants to unload 'is 'orses.'

Shrimp popped his head through the open doors of the wagon. 'Well done, Williams. Come and look at these horses.'

'They look good. Better than some of the rubbish that has been consigned to us. Who do they belong to?' asked Williams.

'I dunno, the British Army. I think they're for officers in the Infantry.'

'Are you sure they aren't privately owned?'

'Only those two at the end of the wagon. That one belongs to a colonel and the other one belongs to some major. The lads told me. But the others have just come over from Ireland and don't belong to no one in particular.'

'Well they do now,' said 65. 'We'll have 'em.'

'Good idea. We'll take these eight and replace them with our horses,' agreed Williams. 'Do you think the plant life will notice?'

'Na. They don't know one end of an 'orse from the other,' said Shrimp.

'I hope they're broken in.'

''Course they're broken. The cannon fodder couldn't do nothin' wiv 'em, else.'

A short, slight soldier with one stripe on his arm strutted up. 'I've come for the colonel's horse. I hope he travelled well, Trooper. You'll be for it if he's damaged.'

'I think you'll find he's in perfect condition, thanks to my soldier here,' said Williams.

The arrogant little man glared at Williams. He opened his mouth to say something, when Turner 65 said, 'Yeah, so take your fucking horse and bugger off'.

'Don't speak to me like that. Who are you?' The little man looked belligerent as 65 bore down on him.

'Never mind who we are; more to the point who are you?' asked Williams.

'I'm Colonel Haven's groom.' The man entered the wagon and located his horse at the back. 'Get them other horses shifted so that I can get mine out, and the one next to him. That belongs to the major.'

'Right you are.' Shrimp grinned.

'And what would you like us to do with the others?' Williams asked.

'Just get them out of my way. Tie them up to the fence over there, someone from the Infantry will come and fetch them. You lot,' he shouted to the soldiers struggling with the ramp, 'hurry up.'

The three cavalrymen led their new mounts off the train and into the crowd of unloading horses and shouting men.

'Where's the captain?' asked Williams.

'Can't see him,' replied 65. 'But them recruits are still standing over there like a bunch of lost sheep. How are we going to fight a war with them dozy lot?'

'Over here, at the double,' Williams shouted as they ambled across the busy platform. 'Come with us and collect the rest of our horses.'

'Steady on. It's me what gives the orders around here,' snapped an aging sergeant. He had arrived in their squadron with the new troopers.

'Sorry, Sergeant, just wanted to give you a hand,' said Williams. 'Didn't see you there.'

'Hmm. Carry on. Take them horses up the platform and fetch the others. Here are the papers.'

'Thanks, Sarg.' Williams turned back to Shrimp and said quietly, 'Now I have the paperwork we'll sort out eight look-alikes and change them. We can match them up against the others. None of these Irish horses have any identification marks. By the time we're on the road no one will notice.'

The three men found eight cavalry horses that either looked lame or were small, but who matched the Irish horses in colour and white markings.

Shrimp and Turner 65 were tying the horses to a fence when two officers arrived.

'What are you doing with our horses, Trooper?'

65 saluted. 'The colonel's groom told me to tie them up here, sir. I hope they're to your satisfaction. One of our best men travelled with them.'

'Thank you. That's what we like to see, co-operation between the different regiments.'

'Glad to be of service, sir.'

The troopers hurried away, but not before they heard the two officers exclaim, 'Good God, these look pretty ropey'.

'I thought they were sending us some decent hunters. Can't see these buggers galloping, let alone jumping.'

'Galloping? I doubt if they'll keep up with the marching men. Where have those damned troopers gone?'

'Keep your head down, 65.' Shrimp laughed as they watched the two officers study the paperwork.

'Well, the descriptions fit. They've got to be ours,' said one of them.

'That bugger is resting his foreleg and looks lame, and this one has a great chunk missing from her forearm. God, what a disappointment. I'll have someone's guts for garters sending us rubbish like this.'

65 and Shrimp couldn't wait to tell Williams what the two officers had said. 'We'll get the farrier to brand these horses' hooves as soon as possible. Then there'll be no argument. Well done, Shrimp,' said Williams. 'We've got ourselves some nice horses. The captain's over there.'

Andrew watched the horses approaching. 'Some of these horses look pretty good, better than I remember them when they were loaded,' he said, tongue in cheek, to Shrimp.

'Yes, they have travelled well, haven't they, sir. Shall we get them saddled up? I thought you would like this one. Is it all right if Williams, the Turners and I take one each of these eight?' Andrew looked at the horses and then at the deadpan faces of the troopers. 'And I suppose you would like Pilson and Clark to have one each of the well-travelled horses, as well, Fisher?'

'That would be nice, sir.'

'Did the colonel collect his horses? I would hate to cause any confusion.'

'Oh yes. His groom collected them. Rather a cocky little so-and-so, if I may say, sir,' replied Shrimp.

'That was Joe Brown... you know, the jockey,' Williams joined in.

'Oh, really.' Andrew paused. 'I think I know the colonel in

question... Infantry Regiment, owns some bloodstock. Haven, I believe his name is.'

'That's right, sir,' said Shrimp.

Quite a... how shall I put it... a force to be reckoned with on the Turf,' remarked Andrew.

'Yes, I believe he had some controversial losers,' Williams agreed.

Once mounted, Andrew assembled his squadron. He had to wait for a battery to clatter past and then led his men out of the gate and away from the station depot.

'Bloody artillery, they're always in the way,' complained 65.

'Don't knock them. They may save our arses, one day.'

'At last you're beginning to speak our language, La-di-dah.'

'That'll be the day, 65.'

The road was congested, but they could hear the familiar sound of guns in the distance above the noise of clattering hooves and the singing foot soldiers.

'This bloody rain, I haven't got a dry bit anywhere on me body, in spite of this mac,' 65 complained.

'Stop moaning, neither 'ave I,' said Shrimp. 'But I've got a good 'orse. I wonder what happened to that little blood mare I rode to the coast. '

'Shut up about your horses. Who cares what happened to that wild, half-mad, frog filly.'

'I do, 65. I remember all the horses I've ridden.'

'Can't be many then, not as many as us.'

'A lot more than you, well over three hundred.'

'We've ridden more than that between us.'

'Yes, between you, whereas I....'

'For God's sake shut up you two,' interrupted Williams. 'It stands to reason Shrimp has ridden more horses than you, he had a livery stable in London.'

'There, see.' Shrimp was triumphant.

'Oh yeah,' retorted 65. 'It weren't yours, it were your Da's.'

'You have to admit these Irish horses are good, though, 65.' Williams changed the subject.

'Yes, I'll give you that. Bloody Shrimp has his uses sometimes.'

***

They rode on towards the sound of the guns. All the new horses from the train, although tired from their journey, pricked their ears and threw up their heads, faltering in their step. The young recruits looked apprehensive.

Andrew halted the men in the middle of a village. He suddenly felt exhausted as he looked over his men and saw the unsettled horses with their frightened riders. He wrote in his letter home that evening: *It seems to be a never ending cycle of training men and horse; as soon as they get used to the guns we lose them.*

He was about to give the order to dismount when he heard the clatter of hooves coming up the village street from the direction of the guns. A squadron of cavalry stopped in front of him. He could see by the muddy and bloodied state of the riders that they had just come off duty in the trenches. Also, seeing the number of led horses, it was obvious that several troopers hadn't returned.

A familiar voice said, 'By Jove, Harrington-West, back again I see. You seem to go missing and then turn up again like a bad penny. I don't know how you get away with it.'

'Dickson-French, I see that you have also returned from your exploits in one piece.'

'We routed the Hun don't you know. I got myself safely home again, old boy. Lost a few troopers along the way, but that couldn't be helped.'

'No, of course not.' Andrew's sarcasm went over the other man's head. 'Well it's nice to see you. I can't wait to hear all about your adventures. I must get on now.'

'See you later, old bean.'

'Not if I see you first,' said Andrew under his breath, but he called out, 'Look forward to it.' He was directed to a farm and was pleased to find that his horses were to be picketed in a barn, for the rain was still falling with remarkable persistence.

***

Shrimp vigorously rubbed his horse down with a handful of straw. 'Come on you lot. Get cracking before they catch cold. Warm yourselves up, too, rubbin' down. We're all cold and wet, just get a move on.'

'Since when do you give the orders?' snapped the sergeant.

'Not giving orders, only advice,' retorted Shrimp.

'Hmm,' the older man grunted.

'Welcome back, Shrimp,' someone shouted.

''Struth, if it ain't Pilson. Good to see you.' Shrimp called out, 'Turners, Williams, here's Pilson. We've brought you a new horse from England. A good 'un; come and look.'

Pilson was impressed when he saw the Irish horse. 'He looks grand, how come?' Shrimp explained as the others gathered round.

'Great to see you. How are you?' asked Williams.

'Just done a spell in the trenches. Got a bit wet.' Pilson removed his mackintosh cape and revealed the state of his uniform. He was covered in mud and soaked to the skin.

'If you lot think you're wet, look at this,' said Williams. The new men stared in awe at Pilson.

'You're bleeding!' Shrimp stared at the large patch of blood on his tunic.

'Not mine, bloke next to me caught it. I'm all right, except we didn't get any food yesterday.'

'Why not?'

'Supplies didn't arrive. Got some today though.'

'You don't have to shout,' said Shrimp.

'What?' asked Pilson.

'Stop shouting.'

'I'm not.'

'You are,' said a chorus of voices.

'Sorry, can't hear... the guns you see. But got some good news for you lads. Stone's back.'

'Where is the little bastard?' exclaimed Len Turner.

'Hiding I don't doubt, especially if he sees you two.'

'Little shit, we'll get 'im.'

'Yes, the captain tried to have him charged with horse cruelty and desertion, but old Falters wasn't wearing it,' Williams informed them.

'And he grassed up Mademoiselle Francine,' added 65. 'If Falterstone won't do anything, we will. Shrimp do you agree?'

'Yeah. We'll Court Martial him ourselves,' replied Shrimp.

'What do you mean?' asked someone.

'Well, in prison...'

'You've been to prison?' sneered 65.

'No I ain't, but I know some who have. They abide by the law of ... Can't remember what they call it, but they judge their own kind. If one of them grasses a man up or breaks the unwritten code, then they punish him themselves. And I reckon Stone has broken the unwritten rules.'

'I agree. We did that at school.' Williams joined in.

'Let's flog him.' 65's eyes gleamed.

'That might be a bit too obvious,' said Williams. 'No, let's think about it, see how the land lies. We'll get an opportunity sooner or later.'

'Na, let's do it now.'

'No, wait,' said Shrimp. 'Williams is clever, you have to admit that.'

'Clever, my arse. If he was that clever he'd be an officer.'

'Leave it to Williams,' said Pilson. 'He's right; I've been in the trenches. There'll be lots of opportunities.'

'All right,' 65 agreed reluctantly. 'But I'll go and thump the little bugger.'

'No!' exclaimed Williams. 'Just lull him into a sense of security.'

'What?'

'Let him think we're his friends. He'll drop his guard then. A little shit like him will go blabbing to an officer if we threaten him.'

'All right,' 65 reluctantly agreed. 'But I want first go at him.'

'That'll be fine. By the way, where's Somerville?' Williams asked Pilson.

'Somewhere around, unfortunately.'

***

'Fucking Hell, it's the middle of the night,' moaned 65, as reveille sounded in the barn at 2.45 the next morning.

'I'm still soaked to the skin.' Shrimp stood up, shivering. 'Let's get them 'orses fed.'

It was raining as they rode towards the front line. Andrew wasn't pleased to discover that Rupert was still with him. He had expected the lieutenant to transfer to Dickson-French's squadron while he had been away.

An NCO directed them to another barn, just out of range of the enemy artillery.

'We've been lucky with our stabling, so far,' Andrew remarked to Rupert.

'Well, *you* are,' Rupert retorted. 'When you were in England we had to picket the horses out in the rain. A stray shell fell on the end of the line and we lost some of them.'

'Then it's just as well that we brought replacements from England.'

'You seem to have done all right for yourself.' Rupert looked down at Andrew's horse. 'I notice that some of your troopers have good horses, too. I've got to put up with this old donkey.' He kicked his thin horse in the ribs; it jogged forwards and Rupert jabbed it in the mouth.

'Don't ride like that. It sets a bad example to the men.' Andrew was thankful as they rode up to the barn and dismounted. 'See the horses settled in,' he snapped at Rupert. He stood sheltering in the barn staring out at the falling rain, thinking about Francine and what had happened while he had been in England. He jumped as a sergeant approached him and said, 'All present and correct, sir.'

The men sloshed their way across a muddy field to a deep ditch that was rapidly filling up with rainwater.

'Is this what you call a trench?' asked 65.

The men slithered into it and stood in several inches of water, leaning against the wet bank, their rifles in their hands. They saw a level field in front of them, shrouded in mist. It wasn't until the mist cleared that they could see the craters and the zigzagged barbed wire. They stared at the enemy lines.

'This is uncanny,' remarked Williams. 'They're so close.'

'I know, one feels that one could reach out and shake hands with them,' replied Andrew.

'Sir, sir!'

'What is it, Fisher?'

'Me rifle's clogged up with mud, what shall I do?'

'You piss down it,' said Pilson. Andrew stared at the trooper. 'You piss down it, sir. The riflemen told me, it cleans the barrel.'

'Well, carry on Fisher. You know what to do.'

'But I don't want to go,' Shrimp whispered to Pilson.

Suddenly there was a whistling noise followed by a thunderous explosion. Mud and water flew in the air as a shell landed just short of the trench further down to their right.

''Struth,' exclaimed Shrimp. 'I do now.'

It was immediately answered by a salvo of guns from behind them. The men instinctively ducked. The exchange of fire continued while the cavalrymen sat on the muddy firing shelf. Some stared at the ground and others held their heads in their hands. They couldn't hear themselves speak as shells exploded in No Man's Land sending up showers of mud and shrapnel.

Shrimp felt a draught and heard the thud as a piece of shrapnel flew into the trench and hit the far bank. He turned to the man next to him and tried to say, 'That were bloody close.' But the words stuck in his throat as he touched the trooper's arm. Shrimp stared in horror as the man's head fell unnaturally backwards, exposing a gaping hole in his throat. By a quirk of fate the shrapnel had ricocheted off a protruding stone in the far wall of the trench, rebounded and all but severed the lad's head from his shoulders.

The men stared in shock at their dead comrade. A young trooper stood up and tried to run away from the noise, his eyes wild with fear. Len Turner pulled him down as a volley of bullets rained over their heads. The lad sat shivering on the firing shelf while Williams hastily threw the dead boy's cape over his body, hiding the hideous wound and the unnatural position of his head.

Andrew looked over the parapet using the homemade periscope that a fellow officer had pushed into his hands. He saw enemy soldiers pouring into No Man's Land.

He gave the order 'Stand to' and then 'Fire!' The squadron leant against the muddy bank and began to fire at the Germans, who were half-walking and half-running towards them. The barbed wire was strung low enough for men to step over, but also just high enough to unbalance them and slow them down, making the enemy an easy target. Soldiers fell screaming as they were hit; the wire hooked into their tunics and held them trapped.

The first few Germans who had successfully negotiated the wire arrived with their bayonets fixed to within a few feet of the British trench. Once they were there they hesitated as if they didn't know what to do. Some reached down trying to bayonet the British while others began to fire at random into the trench. Several cavalrymen were hit while they fired back. The Germans began to fall, some on the brink of the parapet and others into the trench at the feet of the British. A young cavalryman stared with horror into the eyes of a wounded German who was reaching for his rifle.

'Look out, stand back you idiot,' shouted Len Turner. He fired a shot from point blank range. The young trooper was spattered with the German's blood. He leant against the muddy wall of the trench and threw up.

'Disarm the wounded,' yelled Andrew. 'Take them prisoner and watch yourselves.' The men quickly undertook the grisly task of sorting out the wounded Germans.

'Poor bastards,' Shrimp said quietly to Williams, as he turned over the dead body of a young German lad who had part of his face missing.

'It's either them or us,' replied Williams, with a look of revulsion on his face.

Rupert shot an injured soldier. Feeling that someone was looking at him, he turned and saw Trooper Ashton. He remembered how the trooper had watched him kill a wounded German at the ford.

'The captain told us to take them prisoner.' The trooper stared accusingly at him. 'I saw you...'

Rupert didn't let him finish the sentence. He furtively pulled out his knife and put his arm around the trooper, saying, 'I see you're wounded. Sit down over here'.

As Ashton replied, 'No, I'm...' Rupert stabbed him in the chest. He looked around, but in the mêlée nobody noticed. Then he quietly laid the body on the floor of the trench.

***

The squadron were still in their firing positions as the second wave of Germans came over the top. The enemy began to slow down; their numbers had rapidly diminished and there weren't enough of them to make a practical assault on the British trench. They lost heart, turned round and headed for home. Frantically shouting Feldwebels tried to urge them forwards. Shrimp was horrified when he saw a German officer shoot one of his own men. The others turned to face the British again.

Suddenly the British artillery roared into action and the remaining Germans in No Man's Land, including the shouting NCOs, disappeared in a muddy cloud of shrapnel.

The troopers shrank back into their trench, their heads bowed as bits of human tissue rained down upon them.

Silence fell and the men turned to look at each other; some of them were too shocked to speak.

A young lad sat huddled, shivering and crying, clutching his stomach.

'He's shit himself,' announced Turner 65, as Shrimp looked

enquiringly at him.

'Well I don't think you should mock him,' said Williams. 'There, by the grace of God, go we.'

'I'm not mocking him. Shrimp asked me, so I told him.'

'What the devil are you talking about, *the grace of God*,' cried Len Turner. 'I can't see no God. Not in this hell.'

'Neither can I.' Shrimp shuddered. 'Fritz shot his own man.'

'I saw that, too,' said Pilson. 'What sort of people are they?'

'And what about our horses?' asked Shrimp. 'How are we going to charge into battle in this hell?'

'We can't,' said Williams. 'You couldn't ride a horse into battle in these conditions.'

'We'll become cannon fodder,' said Shrimp.

'We are cannon fodder you idiot,' snapped Turner 65.

'What about the horses? What'll happen to them?' repeated Shrimp.

'I don't know,' replied Williams.

'When you have yer 'orse in battle he kind of gives you support. Like a partnership, someone sharing things, helping you.'

'God, you're weird, Shrimp,' exclaimed 65.

'No, he's right,' agreed Williams. 'The horse is a friend. It's comforting to feel him beneath you.'

'You're getting as bad as him, La-di-dah,' 65 mocked.

'Actually, brother, I agree,' said Len. 'I don't want to give up my horse and become an infantryman, do you?'

'No I don't... now you put it like that,' exclaimed his brother. 'Bloody hell, we'll become no more than plant life.'

'That's exactly my point,' said Williams.

The men fell silent. The palls of smoke slowly cleared and the officers, looking through their periscopes, could only see craters in No Man's Land. The advancing troops, the wooden posts and the barbed wire had vanished.

There was a sudden flurry of activity. Officers ran down into the trench and stood in a group talking amongst themselves.

'What's going on?' asked Shrimp.

'I expect we're going over the top,' said 65.

Two young troopers started shivering, huddled together. 65 glanced at them and said, 'Well, they'll get killed, either by Fritz, or by one of our officers. Because if you've seen the Hun officers shoot their men for cowardice, you can be sure that ours will too.'

'I don't believe you,' said Shrimp.

'Please yourself.' 65 shrugged.

The men stared at each other in dismay. The group of officers parted and Andrew approached his men, hurriedly gathering them around him.

'We're launching a counter attack.' The men stared at him in horror. He smiled to himself, thankful that a more experienced battalion of infantrymen were being prepared, and announced, 'Because of our lack of bayonets, we're not going over the top this time.' Andrew felt the relief as pent-up tension left the men. 'But we're here to give them support. You'll fire at any Hun who shows his head above his parapet. You'll also take care to avoid hitting our own men.' A whistle blew further down the trench. 'This is it.' Andrew hurried away.

'Stand to,' yelled an NCO.

The troopers watched the British soldiers, their bayonets fixed, as they scrambled through the craters left by the shells.

As if from nowhere, Germans appeared in the vacated trench and began firing. The leading British soldiers fell, those behind took cover in the lee of the shell holes.

The British artillery fired at the enemy trench. They had aimed too short and hit the sheltering riflemen. The next salvo reached their mark in the German trench. The British continued their advance only to walk into the relentless fire of a Maxim machine gun. Any soldiers left advancing were immediately brought down by shells from the German artillery. When the smoke cleared there was nothing left on the battlefield.

The cavalrymen slumped on to their firing shelf drained of energy and emotion.

At last the order 'Stand Down' came. They marched wearily back to the barn in silence. When they arrived at the makeshift stables they found two British gunners sitting amongst the horses.

'What are you doing here, mate?' Turner 65 was the only man with enough energy left to ask. As the gunners turned round, the cavalrymen recoiled. Both were bleeding profusely from their noses and their ears.

'Fucking hell,' exclaimed Len. 'What's up with you?'

'Guns... Noise... this happens.' One of them pointed at his face. 'Been sent here... 'til the bleeding stops, then we go back.'

'Poor bastards,' remarked Len.

Shrimp hugged his horse and nodded in agreement. Turner 65 couldn't find the strength to comment on the un-soldier-like behaviour of his comrade-in-arms, although he did surreptitiously pat his own horse.

Andrew counted the number of unclaimed horses and realised that he didn't even know the names of some the missing riders, or if they were dead or only wounded. He shook his head and ordered the riderless horses to be led back to the billeting area. They rode in silence, their heads and ears aching, their wet feet numb with cold and their saturated shoulders sore from the recoil of their rifles.

***

The next three days passed in the same way. They stood in the unrelenting rain, the mud became worse and the water level rose in the trench. Neither the Germans nor the Allies succeeded in doing anything other than prevent the advance of their adversary and so the stalemate continued. Each evening the men returned to their barn in the village, wet, cold and hungry. As soon as they had rubbed down, fed and watered their horses, they slept, without removing any wet clothing and with no hope of getting dry.

Andrew returned to the modest comfort of his billet where an open fire awaited him. He sat, almost in the grate, watching the steam rise off his tunic that hung on the back of a chair pulled up to the fire. He removed his boots and wriggled his toes in front of the flames. He poured himself a brandy and, as his fingers began to come back to life, he wrote a hasty note to his parents. He felt angered by what he had witnessed over the past few days and helpless to do much about it. He was too annoyed to work on a report so he took another swig of brandy and decided to send a letter to Francine. He wrote:

Dear Francine, I hope you're feeling better.
We've just spent several dreadful days in the trenches standing in water. Your countryside is being laid to waste and all for nothing. I mourn for France, but most of all I grieve for my men who are being killed and our poor horses who suffer cold and hunger.
Your country needs all the men and women it can muster to fight. They must do their bit if we are to drive away the "sales Boches" as you call them. Many Frenchmen have fled to safety. It distresses me that our boys are ready to die for their country when yours are fleeing to the safer parts of France. Surely the French people who live behind the enemy lines

could help us. If only a small fraction of them became spies or blew up communication lines they would be of immeasurable help. Yours, Andrew H-W.

Andrew felt too tired to alter his letter. He knew his brain was clouded by brandy. He stuffed it into an envelope, deciding to tear it up and write a more agreeable one in the morning. He fell on to his bed and slept. He was aroused, in what seemed to be only minutes later, by someone banging on the bedroom door.

'What is it?'

'A night attack, sir, we're ordered to "Stand to".' His batman put his head round the door.

'Right you are. Thank you.' As he pulled on his wet boots he thought, *'why can't the Hun keep civilised hours?'*

He arrived at the barn to find the disgruntled men saddling up.

'Take the morning feed and give it to the horses when we get to the front line,' ordered Andrew.

The squadron clattered off into the night. Thankfully the rain had stopped, but their equipment was still soaking wet. When they arrived at the now familiar barn, Andrew ordered Williams and Shrimp to feed and water all the horses, but to leave them saddled up.

As soon as they had finished, the two men joined the others in the silent trench.

'Did you know that Stone is here, sir?' Williams asked Andrew as he reported back. He splashed into the water in the trench which came well above his knees.

'No, I didn't,' replied Andrew. 'And be careful, you have just soaked me.'

'Sorry, sir. Didn't see the water.'

'Have you seen him?'

'Who, sir?'

'Stone, of course.'

'No. He's with Dickson-French. He's keeping well away from us.'

'I'm not surprised.'

'Pilson caught sight of him, but the little blighter went to ground. Are you going to charge him, sir?'

'I very much doubt it, Williams. Too much going on.'

The men stood in the stagnant water, which frequently swirled whenever anyone further up the line moved, sending stinking waves lapping up their thighs.

'What a stench,' said 65.

'Not as bad as the château, though, you have to admit,' said Williams.

'Thank Christ, no. That was a bloody awful smell; never smelt anything like that in my life.'

'They're coming round with the rum,' said Shrimp, as two figures sloshed along the trench carrying stone flagons.

'Thank God, about time you buggers.' 65 he held out his tin mug and took his ration. He immediately knocked it back. 'Hurry up, Shrimp, or I'll have yours too.'

'I like to savour mine.' Shrimp sipped his measure, pulling a face with each swallow.

'You don't even like it. Best give it to me.'

'Get lost, 65.'

'You look too young to be drinking that,' Len said to Williams. 'We'll have it.'

'In the immortal words of your brother, "*fuck off*".' Williams knocked his rum back in one.

'If he's old enough to die for his country, then he's old enough to drink that,' said Shrimp.

'Bloody hell!' exclaimed 65.

'What now?' asked Shrimp.

'A turd just floated past my leg.' Shrimp and Williams started to laugh.

'It ain't funny,' said the affronted 65. 'I could catch something off that.'

'Like what? You could attach a message to it and see where it ends up.'

'Don't be so fucking stupid, Shrimp. Why don't you return it to its owner? And you can stop laughing,' he said to his brother, who had begun to giggle.

'Quiet!' shouted a sergeant. This made the men giggle even more, and sent waves further down the trench.

'Why don't you lot put a sock in it,' an angry voice complained from further down. 'I'm getting sodding wet.'

'You could put it *in* a sock,' Williams giggled.

'Yeah, that would be a good idea,' agreed Shrimp. 'Keep it warm.'

'Or you could stick a twig in it and turn it into a sailing boat,' said

Williams.

Len said, 'It looks like a sausage: you could fry it and give it to Stone for breakfast'.

'Good idea. Let's do that,' said 65.

'You catch it then,' said his brother.

'Bloody thing's gone down stream now.'

'Well, ask for it back.' By now the men were laughing helplessly.

'Will you be quiet,' hissed Andrew. 'Williams, what's so funny? What have they lost?'

'Nothing, sir,' said Williams.

'Well keep them quiet.' But the giggling grew worse. 'What is it Williams?' Andrew snapped.

'I think it was that floating turd, sir.'

'What floating turd?'

'The one that narrowly missed your leg.'

Andrew jumped. 'Where?'

'That's just it, its missing.' Williams giggled.

'For goodness sake, grow up. Are you all back in the kindergarten?'

Williams nodded. Then Andrew, suddenly seeing the funny side of the situation, began to shake with laughter. Rupert stared at his captain and stood miserably clutching his rifle. He couldn't see anything funny in the situation at all.

Eventually the laughter subsided. They stood silently in the steadily rising cold water, staring into the dark field in front of them. The minutes turned into hours. As it got light, the temperature dropped. They were all too cold and miserable to think of anything to say.

Turner 65 suddenly broke the silence. 'What's that noise?' They all spun round.

'It's another lot of infantry,' said Len.

'Thank God for that; does that mean we can go?' asked Williams, just before the order to stand down was given.

They struggled to get up the slippery slopes of the trench, but their numb feet and legs wouldn't respond.

'Piss down your legs,' announced 65. 'It warms them up.'

'You're right,' Shrimp agreed after a short pause.

'Yes, it definitely works.' Williams landed on the top of the bank like a beached whale.

Andrew lined up his muddy, wet and cold men and marched them back to their horses. He used all his self-control to make his legs and his feet do what he wanted them to do without having to resort to the warming up methods of his men.

***

'That was a bleedin' waste of time,' remarked 65 as they bedded themselves down, having seen to their horses. 'Not one shot was fired.'

'No. Thank God we can get some sleep,' said Shrimp. But their rest was short lived as Dickson-French's squadron arrived noisily in the big barn to fetch their horses.

'There he is, 65... look,' exclaimed Shrimp.

'Who?'

'Stone.' The men looked up.

'Well, I'll be damned,' said 65. 'I'll get the little runt.'

Stone was saddling his horse. 'Stay still,' said Williams. 'He's looking this way. Don't move.'

'Has he seen us?' Shrimp asked.

'Yes. He jumped and changed colour.'

'They're going now,' said Pilson. 'That's a shame.'

'No they're not,' said Williams. The squadron were ordered to stand by their horses, but not to mount.

'Right,' said 65. 'Who's coming with me? Lucky he's at the back of the formation and not facing us.' Pilson, Williams and Shrimp hastily stood up and joined the twins. Turner 65 told them his plan.

Stone jumped as Williams and Shrimp walked up to the head of his horse.

'Hello. How are you? Good to see you again,' said Williams pleasantly. 'We missed you at the bridge. We thought you must have been killed.'

'No... no... I... I got knocked unconscious. When I came to you'd all gone.' Stone stared at them suspiciously. He didn't notice the Turners and Pilson walking up behind him.

'How frightfully frightening for you,' said Williams.

'Yes... Yes it was rather.'

'I'm glad that didn't happen to me. I must say you've done awfully well to make it back. Don't you think so, Fisher?'

'Oh, yes. *Frightfully* well,' replied Shrimp.

'How come you managed to get into Dickson-French's squadron?

That's where we would like to be, too, isn't it, Fisher?'

'Yeah... Yeah, *awfully* much.'

Stone continued staring at them apprehensively. 'I spoke to Major Falterstone and he understood that Captain Harrington-West had it in for me. So he had me transferred.'

'How terribly accommodating of him.'

'Ye...' Stone let out a scream. He tried to turn round, but Shrimp suddenly fell against him, knocking him sideways.

'Whatever's the matter?' Williams steadied Stone, preventing him from looking behind. When Stone eventually swung round, there was nobody there. He put his hand on his buttocks and snarled. 'I'll get you for that.'

'My dear man, what on earth are you talking about?' asked Williams.

'You know bloody well. You... you bastards.' Stone's face was red with anger.

'Sorry old chap, afraid I don't. Do you, Fisher?

'No, mate, I don't know nothin',' replied Shrimp.

The order to mount rang out. 'You better get on your horse, now,' said Williams.

Stone hastily put his foot in the stirrup and, as he swung himself into the saddle, Williams noticed blood on his breeches.

'I'll get you.' Stone growled, but the two men had gone.

'Whatever did you do to him?' Williams asked 65 when they caught up with him on their side of the barn.

'We just pricked his arse with our knives. All three of us together. That's what he did to the horses, wasn't it?'

'Well done,' said Shrimp. 'You scarpered pretty quickly. He never saw you.'

'Well, he'll have an uncomfortable ride,' said Williams.

'It made 'im squeal.' Shrimp grinned.

'The trouble is he might get an infection from that water in the trench. Then he won't be able to ride and they'll have to stand him down.'

'Not necessarily,' said Pilson. 'We're always on the move, he won't get a chance. And if he does get an infection it'll be painful.'

'Yeah, not 'alf,' Shrimp laughed.

CHAPTER SIXTEEN

Retribution

The men were delighted to have a few days' rest. They fed, watered and groomed their horses, then sat inside the barn cleaning and mending their equipment and uniforms.

They only stopped to listen when the guns fell silent. It seemed strangely reassuring when they started again. The recruits and the new horses had at last stopped flinching at the sudden angry salvos.

A voice rang out. 'Hello husband.' They looked up in surprise.

'Well, if it ain't Clark,' exclaimed Shrimp.

'Harlot,' shouted Len Turner. The men looked on curiously.

'Aren't you going to ask why his arm's in a sling?' asked Shrimp.

'No,' snapped Len.

'You see what I have to put up with,' said Clark. 'He's a veritable monster; oh, he treats me so cruel.' More and more men stopped what they were doing and watched.

'Shut up. You'll get us arrested.' Len looked anxiously around.

'Are they nancy boys?' A wide-eyed lad asked Williams, quietly.

'No, of course not. It's only a joke.'

'I've never seen a nancy boy, only me ma warned me, see.'

'Well, I can assure you that they're not.'

'Oh.' The boy looked disappointed.

'What happened to your arm?' Shrimp asked Clark.

'Got a bit of shrapnel in it. Medic dug it out. It's all right now.'

'Stone's back.'

'Yes, we've seen him. He's with Dickson-French. The cocky little bastard wouldn't speak to me.'

'We've decided to sort him out.' Shrimp went on to tell him what they had done and what they were planning to do.

***

When Stone came back off duty, the Turners, Shrimp, Pilson, Clark and Williams all took it in turns to stalk him. The surly little man kept himself to himself. He fed and looked after his horse and then bedded down under his blanket and slept.

He was obviously in pain when he sat down, but he didn't seem anxious to report to the doctor. He looked around uneasily from time to time as if he knew he was being watched.

The next day he rode off with his squadron as usual. That evening he didn't come back.

'The little bugger's done a bunk,' said 65.

'You're right,' said Williams. 'I've just discovered that he's been reported missing.'

***

Every day while they were resting, Andrew took his men on a march to keep the horses exercised and the men occupied.

Williams approached Andrew as they rode out into the countryside. 'Stone has absconded again, sir.'

'Has he, Williams? Thank you.'

Williams went on to tell him how they had been watching him. 'Maybe we'll get him this time. Most of the squadron want to see him get his just deserts.'

'I couldn't agree more, but he's a slippery customer. No doubt he'll come up with a feasible story if he's caught.'

'If he does get caught, what will happen to him?'

'He'll be shot.'

Andrew moved the men on at a canter across a field and then at a gallop.

The procured Irish horses stretched out and left the others behind. It was an untidy bunch of exhilarated men who joined him when he pulled up by a gate into a wood.

'That blew a few cobwebs away.' Andrew sighed as he watched Rupert bullying his horse. He rode up to him and said quietly, 'For goodness sake ride properly'.

'It's all very well for you, you've got a good horse; mine's a donkey.'

Andrew shouted, 'Anyone who wants to jump that gate, follow me. The others stay here.' He turned to Rupert and said, 'You stay here with the men who don't want to jump.' He ignored the ugly look on Rupert's face, popped his horse over the obstacle and cantered into the wood. He flew over a fallen tree trunk and then leapt a hedge into the field beyond. About twenty men followed him.

'Sir, can we jump that hedge, go through the field, over the next hedge into the stubble? Then we could come back over that post and rail fence and then the ditch.' asked Shrimp.

'I don't see why not.' Andrew set off at a gallop. They all flew over the hedge, galloped across the next field and jumped another hedge with a drop and a ditch into the stubble field. Andrew turned and kept going, clearing the post and rails. He swung left-handed and jumped a dyke back into the field where they had started from. When he pulled up he saw a riderless horse and a soldier sitting on the ground.

'Someone's had a fall. Fisher and Williams go and help, also the Turners, you'd better go too.' The four men cheerfully set off jumping the obstacles again. When they arrived in the stubble field they found a trooper nursing his shoulder. Pilson was holding the loose horse.

'Looks like you've broken your collar bone,' said Williams. 'You'll have to walk back.'

'Sod that,' replied the trooper. 'I'll ride.'

'You sure?'

'I'm not walking.'

Between them they managed to hoist the man painfully back into the saddle and set off towards the post and rails out of the field.

'You can't jump like that.' Shrimp looked at the man sitting on his horse holding his useless arm.

'We'll carry on,' said Williams. 'You go back with Pilson. Go towards the farmyard and take that farm track.' They parted company and jumped the post and rails, but they stopped and turned round as they heard Pilson galloping after them.

'Quickly, come and look,' he shouted.

'For Christ's sake, why?' asked Len.

'Don't argue. You won't be disappointed.'

'Come on,' shouted Shrimp, who was already riding back with Pilson.

They followed him back over the post and rails and stopped under some trees where they had a good view of the farmyard.

'Look, over there,' whispered Pilson. The men stared.

'Well, I'll be damned,' said Williams. 'That farm worker.'

'It's Stone!' exclaimed Turner 65.

'Yes, and even better, he's not in uniform. He can't get out of this one.' Williams grinned. 'He'll be arrested, sure as eggs. Shrimp, you go and tell the captain while we catch him.'

Stone walked round the farmhouse carrying a bucket of water and gave it to a woman. Then he started to cut logs.

'He's working on the farm.' Williams was incredulous.

'Didn't take him long to get his feet under the table,' said 65. 'Come on, after him.'

The four men galloped into the yard. As soon as Stone heard the horses he ran for his life into the house. The men dismounted and followed him.

'*Qu'est que vous faites*?' screamed the woman. Stone cowered behind her.

'Don't hide behind her skirts.' Len snarled and lunged at him. Stone pulled out a knife and jabbed it at the twin who put up his hand to protect himself. The knife caught him on the back of his wrist, leaving a trickle of blood. Turner 65, seeing the blood, became enraged. He lashed out at Stone, hit him on the chin and floored him. All three men then fell on top of him while 65 shouted, 'Give us some rope'. The terrified French woman stared at him.

'*Avez-vous un bout de ficelle*?' asked Williams. The woman nodded and, opening a drawer, took out a ball of string. Williams firmly secured Stone's wrists together behind his back.

'You bastards! May you rot in hell.' Stone's face twisted in anger.

The Turners manhandled their captive out of the farmhouse. Using the lead rope from a head collar, they tied his bound hands to a D on 65's saddle. 65 held the horse, but when the captive went to mount, it jumped forwards and set off at a gallop. Stone's boot became jammed in the stirrup and, as the lead rope tightened, he fell backwards. His body twisted round and his head fell close to the thundering hind legs.

The others mounted. However, as they galloped after the runaway horse it gathered momentum, headed for the hedge and took off. The trooper became caught up in the brushwood. Luckily the horse stopped abruptly as soon as it landed.

Stone had stopped screaming by the time the riders arrived at the other side of the obstacle.

'How come you let go of the horse?' exclaimed Williams.

'I dunno,' replied 65 as he dismounted.

'Well, get him out of that hedge. Is he dead? He's very quiet.'

'No, he isn't.' Pilson peered at Stone, who lay awkwardly entangled in the hedge.

'Here comes bloody Somerville,' announced 65.

'That's all we need.' Williams sighed. They watched him ride up with barely concealed dislike.

'What's going on?' Rupert glared at the men.

The prisoner cried out, 'They're trying to kill me, get me out of here'.

'No, we aren't. It was an accident.' Williams was indignant.

'Me arm's broken,' screamed Stone, as Turner 65 tried to pull him free.

'Is it?' asked Rupert.

'It might be.' 65 looked at the curious angle of the captive's upper arm.

'Untie me hands,' yelled Stone.

'He's a deserter.' Williams felt he had to explain.

'I can see that. I know who he is.' Rupert drew his pistol. 'Untie his hands, I have him covered. I'll shoot him if he tries to abscond.'

Stone looked up into Rupert's angry face. 'I ain't going nowhere. They tried to kill me.'

When the Turners untied Stone's hands they discovered that his left shoulder was dislocated.

'You'll have to get him on that horse again. Turner, you mount first, and then pull him up in front of you,' ordered Rupert.

'I tell you, me bleedin' arm's broke. I can't get on no horse,' yelled Stone.

'Be quiet.' Rupert waved his revolver in the air.

Williams shouted, 'Don't fire, sir, you might hit one of the twins.'

'Don't be impertinent,' snapped Rupert.

'Sorry, sir.' Williams raised his eyes to heaven and Pilson began to giggle silently. They eventually got the prisoner on the horse, in spite of no co-operation and much screaming from Stone.

It was a strange cavalcade that made its way back to the village. Rupert rode in front, taking the credit for the arrest. The others, following behind, tried to keep straight faces.

Stone, sharing Turner 65's horse, stared at the ground and sagged in the saddle, ignoring the taunts from the twins. They rode into the village and up to the square in front of the church where they found Andrew waiting for them. A crowd of soldiers looked on as the deserter was pulled off his horse and handed over to the military police.

Andrew followed the small party of red-capped soldiers as they marched their prisoner to a house in the square which acted as their headquarters. He found the Commanding Officer, Colonel Kettleworth, in his temporary office and explained the circumstances of Stone's arrest.

'It's a clear case of desertion. He isn't in uniform and he's been caught red-handed.' Kettleworth was adamant.

'Yes, and I have reason to believe that he's done it before.' Andrew gave a brief account of the circumstances leading up to the incident at the bridge.

'I see. Bring your witnesses along at...' The Colonel looked at the diary on his desk, '14.00 hours. I want this case wound up as quickly as possible. We have to make an example of him.'

Andrew returned promptly at two o'clock with the men involved in the capture and sat waiting in the corridor outside the colonel's office. They watched as Stone, still wearing the blue French farm worker's clothes, marched past them between two guards. The prisoner's eyes were glazed-over and he seemed to be unaware of their presence.

Andrew was called into the room first. He gave his evidence to Colonel Kettleworth, who sat at his desk between two military police officers. The captain told the court what he had seen as he waited for the men to rescue the trooper who had fallen.

The colonel listened to Pilson's and Williams's evidence. The prisoner stared into space as if detached from the situation.

Andrew was surprised when Kettleworth, after conferring with his two officers, announced that they didn't have time to hear any more evidence. He addressed Stone, saying, 'Do you understand the charges brought against you?'

Stone looked at the officer and said in a clear voice, 'Yes, sir.'

'I find this man to be guilty of desertion and I order him to be shot at dawn tomorrow. March the prisoner away.'

Stone was marched back to a bedroom that acted as his cell. Andrew requested permission to visit him. Two MPs escorted him upstairs and left him with the guards who stood outside the bedroom door.

When Andrew entered the room he found Stone sitting on his bed, staring out of the window. The condemned man neither stood nor looked up. He hardly seemed to notice that he had a visitor. The captain pulled up the only chair in the room and sat down, saying calmly, 'I'm sorry that it has come to this, although I believe you tried to desert before'. Stone said nothing. 'Why did you do it?' Andrew took a deep breath and continued. 'Why did you join the cavalry when you clearly dislike horses?' Stone still didn't answer. Andrew sat quietly studying his face as it slowly changed. The faraway look became one of belligerence. He knew that Stone was listening. 'You're not a coward. It takes some guts to do what you did. I think under the right circumstances you could have made a very good soldier. So why the cavalry?'

The belligerent look gradually left Stone's face and his features became softer. He appeared younger and suddenly vulnerable.

Andrew waited in silence. The condemned man whispered, 'Had to'.

'Why?'

'Me Da made me.'

'Why?'

'He was in the cavalry… in the Boer War. Always telling me how wonderful it were. He thought more of his 'orses than he ever thought of me.' Once Stone had started talking it was as if the flood gates had opened and he couldn't stop. All the time he stared out of the window; he appeared to be speaking to someone on the other side of the glass. 'I'm pleased…' He nodded. 'Glad I'm going to be shot, because me Da won't be able to handle that. It'll destroy him. Not because I'm going to die.' Stone shook his head. 'He'll be pleased about that. No, it's the disgrace of being a deserter that will kill him.' Stone began to snigger. 'He won't be able to brag in the boozer no more about his wonderful son in the King's Own Cavalry. They'll all know that his son was shot as a deserter. He won't be able to show his face.' Stone suddenly started to laugh. The door flew open and the guards rushed in. The prisoner didn't notice them. Andrew said softly, 'It's all right. I'll shout if I need you'. They quietly withdrew.

Stone was still talking. 'He used to beat me if I didn't do his damned 'orses just right. They had the best of everything. All the money went on his bloody horses… And his women. He had other women, too, you know… oh yes, I saw him picking up tarts in the street and then he would go back to me Ma. She were a lady, me Ma. He would get into her bed after he had been with them sluts.' Stone shuddered. 'Well it's me what's laughing now. It's me and me Ma who has the last laugh. I'll go to me death happy, thinking about the look on his face when he hears the news.' Stone giggled. 'The shame, the dishonour… He'll be humiliated… He was a sergeant, see.' Then the trooper turned and looked at Andrew, acknowledging him for the first time. 'You will tell him, Captain won't you? That I was shot and what I did to them horses. And what I did at the ford. I'm sure Pilson has told you.'

'I... Certainly he'll have to be told.'

'Good.' Stone started to giggle loudly. The door opened and a guard looked into the room. Andrew gestured for him to remain in the half open doorway. 'Will I be in the newspapers?' asked Stone.

'You might be. I don't really know.'

'Of course it'll be in the papers. I must be the first cavalryman to be shot in this silly war.' Stone rocked back and forth giggling. Then his mood changed to one of childish curiosity. 'They say I'll go to Hell. But I'm already in Hell, so where will I go?'

Andrew spoke as if he were addressing a child. 'You must ask the chaplain that. He'll be coming to see you later.' He paused and then asked, 'Why did you steal the money?'

'Oh that.' Stone started grinning. 'That were mine. I were meant to find it.'

'Where did you find it?'

'In a chest. In the feed room... at the enclave. I felt it were there.'

'Whatever do you mean?'

Stone grinned and touched his nose. 'Smelt it see. It were at the bottom of a coffer of oats. Me Da used to hide things there, so as me Ma couldn't find them. I knew it were meant for me.'

'What things did your father hide?' Andrew asked gently.

'Money, love letters, booze, betting slips... sometimes I would take them. He didn't like that. That made him very angry. Then he would beat me, but it was worth it to see him worried me Ma might find out about his dirty secrets. He was frightened of me Ma, she being of a higher class than him. She held the purse strings, see.'

'Is your mother still alive, Stone?'

'No. He killed her.'

'You mean he murdered her?

'As good as, he dragged her down to his level and then he broke her heart. She died in childbirth... Eighth baby. She were too delicate to breed like that. He had to have his vile way with her even though he had other women.' Stone trembled. 'I heard him... at it. Then I'd go and take his things, or punish his horses. He didn't like it if I hurt his precious horses.' Stone paused, grinning manically. 'You can go now.' Stone turned away and looked out of the window.

Andrew left the bedroom.

'He's mad, sir,' said the guard as he locked the door.

'Yes, I rather fear that he is.' Andrew watched an army chaplain hurrying along the corridor.

The priest stopped. 'Captain Harrington-West, good afternoon. Dreadful state of affairs, dreadful. Should we shoot our own men? I don't know. I really don't know. Poor man, oh dear, poor man. Nice to meet you. I must get on. Not a very pleasant job, but it has to be done. Guard, open the door please.'

Andrew watched as the man hurried into the room and heard him say, 'My dear boy...'

Andrew was still in the house when the chaplain came hurrying after him. 'There you are, Captain; the poor man didn't want my services. Very odd. He was very odd indeed. Poor soul. I feel I've let him down, you know.'

'No Padre, we've all let him down. I'm to blame as much as anyone.'

'My dear boy! Of course you're not.'

At that moment the door of Colonel Kettleworth's office opened and the CO came out. 'Harrington-West, Padre, I'm glad you're here. We're going to perform the execution now. We can't wait until tomorrow morning. We've orders to move on. I trust you have no objections?'

'On the contrary,' said Andrew.

'Padre?'

'No, not at all. I agree with Captain Harrington-West.'

'Good, in that case you might like to proceed to the wall beside the church.'

'But... The church? I really think... There are a lot of soldiers about, they'll see...' the Padre said rather lamely.

'Quite, we have to set an example. We can't have men deserting nineteen to the dozen.' Kettleworth hurried away.

Outside in the Church Square a red-capped NCO mustered volunteers for his firing squad. He picked men from the soldiers who were milling about.

Andrew's heart sank when he saw that five of his men, the two Turners, Pilson, Shrimp and Williams had all been picked to be part of the twelve-man squad. He cursed himself for not ordering them back to their horses. He could only stand and watch, keeping his emotions in check, as they were issued with the already-loaded rifles. He knew that the men would be told that some of the rifles were loaded with blanks, so that nobody would know who would be responsible for killing the prisoner. Andrew always doubted that theory. He believed that if some of the men with live ammunition were bad shots or one or two chose to miss the prisoner, the condemned man wouldn't be shot at all and the execution would become a farce.

He noticed the tense look on the faces of his men. He saw Williams lean over and say something to Shrimp, who smiled and nodded. That boy has a wiser head on his shoulders than any of us, thought Andrew. Shrimp murmured something to Pilson, who also nodded. Turner 65 looked down the line to Williams and made a remark.

'Silence,' barked the sergeant. Andrew smiled to himself, suddenly proud of his diverse group of cavalrymen.

The firing squad were ordered to "About turn". They stood with their backs to Stone as he was marched out with his hands tied painfully behind his back. A thick rope wound round his body secured him to a post that had been hastily hammered into the ground. An NCO marched forwards and, with a flurry, blindfolded the prisoner. Andrew felt that an elaborate piece of theatre was being played out by the military police which, he considered, was in bad taste.

Before he was blindfolded, Stone looked around and smiled as he watched more and more soldiers flocking inquisitively towards the church.

Once the blindfold was in place, a white cotton square was pinned to his chest, again with unnecessary drama reminding Andrew of a magician's assistant.

The twelve-man firing squad were ordered to "About turn". Andrew watched the faces of his men as they looked at their victim for the first time. Once more he was proud of what he saw. Their first reaction was one of revulsion followed by concentration as the order "Aim", was given. When *"Fire!"* rang out, Andrew noticed the muzzles of Williams's and Shrimp's rifles tilt slightly in the air. The other three cavalrymen fired straight at the target.

An officer ran up to the sagging body of Stone and discharged his revolver into his head. The padre walked up and blessed the body. The watching soldiers began to leave the square. Andrew heard their remarks as they passed him by.

'Poor bastard.'

'Serves him bloody right, deserting coward.'

'To die like that ain't right, though.'

'Well, he shouldn't have deserted, should he? I feel sorry for the poor sods who had to shoot him.'

Andrew saw Rupert standing rooted to the spot. He was white

faced and stared at the body of Stone as it was removed on a stretcher.

'Not much fun,' Andrew said kindly. 'I'm sorry you had to witness that.' He was surprised to see the lieutenant was shaking.

'No... no,' stuttered Rupert. He turned and quickly walked away.

Andrew approached his group of men.

'Cor, blimey! I never want to do that again,' said Shrimp. 'That were 'orrible.'

'I thought you would be pleased to get your own back for your precious horses,' 65 scoffed.

'Yeah. But not like that. That were inhuman. I mean he's one of us, after all.'

'Yes, shooting your own isn't funny. That was the most difficult thing I have ever done,' said Williams. 'I hope I'm never asked to do it again.' He looked at the Turners. '65, come down off your high horse. I know you didn't enjoy it either.'

Turner 65 looked at the ground. 'No I didn't actually. Bloody laugh if you want to. It was the most despicable thing I've done in this war so far. I know the bloody little prick deserved it. I know I wanted to flog him. But to do that, was... was... well fucking awful. Volunteer? I'll volunteer to put my boot up that bloody MP sergeant's arse.'

'Yeah. And all them plant life watching, too,' said Len. 'Bloodthirsty lot. He was one of our own, not a Hun bastard.'

'You did well,' Andrew butted in and the men swung round. 'Walk over here.' He took them apart from the crowd and stopped. 'I want to say that I'm tremendously proud of you.' The men stared at him. 'You've just carried out an extremely distasteful job in a most dignified and proficient way. You're a credit to yourselves and to the regiment. I've been listening to the soldiers in the crowd talking. They're all saying the same thing. That the man deserved to die, but none of them would have wanted to be part of the firing squad.'

'That's typical of the plant life, sir. All mouth and trousers,' said Turner 65.

'That's a bit unfair. They're a brave lot of men and they are all British.'

'Yes, I'll grant you that, sir. They are British, not a murdering bunch of Jerries.'

'Quite, and that's what has made it so distasteful for you. Not only was Stone a British soldier, but also he was a cavalryman.'

The men agreed and Williams said, 'Yes... yes that did make it worse. But I wouldn't want to shoot any British soldier, whatever they had done. It's against everything decent'.

'Me neither, it's like murder, sir,' said Shrimp. 'Does that mean we would be disobeying orders, or being cowardly?'

Andrew looked into the anxious faces of both men and said, 'No. Not if that is what you truly believe. If you're being asked to do something that you find to be totally distasteful to every aspect of your feelings and principles, then no, you're not being cowardly. It takes a lot of courage to stand up for your own convictions, especially when there's pressure to bend or break your own rules.'

Andrew saw the tension leave the two men as they glanced at each other. 'Thank you, sir,' replied Williams.

'I spoke with Stone before he died and I would like you to know that he wanted to die.'

'What?' said 65. 'Then why didn't he let the Hun do it for him, instead of us?'

'You might well ask. It's a long complicated story. But I discovered why he found it necessary to abuse his horse and, at the end of the day, why he welcomed death. He was a tortured soul and he's now mercifully at peace.'

'He'll never be at peace hurting his horse like he did,' said Shrimp.

'You may well be right, Fisher,' replied Andrew. 'But fortunately it's not for us to judge; wherever he goes now is up to the good Lord. I think we all need to put this unpleasant incident behind us. Tomorrow we march north. I suggest you go and see to your horses and prepare your kit.'

CHAPTER SEVENTEEN

Chaos

Andrew's squadron marched north through Picardy towards Belgium. Riding at night, they covered about twenty miles on each leg of their journey. They had the luxury of tea brewed up by the cookhouse staff during their breaks, together with regular meals.

They rested by day and, although they could hear the distant rumble of guns, their eastern flank was covered at all times by the French. They had little to worry about, even the weather was good. There was plenty of fodder for the horses and shady, dry places in which to picket them.

One morning, after they had been riding for over a week, the men lay in the shade of a line of tall trees reading their mail. Andrew sat leaning against a tree, studying a letter from his father. He learnt, with mixed feelings, that his brother Bertram had arrived in France.

He was surprised to find that he also had a letter from Francine. She wrote:

Dear Captain, Thank you for your letter. I'm sorry to hear that my compatriots don't meet with your approval. I have told you that I plan to rectify the matter, for my own part, when I return to France in the near future.

I'm so grateful for your parents' kindness in looking after me for the past weeks. I'll greatly miss your mother when I return to take up my new duties in my beloved homeland. Yours sincerely, Francine du Byard du Moulin.

Andrew stared at the letter, wondering what on earth she was talking about. Then he suddenly remembered that he had written to her on the night he was cold, tired and fuddled with brandy. He had given his letters to his batman to post and forgotten about the scribble to Francine. He went cold as he asked himself, *'what must she think?'* He read her letter again and he knew exactly what she thought. He hastily wrote:

Dear Francine, I'm so sorry you received that letter. I was sure I had torn it up. I don't know what came over me when I wrote it. The only excuse I have is that my extreme tiredness must have muddled my brain.

Please forgive me. Your countrymen are exceptionally brave and I have no right to criticise them.

He assumed that if she was talking about taking up her new duties on returning to France, then she must have already been discussing becoming a spy while she was in England. His first thought was to write and ask his father if she had mentioned it to him. But he immediately dismissed the idea; his letter could be intercepted and that would put Francine in danger. He continued writing: *I must meet you, Francine, I have so much to tell you. When do you return? Please write and say you would be willing to see me. Also forgive me for being so crass. Best wishes, Andrew W.*

***

Andrew then walked to the village, hoping to find some congenial company and to catch up with news of the war. He was delighted to find three Hussar officers sitting outside a cottage with a crate of white wine at their feet.

'Have a drink.' One of them held up a glass.

The other two officers stood up. 'We've things to do, no offence, but duty calls. Have a seat. Potty will look after you.'

Andrew sat down and introduced himself. The remaining Hussar officer, Captain Philpot, poured him a drink, saying, 'We've just returned from digging a trench. They say that eventually it will stretch from the sea all the way down to the Swiss border. Bloody long way, what?' Andrew nodded. 'We Cavalry are being used to fill up gaps in the front line. *Puttying-up* as I call it.'

'So I understand,' replied Andrew. 'Have you any news about Antwerp? I heard that the Belgians wanted to surrender.'

'Yes, the First Lord of the Admiralty... What's his name?'

'Winston Churchill.'

'That's right, he's sent in three naval brigades to hold it. But we believe that they're not very well trained. And how, may I ask, are sailors going to fight on dry land against the Hun? Fishes out of water, what.' Captain Philpot paused and poured himself another drink, throwing the empty bottle to join several on the ground. 'I met a French cavalry officer the other day, who accused us of doing the same thing.'

'What do you mean?'

'Well, he was shocked to see us Hussars in the trenches and said that it was 'derogatory to the cavalry spirit'. I told him that we British will do what we have to do to win this damned war, although he did say that he was impressed by what we were doing and how well we fought.'

'They fight well too. A squadron of French Dragoons did a very good job against some aeroplanes, I heard.'

'Really. Where was that?'

'They were coming off patrol when they found out that some Hun planes were parked in a field, not far from a town called Villiers Cotterets, in the department of the Aisne. Lieutenant de Gironde led them in by night, charged and destroyed them. They lost all their horses. But the men managed to escape back to their own lines dressed as farm workers. Apparently it's the only cavalry charge, ever, against aeroplanes.'

'I don't doubt their courage; trouble is they want to charge everything with their horses. I mean, it isn't practical, old boy, not feasible. Have to adapt. Look at sailors on dry land. Have another drink.'

Andrew sat for a while listening to Philpot's experiences in the trenches. Although the Hussar officer was drunk, Andrew realised that what he was telling him was very useful.

'The only thing that distinguishes us from the Infantry, old boy, is our lack of bayonets and entrenching tools,' Captain Philpot continued.

'We're to be issued with bayonets, I understand.'

'Well they haven't arrived yet. But I tell you what we have been issued with.' Andrew looked curious. 'Four hundred pipes, old bean.'

'What sort of pipes?'

'To smoke. Some do-gooder in Blighty seems to think they're better for the men than cigarettes. I ask you.'

'Good Lord.'

'Exactly. You can't dig a trench with 'em or use 'em as weapons, what.' Philpot leant towards Andrew. 'If you're asked to dig a trench, I suggest you purloin some tools from someone's garden. A spade is more useful than a sword at the moment, unless of course you use your sword to dig the trench.'

'Thank you. I'll bear that in mind.'

'Your glass is empty, let me fill it up.'

'No thanks, I have to get back. Nice to have met you, see you again no doubt.'

'Look forward to it.'

Andrew left him uncorking another bottle of wine.

***

212

Andrew's squadron had twenty-four hours' rest and marched on again the following day. The guns became increasingly loud and the roads more congested.

'Look, there are some London buses. They're transporting troops,' cried Shrimp.

'What you talking about? You beginning to see things? You'll be seeing an angel next,' remarked Turner 65.

'No, over that hill, look.'

'Oh yeah, open-topped buses, so what?'

'Well, it's just nice to see them... Home from home, that's all. Even if they are painted grey you can't mistake them,' replied Shrimp. 'Anyway, look out, here come the artillery.'

'Bloody show-offs. Think they're more important and can push us off the road,' Turner 65 complained as they pulled into a field to allow the battery to gallop through.

'That's because they are important,' replied Williams. 65 glared at him as they were given the order to canter and then to gallop.

They followed the battery, galloping closer to the front line. The artillery pulled away to their right and the squadron kept going until the noise of the guns drowned everything out. They stopped on a ridge and saw below them the familiar sight of the crater-filled No Man's Land laced with barbed wire and littered with the bodies of soldiers from both sides. Palls of smoke hung in the air and the smell of cordite stuck in their throats.

Andrew left his squadron in the lee of the hill. He jumped down into the trench and jostled his way behind firing riflemen looking for the CO. He found him covered in mud. His face was blackened with smoke, one sleeve of his tunic was torn and his other arm was in a sling. The man smiled a lop-sided grin, held out his hand and introduced himself as Major Henry Cornwall. He yelled, battling over the noise of the rifle fire and artillery. 'Glad you could get here. As soon as this racket stops I want your men to start digging a communication trench. We'll have a lull sooner or later, always do. Don't know why. Gives us time to retrieve the wounded and dig. I presume the other side does the same thing.'

'Have you got any tools?' asked Andrew.

'Bloody cavalry.' The major shook his head and smiled. 'Might have guessed you wouldn't have any equipment. Still, not your fault, I suppose.'

'I'll send a few men out to find some,' replied Andrew.

'Good. In the meantime, hold that ridge.' The major pointed away to their right. Andrew sprinted up to the top of the hill as fast as he could and dropped down the other side unharmed. He ordered Williams, the Turners, Pilson, Shrimp, and Clark to go and find as many digging tools as they could and to return as quickly as possible.

The six men galloped back the way they had come. Williams shouted, 'I saw a farm away to the right here.' The others followed him as he veered off the road and down a track.

They clattered into a large farmyard and slid to a halt. The farm looked deserted. They found a barn full of agricultural machinery and there, neatly stacked against the wall, were spades, shovels and pickaxes.

'Right, we'll take all these,' said Williams. 'Get them loaded on to the horses.'

As they returned to the ridge they found the rest of the horses belonging to their squadron picketed in the lee of the hill. The riders stared in dismay; four lads from the cookhouse were on guard, but they knew nothing about horses. They were sitting under a tree, chatting to each other, not noticing the mayhem that was going on in the horse lines.

Most of the animals were tied to a rope strung between two trees, some were hobbled and they were eating the oats from each other's nosebags. Some horses were grazing; their reins had fallen to the ground and were broken. A further ten had been left in pairs tied head to tail; they stood quietly, except for a big gelding which was tied to a mare. He bit her hind leg making her squeal and lash out and then they began to spin in circles.

'What the hell's going on?' exclaimed Williams. Shrimp ran towards the mismatched pair. The mare kicked out with both hind legs, lost her footing and fell over, pulling the big gelding on top of her. The Turners tried to cut the two horses free of each other. Both struggled violently and their steel-shod hooves flew out at random. Len received a kick in his stomach which sent him reeling backwards. He fell with a jolt into a sitting position. He sat for a few moments, winded, and then painfully stood up.

Turner 65 yelled at the cookhouse lads, 'What the hell are you doing? We won't have no horses left at this rate.' But his words were drowned by a salvo from the British artillery.

The men left the two frenzied horses on the ground and quickly turned their attention to those who were plunging and straining at their headcollars. Some horses became entangled in the rope, but it remained tied fast to the two trees.

The four cookhouse lads, ignoring the chaos, turned and fled back to the safety of their wagon.

Between them the troopers managed to calm the picketed horses and none broke free.

The mare and the gelding lay quiet and as Shrimp walked back to them he thought that they were seriously injured. When he cut them free of each other they scrambled to their feet and stood shaking; both had cuts on their legs and stomachs. He led them forwards but they were virtually sound.

'Cor, that was lucky,' he said to Len Turner. Then he added, 'Are you all right? You look lamer than these two'.

'Yeah. I'm fine.' Len walked painfully towards his brother.

Williams watched the injured twin. 'It looks as if you have broken your coccyx. You sat down with such a bang when that mare kicked you.'

'Don't talk bollocks. Of course I haven't. It's me backside what hurts.'

'Your coccyx is your tail bone.'

Len looked relieved. 'Oh yeah. You might be right, it bloody hurts. I don't know how I'm going to ride.'

'Well, you won't have to. We can walk to the ridge from here.'

Shrimp collected up the hobbled horses and those tied head to tail. 'We could move all these over there.' He pointed to a rectangle of trees behind a high wall in the garden of a shelled house. 'Then we could feed and water 'em.'

'Good idea,' replied Williams.

They led the horses in relays to the clump of trees and found a water trough and a pump beside the ruined house. They fed them with the remains of the oats from their saddles. Williams left Clark on guard in the sad remnants of the once well-tended garden and went to report to Andrew on the ridge.

As they approached the front line and walked up the slope, someone frantically signalled to them to get down. They fell on to their stomachs as a hail of rifle fire skimmed over their heads.

'What the fucking hell are you doing?' yelled an NCO. 'Bloody donkey wallopers, got no idea,' he muttered to himself.

The troopers lay were they were as the British artillery fired over their heads. Their target was a German stronghold in a sugar beet factory, set in the middle of the plain. The cavalrymen listened to the first dull boom as the shells left the muzzle of the guns, the scream as they passed overhead and then the crash as they burst.

Eventually the guns died down and the NCO called them forwards. 'What do you want?' he asked.

'We're reporting to Captain Harrington-West,' replied Williams.

'He's over there.' The NCO pointed further down the line. 'His lot have been shooting well; good shots most of them, so keep your bloody heads down. You might be of some use to us after all.'

'Bloody cheek,' said Turner 65 as they ran down the line.

Between the bursts of gunfire they were able to explain to Andrew what had happened. Heavy fire continued for the rest of the day; eventually, as dusk fell, there was a lull and the rations arrived.

Major Cornwall came up from his trench and congratulated Andrew on his squadron's performance. 'Fine shooting, Andrew; you should be pleased with your men. You were firing so fast that our lot thought you had a machine gun. Well done. That last push from the Hun was quite formidable.'

'Thank you. We now have a quantity of entrenching tools.'

'Excellent. You have some resourceful men; not only do they shoot well, but they appear to be first-rate scavengers as well. We'll turn you into infantry yet.'

'I don't think so, Henry, but thanks for your compliments.'

'We'll test your digging skills. Start on the communication trench over there.' He pointed to their left. 'Once it's dark the Hun send up flares every now and then, so be careful of snipers and keep your heads down. Although our artillery usually give them something else to think about when that happens.'

As darkness fell the cavalrymen began digging in relays. The number of tools denoted the number of men digging.

Slowly the trench took shape and by the morning they had dug a reasonable depth and length. They sat on a shelf and rested.

'My backside hurts, I can't sit anymore.' Len Turner stood up just as his brother shouted, 'Keep your bleedin' head down'.

It happened so quickly. The bullet from the sniper caught him in the temple and Leonard Turner crumpled to the ground.

His brother stared at him. 'Get up.' Len didn't move. 'Len, get up. Stop fucking around, get up.' But his twin lay where he had fallen.

Shrimp, Pilson and Williams stared, horror-struck, as Turner 65 picked up his brother and sat him down beside him on the muddy shelf. Len slumped to one side while his brother cradled him in his arms. There was very little blood. Just a hole in the side of his head, and the expression on his face was one of mild surprise. His eyes were almost focused and his mouth was partly open. He looked as if he were about to speak.

Shrimp, Williams and Pilson glanced at each other, not knowing what to do or say, as Turner 65 carried on talking to his brother. When they continued digging, 65 left Len sitting on the self.

'What are you doing? Get digging.' A sergeant shouted.

'It's all right, Sarg,' Williams called back. 'He had a bang on the head. He'll be all right in a minute.' The sergeant grunted.

'What are we going to do?' asked Shrimp.

'I don't know. Are you going to tell him that his twin brother is dead?'

'No fear.' Shrimp vigorously shook his head.

As the trench grew, so they moved Len along the shelf. At last the order 'stand down' was given and they were thankful to be relieved by a company of Royal Engineers. In the chaos and scrimmage that followed, as the fresh soldiers replaced the cavalrymen, nobody noticed Turner 65 carrying his brother. Then the guns started up again while the troopers ran down the other side of the ridge.

They found their horses where they had left them, in the little spinney in the garden of the ruined house. The men were exhausted, but they fed and watered their mounts. Nobody gave a second glance at Len sitting, leaning against a tree while his brother attended to their horses. They were thankful as they took their blankets from under the saddles of the still saddled-up mounts, collapsed on to the ground, their heads resting on their kit bags and slept. Turner 65 carefully wrapped his brother in a blanket and lay down beside him.

***

The troopers were woken by the transport as it arrived with rations and fodder. They got up feeling stiff and hungry and shivered as they did the horses. All except for Turner 65 who lay cradling his brother in his arms. Shrimp and Williams, warmed up by their exertions, returned to see 65 before they went to collect their own food.

Shrimp stood nervously by as Williams spoke. 'Shall we bring you something to eat?'

'No.'

'We've done your horses,' Shrimp added.

'What about me brother's horse?'

'We've done him too.'

'Humm.' Turner grunted.

'Ungrateful bugger, ain't he?' remarked a trooper who was passing by with a friend.

'Loony, if you ask me,' said the other. 'They ought to take that body away from him. It's beginning to smell. I don't know how he's got away with it.'

'What did you say?' 65 sat up, grabbing his rifle.

'Nothin'.' The two troopers hurried on.

'What are we going to do?' Shrimp asked Williams. 'He can't go on like this, threatening anybody who questions him. Or who calls him loopy, 'cos he *is* loopy. He'll get put on a charge and then what?'

'I know.' Williams lowered his voice. 'And the body *is* beginning to smell.'

Turner 65 stood up. His uniform was caked in mud and he hadn't washed, shaved or eaten for thirty six hours. His bedraggled hair stood up on end. He stared with wild eyes at the two men.

'I'll go and fetch the captain. He'll know what to do. You stay with him,' said Williams.

'No, I'll go. I can't control him if he gets stroppy. You're the one who's clever wiv words.'

'All right. But hurry.' Shrimp ran off.

'Pilson,' called Williams. 'Come over here.'

Turner 65 sat down. He turned to his brother and started talking. 'It's all right, Len. I won't let them take you.'

'Bloody hell,' exclaimed Pilson. 'What are we going to do?'

'Shrimp's gone for the captain.'

'Let's hope he hurries, because look over there.'

Williams saw several troopers and a corporal striding towards them.

Turner was also watching them. 'Here come some bleedin' idiots who think they can take you away. Don't worry, I won't let them.'

'65, give it a rest,' Williams hissed.

Turner ignored him and continued his conversation with his brother.

The corporal turned to his entourage. 'He's barmy. We've got to do something.'

'Yes. That dead body lying there. It ain't right and it ain't sanitary,' the man replied.

'P'raps he's pretending to go mad so that he'll be sent home,' remarked another trooper. More soldiers drifted over to see what was going on.

Turner continued talking to his brother.

'You've got an audience,' Williams whispered.

'They can all mind their own bloody business; if I want to talk to my brother it ain't nothin' to do with them.' He glared at the growing bunch of men and yelled, 'Fuck off the lot of you'.

'He can't talk to us like that,' exclaimed a trooper.

'No. He's dangerous. He needs putting behind bars,' said the corporal. The mood of the onlookers was becoming hostile. Turner 65 grabbed his rifle, stood up and glowered at them.

'He's just lost his twin brother, Corporal Smith,' Williams tried to explain. 'Why don't you all go about your business and leave him alone.'

'I lost me best mate, but I didn't make no fuss like that,' retorted the corporal. 'We need to get him sorted before he kills someone. I don't like the look in his eyes.' He advanced on 65 who stood his ground. 'I'm taking your rifle. You're not safe.'

'You can fuck off and take your fucking friends with you.'

'Don't use that language to me,' snapped the NCO.

'It's all right, Corporal, Captain Harrington-West is coming in a minute.' Williams desperately looked around, but there was no sign of Andrew.

'Well, I don't see no officer,' remarked a trooper. 'You're just shielding him for some reason. We ain't going to stand for it, are we Smithy?'

'No, we ain't,' continued Smith. 'I'm taking his weapon and then I'm taking that body.'

Williams stood between the Turners and the group of men just as 65 released the safety catch on his rifle.

'Get out of the way, La-di-dah,' ordered 65. 'I'll shoot the bastard.'

'You see. He's mad and dangerous,' repeated Smith. 'Stand aside.'

'No,' replied Williams.

'You'll have to get past me too.' Pilson joined them.

Clark arrived. He too stood beside Williams. 'You have me to reckon with as well.'

'Don't let them get away with it, Smithy,' yelled someone behind Corporal Smith.

Turner 65 stood over his brother like a dog guarding a bone.

Williams turned to Pilson and said quietly, 'I don't know how long we can keep this up. 65 will shoot someone in a minute'.

The men on either side of the corporal tried to push Williams out of the way. Pilson pushed them back. A lad tripped and fell, hit his knee on a stone and cried out in pain. Then he stood up, lashed out and caught Williams in the face with his fist.

'What's going on?' They all swung round as they heard the voice of authority. Andrew marched up to the group and said to Williams, 'You appear to have a nose bleed'.

'Yes, sir.' Williams brought out a dirty white handkerchief and held it to his nose.

'Who hit this man?' demanded Andrew.

There was a silence. Then a small voice replied, 'I didn't mean to, sir'.

'Williams, take the names of the trouble makers. I'll see them later.'

Corporal Smith pointed at Turner 65, who was sitting down beside his brother. 'But, sir, this man is dangerous. We were trying to arrest him but they wouldn't let us.'

'That's all right. I'll deal with him. Those of you who were fighting will give your names to Lance Corporal Williams.'

He heard some of them say as they gathered around, 'It were Corporal Smith 96 egging us on'.

Andrew turned his attention to Turner 65, who was saying to his brother, 'It's all right, Len, the captain has sorted them. They're going now'.

As Andrew watched 65, he thought for a while. He weighed up the situation and recalled his mother's words about people in severe stress. He decided that it was worth a shot in the dark; in fact, it was his only hope of keeping the trooper from being locked up. If his plan didn't work then he would have to arrest him and have the body of his twin brother taken away for burial. He stepped forwards and said brightly, 'Good morning, Turners'.

'Good morning, sir.' 65 respectfully stood up.

Humouring him, Andrew asked, 'How's your brother this morning?'

65 looked up and smiled. 'He's fine, sir.'

Pilson looked round at the others and mouthed the words, 'What's he doing?' They shrugged and listened to Andrew, who continued: 'Good, I really think we need to get him buried today, don't you?'

65 said nothing but looked belligerent. 'He's not...' he started to say.

'Ask him,' interrupted Andrew, with more conviction than he felt. 'Ask him where he would like to be buried.' There was a long pause while 65 stared at the captain and then into the air. 'Come on, hurry up, it's not a difficult question.'

Turner 65 looked at Andrew and said with relief in his voice, 'You can hear him too'.

'No. I can't hear him,' Andrew replied truthfully. 'Although I know he's there.'

'Yes, he's here.' 65 sighed.

'Well?'

Turner looked unsure and his face began to crumple, then he replied submissively, 'In the garden over there, sir'.

'Excellent. We'll give him a good send off at 16.00 hours this afternoon. I'll see you then, cleaned up, shaved, your hair brushed and having eaten a good meal.'

'Yes, sir.' 65 managed to smile. 'Thank you, sir.' Andrew walked away.

'Bloody hell,' remarked Shrimp. 'What shall we do now?'

'Organise the funeral, of course,' replied Williams. 'I'll get some of the lads whose names I took to dig the grave and then I'll take them off the list. First we'll find out exactly where 65 would like his brother buried.'

'You ask 'im,' said Shrimp. 'I ain't going through all that rigmarole like the captain did.'

Williams approached 65 and said, 'Come and show us where you want the grave.' Turner looked at his brother. 'It's all right,' added Williams. 'Shrimp and Pilson will guard Len.'

While Pilson, Clark and Shrimp sat waiting for them to come back, a trooper ran up with a Union flag and another arrived carrying a stretcher. 'Williams told us to give you these... for Len Turner.'

'Thanks mate,' said Shrimp. When they had gone he turned to Pilson and asked, 'What're they for?'

'To wrap the body in and the stretcher is to carry him.' Shrimp looked puzzled. Pilson added, 'Well, we haven't got a coffin.'

Another man arrived with two pieces of wood. He held the shorter one across the longer one and explained, 'A cross'.

'Thanks,' repeated Shrimp. He looked at the shorter cross section. 'We could carve his name on that. Only I can't carve.'

They looked round in surprise as Clark said, 'I can; what shall I put? '

'What about R.I.P. Trooper Turner 4864. And put the King's Own Cavalry underneath.'

'All right. The Turners are farmers in Kent, aren't they?' asked Clark.

'Yes, that's right,' answered Pilson.

'Well, what if I carved a trail of hops, wheat and barley, as well?

'Good idea, if you can,' replied Shrimp. 'You'd better hurry. We've only got until 16.00 hours.'

'No problem.' Clark began to whittle away with his army knife.

Shrimp stood up. 'You two stay here. I'm going to find something to make a wreath.'

By the time Turner 65 and Williams arrived back, Pilson and Clark had placed Len on the stretcher and covered his body with the Union flag.

65 stopped in his tracks and stared at his brother. The others held their breath. Then he smiled and said, 'He looks peaceful, don't he?' They all nodded.

Shrimp came back with an armful of rose hips, hawthorn berries, holly, honeysuckle and michaelmas daisies.

'Where did you find those?' asked Pilson. Shrimp pointed to the overgrown garden. 'How did you learn to do that?' Pilson watched him as he began to twist them together expertly into a wreath.

'Me Grandma taught me. We used to make 'em for Christmas. What's he doing?' Shrimp looked at Williams, who sat sucking his pencil, writing something down, crossing out what he had written and sucking his pencil again.

'Don't know,' replied Pilson.

***

At five to four that afternoon, Turner 65 and Pilson picked up the stretcher and walked slowly towards the overgrown garden. Clark followed leading Len's black Irish horse. Behind them came Shrimp holding his wreath; Williams carried the beautifully carved cross and a sheet of paper. Andrew brought up the rear with a firing party of six men.

A group of troopers looked up, stopped what they were doing and followed the small procession.

'Who's the body?' asked one.

'Search me, must be some officer; let's go and see.'

There were several mourners already standing at the grave which lay beside a great clump of wild dog roses.

The Padre, wearing his surplice over his uniform, waited for them at the graveside. He welcomed the party with the words, '*I am the resurrection and the life, saith the Lord: he that believeth in me, though he were dead, yet shall he live: and whosoever liveth and believeth in me shall never die*'.

After the prayers, they sang Psalm 23. *The Lord is my Shepherd*. Then Andrew stepped forward to give an address:

'We're gathered here to say farewell to a courageous cavalryman who willingly sacrificed his life for his country. Trooper ...' Several men turned and looked at their neighbours, whispering, 'All this for a trooper?'

Andrew continued: 'Trooper Turner 4864 and many men like him are an example to us all. He fought so that peace will descend again into Europe, enabling us to live together in harmony. Our grandchildren and our great grandchildren will be able to say with pride, "Our ancestors fought in this war and cleansed Europe and the world of evil".

'This is a war to end all wars. Our sons of Britain and the British Empire will not die in vain. We shall see our great country lead the world into a new era of peace and unity.

'Let's use this sad day to honour all the valuable soldiers who fight so bravely for those things we hold dear: our King, our Country and our freedom.' Andrew paused and looked around at the impromptu congregation. 'We'll fire a salute and, in doing so, not only will we pay tribute to our comrades who have laid down their lives, but also send this message to the enemy. '*We shall do what we have to do, and we will win*'. Andrew nodded at a sergeant who gave the order:

'Party.' The firing party raised their heads.

'Present arms.' The entire congregation presented arms along with the firing party.

'Slope arms,' ordered the sergeant. Again the troopers gathered round the graveside followed the order.

'Present - Fire!'

Over fifty men raised their rifles and fired into the air. The shots echoed around the ruined house and the field and bounced off the ridge. The black Irish horse at the graveside reared up on to his hind legs and Clark had a job to hold him. The horses picketed in the spinney threw up their heads but none broke free.

'Reload,' came the order and twice more the group of mourners followed the order and fired on command.

The troopers who had not followed the funeral procession jumped up, grabbed their rifles and ran towards the group of men gathered around the graveside. They arrived in time to join in with the hymn *Onward Christian Soldiers*.

The men who didn't have their prayer books shared with those who did. Turner 65 sang out loud in his melodic tenor voice. He could be heard above the droning of some of the less musically gifted men and the shouted words of the others. The hymn rang out over the fields and the garden. The horses in the picket lines turned their heads and pricked their ears.

When the hymn came to an end there was a hush as Williams stepped forward to recite a poem that he had spent the morning writing. He wasn't expecting such a large gathering and his hand shook as he held the paper.

He started speaking: 'A Tribute and Farewell to a Cavalryman'. He paused and cleared his throat. Then he spoke without a tremor:

'Our beloved son of England lies here, free of pain;
He sleeps in peace beneath this foreign soil,
And makes it part of Kent from whence he came,
He is mercifully released from this vile turmoil.

His spirit will ride proudly through Eternity,
Where the heavens house our valiant steeds.
They galloped into death never shirking their duty
Patiently bearing soldiers ignoring their needs

To these grand and noble beasts now deceased
Slain whilst trusting us; extend our appreciation
Give them our love, our thanks and our esteem
For the services they gave without question

Len, we'll meet again at Heaven's gate when our time is nigh
We'll find peace and clarity at last and you will hear us sigh
As the good Lord gives us the answer, to our... "Why?"
Goodbye 'til then, gallant Cavalryman, fearless rider, goodbye.'

As Williams stepped back, the tangible silence was broken as one man murmured, 'Amen to that'. The word *'Amen'* travelled through the group of mourners like a wind sighing through trees.

Then silence fell as the Padre said the words, *'Man who is born of woman has but a short time to live....'* while Turner 65, aided by Pilson, Shrimp and Williams, carefully lowered Len into the grave.

Andrew gave the signal to his bugler to sound the Last Post. After the Padre had given his final blessing, the men filed past the grave, picked up small handfuls of soil and respectfully dropped them on the body.

Some men muttered, 'Goodbye, mate'. One or two said, 'See you soon' and some patted Turner 65 on the shoulder as they filed past. When the last member of the congregation had left, Clark returned the black horse to the horse lines. Pilson, Shrimp and Williams were about to fill in the grave as Andrew approached Turner.

'Thank you, sir,' said 65. 'My brother and me... well, we're very grateful.'

'You must thank your friends, Turner, they organised it.'

'Yes, sir.'

Andrew addressed the remaining men. 'Well done, excellent job.' He walked away with an inscrutable look on his face.

Williams, Pilson and Shrimp continued to help 65 fill in the grave.

Turner picked up the cross and ran his fingers over the carved trail of hops, wheat and barley. 'That's grand; Clark has put the cap badge on the top as well. Len's proud of that.' He carefully placed the wooden cross at the head of the mound of earth. Shrimp laid his wreath over the top of the cross.

'Thank you, that's not bad for a townie.' 65 looked with pride at the finished result. They left him alone as they went to attend to their horses. Williams glanced back at the solitary figure by the graveside. 65 had sunk to his knees, his body wracked with sobs as the pent up feelings of anger and desolation began to leave his body.

CHAPTER EIGHTEEN

Atonement

Von Meyer was sitting at his desk in Francine's father's study when the door was flung open by a private soldier. Heinrich rose to his feet and saluted as his commanding officer strode in.

'Good morning, von Meyer.' Colonel Spitz sat down and signalled to Heinrich to sit also. He continued, 'We're trying to establish what happened to Francine du Byard du Moulin'.

'We had the castle well guarded. I don't know how they got her away.'

'Don't you?' The colonel looked intently at von Meyer.

Heinrich looked steadily back. 'No. I did hear, however, that she was raped by a German officer, which I found disturbing.'

'She was raped. Not by an officer, but by the two men who were guarding her. Oberleutnant von Krutz has had them shot.'

'That's extraordinary because Schultz Reimer, one of the guards, told me, himself, that she had been raped.'

'They confessed to the oberleutnant.'

'Did they?' Von Meyer stared at the Colonel.

'Yes. They were guilty.' He abruptly changed the subject. 'We had information regarding the intended rescue of the girl. Were you not aware of that?'

'I... I had heard something of the sort, but no exact details. Unfortunately the Frenchmen who rescued her knew the castle better than we did.'

'It wasn't the French.' The colonel paused. 'It was the British.'

'The British!'

'Yes, a certain Captain Harrington-West.'

'Good heavens.'

'You were at school with this man, weren't you?'

'Y..es... Yes.'

'And you used to stay with his family in the school holidays.' Von Meyer nodded. 'I find it hard to believe that you were unaware of what was going on. It seems a very strange coincidence to me.'

'I agree with you, sir. It does seem odd.'

The young private burst into the room. 'Excuse me, sir, but the

Rittmeister is wanted. We go into action.'

'*Soldat*, learn to knock at doors,' the colonel snapped.

'Yes, Herr Colonel.' The private hastily backed out of the room.

Spitz turned to Heinrich. 'You're clearly needed, von Meyer. You may go, but we'll be watching you.'

'Yes, sir. But I understood that I was a good soldier.'

'You're a very good soldier and a good officer. That is why I haven't arrested you…yet.'

'I don't understand.'

'I think you do.' The colonel stood up. 'You'd better hurry. Your squadron requires you.'

***

Von Meyer was ordered to take his squadron north into Belgium. After several days on the road, interspersed with heavy fighting, he found himself in a small Belgian town. He saw to the stabling of the horses and then wearily went to his billet. His heart sank as he found von Krutz sitting at the kitchen table with two officers. A surly Belgian woman was dishing out a mixture of porridge and vegetables. She sighed when she saw another German arrive.

'Is this the best you can do?' snapped von Krutz.

'We have no food,' replied the woman. 'Your army has taken what we had. These are my family's rations for a week.'

'Just eat it, von Krutz. The woman is doing her best. Be grateful; the men only have biscuits to eat.' Von Meyer smiled at the woman.

'I'll be grateful when you get your just desserts. You may have fooled the colonel, but you don't fool me.'

'You're being impertinent, Oberleutnant; what are you talking about?'

The other two officers, who had finished eating, got up from the table and wandered upstairs. The woman looked anxiously at the ceiling as she heard them walking about in the room above the kitchen.

'It's all right, Madame.' Von Meyer told her. 'They won't take anything.' The woman shook her head and said nothing.

'What are you, the Good Samaritan?' Von Krutz sneered.

'You're getting very tedious, Oberleutnant. You'd better say whatever it is that is on your mind.'

'I am talking about the du Byard girl whom your friend Harrington-

West rescued.'

'We don't know who rescued her.'

'It was Harrington-West. We've heard from our source in London that you helped him.'

'That's a lie.'

Von Krutz was silent for a while and then he said, 'We're going after the brother'.

'Whose brother?'

'Harrington-West's.'

'Good heavens, why?' asked Heinrich. 'I thought we had better things to do.'

'His father's in the British War Cabinet. We could do some deals with them.'

'I very much doubt that. The British do not make *deals*.'

'So you know the British well do you? … Of course you do, your mother is English and you were at school there.'

'A lot of German people have British friends and relatives. I believe you do yourself.'

The oberleutnant sat up. 'You have done your homework.'

'You certainly seem to have done yours. What's all this leading to, von Krutz?'

'I hate spies.'

'So…?'

'I mean to catch them and I mean to make sure they are punished.'

'You have several missions to accomplish, do you not?'

'I do indeed. But never fear, I'll achieve them, by whatever methods come my way.'

'Yes, I understand you are good with your *methods*. How do you intend to capture Bertram Harrington-West?'

Von Krutz glared. 'If you suppose I'm going to tell you that, then you must think I'm incredibly stupid.'

Von Meyer paused. 'Not at all. I thought I might help you, then it will dispel your ludicrous notion that I helped with the rescue of Francine du Byard.'

Von Krutz thought for a while. 'Yes… that might be a good idea.'

'What are your plans and how do you know where he is?'

'We have word that his regiment isn't far from here.'

'He's behind the British lines and heavily guarded. I don't see how you are going to get near him.'

Von Krutz paused. Then he said, 'That's where you might come in handy. You could infiltrate the British as one of them, single him out and walk with him to an exposed place.'

'And do you expect me to kiss him, like Judas?'

'Don't be ridiculous. I can send someone else. Perhaps you're not up to it.'

'It seems very easy. When are you planning on this operation?'

'Quite soon. I'll let you know.'

***

As they continued on their march north, von Meyer was becoming increasingly disturbed by the actions of some of his fellow officers and their treatment of the Belgian civilians. Houses were burnt and people were being shot; great swathes of fleeing refugees had been machine-gunned by Germans in aeroplanes.

Heinrich was resting after a long day's march through hostile villages and past farms that had been ransacked. He sat wearily at the side of a lane watching his men picket, feed and water their horses.

He sighed as he heard the familiar voice of von Krutz. 'The British are in the valley on the other side of that ridge,'

'That's pretty obvious. We've been riding towards their guns for most of the day. What do you want?'

'Lieutenant-Colonel Harrington-West is camped just behind the front line.'

'Are you sure?'

'Yes, perfectly sure. Are you getting cold feet?'

Heinrich summoned up all his energy and said, with as much enthusiasm as he could muster, 'So we'll go across tonight and get him out, shall we?'

'Yes. Do you have a plan?'

'I'll ride into the camp wearing a British Army greatcoat over my uniform. I'll bring him out and I'll hand him over to you.'

'Do you have a British greatcoat?'

'I do, as it happens; one of my men took one as a souvenir and I have the hat to go with it.'

'Let's hope they don't notice your boots,' Von Krutz sneered.

'It'll be dark,' Heinrich replied calmly.

That night von Meyer rode Francine's grey horse out towards the

British lines wearing the greatcoat over his uniform. He was accompanied by a guide who told him of Bertram's movements.

'Are you sure he follows the same routine every night?' Von Meyer was incredulous.

'Yes, absolutely,' replied the stocky blond man, who could speak perfect German, Flemish, French and English.

They rode along in silence, zigzagging through the countryside in order to avoid barbed wire and guards. The man spoke again when they came in sight of the lights of the camp. He told Heinrich where to meet von Krutz and then he melted away into the night. A sentry jumped out of nowhere and shouted, 'Halt. Who goes there?'

Von Meyer replied calmly in good English, 'Captain Maitland, 1st Cavalry division. I'm here to see Colonel Harrington-West.'

The sentry shone his torch in Heinrich's face and replied, 'Pass, sir. You'll find him in the bell tent on the left'. Von Meyer rode into the camp. Nobody took any notice of him. Most of the soldiers were asleep in their tents and the sentries didn't see the German saddle and bridle on the horse.

When he arrived at Bertram's tent two soldiers jumped to attention and challenged him.

'I'm here to see Colonel Harrington-West.'

'Your name, sir?'

'M… Meyer,' replied Heinrich.

One of the guards went into the tent and came out accompanied by a major carrying a revolver. He demanded 'What are you doing? Are you alone?'

'I'm alone,' replied von Meyer.

The officer looked around. 'Dismount. Private, take his horse.' Von Meyer followed the officer into the tent. Bertram was sitting at a small table in the centre. He stood up and held out his hand. 'Heinrich, what on earth are you doing here?'

'It's a long story.' The German smiled.

'Pull up a chair.' Bertram called to his batman, 'Evans, some brandy for our friend'. The man didn't seem to turn a hair at the glimpse of the German uniform beneath the greatcoat and hurried away. 'Let me introduce you: Rittmeister von Meyer, a school friend of my brother.' The major and Heinrich shook hands.

'Continue with your story,' Bertram invited.

'I've been sent to take you prisoner.' Von Meyer put up his hand and smiled as the major drew his revolver again. 'Don't worry, I don't have an army at the gate, only a guide, who I suspect is a double agent.' Heinrich gave them the name of the Belgian.

'Thank you,' replied Bertram. 'Men like him can be very useful when one realises what they are up to.'

'I think you need to improve your security; I rode into this camp without any trouble at all. Nobody noticed my German saddle and bridle.'

'Yes, you're right. However, we do capture German horses quite frequently, although I must say they aren't usually as fine as yours,' said Bertram.

'No. He belongs to Francine du Byard. How is she by the way?'

'She has recovered well. She owes you her life, as does my brother.'

Von Meyer looked down. 'Yes, I believe so...'

'But yours is now in danger?'

Heinrich nodded. He told the two officers about von Krutz and the meeting with his colonel. 'They know I did it. They're playing a cat and mouse game with me. As soon as it's convenient and I'm no longer needed, they'll shoot me. So I offered to take you prisoner in order to buy myself some thinking time.'

'Was that your idea?' The major was curious.

'No. Von Krutz seems to have taken an aversion to the Harrington-West family, and of course he knows that Lord Hawkenfield is in the War Cabinet. He believes he'll be able to do some sort of deal with the British Government.'

'The British Government doesn't make deals,' Bertram laughed.

'So I told him. But also I'm a threat because he knows that I know he raped Francine. He has had two young soldiers shot for doing so, when in fact it was one of them who came to tell me that it was von Krutz, himself.'

'This von Krutz seems to be a most unsavoury character.'

'Yes, and he's not alone in the German army. The old-school officers are worthy, principled people and I would happily serve under them. The ordinary soldiers are good and true, but there's an element of unnecessary brutality arising amongst some of the younger officers which I cannot condone. They're doing things that I don't want to talk about. I'm a soldier, I fight other soldiers. I cannot abuse and torture civilians.'

'What are you saying? That you are defecting to us?' Bertram asked.

Von Meyer shook his head. 'No, unfortunately I can't do that. My mother is English, my father German and I feel as if I'm caught between two stools. I've thought long and hard over this; in fact I have thought of little else these past few weeks.' He shrugged. 'I feel that I can no longer continue in the German army and yet I cannot join the British army. I don't want to become a spy.' He looked up and smiled. 'I know I have been behaving like a secret agent over these incidents, but it's not what I want to do. I could not let my childhood friend walk into a trap.'

There was a silence. 'Are you giving yourself up?' asked Bertram.

'No, I can't do that either. I'll return empty handed. I must speak to von Krutz; I am his senior officer after all.'

'But you'll be walking to your death,' exclaimed Bertram.

'All of us here will be walking towards our death, my friend, sooner or later.' There was a silence. Heinrich took a deep breath and continued: 'Talking of honour, I have to tell you that my scout told me that your brother murdered one of his own men'.

The two British officers gasped. Bertram exclaimed, 'That's rubbish! Of course he didn't.'

Von Meyer shook his head. 'I don't believe it was him either, but one of his officers did exactly that.'

'What the devil are you talking about?' demanded the major.

Von Meyer told them about the lost cavalrymen led by Rupert at the beginning of the war. 'The men who Andrew engaged in a battle at the ford were from my squadron. A half-troop of British cavalry followed them into a forest. My men lost them and then, as they tried to turn the tables, the British disappeared. Later my scout came across them and, although it was dark, he saw a trooper fall off his horse several times. The officer dropped behind the rest of the group with the man in question. When the trooper fell from his horse again the officer dragged him into the undergrowth and slit his throat.'

'I don't believe you,' cried Bertram indignantly. 'Your man was mistaken or made the whole thing up. No British officer would do that.'

'So one would like to believe, but when I found the body of the trooper, his throat had been cut. My scout is adamant that the British officer did it. The man had a bad head wound which may have been the reason why he couldn't sit on his horse.'

Bertram drew a deep breath, looked at his fellow officer and said, 'What you say is partly right. Andrew certainly told my father the story of how his junior officer galloped after the Germans and became lost in a forest'.

Von Meyer smiled. 'I was sure it wasn't Andrew. But our side are using the story to discredit your family. And the British cavalry of course. I meant to mention it to Andrew in the castle, but there were far more pressing things on our minds at the time, as you can imagine.'

'Surely you can't believe a story like that?' The major turned indignantly to Bertram. 'It's pure nonsense put about by the Germans in order to disgrace our officers.'

Bertram sighed heavily. 'I certainly hope so, but I will have to look into it.' He asked Heinrich. 'Do you believe it?'

'I'm afraid I do. You see, there was no one else in the area. We found the body just as my scout described. The throat had been cut and the man bled to death in the bushes. If my scout had killed the British trooper he would have shot him.'

There was a long silence, broken by Bertram, who said, grimly, 'We'll get to the bottom of it. If it's true then we need to deal with the officer in question very swiftly.'

'The name on the man's identification disc was Nash, by the way.' Then Heinrich went on to say, 'I must tell you that we know your exact movements, Bertram. My guide told me that you go out each night, without fail, and that you stand in the open smoking a cigarette.'

Silence fell and the major stared at Bertram. 'Is this true?'

'Yes, I'm afraid it is. I don't sleep very well and that walkabout and last cigarette helps me to relax,' replied Bertram.

'Well, you must stop doing it,' said Von Meyer. 'When I return empty handed...'

'You mean you're really going to return?' Bertram was incredulous.

'I have to. I will not desert, I will not change sides and I won't become a double agent. What else can I do?'

'This is suicide,' said Bertram.

'There are no other options open to me.'

'You can give yourself up. We'll make you a prisoner of war and then you'll go to England for the duration. In fact we can take you prisoner now.'

Von Meyer shook his head and smiled. 'No, it's not as simple as that. That is the coward's way out. I have to get back; there are some things I need to say to von Krutz before I die.'

Bertram stood up. 'I understand your attitude. You're a brave man.'

Von Meyer shook hands with the two officers and someone called for his horse. He knocked back the large brandy the batman had left beside him, saying, 'Thank you, I need that.' He mounted his horse and rode out of the camp.

Bertram quietly said, 'Adieu,' as he watched him ride away.

***

When von Meyer arrived at the appointed rendezvous, von Krutz rode out in front of his horse. 'Where's Colonel Harrington-West?' he sneered.

'He wasn't there,' replied Heinrich calmly.

'Yes he was. You were seen talking to him. I knew all along that you were a spy. Arrest this man,' he shouted to his small band of soldiers.

They eagerly pulled Heinrich off his horse. 'Tie him up,' yelled von Krutz.

'How did you get the guards to confess to the rape, von Krutz?' asked Heinrich.

'You'll find out,' snarled the oberleutnant and hit him in the face with all his force.

'You did it. I know you did, but you blamed two innocent German soldiers. What sort of officer are you?' Von Krutz hit him again. Heinrich spat the blood from his mouth and gasped, 'How did you get them to confess?'

'You know what to do,' the oberleutnant shouted to his minions. While two of them heaved Heinrich on to their shoulders, one of them tied his bound wrists to a stout branch of a tree. They walked away and left him dangling with his toes just brushing the ground. By the time they came back burning pains were shooting down Heinrich's arms and coursing into his shoulders.

'I've prepared a paper for you to sign,' said von Krutz. 'It says that you helped rescue the girl and that you also committed other crimes.'

'What would those be?' Von Meyer sneered.

'You stole gold and silver from several churches and a quantity of jewellery from the castle in France.'

'You have been busy, Oberleutnant. And you think I don't know that you'll kill me after I have signed your paper?'

'You'll be begging me to kill you by the time we've finished.'

'I doubt that.'

Von Krutz signalled to two soldiers who removed Von Meyer's boots. They began to systematically beat von Meyer's feet with heavy pieces of wood. Each blow sent his body swinging back and forth and with each swing the weight of his body pulled down hard on his wrists and his shoulders.

When they had finished they left him dangling. Von Meyer bent his knees to take the weight off his broken toes, but soon he cried out in pain as cramp gripped his thighs and calves. He straightened his legs. His toes touched the ground and an electric current of pain shot up his legs.

He had never experienced pain such as this. He had believed himself to be tough and ready for whatever von Krutz had in mind, but this sea of agony was beyond anything he was expecting. The weight of his body dislocated his wrists and his hands became numb. He thankfully passed out, only to regain consciousness with an agonising jolt as his feet touched the ground again. He had to bend his knees and so the cycle of cramp and pain continued. His breathing became shallow and laboured as his body stretched upwards.

Dawn broke before von Krutz strode up to the hanging figure. 'Good morning,' he mocked, waving a sheet of paper. 'Are you ready to sign your confession?' Von Meyer didn't reply. 'Cat got your tongue?' Von Krutz said, as he landed a blow to the Rittmeister's upper body.

Von Meyer managed to say, between gasps of breath, 'God damn you to hell, von Krutz... Putting the blame on other people won't save you... You'll pay for what you've done... In the end'.

'Shut up,' yelled von Krutz. He signalled to his henchmen to continue their beating.

'I ... will be sitting on your shoulder...' gasped von Meyer. He found it easier to bear the pain when he taunted his aggressor. 'Think of me there, when I'm dead.'

Von Krutz walked away, leaving his men to continue with their grisly work.

After the second beating, von Meyer couldn't speak even if he had wanted to beg for mercy and ask von Krutz to come back with his bit of paper. His body was an ocean of pain and his feet were now a mangled mess. His weight was pulling unbearably on his shoulders as well as his wrists. He had to concentrate all his energy into drawing each breath.

Von Krutz's soldiers were sitting a little distance away from him, eating and drinking. Von Meyer braced himself as he saw them stand up. He didn't know how he was going to cope with a third beating, so he shut his eyes and prayed for courage.

When he opened his eyes he expected to see his tormentors standing below him, but instead he saw them mount their horses and, at the signal from von Krutz, turn and ride away at a gallop.

Bullets whistled through the trees which briefly took Heinrich's mind off his anguish. He waited for the thump of a direct hit, but none came, instead he heard the thud of horse's hooves approaching at speed. A squadron of British cavalry galloped straight past him in pursuit of von Krutz. The hope that Heinrich had of either being killed or rescued was shattered.

He began to pass in and out of consciousness. He opened his eyes; the light was very bright, the trees had vanished and the countryside was green. Several riders dressed in hunting clothes passed beneath him. A riderless horse stopped and looked up at him as if inviting him to sit on its back. Von Meyer dropped from his tree and on to the horse. As soon as he landed in the saddle the horse took off at a comfortable gallop. Von Meyer could hear the music of a pack of hounds in front of him and revelled in the sensation of the wind in his face and the feel of the powerful horse between his knees. He galloped on towards a hedge and, as he rode the last few strides he thought he heard a voice shout, 'Hold hard. It's a drop'.

But von Meyer's blood was up, he could hear the wail of a hunting horn ahead and he urged his horse forwards. Suddenly there was a jolt and he felt a searing pain in his feet, his shoulders and his wrists. He opened his eyes and found himself lying on the ground at the foot of a tree, with his hands above his head.

'Have I fallen?' he asked, speaking in English. 'Where's my horse?'

'You ain't got no horse, at least not here you ain't.'

'Where am I?' asked von Meyer. 'What am I doing?'

'You tell us mate.'

'Who are you?'

'We're medical orderlies come to take you in. Who're you? Are you English or German?'

'Yes and no,' replied Von Meyer. Then he cried out in pain as the two orderlies untied his hands and pulled his arms down beside his body.

'Someone strung you up like a kipper and made a tidy mess of your feet.' The orderly turned to his partner. 'Come on Reg, put him on the stretcher. He can't walk, not with his feet in that state.'

Reg asked von Meyer, 'These your boots and greatcoat?' He put the articles on the stretcher without waiting for an answer. 'We've found a grey horse tethered. Is it yours too?'

'Yes. What are you doing out here in the hunting field?' asked Heinrich.

'This ain't no hunting field, this is a battlefield.' Reg said to his partner, 'Whatever they did to him must have blown his mind, he's gone barmy'.

'I'm not mad,' remarked von Meyer. 'You shouted to me to hold hard because the fence was a drop.'

'I said, hold him hard, we'll drop him down.'

'Oh, I must have come a hell of a purler.' Von Meyer passed out again.

When he came to, he found himself lying in a tent in the same British camp that he had left the previous evening. A soldier bent over him. 'The medic has patched you up, but you need to go to the field hospital. The Lieutenant-Colonel wants to see you.' Von Meyer smiled; he had been given morphine and he felt quite comfortable. His feet were swathed in bandages, as were his wrists and hands. He shut his eyes and dozed; little by little his experiences of the last twenty four hours came back to him.

He opened his eyes again as Bertram walked into the tent with the major.

'Well, you have been in the wars.' Bertram bent over him.

Von Meyer smiled. 'I was expecting rough treatment, but I didn't think it would be quite so bad. No wonder the two lads confessed to the rape.'

'This is all at the hands of Oberleutnant von Krutz?' asked Bertram.

'Yes. He's stolen gold from churches, also some jewellery from Francine's château. He wanted me to confess to his crimes.'

'Why would he steal? He comes from a powerful and well respected family. I know of his father, he's an honourable man.'

'I have no idea. Greed I suppose.'

'This time, my friend, we have taken you prisoner of war. You will go to the field hospital and then to England with your fellow prisoners. The Nieuport sluices, at the mouth of the Yser River in Belgium, have been opened. The Bavarians, who were fighting there, are being drowned. Vital areas have been flooded. The rising waters are forcing your countrymen to retreat back behind the river. Our seaward flank has been saved. We won the race for the sea. You'll have a safe passage back to the ports and then to England.'

'Thank you, Bertram. Will you look after my grey horse?'

'I have already requisitioned it for myself.'

Von Meyer smiled. 'Remember it belongs to Francine.'

'I will.' Bertram looked down at him and said gravely, 'Our family owes you a debt'.

'You have repaid it in full.'

Bertram touched his arm, 'Goodbye'. He walked away. Von Meyer closed his eyes and slept.

CHAPTER NINETEEN

A Gentleman's Decision

It was the last morning in November 1914. Andrew was sitting in his billet studying a letter from Francine that he had received that morning. It was dated the 2nd November. He turned the letter over and over in his hands. It had taken weeks to reach him. He looked for the postmark. There wasn't one; in fact the envelope had been addressed in a different handwriting.

Francine had written:

Dear Andrew, I could meet you during the week of 12th to 18th November. I'll be travelling north at that time and I would very much like to see you. I'm sure we have a lot to discuss.

I tend to agree, a little bit, with your observations about some of my countrymen and women, so I forgive you. However, the majority do their utmost, as we do, to rid this country of the vile Boches.

I look forward to hearing from you, and hope to see you soon. Yours, Francine.

Andrew was debating what to do when there was a knock on the door. 'Come in,' he called wearily. He didn't look up as the door opened.

'That's a fine way to greet your brother.' A tall, dark lieutenant-colonel filled the doorway.

'Bertram!' Andrew gasped. He stood up and warmly shook his sibling by the hand. 'Sit down.' He pulled a wobbly chair up to the fire. 'What brings you here?'

'I should have come several weeks ago but I couldn't get away. I wanted to speak to you myself.'

Andrew turned to his batman. 'North, could you scrounge more fuel for the fire and bring some coffee, please.'

'I'll try my best, sir.' The man looked dubious.

'Anything hot and wet would be fine.' Andrew smiled. As soon as the man left, he said, 'You sound very ominous. What's wrong? Is it something at home?'

'No, all's well there. It's about your man Rupert Somerville.'

'Good Lord. What's he done now?' Andrew sighed with relief. 'Is he often in trouble?'

'Not really. He's just a nuisance.'

'He's still with you, then.'

'Oh yes. Although when we're not fighting he gravitates towards Dickson-French and his cronies.'

'Describe his character.'

'The men don't like him. Some are openly insolent. He can't deal with that, so he tries to ignore it. I know that I can't rely on him. If I give him something important to do I have to check up, which is rather a bore. We're busy enough without wet-nursing junior officers.'

'Would you call him a gentleman?'

Andrew thought for a moment. 'His mother is certainly a lady... but his father is rather an odd ball. Given the nature of his behaviour... No, I wouldn't describe him as a gentleman.'

'I see.' Bertram related the story that von Meyer had told him.

Andrew sat staring into the flames and heaved a sigh. 'Unfortunately, Bertram, that all makes sense.' He looked at his brother. 'He did have some blood on his sleeve, I remember. He was very uncomfortable when I questioned him about it.'

'Do you think he's capable of cold-blooded murder?'

'That's a difficult question. I know he was under a lot of pressure. In fact, by all accounts he was in a complete funk. He had just fought a battle and killed a German, which he found to be easy. This man Nash was slowing down the troop and he could have got them all killed. Yes, from what I've seen of his character, I think he would be capable of killing the trooper in order to save his own skin. He would think of it in terms of *putting him down* for the good of the others.' With a look of distaste, Andrew added, 'As one might shoot a foxhound that was slower than the pack'. There was a silence.

'Do you have anyone left who was with him at the time?' asked Bertram.

'Yes, Corporal Clark was there. Sergeant Armstrong, also, but he's in England recovering from his wounds at the moment. I'm sure I could get word to him.'

'Let's see what Clark has to say first.'

The batman arrived with a sack full of odd bits of damp timber for the fire. He produced two mugs of hot, weak coffee made from chicory root and laced with bandy.

'Excellent.' Bertram took a sip of the brown liquid. He glanced uneasily at the hissing in the grate and wrinkled up his nose at the smell that was issuing from the firewood. 'God knows where that wood has been.'

'Best not to ask.' Andrew laughed.

While they waited for the corporal to arrive Bertram said, 'There's more. Father has heard from Heinrich. He told him that a Germen soldier, who is in the same POW camp, saw a British officer stab one of his own men. We've narrowed it down with dates and times to your squadron'.

'For heaven's sake! Now, what are you saying?'

Bertram went on to describe how Rupert had stabbed Ashton. 'The German in question was lying wounded. He had been disarmed and was waiting to be picked up by our medical orderlies. It happened within a few feet of him. He was terrified. He thought the British officer in question would kill him too.'

'Where was this?' Andrew asked. Bertram told him the name of the battlefield. Andrew gasped, 'Ashton! Rupert said he had seen him bayonetted right in front of him. In fact he made rather a fuss about it, said it had affected him quite deeply. A pity it's far too late to examine Ashton's body. A knife wound would be considerably smaller than one made by a German bayonet.'

'Well, I'll put it to him and we'll watch his reaction.'

Clark entered the room and looked enquiringly at Andrew.

'It's all right, Corporal,' said Andrew. 'We would like you to recount what happened when you were lost in the forest after the battle at the ford.'

'That was a long time ago, sir.'

'Only three months,' said Andrew.

'It seems like three years, so much has happened since. Where shall I start?'

'Tell us about a man called Nash.'

Clark told them how the trooper had received a bad head injury. 'The doctor said he shouldn't ride, but the lieutenant insisted. Well, we couldn't leave him there so he had to. The doc explained as how he might drop down dead if he exerted himself. Nash fell off his horse a couple of times as we made our way back through the forest. The lieutenant became very annoyed. Then he decided to ride with him at the back, to help him, or so we hoped.'

'You sound sceptical, Corporal.' Bertram gave him a smile. 'Why?'

'I ... He's an officer, sir.'

'Tell us what's on your mind, Clark,' Andrew asked invitingly.

'Well... he didn't seem to know what to do, for an officer I mean.

Sergeant Armstrong had to take control. Only he did it very tactful like.'

'Go on.' Bertram was at his most charming.

'Lieutenant Somerville became very angry because Nash was slowing us up.' The two brothers looked at each other. 'So it seemed odd that he wanted to help him, that's all.'

'What happened next?' asked Bertram.

'When Nash fell off again, we saw the lieutenant fiddling about, dismounting and that. But they were a long way behind and it was getting dark. The next thing the lieutenant gallops up alone with the two horses. He says that Nash was dead when he hit the ground. The doctor wanted to go back and take a look. Somerville wouldn't let him, said we had to press on and that someone would bury him.' Clark looked at Andrew. 'It fair gave us the shivers, sir, unnerved some of us.'

'Yes... yes, I can see that it would,' Bertram replied after a pause. 'Thank you Corporal, you've been very helpful.'

After Clark left the room, the two brothers stared at each other. 'I think we'd better go and find Somerville, don't you?' said Bertram.

***

They found Rupert in Charles Dickson-French's billet. He was playing cards with half a dozen other officers in a room that was thick with cigar smoke. There was a half empty brandy bottle on the table and some empty wine bottles lying on the floor.

''S' that your man with more brandy?' An officer slewed round in his chair as Bertram and Andrew entered.

'Good Lord! It's the Harrington-West brothers,' said another.

'A pleasure to see you.' Charles hid his surprise well. 'Sit down, have a drink. Shall we deal you in?'

'No, I don't think so.' Bertram was frosty.

'We've come to speak to Rupert,' explained Andrew.

'Go ahead, don't mind us. No secrets here, don't you know.' An officer waved his hand in the air. Turning to Charles, he said, 'C'mon, get on with the game.'

Charles shot a look at Rupert and noticed his face whiten and his hands beginning to shake. He announced, 'All right, the game's over, everything is null and void in this round'.

There was an astonished cry from an officer. 'But I've got a good hand, Charles, best all day, can't stop now.'

Charles looked imploringly at two of the officers. They stood up. 'Sort the money out later. Best leave now, what,' said one of them.

'Thanks, old bean.' Charles shepherded the other disgruntled officers out into the cold winter's day. He was surprised to see Turner 65 and Williams standing outside the front door. He walked round behind the little cottage and saw Pilson and Shrimp at the back door. Although he didn't know their names, he knew that they were from Andrew's squadron. He re-entered the smoky room to find the two brothers sitting across the table from Rupert. The three men were waiting for him in stony silence.

'What's going on?' Charles poured himself a brandy and sat down. 'Would you...? He gestured to the brandy bottle.

'No thank you,' replied Andrew.

'We're here to determine what happened to Trooper Nash,' said Bertram.

'Who's Trooper Nash?' Charles gave a short laugh. He looked, in surprise, at Rupert, who pushed his chair back from the table and stood up.

'Sit down,' ordered Bertram.

'I say, old boy....' Charles began.

'Be quiet, Charles,' said Bertram. He recounted what von Meyer had told him about the ride through the forest.

'And you believe a bloody Hun?' Charles blustered.

'One of my corporals told the same story. I'll get confirmation from Sergeant Armstrong in due course.' Andrew's tone was grim.

'Rupert.' Charles looked at the young officer who sat staring down at the table. 'Defend yourself, boy!' Rupert looked up with a wild look in his eyes. Charles gasped. 'It can't be true. I mean you wouldn't do such a thing.' He saw the anguish on Rupert's face. 'My God! ...' He stopped in mid-sentence.

Rupert's face crumpled. He pleaded with the older man. 'You've got to help me. What shall I do?' He stood up, knocking over his chair, and went to grab Charles's Sam Browne belt.

Dickson-French backed away in disgust. 'I say Rupe, that's beyond the pale. What made you?'

'I had to.'

The older man shook his head. 'That's.... That's cold-blooded murder.' He shivered. 'How could you?'

'Don't let me down, Charlie,' Rupert begged, forgetting that Bertram and Andrew were in the room. 'Please, please, not now.' He stared in disbelief at the disgust on Charles's face. 'What am I going to do? You promised Mama that you would look after me.'

Dickson-French shook his head. 'I can't condone this, old boy. You can't go around killing your own men. Bad form, don't you know.'

'I had to get the others back safe and sound,' Rupert began to whine. 'You must see that. You told me that sometimes we have to sacrifice men for the better good.'

Dickson-French, looking embarrassed, glanced at Bertram. 'Not like that, Rupert old lad.' Charles continued backing away from the boy, who was becoming hysterical.

'Rupert, sit down!' Andrew raised his voice.

The lieutenant suddenly remembered the two brothers and turned on Andrew. His voice became louder and higher. 'It's your fault. You treat me like an idiot. You turn the men against me and you give me silly jobs to do.' He started to fumble with his holster when Williams and Turner 65 burst into the room. They grabbed his arms, seized his gun and pushed him into a chair. He sat struggling to get up, still yelling abuse.

Bertram stood up. He leant towards him and banged the table with his fist. 'Be quiet, Somerville. Try to find a little dignity.' Rupert suddenly fell silent and stared at the Guards officer, who continued, 'There is also the case of Trooper Ashton'.

Rupert started to shake violently. He stared wide-eyed at Dickson-French. Charles asked hesitantly, 'What happened to Trooper Ashton?'

Bertram's eyes never left Rupert's face as he replied, 'During the confusion of disarming German prisoners at the end of a battle, Somerville was seen to stab him'.

Charles sat down heavily, his red and white spotted handkerchief held to his mouth. There was a look of horror in his small pale blue eyes. Bertram continued, 'We all know you're guilty'. The silence in the smoky room was intense; nobody moved until Bertram said, 'Rupert, you know what will happen after a court martial. I believe you have already witnessed one execution.' Rupert trembled. 'The whole procedure is most unpleasant. None of us want that. You have two choices. The first is that you deal with the situation yourself, as a gentleman.' Bertram glanced at Rupert's gun which Andrew had put down on the table. 'Nobody in this room will ever mention the matter again.' He looked at Turner and Williams. 'Do I have your assurance on that?'

'Yes, sir,' replied both men.

'Your mother will be told that you had an accident with your revolver. It jammed and, while you were trying to clear it, it went off. None of this nasty business will have to come to light.' Bertram paused. The quiet in the room was only broken by the rumble of guns in the distance and Rupert's sporadic juddering sobs.

Bertram looked intently at the lieutenant and carried on: 'If you choose a court martial, then the story will be splashed all over the newspapers. Your name will be dishonoured. Disgrace and shame will fall upon your mother and your friends.' He glanced at Charles. 'Your regiment, and, in fact, the whole British army will not look kindly upon you. I expect you'll have to go through considerable hardship and humiliation in a military prison as you await your inevitable execution.'

Rupert looked desperately at Charles who said, gently, 'He's right, old lad'.

There was a long silence. Rupert looked at his gun and then, without warning, lunged forwards and grabbed it. Turner seized his arm and, as Rupert pulled the trigger, the muzzle flew up in the air. The shot, intended for Andrew, hit the ceiling. Shrimp and Pilson burst in through the back door.

'Rupert!' gasped Charles. 'You're making things worse. Please stop.'

'So you are a murderer,' Bertram sneered. 'I think you have just forfeited your chance to redeem yourself. You're clearly no gentleman. One of you,' he addressed Shrimp and Pilson, 'go and fetch the Military Police.'

'No, stop. Please wait,' cried Charles as Shrimp turned to leave. Shrimp looked at Bertram, who nodded.

Rupert sat slumped in his chair, his hands now tied behind his back. He stared at the floor. Charles approached him, saying, 'Think of your mother. You know it would destroy her when the story gets out. Do you want that? You are her pride and joy'. Rupert began to listen. 'You're a huge recompense for your father, who we all know is a tremendous disappointment to her.' Rupert shuffled in his chair, looked up and saw the anguish on Charles's face and looked down again. Charles continued: 'If the story of what you have done comes out, your imprisonment and eventual...' He paused and, with a catch in his voice, said quietly, 'Execution.... Well, it will simply kill her'. There was another long silence. Charles saw tears fall on to Rupert's breeches. Then Rupert nodded his head, looked up and said very quietly, 'Charlie, tell them to leave us alone, please.'

Charles looked at Bertram. 'Would you?'

'Of course. But you must understand that if Rupert leaves the house we will shoot to kill.'

'I realise that,' replied Charles.

'Rupert?' asked Bertram.

Rupert nodded his head. They all left the room, leaving Charles and Rupert alone. The four cavalrymen surrounded the little house with their rifles primed.

As they stood outside in the cold, Bertram remarked, 'Dreadful business. I must say I would like to see him face the firing squad for taking a pot-shot at you'.

'Yes, but fortunately he missed. I've seen an execution, Bertram, and it's not pleasant. I hope he finishes the matter himself. Thank you for coming to sort it out. It would have been very difficult without you. Old Falters would have wanted it brushed under the carpet. We couldn't have that.'

'No.' Bertram looked up at the heavy sky. 'It feels warmer. Look it's beginning to snow.'

'So it is,' replied Andrew. They stood in silence watching the snowflakes filling the sky and muffling the sound of the guns. 'We used to love the first fall of snow. But now, with the men outside in the trenches, not to mention the horses, it fills me with dread.'

Bertram agreed. A shot rang out from inside the house. They drew their revolvers and ran through the front door with Williams and Turner, just as Pilson and Shrimp came in through the back.

They found Rupert slumped in a chair, his hands untied with the pistol still clutched in one of them. Charles knelt beside the body, openly sobbing. It was obvious that the boy was dead.

Andrew said, 'I'm so sorry Charles.'

'He... He did it. Right in front of me... dreadful. I'll never forget it.' Charles swallowed, shook his head and murmured, 'Only thing to do though. Obliged to your brother... Frightful scandal otherwise. I'll deal with things from now on'.

CHAPTER TWENTY

An Intrusion

The two brothers walked slowly and thoughtfully away from the cottage. Bertram broke the silence. 'I must leave now. It's been lovely seeing you. You're looking well and doing a good job, I hear.'

'We're not doing very much at the moment.' Andrew gave a short laugh. 'But yes, it's been a great treat to see you, in spite of the circumstances.' He paused and then asked casually, 'Have you heard what Francine is doing?'

'No, but I meant to tell you that I have her horse. I commandeered it from Heinrich.'

'Oh,' Andrew paused. 'That's good news. I hope you'll take good care of it.' Andrew did his best to hide his feelings.

'Yes, I certainly will; it's a very fine animal.'

Andrew stood and watched while Bertram drove away in a rickety car accompanied by a guardsman. He hoped the dilapidated vehicle would make it to their destination as it slipped and slithered over the newly fallen snow. He turned to walk away when someone called out, '*Capitaine* Harrington-West'.

Andrew spun round to be confronted by a French Cuirassier. He was astonished as he recognised the young officer. 'François, you've joined up. You do look smart. What can I do for you?'

'Is there somewhere private where we can speak?'

'Yes, my billet.' Andrew's heart sank. He was sure it was bad news concerning Francine.

They entered his billet to find that the fire had all but burnt out and talked of banalities while they waited for the batman to rejuvenate the flames.

'What is it?' Andrew could ask at last. 'Is Francine all right?'

'Yes, of course, why wouldn't she be?'

'I had a letter from her but it arrived extraordinarily late. I thought it might have been deliberately held up.'

'Yes. She wondered why you hadn't replied.'

'You've seen her?'

'Of course.' François looked at Andrew's worried face. 'It's all right. She's in good health.'

'Then why are you here?'

'Francine is staying at the Château d'Hautmont on the edge of the Forest of Crécy. That's just north of Abbeville. Her father is meeting the king.'

'Meeting the king! What on earth do you mean?'

'His Majesty King George V is at Boulogne for a few days, visiting his troops. Francine is staying with the Comtesse de Villegrande.'

'You French seem to know more than we do.'

François grinned. 'Francine expressed a wish to see you. So her father had the British authorities jumping through hoops to produce these.' He pulled some papers out of his wallet. 'This is a pass for you, and a soldier of your choice, to go to the Château d'Hautmont.' François brought out a map and showed Andrew the location of the little castle.

'Good Lord!'

'I believe you have 48 hours' leave, starting early tomorrow morning.'

Andrew studied the papers. 'You're right. Well I'll be damned. This is astonishing. And so lucky that you brought all these, I would never have got them through the post.'

'That's exactly why they sent me. I'm stationed not far from here. Madame la Comtesse is expecting you.'

'Then I won't disappoint her. Thank you so much.' Andrew looked through the papers again. 'Even train tickets!'

***

Very early the following morning, Andrew, taking Williams with him, boarded a crowded railway carriage. At last, after having to change to an equally crowded and slow train, they reached their destination. However, there was no transport to convey them any further. They walked in the direction of Hautmont hoping to find a lift.

'I'm looking forward to seeing the place where the battle of Crécy was fought,' remarked Williams.

'I would have thought you've seen enough battlefields to last a lifetime.'

Williams laughed. 'This one is medieval. I don't think there will be traces of any bodies left. Although it would be interesting to dig it up and see what is to be found, but I expect that has already been done.'

'Yes, I'm sure it has. Here comes a farm cart and a pair of horses;

flag them down.'

The driver reined in and Williams asked where he was going. He said he was passing through the village of Hautmont and readily agreed to take them. They thankfully climbed into the back of the empty cart which smelt of turnips mixed with farmyard manure. Fortunately it wasn't long before the farmer set them down at the entrance of a small medieval castle surrounded by a moat. They walked up to the stout iron gates which replaced the old draw bridge.

'What a beautiful place.' Williams dusted himself off. 'I wonder if it was captured by the English in 1346.'

'Don't ask them, Williams. Just ring the bell.'

'Wait a minute, sir. You're a bit dirty. Do you think we smell?' He brushed the dried mud off Andrew's back and then pulled the ornate iron bell-pull. They heard a bell jangle somewhere in the nether regions of the castle.

A butler walked sedately across the small courtyard. 'You must be Captain Harrington-West,' he stated.

'Yes, I am.'

'And this person is your servant?'

Andrew looked at Williams, who was suppressing a smile. 'Yes, quite correct.'

'Come with me, sir.' Andrew followed the man into a salon. He stood with his back to a blazing fire and looked at the dark panelled walls hung with tapestries. He hoped that he wasn't giving off an odour of dung and turnips.

Within a short space of time La Comtesse de Villegrande swept into the room. She was tall, aristocratic and spoke perfect English. 'Captain Harrington-West, what a pleasure to meet you. I've heard so much about you.' Andrew gave a small bow as he took her offered hand. 'Francine is out riding. She'll be back directly. You'll stay the night, of course, but first you'll take some sherry. Your man is being looked after in the servant's hall.'

Andrew sat making small talk while they partook of the wine. He stood up abruptly as Francine, wearing an elegant burgundy-coloured riding habit, entered the room. Her eyes were bright and her cheeks flushed from her ride in the cold December air. Andrew stared at her. She looked stunning.

She walked up to him and he took her hand. 'You look marvellous.'

Francine smiled. 'Thank you, it's lovely to see you, although...'

Andrew was taken aback. 'I'm sorry, is there a problem?'

'Of course not.' Francine recovered herself. 'You look a little tired and rather thin, that's all.'

'But very handsome,' added the Comtesse. 'I'm so pleased you had time to visit; soon we return to Paris.' She addressed Francine. 'Please look after the captain while I have a quick word with the housekeeper.' She excused herself and left the room.

Francine and Andrew stood staring at each other in silence. They spoke simultaneously. 'I...' he began. 'You...' she said, then added, 'No, you first. Please sit down'.

'I wanted to apologise. I didn't receive your letter with the dates to meet in November until yesterday. You must think I'm frightfully ill-mannered.'

'I never thought you were rude. But I was very worried when I didn't hear from you. I spoke to my father and he pulled some strings.'

'Thank goodness you did. Shall I have the pleasure of meeting him?'

'No, I'm afraid not. He's too busy.' Andrew heaved a silent sigh of relief. Francine changed the subject. 'How's the war going? I mean how is *your* war going?'

'Rather boring at the moment, I'm afraid. We're being kept kicking our heels waiting for the *big push*.'

'Will you be in the trenches?'

'We're being used as a mobile reserve. I truly don't know what we'll be doing exactly. We hang around waiting for the order to '*stand to*', which may or may not come. The men are bored and very cold. The horses have mud fever and are thin. I cringe when I inspect them. Most of the poor creatures lived in luxury before they were bought by the army.' Francine began to look distressed. 'I'm sorry, I shouldn't be telling you this. The last thing I want is to do is to upset you with stories about the war.'

'No, please tell me. I have to know.'

'Well...' Andrew paused.

'What is it?'

'Your grey horse... My brother has him.'

He was rewarded with a smile. 'Oh, thank God, at least he's not with the Boches.'

'Bertram assures me that he'll take good care of him.'

'Of course.' Francine turned away.

Andrew was sure that she was hiding her tears. 'You're not still thinking of becoming a spy?' he asked quickly, changing the subject.

A gong rang out from the hallway.

Francine said, 'That's the first gong for lunch. Let me show you to your room. Did you bring your batman?'

'No, I brought Williams.' Andrew smiled. 'He's a better soldier than valet. Anyway I only have the clothes that I stand up in.'

'Marie-Claude was hoping that you would bring Turner.'

'I did think about that. But I came to the conclusion that you would be short staffed and wouldn't want your maid distracted. Luckily he doesn't know where we are.'

'We were so sorry to hear of the death of his brother. She's embroidered a beautiful Christmas card for him. '

'That's very kind. Yes, it was a difficult time for him, but he seems to have rallied well. I admire his courage.'

***

When they had finished their after-lunch coffee and liqueurs the Comtesse suggested that Andrew and Francine take a walk before it grew dark. 'The afternoons are so short at this time of year and the château looks beautiful from the park.'

'Madame, the château looks lovely from every angle.'

'Yes, we love it here. I only hope the Boches don't reach us.'

'I'm sure they won't.' Andrew stood up.

***

They walked under the trees and Andrew looked upwards through the bare branches silhouetted against the pale blue December sky. 'There'll be a sharp frost tonight.'

'Yes.' Francine shivered. 'You mentioned in your letter that you wanted to tell me something. What was it?'

'Let's find somewhere to sit.'

'There's a seat around the trunk of that chestnut tree.'

Andrew sat down and looked towards the east. 'Listen! You can hear the guns. Is there no getting away from that sound? They tell me one can even hear them in the south of England.'

'Yes, so I believe.' She turned towards him. 'I'm sure you didn't come all this way to tell me that.'

'No. The truth is…' Andrew suddenly couldn't say what he had in mind, so he blurted out, 'Are you going to become a spy?'

'What if I am? Why is it so important to you?'

'I would be worried about you, that's all,' he replied lamely.

'Well, there's no need. I'm sure I can look after myself. I learnt some valuable lessons when the Boches held me.' She shuddered.

'I know and that's what worries me. I would hate anything to happen to you.'

'It already has.'

'No. Something worse.'

'You mean there is something worse? I understand you gentlemen…'

'Not to me. I mean… I don't…' Andrew felt embarrassed.

'Your father does.'

'How do you know?'

Francine gave a wry smile. 'So I'm right.'

'Francine, please, my mother and myself, well… we…'

'Don't mind.' She finished the sentence for him. He nodded. 'But the rest of your family would.'

'Francine, I think I'm old enough to make up my own mind. The only thing that worries me is *your* father. He would want a title for you, not a younger son with only a small amount of money.'

'My father will wish for my happiness first. A title would be secondary and anyway, I have money.'

Andrew continued talking faster and faster. 'I've inherited my grandmother's estate in Scotland but it doesn't generate much revenue. I go there for the shooting and the fishing, although I do come into the money that my great-aunt Agnes left me when I'm twenty five or upon my marriage, whichever is the sooner. It'll be enough to buy a country house and also provide a comfortable income, but nothing like the houses or the life that you're used to. I don't think your father will…' He looked at her, the light was beginning to fade and she was staring at the château. 'Francine, are you listening?'

She shook her head. 'What's that flashing light?' She pointed to a small window near the top of the ramparts. 'It's coming from the servant's quarters.'

'Good Lord, its Morse code.' They stood up and began to walk towards the château. 'Three dots, three dashes and then three dots again. S.O.S. What's going on? It's changing now.'

'What's it saying?'

Andrew continued to stare up at the window. 'W, I … then two letters, I again, A and then another letter and an S… another word H, E, R, E. *Williams here.* It's Williams.' Andrew lit a match and let it burn to the end.

The flashing continued. Andrew read the words slowly. 'Be.. ware… Hun below… Come through back door. Where's the back door?' he asked Francine.

'Round here.' She began to run and Andrew struck another match as he followed her. The torch in the window waved and disappeared.

They stopped beside the moat, opposite a landing stage which jutted out from a thick oak door in the castle wall. There was no boat. 'Can you swim?' asked Andrew.

'Of course I can swim.'

'It's too cold for you. Look there's thin ice on the water.' Francine had already taken off her shoes and her coat and was tucking her skirt into her undergarments. She slipped into the water without a sound, holding her coat in one hand. Andrew quickly took off his boots and tied them around his neck. He too slid into the freezing water, also holding his greatcoat and his pistol above his head. The icy water took his breath away but it only came up to his waist. They waded into the middle of the moat where the muddy bottom suddenly fell steeply downwards, fortunately only a short distance from the jetty. Then they had to swim. Andrew managed to keep his pistol out of the water and put it safely on the landing stage as he dragged himself after it. He turned to pull Francine up beside him. They both sat shivering on the rotten wooden planks as the oak door slowly creaked open. Andrew grabbed his revolver. He sighed with relief when he saw Williams standing in the doorway.

'What's happening?' he demanded through chattering teeth, as they entered the cold stone chamber inside the door. Williams shut and bolted the door whilst Marie-Claude handed a towel and dry clothes to both Francine and Andrew.

'A man arrived at the front gate about half an hour ago saying he had a package for the comtesse,' Williams explained. 'When Rougé, the butler, opened the gate the man produced a pistol and marched him across the courtyard. He was followed by three men all carrying guns.'

'Who are they?'

'The leader is short and stocky and definitely German, but not in uniform.'

'Von Krutz,' Francine gasped. Andrew's face turned ashen and Williams continued, 'I don't know who he is. Luckily I was walking along the corridor that goes around the courtyard. This castle is a small version of yours, Mademoiselle. I saw the men with guns and found Marie-Claude. The German has the comtesse and the butler in the drawing room. We listened to their conversation through the little service passage that runs behind the panelling. We heard everything'.

'What does he want?' asked Andrew, but he already knew the answer.

'He wants Francine. He's going to kill the butler if the servants don't find her very soon and then he's going to kill the comtesse. We ran like hell up to the top of the house to signal to you, also to warn the other servants. The cook and the scullery maid are hiding. Paul, the footman, and the parlour maid are in the servant's hall. But the German doesn't know you're here, sir, I'm sure of it.'

'Well done Williams. You did well. We'll have to disarm them. You say there are only four of them?'

'There's a car out on the road. I don't know how many people are in that. Three men are in the drawing room and one is outside the door. One of us could easily shoot him and the other could go down the service passage and enter the drawing room from there. The door is concealed from within. It looks like part of the panelling.'

'I'll go with Andrew,' said Francine. 'Marie-Claude can go with you.'

'Francine, you will stay hidden,' ordered Andrew.

'No, I won't. He has come for me and I want to kill him.'

'Sir, please don't argue. You know Mademoiselle will do what she wants. If she is with you at least you will ...'

'Will what?' demanded Francine.

'Know where she is.' Williams was embarrassed.

'Yes, you're right.' Andrew smiled wryly. Francine gave a short laugh.

'I've brought Mademoiselle's gun,' said Marie-Claude. 'And I have one too.'

Andrew smiled at the little maid. 'Good. This is what we'll do...' When he finished speaking they ran quietly up a stone staircase to the servant's hall. They found the parlour maid on her own, crying hysterically.

Francine shook her. 'Be quiet,' she hissed in French. 'Where's Paul?'

'They summoned him,' the girl gasped. 'He's gone to the drawing room.'

They heard a man crying out in pain as he stumbled down the stairs. The door flew open and Paul fell into the room, his hands pressed to his face. Andrew prised them open and recoiled.

'My God! The barbaric bastard,' exclaimed Williams. The man had a hole in his cheek that had been burnt with a red hot poker. Marie-Claude grabbed a towel, ran to the scullery and soaked it in cold water. She pressed it to his face as he managed to gasp, 'The German. His name is von Krutz. He's going to kill Monsieur Rougé if Mademoiselle du Byard doesn't go in there.'

'We'll go to the drawing room, don't you worry,' said Andrew through gritted teeth. He turned to the others. 'You know what to do.' Williams nodded as he and Marie-Claude mounted the stairs towards the main entrance hall.

Andrew and Francine ran silently up another flight of stairs, led by the subdued parlour maid. They followed a rabbit-warren of service passages until they arrived outside the drawing room beside the chimney breast. The maid hurried back towards the hallway.

Andrew waited; he could hear voices, but not exactly what they were saying. He could see through a tiny hole in the panelling. Von Krutz was standing in the room facing the fire and the comtesse was sitting to his left beside the fireplace. One man was guarding the door to the corridor and the other stood in the middle of the room.

He mouthed, very quietly, in Francine's ear what he wanted her to do, praying that she was a good shot. She nodded in agreement.

They heard gunfire in the corridor. The guard by the door left the room and as von Krutz flew round to see what was happening Andrew burst in through the panelling. He shot the guard who stood mesmerised in the middle of the room. Von Krutz spun round to face Andrew. Francine fired. He dropped his gun, blood pouring from his hand, and ran to the window. Both she and Andrew fired again. The German, who had left the casement open as an escape route, dived through it and into the moat. Francine fired at the swimming figure while Andrew ran outside. He arrived at the gate only to hear a car start up and roar away into the night.

He returned to find Francine with her arms around the comtesse. 'Unfortunately he got away,' he told them.

'Damn, damn and blast,' exclaimed Francine, releasing her hostess. Andrew held her hands. 'At least he didn't get you and we winged him pretty badly. I hit him in the thigh as he jumped through the window.'

'What a terrible man.' The comtesse sat down shakily. 'Rougé, perhaps you would have these removed.' She waved her hand at the dead guards.

'*Oui*, Madame.'

Williams stepped into the room. 'We wounded the man who was in the corridor and we have locked him in a cupboard. He's French and from the village. Paul is sitting outside with a gun in his hand. I have persuaded him not to kill him.'

'Well done, Williams. The French army can deal with him. They can find out what von Krutz is up to.'

'My God! What's that?' cried Francine. Everybody swung round and stared at a small bloody object lying on the carpet under a chair.

'Allow me.' Williams swooped down and picked it up.

'What is it?' asked Francine.

'I believe it's a thumb.' Williams quickly put it into his pocket.

The comtesse turned her head away in disgust and Francine looked at Andrew. 'Good shot,' he said quietly.

***

Nobody had much sleep that night as the French army traipsed all over the castle. The next day, as Andrew and Williams were about to leave, an officer returned to say that, although the traitor had died under interrogation, he had divulged that von Krutz was obsessed with kidnapping Francine. If he had known Andrew was there, then he would have brought more men and taken him too.

'Yes, he tried to capture my brother,' Andrew told the French officer.

'He seems to have got clean away, for the moment. But I don't doubt we'll catch him. He's badly wounded and will need urgent medical attention. Unfortunately the wretched traitor died before we could discover the names of the French spies who helped him. The two dead men are Belgian and come from behind enemy lines, we believe.'

'I presume you have informed the king's entourage at Boulogne of the incident.'

'Of course, *Capitaine*; we told them last night. They're being extra vigilant. But I don't think that von Krutz is in any state to go after His Majesty.'

'No.' Andrew gave a laugh. 'I don't think so either.'

'I'll give you a lift to the railway station, if you would like to accompany me.'

'Thank you. Excuse me for a moment while I say my goodbyes.'

Andrew found the comtesse and Francine in the hallway. He thanked his hostess for her hospitality and drew Francine to one side.

'The French army are escorting la comtesse and myself to Paris,' she informed him.

Andrew opened a door and pulled her into the library.

'What are you doing?'

He caught hold of both her hands. She stared at him in surprise. 'I came here to tell you how I felt about you, but I lost my nerve. Now, after last night and everything else that is happening in this dreadful war, I seem to have found it. The niceties of society appear to have flown away.' Francine began to smile and Andrew felt bolder. 'I love you. That is all that matters.' He looked intently into her eyes. 'I have to know what you feel about me.' His heart sank as she turned away and he released her hands. 'I thought it was too much to hope for; as I said, I'm a younger son and you would expect better.'

Francine spun round with tears in her eyes. 'I fell in love with you the first time I saw you. My feelings have never changed.' Andrew stared at her. 'Didn't you realise?' she asked.

'No, how could I? You were so cold, I thought you hated me.'

'Because I am no good for you, I'm... how you say....?' She gave a hollow laugh. 'But at least I'm not pregnant.'

'Francine.' Andrew took her hands again. 'Promise me one thing.'

'That depends on what it is that you ask.'

'You will never say that again. We will never mention it and, in fact, we'll forget all about what von Krutz did to you. I'll never refer to it again and I'll forbid anyone else to. That includes my father.'

Francine relaxed and smiled. 'I promise. But I still want to seek my revenge.'

'All right, I'll go along with that. But I don't think he'll get far with no thumb and a hole in his leg.'

Francine laughed. 'I hope he's suffering.'

'I'm sure he is.' Andrew folded her into his arms. She smiled up at him and he kissed her. This time she kissed him back and held him tight. Andrew was left in no doubt as to her feelings for him. He broke free. 'I can't tell you how happy you have made me.' She looked away from him.

He gently turned her face towards him and saw the tears in her eyes. 'What is it?'

'I've waited so long for this moment and now all I want to do is cry.'

He put his arms around her again. 'Please don't. Or I shall start too and that would never do.'

She tried to laugh. 'No. A British cavalry captain mustn't cry. I have you for only a few minutes and now I'm going to lose you to the front line. It's too much to bear.' She looked up at him through her tears. 'Please let God keep you safe.'

'Of course He will,' Andrew smiled.

There was a knock on the door and Williams's voice called, 'Sir, they're waiting to take us to the station. We'll miss our train. You must come now.'

Francine gave a sharp intake of breath. Andrew kissed her one last time. She clung on to him, quietly sobbing. He gently extricated himself and hurried out of the room without looking back.

She stood by the library window as the car drove away. The tears coursed down her face and her body shuddered with sobs. 'Dear God, please, please look after him,' she murmured.

The End

6190824R00152

Printed in Great Britain
by Amazon.co.uk, Ltd.,
Marston Gate.